NATASHA KARIS

The Sisters You Choose

Contents

Make sure to check out the back of the book for your exclusive gift from the author.
Or, if you can't wait, check it out today at:
https://www.subscribepage.com/initiation

For all the women who cannot speak.

The Grave

Abbie

It was near dark and pouring rain when Abbie visited her mother's grave for the first time. As she drank long gulps of cider under the shelter of the old clubhouse, the fat raindrops dripped down from the lip of the roof in an endless chant, saying: *go now, go now, go now,* until it was all she could hear, all she could think about.

The streetlight over the park shone a direct line to the graveyard, as blatant and inviting as a neon signed arrow. It wasn't like she wanted to go there to mourn. Or to cry. Or to apologise. Abbie's only urge was to spit on the murderer's grave. Baited by the alcohol, she rose to her feet, resolved to tell the woman under the ground how much she hated her.

Her friends didn't stop her, for most of them used the graveyard when nature called. Earlier, they hadn't acknowledged the anniversary, even though everyone in Ireland, let alone Knockfarraig, heard about her parents' death. After ten years, the gossip in the town had softened to a lingered hum, reduced to a tale of delicious scandal whispered between adults who remembered these things. All her friends knew her story and, if she was honest, most of them were only friends for that reason, liking the status it gave them to hang around with someone like her. Abbie stayed friends with them because they hadn't ignored her like most of the students in the school, instead the gang approached her. Reece asked straight out, 'did your mother really murder your dad?'

It surprised Abbie, that the significant date had gone unnoticed. Only later would it dawn, when a parent would ask how Abbie had behaved, her actions would make sense; as they recalled her quiet mood. She'd hoped for distraction, that the alcohol would help her forget, but her parents' death day had imprinted in the underlining of her brain. Unavoidable, with no alarm or calendar needed, the date marked out in her mind every year.

The graveyard was easy to enter. Even though the church caretaker locked the gates at night, you didn't need an entrance from inside the park. All Abbie had to do was step her foot in the known gap and hop over the dipped wall. Despite the rain and impending dark, the stone slabs still made a shocking sight.

'Come on, Abbie, it's only about five o'clock. No one's going to get you,' she said under her breath.

Needing to sober up by ten meant she always drank early; Maureen didn't react well to Abbie breaking her curfew.

On the other side of the graveyard, it was even darker, for the dead have no need for artificial light. She flicked on the torch on her phone. Not yet evening, the sky still maintained some brightness although the downpour of rain prevented full vision. It took time to get the directions right; being six years old when her parents died, she had memorised a sketch from a site about murders in Ireland, but hadn't factored that every pathway between the graves looked identical. The rain didn't help either.

Three times she backtracked her steps and tried another trail. Twice she stumbled, first over a mound of weeds, next into what she hoped wasn't an unmarked grave, her knees soggy with mud when she stood back up. She kept looking over her shoulder, expecting someone to jump out and attack, to grab her by the leg from under the ground like she'd seen in countless horror movies. The place had her spooked. An overwhelming feeling of trespassing, or to run away, came over her. Only when she was on the verge of giving up, when she turned in what she imagined was the direction out, did her phone flash over the plain headstone marked Gabrielle Ellis.

Fresh flowers lay on the marble; which should have but did not surprise her; her mother had been a famous author, infamous after what she done, with many fans.

All alone, for her father wasn't in the same grave; they buried him in the Ellis family plot, well away in the new cemetery overlooking the sea. Abbie had visited that grave many times.

People always wanted to talk about her parents when they found out who she was. Abbie stayed silent, having learnt over the years not to encourage the conversation. They talked anyway. Everyone carried an opinion. Whether on her mother's books or on her crimes, they conveyed information as if they witnessed the murder, or gathered insider knowledge. In hushed voices or conspiring whispers, as if that made their words less harsh or as if the dead could hear you talk about them if you spoke louder, they brought up the subject with questions they assumed were original when in fact she had heard the stories, or fabrications or some downright lies, many times before. They waited for her response, with their leaned in posture, with their mouths slightly open, desperate and eager for a glimmer of extra gossip, hoping she held the key to the truth and wasn't the little unknowing girl she must have been.

'Did she go into the water covered in blood like they said?'

'My friend lived up the road and she told me she'd never salute you. Marie could tell there was something wrong with her.'

'Evil. Pure evil. She did you a favour by killing herself. You would have an awful life if that woman reared you. Or worse. Imagine if you were *there that day.'*

Abbie never told them how she often wished it was three lives her mother had taken. There wasn't one person in the world who would understand.

Now, looking at the plain slab and grave, she felt underwhelmed. She had built the occasion up in her head, imagining for years the act of facing the resting place, believing that when she finally had the courage to face her mother's demons, to see where she lay, that it would be the start of her enlightenment, that she would feel something, or at the very least something would happen. Unable to discern what she had expected, apart from general disappointment, there was nothing. Stupid. Somehow she'd at least thought her mother's grave would stand out, but it was the same as every other. All the graveyard was, was soggy soil and rows upon rows of other stone slabs that stood as indicators of misery, either for the living now or the dying before they died. There wouldn't be any epiphany or enlightenment or understanding; her mother was no more there as she was anywhere else.

'Long dead and good riddance,' she muttered.

Abbie wasn't a believer in religion or the afterlife or any such bullshit. When you were dead, you disappeared. At the very least, she'd hoped being at the graveside would trigger some memories, but all it brought was frustration.

The rain beat down on her face with such violence she found it hard to see. Abbie's clothes clung to her skin. Despite the downpour, the fresh flowers stood bright on the grave. Who would do that? Only some freak or some fan of her mother's books. She knelt and fingered the flowers. They were an unusual type, a kind Abbie hadn't seen, similar in shape and leaf to roses, but with all the colours of the rainbow on each flower. She fingered the mutated leaves. Real. How was it possible to get a flower like that? Sprayed probably, but touching the skin of the petal didn't smear the colours.

On the slab, the only other inscription was the date her mother came in to the world and the day she left. Nothing else. Aunt Maureen would have insisted. Fresh anger fired. Good. That was what she had been looking for. Some kind of reaction was better than none and anger would do just nicely. Abbie listed the reasons out loud.

'How could you leave me with Maureen? Do you know how angry I am with you?'

It felt good.

'I'm angry about being unloved. For being born to a crazy mother who didn't love me enough not to hurt someone. You didn't care enough to stay. Because of you, there's this cloud of... of stigma that follows me like a smell everywhere I go.'

Riled up, she stood, wanting what she had to say next to have more impact. Her words when she spoke were loud this time. It didn't matter that she was shouting, there was no one else around.

'You were an awful mother. Mothers don't do what you did. They don't kill fathers and then themselves. Mothers don't leave their daughters. Not with aunts like Maureen.'

A foot squelched on the mucky, uneven earth behind her.

Abbie spun around. At first, all she saw was a pair of white eyes. Then, as her own eyes adjusted, she made out a tall, thin, dark-skinned woman. Her long, black curly hair hung in damp ringlets under a black beanie hat.

'Hi Abbie,' the woman said.

The woman was a complete stranger.

Rain

Abbie

'What do you want?' Abbie's voice came out accusatory and uneven, for the woman, whoever she was, had heard her. Conscious they were alone in a graveyard, it would just be her luck that the one time she braved going to the grave, she'd get stuck with some freak. The woman didn't seem fazed in the slightest at seeing a sixteen-year-old shouting at a grave in the rain, quite the opposite actually, for she acted like they had prearranged the meeting.

'I came to speak to your mother. To speak to you too.'

Definitely a crazed fan then. Over the years, she'd seen plenty of them hanging around the town. All you had to do was type in her mother's name and a bunch of forums came up with people giving their take on conspiracy theories, swearing of her mother's innocence, of her talent.

'You don't know me,' Abbie said.

The woman shook her head. 'Don't you recognise me?'

The conviction in the woman's eyes scared her.

'Definitely not.'

'Pity.' The woman wiped some rain from her face. 'I know you, or rather, I did. When you were younger, you spent lots of time around me. Nobody ever showed you a photograph of me?'

'Never saw you before.'

'Why am I surprised?' the woman muttered.

'I'm going.'

'Wait. I'm your godmother.'

Abbie screwed her eyes. 'Wrong. Maureen is.'

The woman shrugged. 'I can show you pictures.'

'Lies.'

'If you say so.' The woman shrugged. She didn't seem bothered at all.

'Did you follow me here?'

The woman shook her head.

'How did you know I would be here, then? I've never come before.'

'I didn't. I know you haven't.'

'What are you, a stalker or something?'

A raindrop dangled and dripped from the woman's nose. Her eyes bored into Abbie's. There was an urgency, but also a challenge in them. She didn't answer the question.

'What do you want?'

'To tell you a story. Or rather, your mother would like to.'

'My mother is dead.'

'Her story isn't.'

'What if I don't want to hear?'

The woman smirked. 'Oh, you want to hear, Abbie. Isn't that why you're standing at your mother's grave on the anniversary of her death? You want answers and there is only one way to find them.'

'I already know everything there is to know.'

'You know nothing.'

A fury stronger than Abbie had ever known ignited inside her chest. Who did this woman think she was to turn up and say she knew more about her life than she did? Abbie searched for a comeback, but still under the effect of the drink, the shock of that stupid woman, that

7

stranger, showing up and ruining the moment she had pictured for the last ten years, had thrown her off course and unbalanced her, silenced her. If words wouldn't come, she would show it another way. Abbie needed a storm off. As she bumped past, the woman tugged at her sleeve, causing her to stumble. The woman caught her, steadied her before she hit the ground, then leaned in close to speak.

'I'm not your mother. I won't take your shit. Don't think I won't fight you until you hear what you need to.' Up close, the woman's eyes were dark brown, and they were studying Abbie. The woman showed teeth. 'But I don't need to, do I?'

The woman let go of her arm and walked off, trailing between the graves. When she reached the path, she turned and shouted back.

'I'm going now to my hotel and you can join me if you want to talk. If you don't, and want to find me later, I'll be at The King's hotel in Crookstown. This is for your ears only though, Abbie. Don't tell your aunt.'

The woman wiped the rain away from her face. 'Know this, tomorrow evening, I'm gone.'

The woman disappeared into the darkness towards the car park. Abbie's chest heaved. Any bet the woman *was* just a crazed fan of her mother's books; they spoke of her as if she was the second messiah.

But she had called her Abbie.

The newspaper's, the forums and fans believed her name was Alexandra. The rare time Maureen had spoken her mother's name was to explain to Abbie her mother released it to give her daughter anonymity when the books exploded. Back when they were a family. Although everyone in Knockfarraig knew her real name and these days, all you needed was a social media account or a trip to the births, death and marriages office to find out who a person was, it still made her wonder.

In the distance, Shawna called her name. She had been gone too long,

8

and from the sound of Shawna's increasing shouts, she was worried. The cleverest option was to go back the way she came, go to her friends, go home and never see that obnoxious woman again. It would be madness to go to the car. To follow a stranger at her suggestion of a message from her mother was certified crazy.

Yet, something forced her on.

It annoyed Abbie that the woman never looked back to check, yet waited when she reached her car with one hand on the passenger door, keeping her back to the graveside until Abbie caught up, as if knowing she would follow.

For that, she hated the woman even more.

The woman swung open the passenger door and when Abbie sat in; the woman slammed it, the whoosh of air like a smack across her wet face. Abbie fumed. The boot opened and closed and when the woman got into the car; she handed Abbie a hand towel to dry herself. They were both wet right through.

'Take off your jacket,' she said, removing her own and turning the heat on in the car. Abbie towelled her hair then wiped her face dry, smearing mascara on the white cloth. The woman held out her hand wide, and as the material dripped down Abbie's arm, she shook off her soaking jacket and dropped it into the splayed hand. Without saying a word, the woman threw it behind both of them onto the back seat. They sat for a moment without movement. The rain beat on the glass in relentless waves, hard enough for Abbie to wonder if the glass could splinter. Abbie welcomed the heat. The woman pulled out and for the entire drive, they drove in silence.

The blast from the rain and the shock of a stranger at the grave had sobered Abbie up some bit, but the drive brought more sobering thoughts. She hadn't even asked what the woman's name was. Yet here she was, letting a random stranger drive her further away from the coast, further away from home. The woman lit a cigarette. Abbie made a point of coughing and waving the smoke away.

'If you don't like it, walk. I'll meet you at the hotel whenever you can catch a bus.'

The woman blew a long stream of smoke in Abbie's direction. To counteract, Abbie opened the window down to its minimum until an onslaught of cold, wind and rain blasted her. The point wasn't worth it; she closed the window again.

'I can't make you out. You're saying you are a friend of my mother's, but I wouldn't say you're being friendly.'

The woman flicked some ash out the window. 'Ditto there, Abbie. Anyway, I wouldn't say I'm known as being that type of person. Gabs would have told you that.'

'Yeah, well, she can't, cos she's dead.'

The woman took her eyes from the road to look at Abbie. Her caustic stance softened for a second, and when her eyes watered, she looked away. She took a long drag from the cigarette and, opening her window wider, threw the last of the cigarette out. 'That she is.'

'Are you going to tell me your name?'

'Sadie,' the woman said, looking straight ahead.

'I've never heard of you.'

'Don't worry.' She smirked. 'You will.'

The King's

Abbie

The road sign read Crookstown. Joined by one winding coast road, it was the next town to Knockfarraig, but unlike that town, which was a collection of zigzagging crossroads that rose upwards giving breathtaking views of the sea, Crookstown was one long street of houses, bars, schools and shops that all faced the beach and coast. Different coloured pastel houses lined in a row when you entered; the pinks, yellows, blues and greens gave the town a friendly feel.

The only hotel, The King's, stood grand and regal. It was impressive, with what looked to Abbie to be about a hundred white framed windows on its front and an awning with marble columns at the entrance displaying fancy plant boxes by the door. Inside though, the decor had seen better days. With worn carpet so thin you could feel the hard floor underneath and was probably older than her; smelt older for sure. Abbie shuddered at what you would find if you peeled back the material; decades of dead people's skin and mildew. For all the numerous windows, once past the hallway, you entered a dark, enclosed room that resembled a lobby. The lack of natural light depressed the room and the decor didn't help either. An old, unmanned mahogany counter lined one wall and murky corners were filled with dumped, battered sofas with grotty table lamps beside them. The only redeeming attribute was the lit fire with two wing back chairs on either side. At one stage it must have been a grand building, Abbie thought, where people flocked to sit and talk and meet. Like, a hundred years ago.

Sadie continued straight to the lift and pressed the button.

'That's not happening,' Abbie said.

Sadie swivelled round. 'What's not?'

'You turn up at my mother's grave and think I'm dumb enough to go to your hotel room. No thanks. I shouldn't even have come here, but I did, so I'll listen.' She pointed to the fire. 'Whatever you have to tell me, can be told right there.'

Sadie sucked in a breath, then bit down on her lip. She exhaled real slow like a mother trying to keep her cool with a small kid.

'Don't you want to dry off?'

'Nope. Being wet doesn't bother me.'

'Fine. Let me get changed. Order me a coffee and something for yourself, not alcohol, you had enough already. Do you want me to bring down a change of clothes?'

'No.'

Sadie banged the button for the lift over and over with her fist until the doors opened. She left without looking back.

According to the loud ticking clock on the wall, it was only six in the evening. Abbie pulled one of the chairs closer to the fire; hoping for warmth and wishing she was dry. She tried to arrange the material of her leggings in a way it would dry the quickest. The mud was too caked in to even attempt to clean. Sadie's instructions to order coffee went ignored for Abbie wouldn't follow *her* rules. The clacks of china and cutlery being laid out came from a room beside the counter.

In no time at all, the lift pinged again and Sadie strolled in dry and different in jeans and a shirt. Seeing the empty table, she shook her head.

'Thanks for that Abbie, I could have killed for a coffee. Aren't you hungry?'

Abbie didn't answer; all her focus was directed on what Sadie was holding. In her hands was a book.

'When was the last time you ate?'

'This morning.'

'So, you're hungry. I suppose you're carb-free or celiac, everyone is these days?'

Abbie screwed her face up at Sadie in answer.

'Two toasties it is then.'

Sadie strolled way too slowly for Abbie's liking, especially with the book in her hand. She disappeared behind the open door, but the voices still carried.

'Hey Jim, I was wondering where you were hiding.'

'Sadie, how's life? I could hear you had company, and didn't want to go to your room, so I said I'd give ye a minute to settle. You're looking for toasties? How 'bout I test out my new cappuccino machine on you?'

'That would be perfect.'

Pleasant Sadie was even more annoying.

'Grand so. Put your feet up and I'll bring it out.'

Sadie sat in the seat opposite Abbie. Then she placed the book on the side table.

'That's why I wanted to go to upstairs. The walls have ears here,' Sadie whispered, nodding toward the other room.

'Why does everything have to be so top secret?'

Sadie looked away, at the fire, stroking the book. 'This is the last story your mother wrote.'

Abbie huffed. 'Is that why you brought me here? Christ, if I wanted to read her books all I need to do is visit the library.'

Sadie kept staring at the fire, kept stroking the book. 'You won't find this one there, you won't get this one anywhere.' She laid her hand flat on the cover and closed her eyes as if absorbing the book. Then she looked at her.

'This is a special edition, exclusive, one of a kind Gabrielle Ellis novel. It is a story that was only ever written for you. Your mother asked me to hand it over when you were old enough and since you're sixteen now, it's time.'

'So, what? You're going to sit here watching over me while I read it. Why can't I take it home?'

Sadie rolled her eyes and tapped the book, her fingers making an exaggeration of her irritation.

'I told you already. It's for you, only you. If you don't want to read it, that's fine by me, I'm here because of your mother, not you.' She hugged the book to her chest, covering it. 'If you don't want to read it, it's no skin off my nose.' Sadie smiled, all smug and sure of herself. She leaned nearer Abbie. 'But you do, don't you?' She sat back into the chair. 'Trust me, Abbie, don't bullshit a bullshitter.'

Abbie's cheeks flushed, and her breath rose. In that second, she despised Sadie more than anyone she'd ever met, more than Maureen even, and that was saying something. Yet Sadie was right; Abbie was dying to read it. There was a standoff between them and as much as she wanted to devour that book, she would not let Sadie see her eagerness. Abbie made a point of not looking at the book and concentrated on the fire. She blurred the flames to unseen, her proper focus on her sideways view of Sadie; it was enough payback to see the flicker of the woman's eyes on her and then to the book. Despite what Sadie said, she was dying for Abbie to read it too.

Her delay wasn't just to get one up on Sadie. Even though that was a good enough, there was another reason for her hesitation. Her head was reeling. Could her mother have written something just for her? Whatever was in that book, she could feel just being in the hotel was the start of something, something bigger than Abbie, and that sent shivers up her. And yet, it was the moment she had waited for because the book might hold answers to the questions that prevented her from sleeping at night, the answers she had given up asking Maureen for.

A spindly man came out with a tray and a broad smile. The way he shook the tray made Abbie wonder if any cappuccino would stay in the cups. Sadie jumped out of her seat and took the tray.

'Jim, this is Abbie.'

'Well, hello Abbie. I hope you'll be as charming as Sadie here.'

'Charming's not the word I'd use for her,' Abbie said under her breath.

Sadie smirked. Not hard of hearing, then.

'Jim knew me when I was a kid. I haven't lived around here in a long time, so we had a great catch up last night.'

Abbie nodded, bored with the small talk now. She eyed the book. Sadie noticed and placed the cappuccinos and toasted sandwiches on the table next to the two chairs.

'Thanks, Jim,' Sadie said handing the tray back in an obvious dismissal. Jim didn't seem to notice or mind. The grin, like him, stayed intact on the one spot.

'We'll eat these then get to it OK?'

Abbie nodded again.

'I'll get out of your way,' Jim said. Still, he hovered.

Abbie scowled, giving him a look she hoped said, *would you just go already?* The man took an eternity to leave. Abbie had half her toasted sandwich eaten by the time he reached the door.

'Why don't you come up for air there?' Sadie said. She hadn't touched hers yet.

'Just want to get to why we're here. The point is to read it, isn't it?'

'It is.'

Sadie picked up her sandwich and ate.

Once finished, Sadie caressed the leather cover of the book once more, then with a slight hint of reluctance, handed it over.

The cover was plain with no title or description. Just brown leather with one gold square rim running around the border.

Abbie knew what she should do. She should hand the book back to Sadie and tell her she didn't want it, that what her mother said or wrote was of no significance to her and demand she drop her home. She should stand and walk out and never more think of what might be inscribed on the inside of the cover. The facts were enough, well documented and transcribed. Before that night, before meeting Sadie, if anyone had approached her and asked if she wanted to read anything from her mother, without hesitation the answer would have been no. Like Pandora's box, opening it would only unleash problems, could only cause pain. But how could she ignore a secret scribe meant only for her, a story Sadie claimed her mother wanted only her to read?

Abbie opened the book, catching the waft of old pages, of dust and ink. There was a note made in black pen on the title page:

My dearest Abbie,

If you are reading this, then you have met Sadie.

This is a story about me and her, but it's also a story about you and your father.

I discovered early on how easy it is to lie. How people prefer to hear your untruths because lies make life run smoother.

The truth is, truth hurts.

This is my truth, Abbie. I want you to know the truth about my death because lies hurt too. There are things you won't like and things I'd prefer not to tell. But I promised to tell the truth when I started to write this for you and I have, no matter how hard it was to recall, or how hard it might be for you to hear.

Sadie will be around if you need to fill in any blanks. If you haven't had the chance to already, please wait and get to know her. The abrasiveness was earned and needed. Her harshness can have a bite, but kindness will kill it.

   Gabrielle.

   Underneath, written in pencil, the writing more slanted, messier, as if rushed.

   As I sit here with his blood on my clothes, I think about how we got to this. I hoped to give you this book as a memory of us, but now I know it for what it is – an apology.

   Please know I loved you.

   Abbie dropped the book onto her lap. There it was; everything people had said had happened was true, yet the confirmation did not instil any satisfaction. Her mother admitting the murder stung. Even though she had never mentioned it to another soul, there had always been a particle of hope inside her that there had been some mistake, some other explanation or reason but here was her mother's written guilt.

   'How can she say she wants me to know the truth about her death when she wrote it while she was alive? How can she have written a note in a finished book, before she finished the story? Are you making a fool out of me?' She flapped the book at Sadie. 'Did you write this?'

   'Four questions there.' Sadie muttered. 'I'll answer one. I could never write like that, like your mother. They are all your mother's words. Just read on. She'll leave nothing out. It's warts and all, for everyone involved. The pieces she needs me to fill are after her death. There's a lot you don't know.'

   Abbie glared at Sadie, who returned to staring at the fire.

   Despite Abbie's want to argue, despite her reservations to snap the book closed and run far away from the hotel and from Sadie, despite her deep hatred for her mother, if she read on she would also learn the truth, her mother's truth at least. Finally, she would find out. Either way, good or bad, reading it would be life changing. Despite how scared she was, her fingers flipped the page to begin the story.

Classrooms

Gabrielle

My story started like most others, with a birth and two parents and a room full of relief and joy. There is too much to say in a limited amount of time to include the unremarkable. What I will say about my early years is important; my parents reared me with love.

Instead, I'll begin where I believe my story really starts, at a pivotal point at eleven years old, on the day I met Sadie. Shoved into a new classroom by the Principal and handed over to a stranger called Miss Simpson, she clasped my hand and announced, 'Please welcome Gabrielle O' Neill, who is joining us today.'

Thirty eyes in a new classroom in a new country that I didn't want to move to, or live in, stared back at me. Out of habit, I smiled, but I didn't want to make new friends; I wanted my old ones back in England. Bolting to the door appealed.

Guiding me by the elbow, the teacher deposited me at a table where a pretty girl with two long plaits that reached her stomach, scooted her chair over, freeing enough room to sit beside her. As I sat, a small girl opposite me, with short, in parts matted, hair the colour of charcoal, and skin the colour of caramel, picked up her own chair and moved it to the space at the head of the table, so she could sit on the other side of me.

As the teacher turned her back on us to walk to the top of the classroom, the pretty plaited one reached over me, tugging the small girl by the arm. 'You're not allowed do that. The teacher wants her to only sit with me.'

By the way the girl recoiled, there was a familiarity in the gesture. Either used to people pulling, or telling her she was wrong, the girl cupped her hands under the seat, ready to move.

In that strange place, it was all I needed. I've always hated anyone being put down.

'She can sit there if she wants.'

I shrugged at the pretty girl and glanced over at the teacher's desk to check if there would be a rebuke. The teacher smiled, then continued reading out loud.

That moment was so important Abbie. But significant moments are often distracted by insignificant tasks. This time was no different. My primary concern right then was the fact I didn't have any books to read from yet.

'I'm Sadie,' the small girl whispered, turning her page and moving her book closer to share, her nails bright white against that caramel skin.

'Gabrielle,' I whispered back, placing my pale, blue veined, scrawny hand on the other side of the book, catching the page as she turned it, completing the task.

And that was that. A bond formed, an alliance made. Sadie became my shadow. Anywhere I turned, she would be there hovering, waiting for permission to approach. Her uncertain eyes terrified of a reprimand I would never give. If I had been older, I might have labelled her a weirdo, if younger, her stares might have freaked me out. What I was, was grateful. In leaving the life I knew behind and facing the uncertainty of being the English girl moving back to Ireland before even knowing anything of the divided history, I was thankful to have someone by my side.

We were opposites in every way. I was loud while she stayed mostly silent until she erupted. Easy going compared to hostile. Calm opposed to anxious. Due to early puberty, at eleven my breasts and hips had already developed, making people treat me different, expect more, my body alluding to a ripening I didn't yet understand. Standing at the front, I must have looked like a woman amongst children. The tallest in the class, whereas Sadie was the smallest by far. Was it fate that placed me at her table in a seat across from her or just a clever move by a teacher who saw something needed by the other in both of us?

Sadie took one look at my too high on the leg, too short for school, skirt and knew she loved me. Whereas I'd first noticed her the day before, standing outside the school gates. It wasn't her beautiful skin or messy hair that made me notice her, although she stood out in a sea of white. Rather, it was her stillness, her difference of composure. Sadie, unmoving and sad, stood out amongst the madness of the kids rushing around and I liked that, liked her, because I stood out too.

After that first day of school, Sadie insisted on walking me home and I noticed her delight when she discovered I only lived about ten minutes away.

My mother was relieved when she saw there was a girl already in tow. I allowed her that as an apology for how much I had shouted and struggled when I refused to go to school earlier that morning. Imagine, a nearly six-foot girl being dragged by a woman already smaller and thinner than her daughter, her face bright red as the young girl pushed and fought against her efforts. The five-minute walk took an hour, with me losing for a while and then wriggling from her grip and sprinting down the path. My mother would catch up and we would start grappling again. The primary school complex was long, with all the rooms on one level. I didn't notice or care about the multitude of windows that could see our struggle and anyway, it only ended up giving me more kudos amongst my peers. Before I walked into class, I'd already gained the reputation of someone who didn't listen to her parents, of someone that fought back. They didn't have a clue that the only reason I fought my mother was because the sheer terror of walking into the unknown was worse than the embarrassment of being seen. Eventually, though, she defeated me. Stood at the entrance of the school, worn down, I finally gave in. Even an eleven-year-old knows it's futile to keep fighting the inevitable. I had to go to school. Even though she was the winner, there was pain in my mother's eyes as she wiped away my streaks of tears, and slumping my shoulders, I relented.

'It will all be all right, Gabrielle, I promise.'

But nothing was right. I was alone in the world and only I could walk through those doors. I hated my mother that day, for forcing me to go when she could see how terrified I was. Until that day, she had been my protector. The person who rubbed my forehead in the middle of the night until I fell asleep or when I got scared, or when sick, who held my hand and did everything in her power to take any pain away. All I could see that morning was how my parents had ripped me from the life I knew.

That day, Sadie walked into my home and from then only left it to sleep or get changed or when her parents demanded her to return. She walked into a half-finished home, a home that embarrassed me because it needed a whole do over. A complete change from the beautiful house we lived and made memories and adored in England. All I saw was a house in need of renovation, with quickly bought shoddy furniture. Sadie didn't, though. She loved the dinginess and the relaxed attitude we had regarding the treatment of our furniture. Her mouth gaped in shock when I tucked my feet under me on the couch. Once, she tripped and spilt the entire contents of her drink on the floor. Sadie dropped onto her knees onto the manky grey carpet to clean it up, trying to scoop the liquid out into her glass. 'I'm sorry, I'm so sorry,' she said.

'Don't worry, it's coming up anyway,' I said. Back then, I thought her shock was amusing. At eleven, you don't wonder why something so minor would worry a person. Our relaxed attitudes must have been inviting, our acceptance of her with her moods and her insecurities were like a magnet to Sadie.

After that day, there were countless times I came down the stairs and found her in my kitchen, invited in by my father who'd already left for work, her small legs swinging high off the floor, eating the last bowl of cereal. She would beam when I complained there had been half a box there the night before. With a full mouth, she would say sorry with bits of cornflakes dribbling down her chin. She would then shovel in the last few spoons, one after another, in case I would try to take them. I forgave her for that. I always forgave Sadie for everything.

Nails

Abbie

Abbie pretended to carry on reading but slid her eyes towards Sadie. Even though the woman sat with her legs up on the table, currently extracting what looked like dirt from her nails, she still managed to look hostile. It wasn't in Abbie's imagination either; the act of putting legs on a table was aggressive in itself, and then there was the quick, forceful way Sadie removed the dirt as if she was furious to find it there, her brow furrowed in concentration, her mouth in a grimace. Gabrielle's words came back.

The abrasiveness was earned and needed. Her harshness can have a bite, but kindness will kill it.

Those nails. Abbie saw the whiteness her mother mentioned, opaque against dark skin, her fingers thin and bony, with silver rings on every second finger. *I always forgave Sadie for everything.* Had Sadie done wrong to Gabrielle? Had she hurt her mother? Sadie looked up, as if noticing Abbie's attention or the fact she had stopped reading and the grimace left for a minute and a blank expression came over her, gauging what she wanted, seeing if she needed to talk. Abbie instantly dropped her eyes, not wanting to be interrupted and carried on where she left off.

Dialects

Gabrielle

When you are surrounded by love as a child, there isn't much need to search or strive for anything. If you are content, there's no urge to change your life. Love, laughter, happiness made up our days. Course, there were fights and hassles too, I'm just trying to get across, when you felt that much love, as a family we didn't need to do much outside of it. No matter what, we all gravitated home. You'd find us all in the one room on top of each other watching television, with one of us allocated our version of a throne, which in our house was the length of the couch, with our head on our mother's lap. The other sought-after spot was wedged into the single seat with our father, squished into his arm and loving it. The other two kids relegated to either the couch with the chosen one's legs on top of their laps or splayed out on the floor on their stomach as if ready to swim. No wonder Sadie wanted a part of it.

Don't get a false impression, we weren't like the perfect family or anything. We swore. My brothers fought at any opportunity; all dives and punches and wrestling moves. My little sister danced and shouted and whined and followed me everywhere. Silence was definitely not a viable option in those early days. We dropped things, we made a mess. My mother's constant gripe was we didn't help enough; when the complaining hit a crescendo and we started to, she'd take whatever was in our hands and shoo us away. 'Go on, play,' she'd say with a resolved sigh. 'You won't be kids much longer.'

My father, your grandfather, wasn't afraid of hard work. As a builder, his hands were his weapon, there wasn't anything he couldn't fix or figure out. He couldn't stay still and even at home on a day off, he grafted. What I loved most was his smile, or the way he lit up when he saw one of us, as if we were the surprise he waited for. He created a successful building business from nothing. I loved listening to stories of how he left Ireland on a boat when he was twenty two with only hope in his pockets. With work scarce in Ireland, England held jobs and opportunities and, more importantly, more significantly for me, my mother.

I loved my family. We laughed a lot. Before Sadie entered our lives, I thought that was normal, that every family was like that, not should be. When Sadie came along, I realised how precious and not guaranteed that is.

Sundays were our day. When no one worked and we could all be together, when every one of us kids would filter into our parents' bedroom one by one until we were all piled on top of each other in their double bed, a jumble of legs and limbs and elbows and we would cuddle and chat and laugh. We spent hours in that bed all squished on top of each other, until someone got hungry or needed to pee or just got sick of the moving, jutting bones or bumps to the head. Despite my parents protestations they didn't move. We knew they loved it really. My mother would focus on each of us in turn, stroking our hair as one regaled stories of the week. Like I said before about significant moments being lost, at the time that was our normal, and we had no reason to believe they'd ever end. I think about those times now. I miss them.

* * *

'Tell me their names again.'

Sadie pointed at a collage of photos I had stuck on my wall, I didn't have to ask which one she was talking about, the question had become a regular occurrence.

'There's Mandy, and Cheryl and Janine. Tina is the girl in the back with me, obviously.'

'Where is the photo taken?'

'At the back of the Wimpy.' I repeated every time. The lyrics, *ooh Aah Paul McGrath,* played from the small radio.

'I'm sick of that song, it's all we've heard for months. The world cup is over, you know?' I said, lowering the sound.

In the picture we held silly string spray cans. Some of the string hung from our hair. All smiling, all caught up in the moment. It had been a day of fun, bordering on hysteria, and I understand now as an adult, we didn't have the capacity, didn't have the words to vocalise what was happening, so the giddiness was the only way we could say goodbye. The magnitude of the day had not taken over yet, that would come later, on the plane when my voice caught in my throat cutting off all noise, as it dawned I would never speak to them again. When I realised that I never told them all how much I loved them and how much I would miss them. On the day, I had wanted to ask for their addresses but stopped short of saying it, not wanting to sound silly. On the plane, I kicked myself for not having the courage. All I had left of them was that photograph, developed as soon as I arrived in Ireland, where those first few days I had held on to it like a comfort blanket until I'd pawed it so much, it curled at the edges. Knowing it wouldn't survive much longer, I turned it into art. It remained in the centre with different images surrounding it in a circle until I had a poster of pictures looking out. The only time I looked at it was when

Sadie questioned me. It hurt to see the girl in the middle, full of fun, so ignorant of what lay ahead.

What determines a person? When everything you know is gone, what makes you still you? My bed, my house, my school, my friends, all changed. Everything was different. Everything was replaced with something else and for a while I believed they were replaced with lesser things. And I didn't want that life. I wanted my old life back.

How can I describe what Cork is like to a stranger, or to someone who hasn't lived anywhere else? For a young girl the accent was hard to understand with its sing song tones or different dialects depending on what part of Cork they originated from. There were many differences, the north side of Cork use different sayings from the south side. Sarcasm was used a lot and was often confusing. A place where '*I will, yeah*' meant no. They talked fast. I'd never heard words spoken as if they were dancing before, but that was what it was like, the words going up and down, stopping and starting.

Quick enough, I learned Cork was different from England in many positive ways. For one, being outside opened out. Before, loneliness had been an accompaniment I hadn't realised I carried. In England, play dates or chasing in the street were strictly forbidden, the rules only softened the year before we moved when I was allowed meet with friends for an hour.

At home, my two younger brothers played with each other mostly, who mainly communicated by beating on the other or wrestling or playing football. With the boys, girls weren't allowed and my sister was too little to have anything in common with, which also meant my mother's time was consumed by her. So, I read. Or painted. Or watched television. Or climbed trees. Or bugged nature. Mostly, I imagined, dreaming up worlds and people with intricate plots and dialogue. All in my head for I didn't write it down yet, but I guess I fed the writer even then.

In London, my town consisted of built up streets and back gardens, while in Cork, there were fields, farms, flowers and green everywhere. Best of all, there was water. To have a beach near my home was a revelation. Abbie, I've always adored the sea.

In London, beaches meant long rides in hot cars. It meant traffic, full bladders, car sickness and unrelenting boredom, then packed beaches full of windbreakers, chewing limp sandwiches while trying to ignore the gristle from the sand, sipping warm lemonade with barely any available space to sit on the sand, let alone watch the calm water. In Knockfarraig, even on the hottest day, the amount of plentiful beaches nearby meant they were never full. With beach on my doorstep, you couldn't keep me away, though my parents drew a line at me swimming without them.

For them, Knockfarraig was judged safer, allowed to roam, we hung out by trees or lay on grass or sand.

Girls called to my house relentlessly. Girls separate or grouped together. I spent most of that time silently terrified, because the main topic of conversation revolved around boys. No matter what I tried to talk about, the girls steered it back to asking me questions about the opposite sex. I didn't understand the obsession. Yes, I knew boys, for I had gone to a mixed school. According to my classmates, this elevated me to expert status. But I hadn't known anything for I hadn't seen boys as different at all. Once the girls discovered I didn't hold the secret to what made males tick, the knocks at the door petered out. In my previous life in England, everyone was put in two piles; my friends or the people that weren't so friendly, regardless of being girls or boys. I didn't understand why gender was a big deal. This made me different. I watched the girls turn giggly and dumb when boys approached or passed and I didn't understand I was supposed to do the same. I didn't get it. Watching the boys shoving and chasing the girls and then asking them to come down the back of the fields freaked me out. Even though I'd learnt of the mechanics of sex and believed I understood it, I had never saw aggressive sexual behaviour before. The big London kid was enlightened, and I didn't like it.

Another thing that struck me as odd when I moved back to Ireland was that it was so, how do I put this?

White.

The culture in London was diverse. Used to the smell of spices from Indian food wafting through my garden, I would follow my nose and scale one of our trees dividing our houses, climbing the metal mesh in order to figure out what the indescribable scent was. I learnt to ask questions without asking questions, how admiring my friend Meena's satin trousers led to her telling me as a Muslim she covered her legs. Or when I bit into a dessert, if I stated the obvious, saying, 'it's spicy', they would elaborate, informing me if it was cardamon or turmeric or ginger. Early on I relished the differences, the smells, the traditions and different colours. The natural inquisition of a writer was there even then. Everything I learned, I stored for another time, for when or who, I didn't know. One of my closest friends was a daughter of German and Indian parents which resulted in an interesting combination for dinner. I drove to school with a Chinese family. Afternoons were spent playing with a Scottish family up the road or two doors away with a family of Nigerian heritage.

All I saw after I moved to Ireland were white faces. Shocking, at first, it felt like living in an alternative universe. No matter where you went, you could count the non white people on one hand. Maybe that was why I gravitated to Sadie; she reminded me of England, she reminded me of what I had left behind, of what was normal, of what I had viewed as normal.

When Sadie was around, I watched white people watch her. At the time I didn't label it as racism, more like wary dogs sniffing at a stranger, showing a fear of the unknown; coupled by most with a willingness to understand, with an undercurrent mix of terror. We would both straighten when adults did that, because like dogs we didn't know how their reaction would go – would they wag the tail or bite? Usually it wasn't blatant. There was no shouting or harsh words, no outright hostility. It was more subtle, more friendly. There was a lot of ignorance back then, of talking to her instead of with her, talking to her as if her skin affected her like a disability. Some spoke louder or stepped back when she walked by. As an adult, I understand there are many forms of racism; that a smiling person can still be guilty of discrimination; that an abusive sentence can be admonished in the politest of ways. Writing this, I think of how it must have felt for Sadie, to be labelled different, to stand out everywhere she went, but if you want to know more about how it was back then, ask Sadie, for I can only tell you how I saw it – Sadie is the only one who can tell you how it felt.

In a different way, I felt it too.

Racism wasn't just about skin colour back then. When I spoke, the majority of strangers' reacted by recoiling at my accent. English people didn't instil fear of the unknown to the Irish like people with a different skin colour. In the time of Margaret Thatcher, of poll tax and the IRA, the English were well known and for the most part in Ireland, despised. Many people felt it was their business to inform me, an eleven year old girl, about the famine, or a recent bombing, or what happened in 1916, in a voice that insinuated a level of blame, of something wiped or disregarded by the English history books. And for the first time in my life, I knew what it felt to feel real shame for being me. I was the only one who seemed to see I hadn't been responsible. Even as an adult, I took an intake of breath any time someone questioned where my accent was from. It always baffles me why humans need to label people in order to understand them.

One morning, Sadie sloped into school late, which in itself wasn't unusual, but, she didn't look in my direction as she passed, didn't say anything and although long bouts of silence were common with Sadie, on this morning she acted more subdued than usual, with her chin almost resting on her chest. My first inclination was to approach her, but by then sitting next to each other had proved too much for the teacher and two tables separated us.

The first lesson was an art task. On each table one coloured paint sat between a white and black. Each group were allocated a different colour. Red was mine. The rules, the teacher explained, were simple. You could draw anything with the primary colour. Black and white were only to darken or lighten the assigned shade. Straight away I set to work. Out of everything in school, I loved tasks like this, the creativity distracted me from feeling lost. First, I mixed red with white until pink appeared. I dotted weeping willow buds on the paper. Next a darker shade made lines of the trunk. With a delicate touch, I barely made the edge of the water running across the page, vertical minute lines portrayed a perfect lake edge. Then, all I needed were only a few horizontal lines to display the water. After that, a blush pink sky with a blood red peeking from the horizon showcased it all. Once finished, the picture made sense. It looked like that pink sky veiled the tree and water with a red and pink hue.

Leaning back in the chair, I appraised my piece. It was exquisite. To this day, it is still the best piece I have ever done. The teacher's mouth dropped open when she saw it. She looked at me as if seeing me for the first time.

'Can I take this?' she asked.

I shrugged in answer as if I didn't care but she took something precious from me when she left. In her hands she held the light I poured out from inside me. For the first time, I had unlocked something inside and left it on the page. When the bell went for lunch, Miss Simpson stood.

'Gabrielle and Sadie can you stay behind please?'

Sadie's eyes met mine for the first time that morning, flashing a puzzled look for a second, then remembering either what had happened or where she was, scowled. We couldn't be in trouble as we hadn't even had a chance to speak to each other. Sadie sat still, her head tucked into her chest. With her arms folded, I heard her huffs from across the room. I giggled at her hostility. How could such a little girl strike such uneasiness in others? As I approached Miss Simpson's desk, the rest of the class emptied.

'Sadie, come here please,' Miss Simpson said in a soft tone.

Sadie pushed her chair back, causing it to screech. Still with arms folded she stomped to the table. Her head stayed tucked into her chest, her eyes stayed fixed on the floor. The way she wouldn't look at me, you'd swear I'd done something. *Had* I done something? In front of Miss Simpson's desk were two paintings side by side. One was mine.

'Tell me what is different about these?'

Mine, so delicate and soft. You could almost see the leaves of the weeping willow swaying in the gentle breeze as the sun set. The epitome of calm and serenity. Sadie's table had been allocated blue. Her picture was one massive circle. Masses and masses of circles on top of each other. Different shades of blue hinted at previous circles, still trying to escape from a primary mound of almost black. The frantic effort had worn away some of the paper. If mine was the epitome of calm, Sadie's painting represented utter rage.

'Emotions were never so true in a painting.'

Miss Simpson took both our hands and laid them on the desk beside the paintings. She placed a hand on top of mine, then moved Sadie's on top of ours and, putting her other hand on top of Sadie's, created a stack.

'This task shows what happens when you mix light with dark. That's what you two do, you balance the other. You both need that. Always

32

be there.'

Sadie and I locked eyes until the anger in her thawed a little and she allowed a smile. In the classroom window I caught sight of our reflection. In every way we were opposites. Sadie's dark skin next to a complexion so pale it made milk look colourful. Her black matted hair compared to my sun streaked, long and straight, light brown. My excessive height compared to her smallness. My curves compared to her childlike frame.

The teacher was right. Our physical differences aside, we needed each other. Sadie needed my light, and I learned from her darkness. It drew me to her, because I always placed others happiness before my own, always prioritised another's feelings as more important than mine. Sadie showed me it was possible to feel, to show a negative emotion and survive. Without apology, she was fine about being miserable.

The problem with mixing light and dark though, is one eventually needs to take over the other. Which one would win was up to us.

Cubicles

Abbie

Abbie was going to vomit. Moving the book to the safety of the side table, the bile rose quickly.

'Bathroom?' Abbie managed.

Sadie pointed to a door just beside reception with no look of concern.

Abbie barely made it to the cubicle when the vomit came. A film of clamminess broke out on her forehead and the place spun. She vomited again and when the retching ceased, she rested her head against the plywood wall in relief. She sat on the cold floor and waited for the stomach spasms to stop.

The door to the ladies whooshed. Black boots caked in mud stopped outside her door. Through the gap underneath a hand appeared, shoving a small tumbler of water through.

'You done?'

'I'm fine,' Abbie answered, wishing the woman would just go away. 'I just need a minute to myself.'

Sadie's sigh was loud from outside the cubicle.

'I get it, you know? It's too much. Meeting me, finding out Gabrielle wrote you something, finally getting to speak to her, in a way... well, at least to hear from her, it must be... a lot. I shouldn't have given it to you after you'd had a drink.'

34

Abbie stood, the sickness gone. She opened the door with a jerk, wanting to tear it off its hinges.

'You know nothing.' Spittle flew as she spoke. 'You think you know me so well? That you can turn up and pretend you know everything about me just because I needed to puke. You make out like you're doing me this favour by appearing out of nowhere with that stupid book, but I'm the one doing you the favour. I'm only reading it so I can get to the end and rip it up in front of you and say what a waste of my time it was. And so far, what a load of self-important drivel. All I'm reading about is you and her and it's boring. I thought she was a writer.'

Sadie closed her eyes and stood back as if someone had hit her. She spoke slowly, as if she was trying to compose herself.

'Which is why I should have waited for you to read it sober. It's tainted your view.'

'No, what's tainted my view is a mother who murdered my father. I think that would taint anyone, no?'

Sadie's eyes opened and when they did, it was time for Abbie to take a step back. Sadie looked like she was going to launch at Abbie. It ran through Abbie's mind how alone she was in the bathroom, how vulnerable she was being there with a stranger. How stupid.

Sadie didn't launch though, instead she turned and walked to the sink, twisted a tap and splashed water on her face. She dabbed her skin with a paper towel. Without looking at Abbie, she passed her, only stopping at the door after she opened it.

'Leave then. No one is forcing you to stay. If you think what your mother is saying is a pile of dung, then just say. I'll drop you home and disappear from your life. You never have to see me or the book again. I'm not playing a game here Abbie, you either want to know what happened or you don't. Drink the water. Think hard about what you want because whatever you decide there is no going back from it. Make the decision. Make the right decision.'

Sadie left. Abbie's first urge was to catch the glass and fire it across the room. Who was this one to tell her what to do? Right then, she hated Sadie, hated how self-righteous she was, how composed, how condescending. What she would give to walk out of the hotel just so she could see the look on the woman's face because it was all a front. Sadie *needed* her to read it.

Abbie leant on the counter and stared at her reflection. Her hair, although dry, hung in clumps from being rained on. Her mascara had smudged a little. Whose eyes were hers? Were they from her mother or her father?

Sadie sat in the same chair and didn't look up when Abbie sat. She never said a word when Abbie picked up the book. Never moved or looked her way, just sat staring at the fire as if it was the most normal thing in the world to wait as a person read.

And Abbie did, because as much as she already disliked Sadie, as much as she hated her mother, she just had to know.

The Christmas Present

Gabrielle

Two days after my first Christmas in Cork, I handed Sadie a box.

'For me?' Sadie had seemed more downbeat than usual, so I beamed at the change of her mood.

'I didn't get you anything.'

I flicked my hand at her, batting away the need. She picked it up and ripped the wrapping and seeing the silk scarf and a wide toothed comb inside, stroked the soft material. 'It's beautiful.' She picked up the scarf and held it to her neck. 'Does it go like this?'

'No silly, haven't you seen one before?'

Sadie looked at me as if I was talking in another language.

'Like, your mum must have shown you?'

Still, she looked at me with the same confused, blank expression.

'It's for your hair. It stops the hair cracking or something? My friend Tina, in England, showed me one. You wear the scarf at night wrapped around your head and it keeps your hair soft. She had a proper one, like a cap but I couldn't find any in the shops and I only had enough pocket money for one of these but I think it should do the trick.'

Sadie was staring at me like I'd said something upsetting, as if frozen to the spot with the scarf still up to her neck.

'I can take it back, it was just that you said last month how you couldn't brush your hair and I wanted to help.'

I didn't understand. I tried to decipher what I'd said that could have offended. Was it because she thought I didn't like her hair, that I thought it was dirty? Sadie swallowed hard, then smiled. 'What do I do with the comb?'

'Tina's hair matted sometimes, when it did she'd moisturise it to work through the knots. They'd cover her hair in conditioner and leave it on for ages and when it was ready, first her mum would go through the hair with her fingers, then with the comb. Her mum showed me once, how to untangle it. If you wanted, I could give it a go?'

Sadie touched the top of her head. 'It's a mess,' she said, barely making sound.

'It's pouring rain. We've nothing better to do.'

Sadie kept her head down staring at the floor for the longest time. I knew not to push. After a few minutes she nodded, then took her clips and hair ties out. Even after she removed them, the hair remained in the same spot. As I touched it, Sadie flinched. It was one giant mass, so my fingers couldn't break through. There were white flakes everywhere, her scalp was dry and shedding.

It was so sad to see my friend's hair like that, reminding me of each night when one of us lay on the couch and my mother stroked ours. No one had stroked Sadie's, no one had brushed it in a long time. Yet, I knew it was important Sadie didn't pick up on my feelings. If she noticed how her appearance upset me, she would jump up and make an excuse to leave because she hated anyone feeling sorry for her.

'Right. First thing is mum's conditioner. I'm gonna get magazines and some snacks for us cos once I start, I don't think we're moving for a while.'

Through all the hours she sat in the one spot, Sadie didn't complain. As I slopped and slathered, smothered, tugged and smoothed and eventually, thankfully, untangled. Looking back, it became a personal vendetta; I went silent, into the grooves of the hair, figuring out the puzzle, finding the ends and loosening, setting them free. Jigsaws were my favourite thing growing up, and it stood to me for this task, as if each one had been accomplished and built up to prepare for my Everest, because I knew how important it was for Sadie.

By the time of her curfew, I was only through half of her hair. Without washing out the conditioner, Sadie promised to sleep with a towel wrapped around her head, in the hope it would absorb the moisture.

She called early the next day and we got to work, even though our backs were creaking and our necks hurt and we needed to take breaks every so often to stretch our limbs, we didn't complain. At the end of that day, I ran my fingers through the last strand of knot. The feeling that ran through me Abbie, that accomplishment, has happened only a handful of times in my life: when I wrote a line I was proud of, when I finished a novel, when I looked into your father's eyes as they announced us husband and wife, and with you, when they handed you over for the first time.

In the mirror, Sadie's face was a picture. After we dried her hair, she shook her head, this time the hair moved, once straightened and stretched out, it reached her shoulders. She tilted her head from side to side and giggled.

'You did it.'

'Both of us did.'

'My mother said she was going to shave it off if I didn't do something. If I brushed it, she would see how bad it was so I pulled it up and left it in the bun and just smoothed the sides down with Vaseline or water. I knew it was bad but I didn't know what to do. Do you know why?'

I shook my head.

'Me neither.'

We stood in front of the mirror. The brightness that had been behind the smile faltered a little.

'Why am I so ugly?' Sadie whispered.

'You're not. You're the most beautiful person I know.'

'Everyone else thinks so. My mam says I look dirty, that's why people don't like me.'

'I don't think you look dirty at all. I think you look yummy. Your skin reminds me of my favourite thing in the whole world, caramel.'

Sadie giggled.

'I wish my skin looked delicious. Mine doesn't make me wanna lick it, all you can see is my veins and stuff. Don't listen to your mam. The others, the strangers, they just don't know how to deal with you Sade. You're different, so they stare, like they'd stare if there was a man in heels or a dog dressed in human clothes or the way they change when they hear my accent. Different isn't ugly. Different means you stand out. In England no one would look twice at you.'

'Maybe I should run away to England then.'

'If you want to I will.'

'You'd do that for me?'

'Anything. Always.'

We leaned our heads together and Sadie's smile grew wide again.

The Jennings

Gabrielle

From early on, Sadie begged me to visit her house. As my first time going to a friend's place in Ireland, I agreed with nothing but eagerness. It had taken some time, what with getting settled in the house and once my mother took a job in a factory, I was on babysitting duty most weekends. So, it was some months later when Mrs Jennings opened the door.

On seeing me, her smile turned, the sides of her mouth almost touching her jaw. Mrs Jennings took one look and decided she didn't like me.

I wasn't smiling anymore either though, for Mrs Jennings was blonde. And white.

She leant her hip against the doorway, the rest of her body staying in the middle blocking the way in. She folded her arms. 'So, you're the girl Sadie won't stop going on about.'

I didn't answer, my mouth wouldn't close and anyway, I wasn't so sure it was a question. The next one was though; Mrs Jennings bent nearer to me, so she was closer to eye level, screwing hers up.

'How old are you?'

'Eleven,' I said, slow and unsure. Somehow, I could tell this was the wrong answer but I couldn't understand what would be the right one.

Her eyes lingered on my jumper. On my breasts. It was only then I understood she had expected a different eleven-year-old to greet her, a girl as small as Sadie, when what she got was a near six-foot girl with adult curves, with breasts and bras and periods. In her eyes, I was too old for her daughter. Despite my young age, I understood what she thought she saw: corruption and waywardness, that I would lead her innocent daughter astray.

Abbie know this; there is something in me that always backs the underdog, that believes in treating people fairly and I can't stand back when someone is acting unjust. So, when faced with a woman who in one second had labelled me as a troublemaker, instead of cowering away I stood straighter.

From that moment on, I judged her too. I saw the blonde hair smoothed in a perfect blow dry. She wore red lipstick, thick enough that when she sucked on her cigarette, it left a bright red rim around the filter. Her nails were painted a cherry red; she kept them long and filed to sharp points. It shocked me that her legs were on show, her skirt stopping mid way up the thigh. Lacking in height, the short length coupled with the high heels gave the impression her legs were longer than her height alluded to. I tried to remember if I'd ever seen my mother in a dress. What I noticed most was behind the heavily kohled eyes, anger blazed from them. Straightaway Mrs Jennings saw me as an opponent, as someone on an even level mentally, but on that point she was wrong. Despite my appearance I was still just a young girl needing as much love as her daughter. And that was before I opened my mouth.

'Sadie tells me you've come from England.'

Her nose wrinkled when she said the word England, as if it wasn't worthy of sitting on her tongue.

'Yes, Mrs Jennings.'

'Where? Where in England?'

'London.'

There was the wrinkle again. It didn't suit her. 'Big city. Why here?'

'Why live here?' I repeated, unsure what she meant. Mrs Jennings still stood at the door blocking my entrance.

She pronounced each word slowly as if talking to a much younger child.

'Yes, that's what I said. Why did you move here?'

It was the first time I was asked that question, but surprisingly not the last. My answer became my go to.

'My parents are both from Cork. They only moved over to England for work. We came back cos they wanted us to be brought up Irish.'

Despite knowing we were now enemies, I was relieved when I was awarded a smile for the right answer. See what I mean about me needing to please? The door opened wide. Granted entry, I knew by her sneer I wasn't granted approval. We were rivals from the start of our story, Sadie's mum and I.

That day, I learnt you could be judged by people on one meeting, how your whole existence could be determined in one glance. It gave me an inkling into Sadie's life, it showed how someone could be frozen out of her mother's company if she saw fit.

Sadie appeared, standing behind her mother, her feet going on tip-toes and back down again, bobbing from air to ground, her excitement evident with no trace of nerves. I wondered if she had listened to the exchange between us and if so, what did she think? She didn't seem embarrassed at all, it was as if that type of exchange was normal.

When her mother stepped out of the way, Sadie gestured to enter a room, but I waited for her to move before I followed behind. Two much older boys sat on a couch watching TV, they nodded a hello but ignored us after that, turning back to the show they were watching. They too were white skinned; as pale as me. One wall was lined with shelves full of antiques you would be afraid to pick up but wouldn't want to touch anyway. I wondered if the couch was as uncomfortable as it appeared, but I didn't find out as there was no invitation to sit down. The grand lamp in the corner, with its glass beads and gold work was too ornate for a house with children in my eyes, and wouldn't have lasted five minutes in my house. The room spoke of money long spent and never upgraded.

'Can I get you a drink Gabrielle?'

'Yes please, Mrs Jennings.'

'Don't call me that, it makes me seem so old.'

She didn't offer an alternative.

'Milk or water?'

'Water, please.'

Everything she said to me was in a nice manner. On the surface, everything was nice. As time went on, the woman was so amiable sometimes I would question that first day. Then I would catch a quick glance or I'd notice a blink and miss it sneer, or see Sadie flinch and it would convince me all over again.

That day Sadie didn't seem to notice any uneasiness, and by the way she pulled at my sleeve, she was too eager to show me around. We bounded the stairs to her bedroom, the box room, like mine. That's where the similarity ended. The first difference being the lock on the outside of the door, not the inside. I had never seen that before. High on the door, I needed to tiptoe to reach the sliding lock, so it would definitely be out of Sadie's reach.

'What's with the lock?'

Sadie rubbed her arm, as if struck. She didn't answer. Not wanting to push, I changed the subject. 'Are you going to let me in or not?'

She grinned, opening the door. The second difference between our bedrooms was the bareness of hers. There was nothing but a bed and a wardrobe. The bedspread was a blanket that was so old I could smell rotten, damp wool and dust from the doorway. Sadie jittered with excitement. About what I couldn't understand, until I spotted the one picture on the wall stuck with Sellotape. The sketch was a close up of our faces, smiling with our heads touching. It was the only colour in the room.

'Sadie, that is so good. Did you do that from memory?'

She nodded, proud out.

'I know it's not the same as your room, but at least I could finally put one up.'

'What do you mean?' I asked vaulting on the bed for a closer look.

When she winced from the noise, I sat straighter, in apology. Sadie stayed standing, fingering the corner of the blanket.

'My mam doesn't like anything on the walls, says it's a distraction from my study, but I kept on and on until she let me.'

A lump lodged in my throat at how proud she was. At how happy it made her to be allowed one picture on her wall. The coldness in the room made me shiver, not from lack of heat but the lack of warmth. Then, I couldn't put a finger on why, it's my adult eyes that knows the reason now, Abbie.

'You can put some on mine if you want?'

'You'd let me?'

I shrugged. 'Course.'

'Cool,' she said, climbing onto the bed and sitting next to me. As much as I was dying to, I couldn't tell her I wanted to run to my own rundown, untidy house, to my room with its pictures stuck on the walls, to my manky carpet and my parents with their unlimited acceptance. But I didn't say any of that to Sadie. Right then, she needed my approval and if I spoke of wanting to leave, she'd be wounded. After about an hour, she got bored, and only then did I suggest going home. As we descended the stairs, a man appeared in the hall.

'Yay, you'll get to meet my dad,' Sadie said.

A tall, round man with longish light brown hair and glasses stood at the bottom of the stairs, taking up the entire space.

Up until then my logical assumption had been that Sadie's father was black, and when the man wasn't, it struck me speechless. Not one of Sadie's family had any dark features at all. Her father smiled.

'So, this is the famous Gabrielle. Come on, let me have a look at you.'

I walked nearer and stood, uneasy. He folded his arms and let me stand there. Sadie stopped beside me. He stared for a long time, running his eyes up and down my full length, only stopping when I crossed my arms over my chest.

'It's like little and large,' he said shaking his head and smirking.

I reddened, his scrutiny heating my skin. He noticed.

'You're some big girl.' He stared at my breasts, not stopping this time. 'Come on, do a twirl for me then.' He took a swig from a bottle of beer. By this stage I could feel the burn of my cheeks.

'I'm only kidding. Surely you can take a joke? How old are you though really? Twenty?'

My skin flamed hotter.

'Jeez, Doreen, we have another sensitive one.' He called out to the kitchen.

'What a sight the two of ye are.' He shook his head. 'Like some comedy act or something.'

His grin was wide and open and held no anger yet his words were thick with menace. Sadie pulled on my sleeve. 'Come on, let's get out of here.'

'What are you two up to?'

Sadie piped up. 'Gabs asked me to go to hers.'

Mr Jennings kept his eyes on me.

'OK. I don't want you to be late Sadie. Not one-minute past seven. Understood?'

'Understood,' Sadie repeated.

'It was nice to meet you Gabrielle, maybe the next time you'll talk.'

I fought the urge to run without answering. 'Yes. Bye Mr Jennings.'
'She speaks. In a British accent no less. Well, goodbye Mrs Gabrielle.'
As the door closed, I took a breath.

To me, Sadie's father was by far scarier than her mother, for Mrs
Jennings at least laid her cards out. There was a threat in his laughter
and a meanness behind his jokes. As time went on, her brothers always
bypassed me, as if I wasn't even visible, probably only due to the age
difference but it only fed my hidden insecurities, and added to the
unfriendly vibe. Whatever it was, I avoided the house as much as I
could.

As I tried to sleep that night, I tried to work it all out. All her family
looked nothing like Sadie, with their blue eyes and lighter blonde to
brown hair. Yet she couldn't be adopted; their faces were the same;
the features familiar, the same shape eyes, the same upturned nose
and high cheekbones of her mother, the same misery although that
was something I guessed could be taught or learnt. Was that the issue?
Sadie's skin was a different colour to her family; she called her father
her father, her mother her mother, yet the rest of her family were
white and Sadie was not.

In the days that followed, I never asked her, and Sadie never
mentioned it. Any time I did broach the subject, she would become
very still as if afraid. After that I couldn't ask her. Not then anyway.

Slang

Gabrielle

Those first years, I was everyone's protector. For my brothers, as their older sister I was always prepared to scare an older boy away or with my sister, I would pull her from harm or just sit down and play dolls. In Sadie's case, I would stick up for her when someone tried to strip her down. It never occurred to any of us that nobody was minding me.

It wasn't until the summer, about eight months after moving, that I noticed the bruises. When the hotter it got, the fewer clothes Sadie could leave on. Most could be passed off as part of the rough and tumble of our excursions, for I had bruises too. Some of Sadie's were different, though; on one occasion, I trailed my hand on one of four reddish round dots spaced out evenly on her arm.

'How did you get that?'

She turned and shoved my hand away. End of conversation. Sadie was an expert on how to shoot a subject down. She walked in circles, avoiding me, until she bent down investigating a spot of grass that caught her interest. I waited, knowing she needed a moment before she would talk. Then the frown changed, and she gave me the brightest smile. I swear Abbie, when Sadie done that it was like the sun shining during a storm.

'Race you down to the shop, I found a pound.'

At twelve, Sadie already perfected the art of deflection.

We spent our summers rolling down grass hills, making daisy chains and sitting around bored. On a good day, some money would line our pockets for penny sweets or ice cream at the beach. Or when we didn't have money, we would walk down to the one shopping centre in the town and amble around the stores. Or on a hot day, we would sit and watch the waves, itching to swim. That was one order I didn't rebel against my parents, no matter how hot the day, or how much the water called to us. Except for taking our shoes off and wiggling our feet in the water, each time, more of our legs got wet.

We didn't frequent the bandstand or the woods yet, as the teens that hung around there were too threatening, and we banished the playground for being too young.

On the days Sadie was grounded, I read. Which meant I read a lot.

Being popular for a while, the other girls in our class invited us to a clearing with trees next to the playground, which was still open enough to feel safe.

One day, I made my way there and two of the girls, Marissa and Ellie, huddled with Sadie, on a large rock with their backs to me. I snuck up behind them, determined to give them a scare. Marissa's hand hovered over Sadie's. Her hand turned into a claw, digging her nails into Sadie's skin. Sadie winced and tried to take her hand away, but Ellie cupped her other hand underneath so she couldn't.

'What's going on?'

Both girls dropped Sadie's hand.

'Nothing. We're just seeing who can take pain more,' Sadie said, grabbing me around the waist and steering me towards the tree. 'Look what we made. A swing...'

For the rest of the day I watched them, but Sadie acted like nothing at all was wrong, so I let it go. Their take on my use of language was enough to distract me.

'Want a go?'

'I think if I try to swing on that, I'll most probably end up on my butt.'

'Most probably?' Marissa repeated, laughing. 'What is, like, most probably? That doesn't even make sense.'

Sadie clasped her hands together. 'Let's teach her some sayings.' She pulled me down to sitting. 'So, a guy is a feen, and a girl is a beeor,' she said it as be-oar put together. 'And your old laid is your mum.'

'Yeah, an old doll is a girlfriend. Or you can call someone "yer wan." Like, look at yer wan.' Ellie said.

'There's some that have loads of different meanings. Like if you like someone they are a flah, you'd say it like, "he's some flah", or if you do *it*, it can be called flahing, but if you're flahed out you're tired. Langer is another one. If someone is an asshole, they're a langer, but if you're langers, you're drunk.' Sadie said.

'A boy's thing can also be a langer,' Ellie said.

'That's pure rotten. I'm gonna get the gawk,' Marissa said.

'What's gawk?' I asked.

'Puke,' Ellie squealed.

Sadie bent over at my confusion. 'I'm weak.'

'What, you feel sick?'

'No, from laughing.'

'Look at her, she's allergic,' Marissa said, cracking up too.

I folded my arms.

'Your gaff is your home. A shift is a kiss.'

'No moo-lah is another.'

'What's that?'

'No money. Honey.'

'You see, stick with me and I'll teach ya, cos I'm double wide.'

'Come on!' I said.

'I'm no fool, like, I extra watch.'

'Observant, you mean?'

'Chalk it down, girl,' she said in a singsong voice.

I kept mine monotone. 'Chalk it down. Are you making these up? Everyone will laugh at me if I repeat them.'

She cackled. 'You're gas.'

I stormed off.

'Ah, come on, we're just ball hopping,' Sadie shouted after me.

Abbie

Abbie put down the book. Sadie still stared into the fire.

'Why am I reading about what ye done as kids? How is that meant to help me?'

The fire played with Sadie's eyes, making them appear to water.

'Because you need to know the reasons behind the decisions that were made. Your mother wanted you to know who she is, who she was, I mean.'

Abbie could see a fraction of the little girl her mother described in Sadie. It was true, she supposed, that in these details her mother had found a way to be heard after death. Not a stranger anymore, not just a murderer, but a living voice. Abbie wouldn't show how much that meant, how the loneliness she felt growing up in Maureen's house was now replicated on the page by the woman who caused the loneliness. The source of all blame was speaking to her in a mass of words placed deliberately on paper. Thinking of that house alerted her.

'What time is it?'

Sadie took out her phone from her pocket. 'Nine thirty.'

'I have to go. My aunt won't let me out tomorrow if I get in past ten.'

Sadie stood and held out her hand, until Abbie with reluctance, handed her the book. 'Come on, I'll drop you back. Remember though Abbie, don't mention this to Maureen.'

'Do ye know each other?'

Sadie gave one quick jerk of her head in answer.

'The book will explain better than I could. Let's just say if you want to be allowed out tomorrow, I wouldn't mention me.'

Knowing her aunt, Abbie wouldn't say a word.

'What's the earliest you can get out?'

'Maureen couldn't care less what I do during the day, it's only at night she freaks.'

'Pick you up at nine, so? You'll have a long read.'

'I suppose.'

Sadie drove her to Mariner's Park without a need for directions, and once reached, she pulled in to a space ten houses down.

'Just in case Maureen's watching from inside.'

'That wouldn't surprise me.'

Sadie pointed at the house. 'Do you have a sea view from the windows?'

'From the top ones. If you want views, you're better off at the road above, Mariner's Way. We'd often walk up there and sit on the green and have a picnic.'

'The house by Scart's End had some view. After your mother's first book blew up and they bought that house, she wrote all the others while facing the water. I told her if I had that sight I would never write a thing because I'd be too busy watching the waves. Does Maureen still wear the twinsets?'

Abbie thought for a moment. 'You mean the cardigan things?'

'Yeah, with the exact matching colour or pattern of the top underneath.'

'Yeah,' Abbie said, giggling.

'Thought so. She was wearing them at ten, but she was the kind that would wear them for life.'

'You knew her when you were ten?'

'Course, Knockfarraig is tiny. She's my age. Your mother knew her before she knew your father. Let's just say we have history.'

'Like? Come on, give me something.'

Sadie leant forward on the steering wheel, as if deciding, then faced Abbie, drumming her thumb against her lip, thinking. Her thumb stopped.

'I'll give you something. Remember the pretty girl with the plaits the first day your mother sat down at my table? The girl who told me not to sit there?'

Abbie nodded.

'That was Maureen.'

Drive

Abbie

Abbie didn't sleep well. The image of a tall girl standing with a short skirt in front of a classroom of strangers kept halting her dreams. In the morning, she tiptoed out of the house. Despite what bravado she had in front of Sadie, her aunt was a control freak and would demand to know where she was going so early on a Sunday.

At the end of the street, Sadie was already there waiting with the engine running. She didn't look at her when she got in.

'You're late,' she said.

'It's five past. Anyway, you're lucky I'm even here, I was tempted to tell my aunt you were waiting outside.'

That got the desired reaction. Sadie flashed a snarl, then looked away, as if trying to compose herself. Abbie smiled at her win. It gave her a chance to study the woman, now that the rain didn't camouflage, or the dark room didn't shadow, Sadie's features were clearer. She looked like she hadn't slept well either, with dark circles under her eyes and a puffiness to the lids, like she'd been crying. The woman was bony rather than skinny. All angles. Sharp and full of edges. Wearing a short leather jacket with a grey light hoodie underneath, she had the hood now drawn over her head. Loose jeans finished her look. Her black, curly hair escaped out of the hood ending almost at her waist.

If Abbie passed her on the street, she would think she was cool, but, Abbie reminded herself, Sadie was not cool.

'Where have you been all these years?'

Sadie ignored her.

'If you were anyway decent you would have checked in on me. If you cared at all you would have showed you did. You're as bad as my mother and she was a murderer.'

Sadie dived at Abbie, just stopping short of their noses touching, making Abbie recoil. Sadie's eye's lit up when she saw Abbie move. Then, she pushed in further. 'Oh, no. I'm much worse than your mother.'

Abbie's breath hitched, but she brazened out her stare. Then, something changed in Sadie, and her features softened, and the fight went out of her and she sat back in her chair and blew out a long breath.

'What has Maureen said about me?'

Abbie straightened the creases out of her coat, more to compose herself than anything else.

'Nothing. She's never once mentioned you. Up until I saw you at the grave yesterday, I never even knew you existed. Maureen doesn't talk about anything got to do with Gabrielle.'

'Does she talk about your dad?'

Abbie nodded. Sadie sucked in her breath.

'Why can't I tell Maureen about this? What have you got to hide?'

'Tell her if you want. I'm just asking you to wait until you have all the facts cos we both know if Maureen does find out she'll put a stop to you reading it. If you want to tell your aunt after, I won't stop you, I'll even come with you if you want. If you tell her now, you'll never get the answers you've been looking for.'

'You don't know me at all. You haven't a clue what I'm looking for.'

Sadie's head rested on the seat, looking straight ahead. 'You are your mother's daughter. Of course, you have questions. Don't act stupid

Abbie, you're cleverer than that.'

'What questions do you suppose I ask?'

'OK. If you want to play that game.' Sadie shifted sideways in the seat. 'How about Maureen? Ever wonder why she doesn't work?'

Abbie shrugged. 'My grandparents are rich, they've supported her while she raised me.'

Sadie snorted. 'Please. Your grandparents ran out of money twenty years ago. They fought their house repossession for years. And if you don't believe me on that, there's plenty of court documentation to prove it. So, I find it very strange how they won't even let you say Gabrielle's name when she was the one who bailed them out when she was alive and since she's dead they have no problem living off her royalties.'

'That's not true.'

'Isn't it?' Sadie asked, arching an eyebrow.

The woman was infuriating.

'How come you're tall?'

Sadie screwed up her eyes, her nose wrinkled as if confused, Abbie wondered if it was the same way Sadie's mother looked at Gabrielle all those years before.

'What do you mean?' The wrinkle flattened and the eyes softened. 'Oh, cos your mum said I was the smallest in the class?'

Abbie nodded.

'I had a growth spurt at seventeen, had to wait 'til then for my period as well. Slow developer, but I caught up.'

'Did you know my dad?'

Sadie's eyes flickered. 'Yes.'

'And?'

'And what? I knew your father. What has Maureen said about him?'

'That he loved me very much. That he was handsome.'

Sadie picked at a nail. 'Both true.'

'She also said he was funny and my mother was evil and she's rotting in hell for killing him.'

'Sounds about right for Maureen.'

'Did ye not get on?'

'Funny, but I seemed to rub her up the wrong way.'

'You? No way.'

They both smiled at each other until Abbie remembered, quickly changing to a scowl.

Do you have any memories of your mum?' Sadie asked.

'Nope.'

'You were six, you have to have some.'

'I don't remember anything.'

'They both loved you more than anything or anyone.'

'Yeah right,' Abbie said as harshly as she could, but the eyes raised to Sadie's were hopeful. She hadn't expected how much she'd want to hear more.

'Tell me. How *is* life with Maureen? Do you get on?'

'What do you want me to say? That Maureen's a cow?' Abbie shrugged. 'She took me in when she didn't have to. She said they hounded us. People would call night and day to catch a look at the freaks. They abused her on the street saying she should have known my mother was suicidal and unfit to keep a child, that the best place for me was in care. It would have been easier to give me up but she carried on. Maureen's done the best she could, I wouldn't say I've been the easiest.'

'Never,' Sadie said in mock surprise.

'Leave it,' Abbie warned. 'Where was your family home?'

'Not too far from your mother.'

Abbie shrugged, unsure.

'What? Don't you know where she lived?'

'No.'

'Jesus Christ, you weren't joking when you said Maureen didn't talk. I'll show you later, OK?'

'OK.' Abbie shifted to look out the window. She could feel Sadie's attention on her.

'Feck it, I'll show you now.'

Sadie drove in the opposite direction to the hotel. Near the primary school, she passed several parks then pointed.

'That was your mother's park,' she said and turned into it. She pulled into a parking space five doors up. 'That's the one.'

It was just an ordinary generic semidetached house, with a front garden, and a gate and a garage. Its windows were fogged from the cold window meeting the heat from inside. Abbie tried to imagine a tall terrified girl looking out that window watching the other children walk to the school. You could see them from there, she was sure.

'Do you know where you lived before?'

'Before my mother killed my father?'

Sadie pursed her lips.

Abbie nodded and twisted her fingers in her hands.

'Sold it. Maureen thought there was too many bad memories there.'

'That was a beautiful house. It stood alone on that cliff for a long time, until they built all those other glass copies. Do you remember it?'

Abbie shook her head with such force it hurt her neck. She didn't want to talk about that place. Not yet anyway.

'Not now, I get it. Better to wait.'

Sadie drove to the top of the park and then turned around. Pulling out of the road, she drove parallel with the school, passing a number of road entrances. When she reached the end of the long road, she turned right and drove up the long hill, passing different estates on either side. After a couple of minutes she turned left, then right, then left again, and, after passing a number of houses, stopped. 'And there was mine.'

'Have you family still there?'

Sadie sat and stared at the house. 'Not anymore.'

As Sadie drove, Abbie wondered how many times she had passed her mother's house on her way to school. Every day, for years. Maureen had kept the information from her, making her wonder what else her aunt kept hidden.

'I don't want to go back to the hotel.'

Sadie sighed. 'And I don't want to bump into people, Abbie. There are reasons I haven't come back here.'

'Do you hate it that much?'

'Yes,' Sadie said her mouth forming a straight line. 'I didn't always. Knockfarraig was both my hero and my tormentor. Parts of it I miss. You know the area around the secondary school?'

Abbie rolled her eyes.

'All right sorry, forgot you still go to school there. You know behind the school you have the woods?'

Abbie nodded.

'Up on the hilly part, right on the top where we were alone, I loved catching a glimpse of the water from that height. Or, in the summer, we would just hang by the beach all day. You could do that back then, hang out with your friends by the water. Can't say the generation today would be left by their parents, I don't know how many times one of us almost drowned, or nearly got hit by a car.'

Sadie pulled in to a parking spot and faced Abbie.

'Those summers with Gabrielle were something else. There was something in your mother that made me come alive. She was the best of us Abbie. Everyone knew it. There was some part of her that pulled out the best in people. Me. In your father. Even in miserable Maureen. And everything she put her mind to she accomplished. You'll see, you'll feel it in her words. She's not the woman she's been made out to be. I loved her. More than I've ever loved anyone.'

Had Sadie been in love with Gabrielle?

'Where did you stop the book at?'

'You teaching her Cork slang.'

Sadie's head went back, and she laughed. 'Ah, we used to mock her terrible. Truth was, I loved her accent. It made her exotic. Here was this girl talking like a posh show from the telly. I loved the way she pronounced words. I would drive her crazy getting her to repeat certain sentences over and over.'

'Do I look like her?'

Sadie didn't regard her, shoving her hair away from her face instead. 'Christ, you've seen pictures Abbie, I don't know. You have seen pictures?'

Abbie bit down on her lip.

'Jesus, Maureen can't stop you with everything. All you have to do is a quick internet search and her face will be there.'

'Forget it,' Abbie said, unbuckling her seat belt. 'I don't want to go to that stupid hotel.'

'There are going to be parts you won't want to read in public. How about we start reading it there and if you want to leave or go someplace else, we can?'

'Fine, but this time let's go up to your room instead.'

'Good idea,' Sadie said, smirking.

Her room was just as battered as the lobby, with dated mahogany chairs with worn away varnish at the arms, the seat puckered and embedded with creases. The place was clean though, and next to the bed was a table with a kettle and a pile of biscuits, crisps and cakes.

Sadie followed her gaze and pointed at them. 'I bought provisions last night on the off chance you'd want to come.'

Was she that predictable? Abbie shirked the thought off, now that she was in the room she was eager to get to her mother's words. The book sat next to the pile of junk food. Abbie slipped into the puckered chair and flipped to the right page.

'I'll make you a cuppa,' Sadie said, but Abbie didn't hear. She was already listening too hard to her mother.

Shelter

Gabrielle

I'd like to tell you life got easier once I settled in Knockfarraig, but I guess you've learned by now Abbie, nothing is ever plain sailing. Like I've wrote already, I had friends and lost them through no choice of my own, and in the aftermath, Sadie was my saviour.

In England, I loved school. Loved the structure and the knowledge, whereas Ireland was different. For a start, there was another language to contend with. That first year, for some strange reason the principal decided that the best way to deal with the obstacle of me learning Irish was to ignore it. So, instead of giving me tuition, they instructed me to do my own thing while the students were being taught the subject.

This was a mistake.

It became normal to ignore the teacher, I learned to zone out the lesson, to make my own rules. With the spare time, I drew and dreamt and found it hard to settle back to the workload after. That first year with Miss Simpson spoilt me, because she encouraged my art, giving me ever increasing projects and let me unleash my creativity in the time. While I painted a mural on the back wall, the students threw jealous looks while they were instructed in Irish. I wish I could say the words filtered through and stuck, that a cúpla focal slipped through but it didn't, not then. As I sketched or painted, the classroom dulled and I found it easy to block out the noise. It taught me well, for as a writer I have to block out the distraction of real life.

That first year was a gift; a classroom of dreams. It lifted me, and defined me in many ways, it gave me a chance to form friendships and settle into Ireland. The next school year was a crash landing back to earth. First, they separated Sadie and I into different classes, placing me in Mrs Murphy's class. A woman who taught every subject in Irish.

There was no effort made to teach me. Mrs Murphy shouted words I couldn't and didn't want to comprehend, although some I had to, like, 'Suigh síos!'

It made me retreat, made me despise the language. It was only when I met your father that I recognised the beauty in Irish, when he would whisper, *grá mo shaol,* the love of my life, or when you were born, he would call you *an cailín álainn*, the beautiful girl.

Back then, the Irish didn't sink in. Mrs Murphy, decided it was an attitude problem on my part and moving me to the front of the class, demanding I sit and watch. As she spoke fluent Irish, she thought somehow it would penetrate, filter through, but her stern way of teaching didn't work. If she had given me a one on one lesson for even ten minutes, given me a starter in *as gaeilge*, I would have lapped it up I'm sure, but it wasn't to be. Instead, unable to dream with the constant barrage of instruction in a language I was eight years behind, I deflected her words, zoning them out and acted like I didn't care. Boredom will make you do strange things. Back then I couldn't explain how her shouting made me feel worthless, made me feel like I should be cleverer, that I should have picked up the information quickly, that really, I was what she implied: a dunce. Instead of trying, I turned my back on my school work. I rebelled, got cheeky, got punished. Hours were spent in the corner facing out the window where I'd tell myself I didn't care, that it was better than looking at her ugly face. The truth was if I was being punished, I couldn't be involved in the lesson and I could avoid being asked the questions I had no answer to. What I did learn that year was, if I didn't do what I should, if I stood against what was expected, people associated it with confidence. Abbie, I was never confident. Inside, I knew the truth. I was not worthy.

Abbie, I hope you don't think the same about yourself. If I was with you, if I could teach you anything, I would teach you to believe in yourself, to know you are worthy. Over everything else, I wish, I hope, you learn that, and that you have a good life.

Abbie

Abbie blinked her eyes rapidly to stop the sting of tears. She didn't want to react, or alert Sadie causing her talk.

Gabrielle

Life wasn't very good for Sadie either. Placed into different classes, she retreated. On our lunch breaks she would have worked herself into such a huff all morning that she wouldn't be able to soften out no matter how much I tried to coax. By the time the bell shrilled to return, she would stand with her mouth gaping and her eyes teary from the injustice of it all. Sometimes I had energy for it, sometimes I didn't. On those days, I moved on and played with others, gravitating to other loud, fun girls who didn't mind getting in trouble. The separation Sadie worried about was already starting. Looking back, I think she saw us fragment before I did, yet she didn't know how to vocalise it. Used to keeping secrets, she kept her mouth shut.

When you're hurting, it's easier to ignore other people's pain. It can even be a comfort to know someone is worse off than you, like a messed-up indicator of how awful people's life is. I'd like to say I helped Sadie more back then, but I didn't know how to probe yet.

Instead, I tried to distract her from her misery, with fun and trying to get her to laugh. I'd like to think my room was her haven. There were times I knew it was.

As a writer I'm aware of show versus tell. I've been telling a lot here Abbie, so I want to show you something. Imagine a tall, thin yet curvy, twelve-year-old who doesn't quite fit in. Then imagine her standing outside her friend's front door. As she is about to knock, the girl's brother opens it, seeing her silhouette in the glass. He doesn't say hello but he doesn't frown either, because to frown would mean she is significant to him and she isn't, she means nothing at all; she is invisible. He just continues up the stairs on whatever mission he is on. From his silence, Gabrielle knows her presence hasn't been announced but she walks into the hall anyway. She stands there a while, but no one comes. She ventures into the living room. There's no one there. At the other end of the long room, the door leading into the kitchen, is open. Gabrielle hears voices coming from there.

'Why are you going away this time?'

'You know why.'

'Are you going to leave money? Enough money, I mean?'

'I'll leave you what I have.'

'And I'm meant to live off that for however long?'

'Don't start.'

'I won't be able to cope with *it*. You don't have to put up with the constant questions, the whinging.'

'I'll talk to her.'

'Don't go. We can fix this. I'll try harder, I'll make life easier. Nothing's been the same since... I should never have gone through with *it*. We were fine before *it* came along.'

'We were never fine.'

'Yes we were. *It* broke us. Having another one was too much.'

I gagged. There could only be one person they were talking about.

'It' was Sadie. The way they spoke about her, was disgusting. What if Sadie had been listening? Who was to say she hadn't heard them too? I tiptoed back to the hall and coughed loudly, leaning my back against the cold radiator. My cough had the desired effect. Mrs Jennings opened the door. A hand went to her hair. It hadn't been blow-dried and stuck out in parts. As soon as she spotted me, the woman I'd just heard begging disappeared, and she was back in charge. Folding her arms, with half slits for eyes she regarded me.

'Gabrielle, why are you hovering in the hall like a burglar?'

'Seamus opened the door. I thought he went upstairs to call Sadie, but I'm not sure. I didn't want to barge in while you were talking,' I smiled sweetly. That would shut her up.

'Well, you should have knocked, it's rude to eavesdrop.'

'It is,' I said over emphasizing my first word with a smile.

'Go up and call her,' she said, but her reddened cheeks were undeniable.

Not to keep it one sided, let me show you an example of how stubborn Sadie could be, of the dynamic between her and her mother.

My brothers were obsessed with a cartoon character called Donnie The Destroyer. Once a week, on a Saturday morning they all crowded on the couch to watch the next set of adventures from Donnie. Then it was announced that a Donnie The Destroyer movie was going to be released. My brothers marked the date on the calendar and every day they marked it off. Tickets were bought and the countdown began but there was one problem that stood in the way. Me. I didn't want to go, arguing I was too old, but my parents' argued back that I was too young to stay on my own.

'I'll just call to Sadie's,' I said. Job done. My parents checked with Sadie and she jumped up and down, in answer.

On the evening, I waved them goodbye and trailed the road. Black clouds hovered from above. As I rang the doorbell, the sky began to spit. Mrs Jennings answered the door and nodded in greeting. By this stage, her father was long gone, another subject that was completely out of bounds with Sadie. With his disappearance, all effort had left her mother while in the house. That day, she wore a housecoat covered in stains. Her hair was dishevelled, wavy in parts and smoothed down in others; a far cry from the woman on our first meeting.

'Sadie,' she shouted. 'There's someone at the door for you.'

Sadie ran down the stairs. 'Leave her up, Gabs is going to hang out in my room, her parents are gone out, remember?'

That's how often I called Abbie. It was such a rare occurrence Sadie showed that level of excitement when I did.

Mrs Jennings lit a cigarette. 'Sadie, what have I told you time and again? There is no playing or coming inside until you do your chores. It's your choice. You either do them now and meet Gabrielle after, or you go out for your allocated outside playtime and complete your chores when you come in at seven.'

The rain dripped heavier on my back.

'I'll help you with your chores, Sadie,' I said.

Mrs Jennings shook a finger at me, from the same hand holding the cigarette. She then took a long drag and exhaled in my direction, making me cough.

'No, Gabrielle, you won't. Sadie needs to take responsibility for her own tasks. She should have done them earlier if she knew you were coming.'

'How could I do them? You made me study. I told you she was coming.'

Mrs Jennings jutted out her hip. 'If you give me cheek, I'll take away your time all together and you'll go straight up to your room alone. Now, what will it be?'

'But her parents are gone out. There's no one at her house. She's got no keys.'

'Sadie, Gabrielle is a big girl, there's plenty of other friends around here she can use for shelter. No. What I said still stands. Make your decision Sadie, I'm not standing getting cold any longer.'

Sadie squeezed past her mother's bulky frame.

'I choose Gabrielle,' she said.

Mrs Jennings closed the door on us at the exact time the thunder clapped and the heavens opened. Within seconds our hair was clung to our heads. Even our eyelashes dripped.

'Let's call to Eileen,' Sadie said running ahead. Eileen was only young but we often played with her if we were bored. The house was pitch dark. No one was there. We rang the doorbell anyway. Lightning flashed.

'Bet they went to Donnie The Destroyer too,' I said. 'Sadie, lightning scares me.'

'Follow me,' Sadie said.

I followed as she ran down the hill, and instead of turning left to go to my house she walked straight on towards an old warehouse, cutting through a length of bushes that separated the building from the road by mesh fencing. She trailed her hand along the area, until she stopped and pulled the mesh away.

'Come on.'

I followed through the bush, then the muck and leaves, until we broke free on the green hill directly in front of the building. It looked old and creepy.

'Why don't we just go to my porch? If you wanna go home, I don't mind.'

'No way,' Sadie said, continuing on, even as the rain lashed and attacked our faces. Our jackets were soaked through and my fingers were numb. Instead of going near the old building, Sadie led me to a shed, behind it. Sadie pointed to a wall with one long plank serving as a bench. More importantly, the roof extended out. We ran to the shelter, laughing deliriously, shedding our coats and shaking the wet from our hair, then huddled together for warmth. The roof stopped the majority of rain except when the wind blew in our direction. It was still bitter cold.

'Sadie, you don't need to stay. Go home.'

'No way, she's not winning. I'm staying 'til exactly ten minutes to seven and I'm not leaving one minute earlier.'

'But it's freezing.'

'I don't care. She won't win.'

'It's not a game.'

'It is. With her it always is. This is the only way I can beat her.'

Arguing with her was pointless. By the straight line of her mouth, I knew she wasn't going to talk more about that subject. Instead, I tried to lighten the mood.

'What do you want to be when you grow up Sade? When we're the adults and get to make the rules.'

'I don't know,' Sadie said, sullenly speaking to the rain. By now I knew her sulks, they had different forms, the darkest being any that involved her family.

Sadie's features never changed, she continued to stare down the rain.

'Whatever I do, it'll be miles away from here. The minute I do my Leaving and turn eighteen I'm running from Knockfarraig and never coming back.'

'Would you leave me?'

'Would you come with me?' Wary eyes watched mine.

'I love Knockfarraig. When I moved here I thought I'd hate it, but I don't.'

'If I stay in Knockfarraig it'll kill me. I won't survive. Or I swear, I'll kill one of them instead.'

'You're so dramatic. When you're older they'll have no power. You won't have to listen to them.'

'You think?'

'I know.'

Sadie slipped her hand in mine. She sang then, her voice cutting sharp sounds through the dripping rain. Even if I knew the song, it felt wrong to join in, as if she needed to let her voice out, needed me to hear her.

'Won't you hear my prayer? I have called you and asked you, are you even there?'

She petered off. After that, I could tell she needed silence, so I sat and listened to the rain battering the ground and watched the puddles deepen.

'What time is it?' she asked, eventually.

I checked my watch. 'Six thirty.'

'Right.'

She jumped off the bench and struggled to pull on her coat, the wet material sticking to her arms. Once done, she stepped out of the shelter.

'What are you doing?'

'I want her to think we were out in it all night. Let her worry I'll get pneumonia. She'll freak at the thought of having to pay the doc's bill.'

No matter how much I reasoned or cajoled she wouldn't budge from her stance. That was Sadie. If she made a decision, you couldn't sway her. The rain soaked her in seconds but for twenty minutes she stood, with the rain pouring down her face, dripping from her nose. Only shifting at ten to seven, when we crawled back out, saying goodbye at the fence.

'I'm sorry I can't bring you back. What'll you do?'

'I'll go to my porch. There's no way I'd stay here on my own.'

Sadie trudged the road spreading her legs as she walked so the wet cold cloth wouldn't touch her skin. She walked with her arms wrapped around her body, but I could see she was shivering even from far away. In all my time with Sadie, she never backed away from an argument, but that never meant she won.

To my relief, when I reached my house, the lights were on. Shocked at the sight of me, I folded into my mother's arms while my father ran for a towel. They fumed and spoke angrily about 'that woman' and I closed my eyes and let them love me with their fussing. Abbie, I was so relieved to be part of that family. I hated to think of the reception Sadie would get in comparison.

As a result of Mrs Jennings refusal to let me inside her house, I was treated to my own key. From that day on, we would never have to stand in the rain again. As for Sadie, she was sent to the doctors and stayed out of school for a week with bronchitis. She never mentioned what happened although her grin when I saw her next made me wonder whether she had played along. Sadie one, Mrs Jennings nil.

Not for long though, never for long.

In January, we took the entrance exam. Required to start all secondary schools, we were reassured it was just an assessment of our capabilities. With the majority of students enrolling in Knockfarraig Secondary School, the entrance exam was only required to determine the class and level each student needed. Everyone was excited about it being a mixed school, for me I was looking forward to not being around all girls anymore. Still, I was nervous. It was our first real exam, the first with forms and timings and extra teachers and instead of taking it in the classroom, we had to sit in separate tables and desks in the school hall. As the teacher handed out the forms, I concentrated on lining up my pencils, ruler and eraser. I heard Sadie before I saw her.

'Miss, there's been some mistake.'

Her hand hovered, stabbing the air with urgency, while the teacher made her way back. Chairs shifted and papers ruffled. The teacher took a form from the head desk and quickly made her way to Sadie. She flicked her pages and for a minute all I could hear was indecipherable whispers.

'No that's not right, I'm going to Knockfarraig,' Sadie said, her voice high.

Hushed voices followed. I held my breath waiting.

'I'm not doing it. I'm not going there. Give me the paper for Knockfarraig. I'll do that.'

The teacher shushed and cajoled but when that didn't work, she tried to remove her from the room. Sadie held on to the table. Another teacher came over. 'We'll ring your parents and sort this out. Sadie it isn't fair on the other students to disrupt them like this. Let's move you to a phone and we can fix it OK?'

'You won't,' she said, openly sobbing. 'She'll make me go. She'll get her way, she'll take me away from everyone, I know she will.'

The other teacher grabbed Sadie by the waist and lifted but Sadie still clung on to the desk until she was horizontal in the air, only letting go when the table toppled over and she had nothing left to hold.

I'll never forget the pain in her face, how when our eyes met, the fear made her eyeballs bulge. Her mother had enrolled Sadie in a different school to separate us and there was nothing we could do to stop her.

In that hall, I pictured Mrs Jennings, sat at home drinking her coffee. With a cigarette burning down in her fingers, smiling at the thought of Sadie finding out she was going to another school. As Sadie looked around at all the black headed paper with the Knockfarraig Secondary crest, hers was the only piece of paper that displayed red.

Heralded by two teachers, Sadie was carried from the hall.

Standing up, I was about to follow when Miss Simpson touched my shoulder, and softly pushed me back down, and whispered, 'I'll go,' then walked out after her. Torn between running after Sadie and starting the exams, I panicked. In the end the decision was made for me; Sadie walked back in raw faced and snivelling, held up by Miss

Simpson.

Afterwards, Sadie didn't wait to talk. She stormed out the door before any of us finished.

Later that evening she stood at my door a broken girl.

'She smiled, Gabs. When I asked her, she actually smiled.'

It only confirmed what I often wondered; her mother enjoyed Sadie suffering. As she collapsed in sobs, I held her.

'What did she say?' My mother asked, coming into the hall.

'She said she don't want me in a mixed school and Crookstown is better.'

'But your brothers go to Knockfarraig, don't they?'

'She said it's no place for girls. It's not true, she just wants to keep me away from everyone.'

That night I worried what she would do so I walked her home. There was no suggestion from either of us to go in. I walked away before she rang the doorbell, afraid of what I would say to her mother if I saw her.

The house phone rang at nine o'clock just as I was about to go to bed.

'Can you tell Sadie she is grounded and to come home immediately.'

It took me a moment to understand.

'Mrs Jennings, Sadie's not here. She hasn't been here since seven.'

'Funny. Put her on the phone.'

'I swear she's not here.'

There was silence.

'Well, when you do see her, tell her to come home immediately.'

'I'll ring around, if I hear from her, I'll ring you straight away.'

'Do that Gabrielle.'

A chill ran through me. I reran Sadie's lost look in the hall, the desperation in the way she clawed at the table, the hopelessness we both felt about the situation. Would she do something irreversible? I hoped Sadie was just trying one last attempt to convince her mother.

That she had ran away to prove her point. It hurt that she hadn't told me what she was going to do. Or run to me. There were no answers. She was gone.

It was different back then, there were no mobile phones, no way to text. If you rang someone, they had to be home to receive the call. Still, we rang everyone we knew but there was no sign. Sadie was a creature of habit. You could usually follow the path she left to my house, but this time Sadie just vanished.

'Let's go look Gabrielle,' my mother said, her voice soft with concern, and I knew then she loved Sadie as much as I did. We walked the streets of Knockfarraig with no joy. We tried the bars and shops, the area behind the shed we spent that rainy evening, anywhere we could think she would go for shelter on a cold night. There was nothing. It was so dark out there. That night I slept with my light on in the hope wherever Sadie was she would see the brightness and find her way home. My dreams were of Sadie running and crying with blood on her hands.

The next day carried on and the worry stayed in the pit of my stomach. My friend was gone, and I had no way to find her. In school, I kept looking at her empty chair. It hurt that she didn't tell me of her plans, that she still wouldn't tell me. Or that she didn't creep in to the house in the night. What if she couldn't? After another day of school, our last day before the midterm, a day Sadie termed the best as it was such a doss, I was beside myself with worry. Two days without going home, two nights without a bed. That evening, I rang her house again.

Mrs Jennings clipped phone voice answered.

'Jennings' residence.'

'I'm sorry Mrs Jennings I've tried everywhere, I've rang everyone I can think of. I can't find her. My mum was wondering if you've rung the guards?'

'There's no need, she's home.'

The relief stunned me. The other side of the line stayed silent. 'Did she just come in?'

'No. Last night. She's grounded, she isn't allowed speak to anyone.'

'We've been out looking for her.' What I held back on saying was: *you could have rung.*

'With all the commotion, it slipped my mind to tell you.' Her tone implied she was anything but sorry. 'Apologise to your mother for me and thank her too.'

The phone clicked.

Even though it was midterm, I didn't see Sadie for two weeks. Every time I called to the house I was sent away by her brothers. Her mother or Sadie never answered the door.

And then at the start of the third week, on the first morning back to school, there she was, sitting at my table eating a bowl of cornflakes. I ran over and hugged her so hard the chair toppled us both onto the floor.

'Where did you sleep?'

'Behind the shed.'

'But we checked there.'

Nodding her head, she sat back on her chair and scooped piles of soggy cornflakes into her mouth as if she hadn't eaten in days, spraying bits everywhere when she spoke. 'When I heard someone coming I ran. My brothers showed me the place when we were younger and it would be just like them to want to dob me in. It was only after, I wondered if it was you. Anyway, I was fuming, I needed to be on my own. I stayed up all night. If I went to yours, they'd look. I knew you'd convince me to go home.'

'Where did you go?'

'Bussed it to the city for the day. When I ran out of money I went home.'

'Was it worth being grounded for the midterm?'

Sadie smiled that sunshine smile, 'For one day I was free.'

I'd love to say I did something after that, like reported Mrs Jennings or got revenge or even confronted her but what could a twelve-year-old do?

I'm not going to go on about the rest of primary school, you know what it's like to grow up Abbie. We survived it, that's all I'll say about that.

Sore Neck

Abbie

Her neck ached from craning.

'I need a break from reading. My neck is killing me and my eyes are going blurry.'

Sadie peered over her magazine. 'If you want to finish it by tonight, I wouldn't stop.'

'Even in school we get breaks.'

Sadie sighed. 'What time is it?' She checked her phone. 'Just gone eleven. How about you lie on the bed and rest your neck while I make you a coffee? Eat a biscuit or something, read for a while and then, in an hour, we'll have some lunch. You'll regret it if you don't read it all.'

'How do you know what I'll regret? You don't know me.'

'I know you're a smart ass who thinks they know everything. I also know *you* know shit. You've no idea how lucky you were to have a mother like her. What I would have given to be loved the way your mother loved you. Now here's an opportunity to fill in the blanks and find out how much, to let her tell you in her own words how much she loved you and you're so uninterested... you act like you just don't give a flying fuck.'

Abbie crossed her arms.

'For someone who asked me not to judge, you're pretty judgy

yourself.'

Sadie flicked over a page of the magazine without looking at it.

'Never said I wasn't. Believe me, in order to survive, I have to sum people up quickly.'

Sadie stood and at the counter, opened a bottle of water and poured the contents into the kettle. Abbie listened to the glug as it filled, to the snap of the lid closing, to the pop of the kettle sitting in its cradle as the switch flicked. All the while, Sadie's back was to her as she set about getting cups.

'What if I don't want to know?' Abbie cringed at the way her voice travelled. She meant for it to sound bitchy, but out loud the neediness in her tone was all she could hear.

Sadie didn't turn, but she seemed to bristle. Yet, she smiled at Abbie when she handed her a coffee.

'I won't promise you anything cos I can't say if you'll be happy by the end or whether you'll regret it. All I can say is it's the truth. Me, I wouldn't be able to stop. I'd have to read it, but then again, I'm a nosey person. Maybe you like being ignorant. No offence.'

It was Abbie's time to bristle. 'It doesn't mean I want to stay ignorant. Just... what if knowing the truth makes life worse? What if knowing my mum loved me makes me unhappier? It's not like at the end of this I get to have her here. It's not like we can make up and hug and live happily after. The story is always going to end the same way, with both my parents dead.'

Sadie blew into her cup, thinking. When she spoke, it was in a softer voice than Abbie had heard from her before.

'Who says that has to be the end of the story? It won't be the end of yours. It's not like you'll drop dead after the last page, is it? You say you don't remember your mum, so who are your parents to you really at the moment? They're strangers. Reading this, they can be real. At least you'll get a sense of them, of who they really are.'

Sadie studied her.

'Look, maybe you're right, maybe you should stop reading. I've done my bit. If you'd prefer, just close it and leave it be. By delivering the book, my duty is complete. You know your mother's wish. It's on you, not me if you don't.'

'What would you do?'

'Honestly?'

Abbie nodded and both of them seemed surprised that she cared what the other thought.

'If it was for your mother, I'd sit down and read that straightaway and I wouldn't stop until I finished. I'd devour every word, Abbie. Then I'd reread it and savour the gift she'd given me. Then again, if it was from my mother, I'd burn it.'

Sand

Gabrielle

The years spent lost in the unknowing of the Irish language set something off in me. Before, in England, the thought of the teacher's wrath made my skin go hot and clammy. In Ireland, I learned if you challenged someone you wouldn't drop down and die. Being punished didn't mean your life was over. That fact was a revelation.

There was such a tight rein over Sadie that she was never allowed to rebel. Her curfews were rigid and if she stepped over by even a few minutes there were harsh consequences. Some I found out about, some were only implied.

Sometimes she used us as a brunt for her anger, when she'd shout at us for cheating in a game, or kick stones in the garden, or snap when we dared ask her how she was. Whatever she did, we never retaliated, knowing she needed a buffer to let out. My parents gave up trying to communicate with her mother and stepped back, knowing if they pushed further an outright ban would be made on the house. All we could do was offer a place of refuge on the times she was allowed out. Sadie got thinner and quieter and every time she entered, she walked with a stoop and her head down. As time ticked on she would unfurl, until by the end she would be smiley Sadie once more, only to have to go home again. I used to hate seeing her drag her legs to prolong the journey.

There's a scientific reason for the teenage years, I've read. It's got to do with a chemical explosion as your hormones work overtime. Also, as the brain develops, empathy is at an all time low. It makes sense. Due to those years, I certainly entered adulthood with a few regrets. Sadie couldn't. She had to suppress those emotions. If you are in a similar scenario ever, find a way. Find an outlet to get rid of the feelings of suppression. Suppressing the suppression only compresses it more. It's like a ticking timebomb. Just ask Sadie. Or, later, me.

My artistic streak continued in my bedroom as I grew older. Each year I changed my room. One time I painted it wall to wall black. Another year I found fluorescent yellow paint in a bargain bin in town. With the first stroke, I understood why it was so cheap, for as soon as I started one wall the worst headache came upon me. For effect, and due to stubbornness, I carried on but afterwards, each time I walked into my room, a headache would switch on like the bright light bulb it imitated. The colour lasted three days, painted over with the spare black I had gathering cobwebs in the garage. When I started going to clubs, I collected the flyers and stuck them to the walls. Eventually they became wallpaper, a collage of music and clubs.

When I'd finally had enough, I took that black paint out again. On the ceiling, standing on the tip of my toes with a tiny brush, I painted the night sky. It took me months, but it was good, because at the time I needed the distraction. One time, when Sadie was allowed join us on a trip to Galway, I found a store that sold plastic stars that shone in the dark, and at night when the darkness took over, their glow got me through.

As far back as I can remember, I've always been scared of the dark. It's when bad things happen. Even as a child I knew this, even though I was safe in that house in England and again in my childhood home in Ireland, I knew it. I think now it may have been a warning, a premonition, even as a child I knew there would be danger in the dark for me. Even as an adult, there is something terrifying in facing the night alone. Or together, with demons, is worse.

Sadie was dealing with her own troubles. Secondary school meant longer days in class, Knockfarraig secondary was only a ten minute walk but Crookstown was a whole other town away. Although walkable, weighed down with a heavy school bag, Sadie had to rely on unreliable buses to get home. With extra homework came an earlier curfew so there often wasn't enough time to make a visit. Sadie found it difficult to make new friends at the best of times, and without her friends' support, she found it impossible. An outsider from the start, Sadie worried the girls in her class thought she was strange. The teachers in her school labelled her difficult and she made it her business to live up to their expectations.

The only saving grace was the guy her age who travelled on the same bus. After weeks of eye contact, one day he sat next to her and struck up a conversation. Dying for any type of affection, Sadie relished his attention. His name was Barry, he had a dimple on his left cheek and smelt of chewing gum and when he slipped his hand into hers, she loved him already. When he suggested they go on the hop from school and hang out she didn't hesitate. Barry was her first proper kiss, her first fumble, the first guy to tell her he liked her. That night, breathless with excitement, she told me all about her perfect day.

The next day in school, Sadie discovered she'd picked the wrong choice. Saffron Hartigan, a girl she'd never spoken to, also happened to be Barry's girlfriend, tore her nails into Sadie's scalp, catching her by the roots and pulling her along the ground with such force she still has a scar on the side of her head from where the hair came away. It didn't matter that she hadn't known he was seeing someone else. After that she became enemy number one. Day after day, the group of girls came for her. School, once a haven, was now another place to dread.

She couldn't even cling to me. In my school, I discovered new friends who hung out on the far side of town on the weekends. Sadie couldn't. Her mother refused to give her the bus fare. Even when I offered to pay, Sadie was too afraid to defy her mother. Sometimes I stayed at home for her but most of the time the draw of losing out on excitement was too much. I left her behind Abbie.

A pattern formed where anyone she came in contact with told her everything was her fault. Contempt and scorn always walked side by side with Sadie. She didn't deserve any of it. How could I convince her when I couldn't convince myself I didn't deserve all the bad times ahead?

By then Maureen hung around with us. The two girls only got on when they sided with each other to prove a point to me. It was the only thing that could bond them. Thankfully Maureen lived on the other side of Knockfarraig, so we didn't see her too often.

Despite our differences and change of school, we always clawed back some time together. In the summer, we woke before the sun rose, for the beach unless the weather stopped us. Every Saturday. On those mornings, Sadie would sneak up to my room so not to wake the others. All I'd need was a tickle of my toes, then I'd grab a towel and swimsuit and we'd set off. If she was grounded, Sadie would still dare the journey, just making sure to be back before her mother woke, which on a Saturday wouldn't happen before ten. If she wasn't grounded, we were free for the whole day. We were masters of our world lying on that sand. The beach only ours, with the sand and the tide out far in front of us. There, our secrets would lift from our shoulders, drifting away with the wind, taken far away by the waves and set free for another week. We would wait for the sunrise, lying on those towels as the sun warmed our souls and skin. As an adult, I think of those days. When the stress becomes too much, I remember those times I didn't need to be anywhere or think of anything else. In those moments, there were barely any words between us, there didn't need to be. The only sound required was the pull of the waves, the intake of our breath. The only requirement was the other beating heart beside us for right then, right there, we were never alone. It was the only time we didn't have to pretend to everyone else. On that beach the mask could be removed. The sea would take our imperfections, our mistakes, salting our wounds as we dived in, the water absolved our previous grievances.

When I die, it will be in the sea. I want my final breath to be under the water.

Abbie

Abbie nearly dropped the book.
She knew then.

Gabrielle

On the rare occasion my family wanted to do something together, the only activity we agreed upon was a trip to the woods. The boys loved the swing that hung on a branch of an old tree, where they could spend hours competing about who could launch higher over the lake. Lily loved sitting in the flowers, picking the perfect bouquet which she would present to our mother, who would always act surprised, as if she hadn't just watched her picking them for the last thirty minutes. Dad and I loved to hike, getting lost in the trail, where one would hum while the other had to guess the song, or he would point out an unusual tree or flower. It was the seat for Mum. Directly next to the field of flowers Lily loved, it also overlooked the lake and the tree so she could sit and watch the view while at the same time keep an eye on all of us. Usually, we finished the trip with a picnic by the car park. One time, the boys brought a tennis ball and as we ate, they volleyed it to each other back and forth, trying to catch the other unaware. Competition was always high between the two, which meant it didn't matter what else was going on - they could eat, chat, drink, and pretend to focus on something else but when that ball was thrown, the other was waiting.

Limp, discarded bits of bread lay on paper plates. A piece of ham, curled at the edges, turned purple in the heat. Lily munched on a grape. The boys ball went back and forth throughout.

'Boys stop it for a while will ye?' Dad said. 'Pass me the water.'

Mum passed the jug without looking up, while still heaping some salad onto her plate; a requirement she insisted on bringing for every trip even though she was the only one who ever ate it, then complained about the waste after.

'So what's this I'm hearing about giving cheek to the teacher, Sam?' Dad asked.

Sam scowled. 'Ah, Dad, it's not fair, Miss Hastings has it out for me all year.'

'Does that mean you can call her saggy tits?' Dad said raising his tone.

Sam went puce. Lily shouted. 'What's saggy tits?'

Mum tickled her under her arm. 'It's what happened to mum after she breastfed four kids.'

'You're not helping,' Dad frowned.

'Sorry,' Mum said, hands up in the air.

Darren threw the ball at Sam. Distracted, Sam's reflexes were off. Although he still caught it, it slipped out of his fingers and bounced straight into the cake mum spent all morning baking.

'For Christ's sake what did I tell you about the ball,' Dad said picking it up and vaulting it into the woods, spraying bits of icing as it flew.

'Dad!' Darren said, standing to retrieve it.

'Stay there. You're to stop that messing.'

'I'll get it,' I said, glad of the excuse to get away from the argument.

Before he could stop me I ran into the dense grass, ducking my head to avoid a branch. The grass was thicker there, a part of the trail walkers seldom used, as it lead nowhere and didn't have any path. Every time I had tried to explore in the past, my father or mother had called for me to go the other way. Now was my chance to investigate. I retrieved the ball fairly easily, the bright yellow sticking out between the tufts of grass. In the distance, Dad's raised voice still carried, for when the rare sound did erupt from him it took a while to settle back. Better stay here, I thought. Walking further, I noticed indents in the grass, like tyre tracks, as if someone had drove between some gap in the trees from the car park. I followed and sure enough, hidden from the clearing was a car. Careful not to be spotted, I ducked down, for my instincts told me any car that drove in this far didn't want to be noticed. At first, the car appeared empty. When I was just about to turn back I heard a soft moan. It was not the sound of someone in trouble, not the sound of a hurt animal or danger. Curious it drew me towards it. On the closer inspection, the car was moving. The engine wasn't running. Instead of rolling forward or backwards, it was rocking. Nearer, I made out a figure. Two figures. The tips of their heads only slightly visible from the back window. The male more so, as he leaned upwards, displaying his black face and shirtless torso as he looked down on the woman under him, her blonde head bobbing. I edged closer to a bush, hiding behind it, shifting my view from the back to the side. I couldn't see the woman's face, but the man's was clear. The look on his was a mix of determination, of satisfaction, of being totally lost in the moment. His face looked as if he was in pain, and the noises coming from the car were primal. The woman's knee knocked against the window and her leg rested on the seat in front. She still had her shoes on. Gold mules with a brooch on the toe.

'Gabrielle, where are you?' My mother shouted. I crawled away, afraid the couple would look up. Once safe, I stood and ran.

On the way back, the mood in the car was subdued. The argument I thought I missed had gone on for ten more minutes while I finished my lunch. Most of us picked at cake until we gave up trying to pretend the trip wasn't ruined. In the car, Dad still prickled and my brothers knew better than to start messing. Lily, still eating her lunch, spilt the bits of cake she hadn't finished at the clearing all over the car. In her rush to pick up the crumbs, she also knocked over her open bottle of lemonade covering the chairs, and herself too. Screaming with sticky liquid, Lily waved her hands, flicking the lemonade on us. Dad, who by that stage had turned a shade of purple, pulled over at the petrol station. As he was ignoring the boys, he asked me to run in for napkins, a packet of baby wipes and a plastic bag. Closing the door on Lily's squeals and my fathers shouts to hurry, I grabbed some napkins from the coffee dock, and the first pack of baby wipes I could see and rushed to the queue. A woman in front was arguing in whispers with another woman behind the counter. The writer in me edged closer to hear.

'You've taken them before.'

'The boss says we can't anymore, sorry.'

'What am I supposed to do?'

'I don't know,' the cashier said, picking up a piece of paper as if busy, hoping to end the conversation.

'But I've come all this way. Don't you understand I have mouths to feed?'

The cashier's mouth softened.

'I do. But I can't cash it here anymore. You'll have to go to the post office Mrs Jennings.'

As soon as I realised who it was, I backed away, bumping straight into a man big enough to block the entire aisle. I tried to scoot past, but he was too wide to even turn. Stuck between them, my only hope was to sneak past the gap. When I turned, Mrs Jennings faced me.

'Get a good look?' she said. There were tears in her eyes and she was wringing her hands.

'I wasn't trying to listen, I didn't know it was you.'

I looked away from her, to the floor. Her shoes were gold mules with a brooch at the toes.

'It was you,' I gasped. 'In the woods. In the car.'

Mrs Jennings face contorted, her eyes widened.

'You will ruin my family. Any chance of saving my marriage will be gone. You'll break Sadie's heart.'

Before that day, I had never saw her emotional, never contemplated that she was capable of feeling pain. 'Don't tell.'

'I won't.'

Mrs Jennings covered her face in her hands. 'You will. Of course you will. You'd love to have that on me.'

'When I promise something, I promise.'

The woman dropped her hands. Looked warily at me.

'If I tell you I won't say anything than I mean it. What happened in the woods is your story to tell. If Sadie finds out, she won't hear it from me.'

Mrs Jennings tipped her head, about to walk away.

'One thing though. If you ever touch her again I'll kill you.'

'Sorry?'

'I'll keep your secret but if you ever hurt her again, I'll hurt you.'

I ran then, back to my noisy, messy car. From that day, I never saw another bruise. If only that could stop Sadie being hurt.

Until the moment Sadie reads this, I kept that promise. I'm sorry Sadie. For I don't want to hurt you but maybe it will help make sense of your mother's ways. I don't know if she loved the man she met that day, or if he was Sadie's father. Or if she was lonely after her husband abandoned her. Or why she had to go to that petrol station to cash a cheque. What I hoped for at the time was the man was Sadie's father, and he had given Mrs Jennings money to support Sadie and if not revealed by me, then one day he could form a relationship with her. It made me wonder if Mr Jennings was sending any money home. All the refusals to let Sadie buy clothes or bus fare made sense after that. Before, I questioned if she did it out of spite, after I understood she was doing it out of necessity. Money wise, anyway.

Over the course of my life, I've learnt even the people who do the nastiest acts aren't born evil. Even monsters love something or someone. They are still kind to *someone*. Everyone has two sides, we can all be different variants of ourself to different people. Monsters take hurt and deal with it differently. Monsters learn to transfer the pain to someone else.

I asked Sadie once if her parents hurt her and she looked at me with genuine surprise. Not at my asking, but at my question. She never answered. And if she had what could I do about it anyway? Back then, neighbours heard arguments and stayed silent. It was normal for kids to be left on their own while the parents went to the pub.

How can I describe the abuse? It wasn't the physical, because that was dealt with solely by Sadie and was never shared. Over the years I have tried to pick at it, tried to reason out what I saw, tried to understand it, wondering if it was even real. There was nothing of weight to pick up: no blood, no evidence that Sadie didn't explain as some other accident, no slip of the mask in my company, no once off occurrence that you could decipher and pour over the details. What happened was normal. What happened was her normal. As a teenager I couldn't back up what I felt was happening, I couldn't fight back against adults that were meant to know what they were supposed to be doing but now, as an adult, as a mother, as a writer, I can.

It was the stripping of her importance. The devaluing. The hatred. Once, I read a book about a mother who picked out one of her children, to attack, abuse and under nourish at any opportunity, treating the child appallingly while she doted on the others. And the children accepted it because they knew if they didn't, they would be ostracised or even worse, replaced as the new one. This is the only way I can describe Sadie's life. She was the runt, the scourge on the family. The one supposed to feel shame and expected to. So, Sadie got angry with everything but the people she was afraid of. She broke things that would never be linked to her or her family. Her knuckles would often be grazed from where she had slammed the wall in frustration. She'd shoplift then give the things away so they wouldn't be discovered in the random searches of her bare room. Anger served her well. Sadie took the hurt and deflected it by any means necessary. After that girl attacked her in school, Sadie learnt to fight back and she fought dirty if needed. Sometimes it was needed. She clawed, scratched. She ripped people apart with her tongue. Sometimes unwarranted, often at the wrong people.

Anger was never my friend. No matter how much I tried, I couldn't use that emotion for my benefit. Instead, I took anger and internalised it.

It is a very strange concept to imagine when you read this you'll probably be a teenager. I look at you now beside me asleep as I write, and all I can do is smile. Beauty oozes from you Abbie. Your pale skin is the exact pigment of mine. A colour I spent my life despising. Yet, on you, it is this beautiful, smooth, luscious design, as delicate as porcelain, as flawless as a painting, the most perfect alabaster hue. In your beauty, I now see my own and I'm grateful for what you teach me. For I have learnt a child teaches more than any adult. Because of you, I love more, care more, am more than I could ever conceive. Every pore overflows with fun and wonder and excitement. Each day I have, I'm thankful you are in my life. I can't imagine you ever being mean or answering back or saying things that are hurtful. Of course, you will. Those years are purposeful; part of a bigger plan you have to go through. Some innocence has to be shed to enter adulthood. Pleasure sought, vices tasted, boundaries moved, relationships tested and cheating death are requirements for passage. A teen has to encounter a level of regret or guilt. There is no such thing as an innocent adult. It's normal, whatever you're feeling is normal. And I want you to know, I would have loved you regardless. We might not have liked each other for a while granted, but I still would have loved you.

The Stroke

Abbie

Blocking her face from Sadie, Abbie wiped at her eyes. Before reading, she couldn't have imagined the power of her mother's words. It was a sucker punch of love. A suspicious shroud of affection.

A flicker then, of a memory settled in of a big bed, of sprawling out, of a hand stroking her hair, of a song sung. Whenever she had remembered it before, she'd assumed it was Maureen, but now the image was clearer. A shaft of light on her arm from the big windows that must have been in Scart's End. A pillow patterned with flowers she'd never found at Maureen's house. Only now did it dawn that it was her mother's hand. It was her mother's voice.

At the time her mother wrote the page she'd just read, Abbie had been beside her. That page, those lines were evidence, of at least one instance when her mother smiled after looking at her.

Beauty oozes from you Abbie. Your pale skin is the exact pigment of mine. A colour I spent my life despising. Yet, on you, it is this beautiful, smooth, luscious design, as delicate as porcelain, as flawless as a painting, the most perfect alabaster hue. In your beauty, I now see my own and I'm grateful for what you teach me. For I have learnt a child teaches more than any adult. Because of you, I love more, care more, am more than I could ever conceive. Every pore overflows with fun and wonder and excitement. Each day I have, I'm thankful you are in my life.

She wasn't sure if she could continue reading. The words dislodged something, unravelled her wound up nerves, making her afraid if she tried to push further, she would come loose completely. It was losing it in front of Sadie that kept her going, because she would rather die than give the woman that satisfaction. Bound to the book now, a need had opened out stronger than anything else she had ever felt in her life. She needed to know. Abbie had to get to the end and find out what happened to her mother.

Denial

Gabrielle

In my later teenage years I became a little lost. No, hold on, I swore to you I wouldn't lie; I *was* lost.

From the day I left England, I felt like an outsider; no matter where I was, I didn't fit; no matter how much I tried to blend, even with the friends I made, I was different. Until I discovered a way to melt into the mix.

There is a cycle when taking drugs – the high and come down polar opposites from each other. Every person knows this happens with harder drugs like heroin but the high from ecstasy can be so uplifting that it's worth the low, and you long for it, long to reach that level of living again, because it was like I only truly lived then and everything in between was just a half life; a waiting for existence, a counting of hours and days until I heard that beat again and took that pill and danced in a dark room where I could dive under the music.

For a long time Sadie didn't know. It was my secret thing, a delicious tightrope walk of who I was with her compared with my other friends. It was separate, even when she did find out, I would never offer Sadie drugs or take them in her presence. Too protective, I would have been horrified if she ingested the same as me, yet I wanted her to experience the club, to lose herself to the music, to feel free for even a moment.

After months of begging, Sadie fabricated an elaborate story about a 'sleepover' in a school friend's house to her mother and, for once, she consented.

Excited to share my love of the place, I watched every reaction from Sadie, wanting her to experience the same feeling as she walked up the metal stairs, the clip clop of our heels, the swish of our skirts as we moved fast, of the crowds as they swelled towards us like a wave as we entered the room, like a soft fog of love swirling around us, pointing to the dark corners where you could hide or get lost in someone's arms, with the pumping beat so loud it made you bounce, so loud there was no point in trying to talk.

The reaction didn't come. That night I whooped and jumped and tried everything to pass over the feelings of freedom that ran over me, that ran through me, wanting them to pass through her too, to feel it too. If anyone needed to escape it was Sadie, but she was never one to do the conventional, expected thing. The longer we stayed, the more Sadie's shoulders curled inwards.

A song I loved came on and I allowed it overtake me, closing my eyes and letting the music filter through my body. Without any drugs I felt myself raising, when I opened my eyes Sadie wasn't in front of me, wasn't standing next to me. After scanning the crowd, I found her sitting on one of the few benches lining the walls, holding her head. I fought the urge to shake her down. As I sat beside her, she didn't look up. Two guys wobbly on their feet stood in front of me peering down at Sadie. She hadn't noticed them or me. With her head in her hands, her dark legs stretched out in front, bare and gleaming under the strobe lights, the two men grinned and elbowed each other, their leering faces as they ducked their heads low, as they tried to get a look under, tried to see more than they should, their shouts travelled over the music.

'Ya reckon it's the same?'

'What?'

'Black pussy.'

'I heard when you open it out it's bright pink inside.'

'The black one's are right goers. She'll ride ya for hours, boy.'

'Tenner I'll find out.'

Without another thought, I'd jumped up and slapped the nearest guy across the back of the head. He swerved to the side then ricocheted back, raising his arm to punch. When he saw his attacker was a woman he stopped, stunned. It bought me enough time. I snarled at him, when I'd never snarled at anyone before.

'Get away from her or I'll cut your balls off.'

In that environment, you could never show fear. You had to show your worst, you had to show what you were willing to do. In that scenario, it worked, the two guys backed off, disappeared into the crowd. My chest heaved as I watched them go, afraid to back down, afraid to turn and not face them, I waited a minute before checking on Sadie. When I did, her head wasn't in her hands anymore but hugging her legs. The strobe lights illuminated the whites of her eyes, showing multiple streams flowing down her face.

'You all right?' I asked kneeling on the floor, placing my hands on hers.

Sadie looked at me, and I knew by the way she did I wasn't the only one to have overheard.

'I want to go home.'

The words were stolen by the music but I understood. Without sound, I heard every syllable, every pronunciation, every bit of meaning.

Even in the club she couldn't disappear. My accent could blend, could silence, could go unnoticed. Her skin was always seen. For Sadie, there was nowhere to escape, no place ever to get lost in the crowd. Sadie would stand out everywhere she went and here's the truth Abbie, at that moment, it annoyed the hell out of me. Instead of changing it, or trying to change it, I blamed her for not sliding over their comments, or not ignoring it, for not seeking fun, or pretending to, at least for not letting go. My friends at these clubs wanted escape, wanted the laugh; the craic always the priority. Sadie reminded me of what life was like outside of those thumping walls, representing real problems, real lives. In that moment, I resented her for ruining my special place, the one place I could go where worry wasn't allowed. Denial beat everything else in there. Denial was the only way to survive. We left early that night. After that, I stopped asking her to come, and she never brought up about going to the club again.

Instead of supporting her, I chased fun. I wanted to escape my body, my brain, my English accent. In there, I didn't have to be the good daughter, the reliable friend, the girl who sorted out her siblings problems, the babysitter, the studying student. I could just be the dancer, the girl who got lost in the music, who blended and flowed with sound, where colours blurred and meant nothing, yet meant everything, where everyone was one.

With everything in life there are opposite poles and the other side has to have their moment and as time went by, the comedowns caught up. No one warns you about the down side to partying, no one you listen to anyway. They don't tell you how you will go home aching from dancing all night, how you'll wake up in the same clothes from the night before, how you'll smell from drink and sweat and shame. How your cheeks will ache from chewing on them and smiling. How your gums will bleed from gurning. How you'll look at yourself and not know who you are. How you won't know how to turn it around.

Abbie, I've made many mistakes. I took the wrong turn more times than the right. Everyone thought I was so steadfast but inside I was just a mess. Pretence has weight; I was good at hiding it, so good I convinced even myself I was doing well. For I was the one who looked after everyone, who stood up for them when they turned speechless, who listened when they were distraught, who held them as they cried. Back then, I was solid. Back then, I didn't comprehend that I would ever need the same, so I never asked and nobody ever knew better to try.

One of those occasions was an all-night party we went to after the club. It was a friend of a friend's place, as it always is with these things. I'd gone at it pretty hard in the club with alcohol and the cab journey made me queasy. The others disappeared into corners or different rooms as soon as we arrived. Left on my own, I searched for the bathroom. After a few failed attempts at opening the wrong doors I eventually found the bathroom upstairs. There wasn't a lock on the door. Even in my drunkenness, I threw my bag down on the floor so that if someone tried to come in, it would block it a little, buy me a little time to sort myself out. As I finished, the door handle moved, so I shouted, 'hold on, someone's in here, I'll only be a second.'

Pulling my knickers up and fixing my dress back over my thighs, it still wasn't fast enough. The door opened, and a guy appeared.

'Someone's in here,' I said, placing a hand on my side of the door to block it.

'Sorry, never heard you,' the guy said but he didn't stop poking his head around the door. He was over six foot and broad, with a neck bigger than my thigh. He eased my hand away like it was made of plasticine. As he stepped in, his large frame and the door pushed me back against the sink. He closed the door behind him.

'Let me pass,' I said.

He stuck out his hands in the air front of him.

'Chill a minute, we're just talking, there's no need to be funny.'

After countless vodkas, I was drunk but not numb enough to feel prickles on the back of my neck. The only thing I could do was brazen it out.

'Chill? Why would I chill when you just barged in after I telling you I was here? That's pretty unchilled if you ask me. Now, you've pushed me out of the way and closed the door, standing in front of me blocking my way. Let me out.'

He shifted his bulk so his stomach touched my chest. He spoke low. 'Don't piss me off.'

His features were slippery, sliding from one expression to another. On some type of drug definitely. Black eyes that should have been blue. The grind of the jaw where the gurning had turned menacing.

'Why do you have to be like that? I just wanted to be friendly.'

On the wrong side of the bathroom to run, I looked around for anything that could be used to defend myself. Edging away from the sink, I leant on the window.

'Let's start again. I'm not trying to be like anything. You freaked me out standing there. We can chat if that's what you want? Why don't we get out of here, talk outside?'

Here's a tip for you Abbie, if you're ever in a not so nice situation, be cool first, be nice, for it might diffuse the situation. I hate that this is the truth – that as women we have to make ourselves smaller, dumber, more docile, more weak just to get out of a situation. Believe me though, if you can, this works better than confrontation with a man. Especially with a six foot tall and nearly as wide, drugged out guy. Flattery may get you somewhere: reasoning, joking, anything that gets him to soften, to lower his guard, whatever's needed to get you out of that sweaty, claustrophobic bathroom. Leave desperate measures to the last resort – leave that to shock tactics if necessary.

'Here's grand. I don't want to go outside, right here's perfect,' he said while stepping towards me. His top lip curled up in a slight smile, revealing teeth. That smile told me his secrets. He thought he had me summed up, as soon as he clocked the drunk me, probably from the moment I staggered through the front door. For him it was easy, for him it was job done.

He tugged at the bottom of my skirt, jerking the material higher up my thigh. I closed my eyes when I felt his hand rough against my skin. My breath hitched. His fingers kept moving up, until they reached the crotch of my underwear. I clamped my legs shut.

What to do, what to do, what to do?

'No. I don't want that. I don't want you to.'

He tugged, pulled at the material until he slipped a finger inside the fabric. Bile rose up my throat. I pushed him gently on the chest.

'I said I don't want that.'

He shoved me against the sink, hoisting my leg on the basin, now yanking the material, ripping it in two. I felt the cool air, exposed and open. He held my thigh hard enough a purple welt formed. He wasn't looking at my thigh, or my face, he didn't care what I looked like or how scared I was. He slobbered on my neck, his other hand working up to my breast. I froze. I stopped breathing. When he squeezed my nipple, my breath hitched in pain, acting like the ammonia in smelling salts, forcing me back to the room, to my body. He nudged my thigh with his thigh, to free his hand.

Do not let him touch you there.

I leant to one side and just as his finger touched my pubic bone, I sprayed him in the eyes with a can of deodorant that was on the window sill. As he fell, as he let go of me to wipe at his eyes, I kicked him in the balls for good measure, making sure to push him, so he fell away from the door.

Like I said, be cool first, be nice, for you might diffuse the situation. But. When nice fails, feel free to use whatever you can. Do whatever is necessary to get out of that room because otherwise, you will leave there a different person.

As I opened the door and escape was in sight, he grabbed my leg causing me to fall down with my skirt over my head, exposing my bare bottom to the people standing in the hall. I kicked at his face until he let go. I didn't care what the onlookers saw. As quick as I could, I ran out of that house, not even stopping to call out for my friends in the other room.

Remember this story, Abbie. Use it as a reminder that there are always people around who try to prey on the vulnerable, or on a girl too drunk or too out of it. Remember these men, these predators, for they wait in the background until you're alone.

There are many different forms of predators. Men who will watch you become incapacitated and then strike. Some wait until you're on your own or can't defend yourself. Some have no interest in you when you are drunk and will wait until you sober up so you remember every detail of what they put you through. Others use the power of their voice, or their charm, and will say anything to persuade you they are trustworthy to get you where they want you. Or there's the kind that attack before they say anything at all. Who hide in the shadows and catch you unaware. Some swear they love you. Others set you at ease first, so you drop your guard. One type will get off on your fear. Sneaky ones put something in your drink. The last, possibly the worst, will list the ways it's all your fault, how you caused what's happening. Drinking makes you vulnerable to them all.

Remember this story, because it plays a part in my future.

That night, I came home to find my mother on the last step of the stairs. For once, we didn't fight. There were no angry words, no chastising. Instead she shuffled over on the step and I sat beside her. She looped her arm around me and I rested my head on her shoulder.

'I'm sorry.'

'Something happened? I woke up to this feeling like you needed me. After that I couldn't sleep so I thought I'd wait.'

'Thanks.' I slipped my hand into hers. 'I had the worst night.'

'You look tired. Are you tired of it all yet?'

I nodded.

'How's this for an idea?' She turned to me, brushed my hair away from my face so I could see her properly. 'What about if we gave you an incentive? If you stop all this... this going out, we'll save up and next year, next summer, after your Leaving Cert, if you start studying we'll take you and the lads across Europe.'

'Like a holiday?'

'Like an extended trip. We can plan out all the places you want to go. Take a month or so, however long we need.'

'You'd do that?'

My mother stroked my face. 'If it means getting my girl back, I'll go anywhere.'

It wasn't about the trip Abbie. I agreed because I could no longer deny what I was doing was impacting on the rest of my family. All the worrying, the waiting, the checking me for signs of drugs was ruining my parent's life as well as my own. From that day on, I didn't touch another drug.

Remember this story too Abbie, for that trip changed my life.

Scones

Abbie

Abbie ran through the times she had been scared in male company. Last year, when she'd tried alcohol for the first time, a guy, a stranger, had been hovering around the park. She'd noticed him throughout the night but as the pleasant veil of numbness had snaked over her from the drink she hadn't cared enough to notice where he went. When it was time to go home, she had stood unsteadily. None of the lads had to go home early, so she walked out of the park alone. It was only when she reached the worst part, the darkest spot, where the floodlights were broken that she heard the footsteps behind her. Before turning around, she knew it was too late to run, knew already who it was going to be. The man grabbed her by the sleeve and tried to pull her into the bushes and Abbie didn't know where it came from but she screamed a sound she had never heard come out before. It could be heard from the other side of the park. That time it worked. That time the man ran. After her escape, all she wanted to do was go home, to reach the safety of her bed but after what she read she wondered, about predators. Was that a once off for the man? Or had he made sure the next time the girl wouldn't be able to scream?

Looking around, Sadie kept her hotel room neat. Sadie's nose had twitched the first time Abbie placed her cup on the counter, away from the coaster, so, she had purposely missed it each time since. After that, she'd crumpled the duvet shifting back and forth, deliberately puckering the cover and revelling at Sadie's failure to hide her annoyance. Yeah, she had her sussed. Yet she didn't understand why she done it, why she wanted to annoy her. Was it because this woman had been closer to her mother than she ever would? Sadie shared stories with Gabrielle Abbie would never hear. At the same time, the woman had given her a glimpse of her mother she would never have had if she didn't turn up.

There was no way she would say thank you though.

Abbie tried to picture Sadie sitting in a club, hearing those men talk about her like that.

'Have you read this?' Abbie asked.

Sadie, lying on the bed, opened her eyes and sat up slow. 'Yes.'

'Did you mind the things she wrote?'

Sadie's smile didn't reach her eyes. 'She saw me more than I saw myself. Your mother wrote about things I could never speak of, in a way I will never voice. Things I thought I hid.'

'Why do you have to go later?'

'I have work.'

'Where do you live?'

'I'd rather not say.'

'Seriously?'

'Seriously. Until you finish the story at least. Until you make a decision.'

'What decision? What am I going to hear?'

'Why don't we go for a walk and clear our heads? I could do with some salt air.'

'My mum was right.'

'About?'

'You are a master of deflection.'

Sadie grinned. 'Your mother was right about everything.'

'We'll see.'

'That we will. I'd say you're about a third through. How about we go for a quick walk then pick up lunch? We'll bring the book and you can read when you want.'

* * *

Sadie parked the car. 'We should be safe enough here.'

The sea roared and crashed against the rocks. The wind pummelled Abbie's face and chest as she got out. She pulled her jacket tighter and closed the zip. 'Good idea for that walk Sadie.'

'Hold on,' Sadie said and ran to the boot. She handed Abbie a fleece and scarf.

'You'll need them,' Abbie said.

'Nah, I've a windbreaker and I'm not a whinge bag like you.' Sadie smiled.

'If I remember correct, there's a restaurant down the end of the pier. How about we go there?'

Abbie shrugged in response; it was too windy to talk. The waves were wild. They crashed violently against the stones and even though the women walked on the road rather than sand, the wind and waves were forceful enough for the spray to reach their faces. Abbie liked it, the droplets formed a veil on her skin. Even so, she picked up the pace, falling in step beside Sadie, eager to read on. It wasn't just a breeze but the type of wind you had to lean into to walk, making her almost horizontal in order to move. The violent air made them gulp and gasp. The sand whipped enough they both held their hands up to their eyes to stop the grit landing. By the time the restaurant came into view they were running for the door.

At the entrance, they both stopped and waited for the other to enter. Abbie ducked in first, glad to be out of that consuming wind. Sadie's dark skin was slick with rain, her eyes watering yet vibrant. The restaurant was no longer, now a bar with trendy lighting and modern wooden furniture. A man appeared behind the counter.

'How's it going?' he asked.

'Looking for a bit of grub,' Sadie said.

He looked at his watch. 'It's still early. Chef's not in for half an hour but I could make you up something?'

'No rush. It suits us to wait. Will get us out of the cold for a while.'

'Yeah, the radio just said it's about to get stormy, could last a couple of hours.'

'Well, we'll just knuckle down here, if that's all right? I'll have a coffee... a cappuccino. Abbie, what do you want?'

'Same.'

'We do scones if you fancy a snack?' The bar man asked.

'Grand. That wind gave me an appetite,' Sadie said.

'I don't have much money on me,' Abbie whispered to Sadie.

'Stop will you, on me,' she said, then to the barman, 'make that two.'

They walked to the furthest corner, both having no need for eaves-droppers. Even though conversation with them was always short, Abbie felt like talking.

'Did you stay in Crookstown cos you went to Secondary there?'

'Kind of. To be honest that school has just as many bad memories as Knockfarraig, but at least no one knows me there. Except Jim at the hotel, he was nice to me back then. Some girls were giving me hassle one day and as I ran past, he whistled and pointed to come inside. Scared more of them than a stranger, I ducked in. Hiding behind the wall we both listened to them going past. One of the girls shouted, *where is the black bitch?* I burned with shame but he, Jim, didn't say anything and just pulled out a chair and offered me a free muffin and man, they were the best chocolate muffins with cream I ever tasted.' Sadie looked up at the ceiling reliving it and when she looked at Abbie her eyes were bright. It changed her whole face when she smiled.

'He heated them, so the cream melted into the warm chocolate becoming this big pile of gooey mess. He was lovely. He listened. After that I used the place as a refuge, every day without fail I raced from school to the hotel and when I didn't have any money, instead of asking him for something to eat, I'd clean and Jim, who would have given me free muffins for the rest of my life for nothing, sensed I didn't want charity I'd say, so he let me, even though I probably was a hindrance rather than a help. I'd keep busy, waiting an hour or two until I knew the girls would have got the bus or gave up and went home. They never figured out where I went to. My mam thought I was staying on in school to study so didn't give me hassle. Any time not spent in Knockfarraig with Gabrielle or under mam's feet was a bonus for her and any time I didn't have to spend in that house was a bonus for me.'

'Was it that bad?'

Pain screwed up Sadie's features. Abbie changed direction. 'At the school?'

Sadie picked at a nail.

'Everything was horrific at that time.'

'So, you can imagine how someone who's mum is a murderer would be treated?'

Sadie nodded.

'Reading your story is like reading my own. Growing up with the Ellis's was like facing a blank wall. For years I believed I must have done something. Or that there was something they knew that I didn't. I thought it was me, that I was born broken and everyone knew. You can't miss what you don't have but when I would see other kids running to their parents or getting hugs, I wondered what that must feel like, and I wished for that. Maureen cried all the time when I was small and early on, as far back as I can remember, I knew she wasn't my real mother, that she had no other choice but to take care of me. I felt every bit of her burden, every bit of her frustration making me tiptoe around her. She didn't explain what happened. After a few days I figured my parents were gone and wouldn't be coming back. It was easy to work out I couldn't mention my mother from Maureen's reaction but I thought they left because I was impossible to love. In school one day, when I wouldn't give Becky Coughlan my new pen with the feather on top, she said no one liked me because my mam killed my dad.'

Sadie looked right at Abbie. 'Kids can be cruel.'

'You know what? Becky did me a favour. After that all the weird reactions made sense. After that I understood why each mother pulled their kid away from me when we linked arms leaving school. Why every time I invited another kid on a play date they refused. Why no matter how I tried to fit in I didn't. On a regular basis, Maureen let me know she didn't choose the role or how much she didn't ever want children. I grew up knowing no one wanted me.'

'That sounds like Maureen all right. She was always spiteful. Somehow she always knew the exact thing that would cut a person in two. Even with you she had to win.'

'Did you try to get me?'

Sadie nodded again, then flicked her eyes to the fire. 'I'm sorry, I should have waited to say anything. For years I've hovered in the background. I've always kept a close eye, promising if l saw the tiniest bit of meanness I would grab you and run. If I thought she treated you bad then I...'

The barman approached with a tray laden with scones and cappuccino's. Sadie took both cups, handing one to Abbie, then smiled at the man as he laid the rest of the contents of the tray on their table, waiting until he was nearly back at the bar before speaking again.

'These last few years she seemed happier, a few times I even saw her crack a smile. Maureen was always miserable, loved being surrounded by misery so don't you ever take the blame. Outside appearances mean nothing I know, so I watched you, when I could. There's a gap in your fence and I used to sit for hours watching in the garden. You would sing and play, you seemed a carefree kid.'

'You spied on me?'

'I kept an eye on you,' she said through gritted teeth.

'This year I saw a change, a darkening, and you seemed to struggle. Maybe you just couldn't hide it anymore. Yesterday, I laid those flowers out for your mum and as the rain got worse, I went to leave. By the wall, I heard a thump and when I looked back, I saw you vault it. At first, I hid, not wanting to get in the way but then I heard you trying to talk to your mother and I knew, it was the sign I'd been waiting for to approach you all these years. A sign from your mother it was time, I guess.'

'I don't believe in signs.'

'Funny, I didn't either before your mother died.'

'What was she like?'

Sadie arched a brow.

'I know she's telling me what happened in the book, but what was she like in person?'

Sadie smiled, the first proper smile Abbie had seen her make. It made her look different, younger.

'Now, there's someone I would talk about all day. You know the way you'd hear of people lighting up the room? I always hated that saying but in her case it nails it. I used to watch her work her way around a crowd, watch other people as they straightened for their turn to talk with your mother. When the books took off she took it in her stride, even in an autograph line a mile long, she had a way of making the grumpiest of people smile. With me, I tended to drag people under when I spoke to them. Not your mother, she did the opposite. Life was always... positive with her. People could tell her anything and she would look at them as if it was completely acceptable. She'd wink at me when someone particularly grumpy approached and would say 'kill them with kindness' and she would. I could never do it. I'd watch her as she'd turn those cranks into different people altogether, like some superhero. Don't get me wrong, she had her faults. She got loud when she drank or was nervous and she liked the sound of her own voice too often. Her choice in men wasn't the best, she always picked the dickhead. Sorry.'

Abbie's cheeks burned. 'Was my dad such a dick he deserved to get murdered?'

Sadie jerked her head backwards and stared at the ceiling. 'Just when I think we are starting to get somewhere.'

She looked at Abbie. 'Actually, I liked your dad. For once I thought she picked right.'

'Sorry.'

Sadie sighed. 'Don't be. Your head must be reeling trying to take all this in. I don't blame you for biting sometimes. You're handling it much better than I would. If a woman I never met gave me a story from my dead mother they'd hear me roaring all over Knockfarraig.'

'Lucky I'm not you so,' Abbie said eating a crumb of scone. 'Have you any children?'

Sadie shook her head. 'You may not believe this, but I have some trust issues.'

'I'd never guess.'

Sadie poked her tongue out at Abbie.

'Tell me about you. Are you happy in Knockfarraig?'

'As much as I can be I guess. Reading about what my mum said about loneliness... I can relate. Over the last year I've hung out with some friends but I don't know, sometimes I feel like there's this gaping hole inside and nothing fills it.'

Sadie nodded. 'The teenage years are hard, I hated that time in my life. Even though I talked so much about my problems with your mother, I held back too. Everyone has secrets Abbie, everyone has things they are ashamed of. I just hope the shame hasn't hurt you too much.'

'In fairness, you can't live without shame when my parents died the way they did.'

'I'm sorry. It must have been hard for you,' Sadie said. She looked like she meant it.

'Don't be. It wasn't your fault.'

'I wish I could have taken you away. Kept you safe.'

Sadie bit down on her lip. Hard enough that Abbie was convinced blood would appear.

There was something Sadie wasn't telling her, Abbie thought.

Eighteen

Gabrielle

After years of waiting, the only way Sadie wanted to celebrate turning eighteen was for the two of us to go to a bar together. For mine five months earlier, my parents organised a party in the house so she was yet to go to a bar legally. We hopped on the bus to town and vowed to walk into the first pub we spotted. Although the first we set eyes on wasn't appealing, with paint chipping off the wall and the sign hanging lopsided above a doorway whose frame looked like someone had tried to kick it in, Sadie shrugged in acceptance.

'At least it'll be memorable.'

Inside, the place was almost pitch dark, and the dark grey, sticky carpet and the once patterned fabric faded to brown of the seats didn't help lift the place. Yet, I'd never seen Sadie as excited. We took two high stools and as Sadie fiddled with her wallet, I placed my hand over hers.

'My shout.'

'Best birthday ever,' Sadie said, shuffling in her seat as if dancing. 'I can't believe I'm actually eighteen. I'm nearly there, nearly free.'

'What? You following through and moving out?'

'As soon as the Leaving's out of the way.'

'Wait for college though yeah?'

'We'll see.'

A miserable looking man behind the counter ignored us. I took out a note. The man didn't move even though there was no one being served.

'Hiya can we get a drink?'

He sloped over. Looked at us and barely touching the note, shoved it in my direction.

'Your money's not welcome here.'

I laughed to make light of what he said, desperate to keep the conversation upbeat.

'We have I.D.'

The man folded his arms and watched a match on a tiny screen in the opposite corner of the bar.

'I don't care how old you are, you're not getting a drink.'

Sadie looked like she was about to cry. The man had clearly taken a dislike to us. His back now turned, his shaved head shone against the overhead light.

'Why?'

He tilted his head back. 'I don't like your sort.'

Sadie looked down at her hands, one finger stroked her skin and when she tugged on my sleeve to go, her face was full of shame. 'Come on, it's not worth it,' she whispered.

That was enough. To see my friend, excited one minute now hanging her head in shame caused heat to flare from my nostrils.

'What? So you won't serve us because she's black? She's Irish,' I hissed.

That got his attention. The man scowled and lurched nearer.

'I said *your* money isn't welcome. She's Irish, you're not. We don't serve English scum.'

I reeled back. Then I curled the note into a fist. Sadie tried to mount the counter but I hauled her off.

'Don't Sade, he's not worth it, let's go to a better bar for your first drink.'

Outside, I turned to her and she turned to me and you know what we did? We laughed. That was our relationship, Abbie; when we looked at each other, we saw a survivor and it reminded us that together we would survive again and that sometimes laughter is the only way through.

We were opposites, but in so many ways, the same.

Thump

Abbie

Her phone ringing startled her enough that she nearly dropped the book.

'It's Maureen. I have to answer it,' she said to Sadie.

Before the phone reached her ear, she could hear Maureen. 'Where are you?'

Only then did Abbie remember.

'I'm out. Don't worry I'll be there. What time is the mass?'

'Twelve thirty. I told you a million times.'

'Maureen, chill, I know, I'm just checking to be sure.'

Sadie pretended to busy herself, stacking the empty cups and cutlery.

'I want you back straight away to get ready. You can't look messy, disgracing your father's memory. It's bad enough that it's a day late, you'd think Father Barry would have made an exception.'

'What about my mother's memory?'

'What did you say?' Maureen's voice was thick with emotion.

Abbie thought of the woman's tears, of her sobs late at night when she thought Abbie was asleep.

'Nothing... look I'm sorry I made you worry. Promise I'll be back soon.'

'Fine.'

'I have to go. With everything going on, I forgot about the mass Maureen organises every year.'

Sadie widened her eyes. 'Right.'

'She needs me.'

Sadie held her hands in the air. 'OK.'

'It should only take a couple of hours at the most. They'll make me go for a meal but after they've had a few drinks, I should be able to slip out. Will you stay? I can come 'round after.'

'I need to leave by seven.'

'That gives me loads of time. I'll get back at three thirty, tops.'

'All right.' She picked up the menu. 'Looks like I won't be needing these.'

'Stay. I can find my own way back.' Abbie said, prickling.

'No, no, wouldn't do to keep Maureen waiting. Celebrating your father, I take it?'

'It's an anniversary mass, yeah.'

'Will your mother's name be called out?'

'What do you think?'

'Knowing the Ellis's the only way they'll mention your mother is to curse her to hell. Enjoy your day.'

Abbie stood. 'I don't know why you're taking it out on me, it's not like I have a say in anything.'

'Oh, you can have a say.'

'Say's the woman hiding out in Crookstown rather than bumping into them.'

Sadie pursed her lips. 'That doesn't make it right. This town only talks about your mother as if the way they died was all she did. Did you know they used to do tours of Knockfarraig based on landmarks of her books? Now they've erased her. Thanks to your family, who made sure every remnant of her was cancelled. You won't even find her books in the bookstore anymore cos they're afraid your grandparents will cause another fuss. They've been vile about her, do you know that?'

'Again, your talking like I have some say.'

Sadie stared at her. 'Why can't you remember Abbie?'

Abbie looked away. 'I've asked myself that many times. Maureen says it's because I needed to forget the trauma.'

Sadie narrowed her eyes. 'What trauma?'

Abbie shrugged.

'That fucking family. Come on, let's go before I get so angry I ram the house.'

In silence, Abbie braced herself against every bend. The wind still howled and the rain pelted down but it didn't stop Sadie driving fast, her knuckles wrapped so hard against the steering wheel that Abbie was sure she was trying to snap it in two. She parked with a screech and for a moment Abbie thought she wasn't even going to look at her.

'I think it's best if I head off now, no point hanging around this place for hours in a storm.'

'Don't do that, it's not fair.'

'What's not fair is them lording over their perfect son, perfect brother, your perfect dad.'

Sadie thumped the steering wheel making Abbie jump, then covered her face in her hands and sat back in the chair, taking a few breaths. When she spoke again, she had regained composure.

'Bet you kept memories about him though, yeah? Bet they haven't stripped them away, haven't tainted and twisted the memory of him, have they? What's not fair is you expecting me to wait around, in a town with too many bad fucking memories. I'm not doing it, I can't.'

'Hold on, I'm being unfair? You show up here and demand to be listened to, telling me my whole life is a lie and I'm the unfair one? Pot calling kettle...'

Abbie stopped.

'Black, is it?' Sadie spat.

'I didn't mean it like that.'

'I know what you mean.'

They stared at each other, both catching their breaths.

'Don't go back.'

'I have to. I have commitments.'

'Couldn't you delay them, pull a sickie or something?'

'You have school tomorrow.'

'I'll go on the hop.'

'No.'

'How could you think it was possible for me to read a huge book in two days? To take in all of your lives quickly like that. Two days to get my head around you even existing.'

'Some time apart will give you time for it to sink in.'

'*You* did this. *You* turned up and dropped this bomb and then tell me I have to have it sorted by the end of the day. Surely my mother would have expected more from you? Don't you owe her more? Don't you owe me?'

Sadie clenched her fists but then dropped them. Her shoulders dropped in defeat. 'I'll come back.'

'At least wait for me until later. Let me finish a few more chapters or leave me the book?'

'That's not happening.'

'Please Sadie.'

Sadie softened when she saw Abbie's hope crumble. She shifted sideways in her seat.

'Look, chill. I made a promise, and when I make one, I always keep it. It's my way or nothing. I'll wait till seven and if you're not finished the book, I'll do what I have to do then come back.'

'Promise?'

The two women stared at each other.

'I already have. Now get out before Maureen sends out a search party.'

Abbie didn't look back when she got out of the car, but Sadie wasn't waiting around either. She took off as soon as the door closed.

Sermon

Abbie

'Where were you?' Maureen asked, expecting a fight.

Her foot rested on the first step of the stairs.

'Just out with some mates, I was on my way when you called. It's not like I'd forget.'

Maureen's eyes were bloodshot red. With her blonde hair styled and her back straight and her best jewellery sparkling, you would think it was all about her appearance but the usually perfect eye makeup was smudged. Abbie softened. This time of year was hard for Maureen too. Sometimes she forgot that her aunt not only lost her brother but became a mother overnight. Not an easy task and one she didn't have to take on. Nobody else stood up to the plate. Not Sadie, her supposed godmother, nor her grandparents. A flash of anger returned, for no matter what the book said, Sadie hadn't been there for her and Gabrielle had ruined her family.

The house wasn't the biggest, but it was in one of the nicest areas in Knockfarraig. Inside the decor was stylish and filled with expensive pieces. Even after all those years, Abbie still felt like a guest. In her bedroom, there was a bespoke bed, designer flowery curtains with complimentary pale pastel colours on the walls all designed and chosen by her aunt. Bar a few books on her locker, there wasn't one thing that Abbie chose on display. To blame Maureen for that would be wrong, because up until that day Abbie had never thought of putting her personal taste somewhere in her room. It made her think of her mother's mark on her own walls, of posters and fluorescent paint, of black ceilings and glow in the dark stars. So often, Abbie talked herself out of projects because she didn't know how to perfect it. Her mother hadn't been afraid to mark the walls with her mistakes. Her mother hadn't worried about imperfection.

The church was located right in the middle of the town. Designed as the main feature of Knockfarraig and built when Irish peoples' whole life revolved around Catholicism. Even with the power from the church now sated, the pews were full, for people always searched for a sanctuary when troubled. Inside, it's ornate high beams and grand ceilings took precedence over the altar. Stained glass windows filled the tops of the walls spilling multi-coloured light onto the cream flooring, it's rainbow shadows were always the most-godly thing in the church for Abbie. More so than the statues whose eyes seemed to watch, to judge, following her. Despite the statues, Abbie loved the church, from the time she entered, a peace would come over her until the time she left. Fr. Barry was very likeable; he spoke instead of preached, with a lively voice too, which made a difference, so many priests she heard had a melodious voice on purpose, which coupled with the gospels and sermons would just send you into a day dream. Maybe that *was* praying though, maybe you were meant to drift off in a hypnotic state, in order for it to work. On this occasion, she prayed for the first time for her mother. Not to forgive her, for even after reading, forgiveness was a long way off and still dependent on what else the book contained. What she did ask for, was that one day she might understand.

There was no hand holding from Maureen. The woman sat straighter than the seat with a linen napkin clutched in her hand. The last standing members of her father's family sat along the pew, her grandfather and grandmother as rigid as their daughter. Abbie jerked her head away when her grandfather turned in her direction, not wanting to see another frown; she had given up the thought of gaining any insight into her parents' life from them; learning the hard way about their wall of silence. Why were none of her mother's family ever at the anniversary mass? Why had none approached her over the years like Sadie? Before reading the book she hadn't even known she had aunts or uncles other than Maureen. Had something happened that wasn't reported on? Had her mother fallen out with them and they wanted nothing to do with Gabrielle's daughter? So many unanswered questions and for the first time some, at least, were being given.

Abbie hoped they were going out for lunch after as she didn't like visiting her grandparents' house. It had become a shrine for her father. A caricature smiled out from every wall. Holding medals and winning races, in uniforms or graduation gown, in business suits or shirtless and handsome on holidays, in every one looking happy and accomplished. Yet it didn't get him anywhere. He still ended up dead. Even worse than a dead parent staring out from a picture, was the way her grandparents looked at her. Only once when she was much smaller, did she dare ask her grandfather why he didn't like her. As soon as she'd said it, he'd moved away, as he always did when he noticed she neared, and she thought he was going to ignore her like all the other times, but as he disappeared out the door he said, 'You're just like your mother.'

Her father's dead spirit hid in the silences in that house, hanging dank and dense thickening the air. They spoke of him as if they were robbed, their son stolen by the same blood that flowed in Abbie's veins. It was never said, they didn't blame her outright but the accusation lay in the unsaid words, in the way they looked at her when they asked how school was or how her grades were, in the forceful way a plate was lifted, or in the crossing of arms as she entered the room. It was in their short intake of breath or the snap of the head to stare out the window when she spoke, as if they wished for anyone but her to be the person talking. It was clear they despised her and for that reason she had never wondered why they didn't offer to take her as a child; her grandfather didn't need to say anything, the man would get up out of his chair the minute she sat down, her presence enough to cause rage. They were cold people. After some years she had given up even trying. All her life she had thought they were that way because of their son's death but was it possible they had been like that before? Sadie had alluded to that.

Whatever the truth was, soon they would join their son and not much longer by the feeble way her grandfather and grandmother shuffled and struggled. Both on borrowed time now, she reckoned, and it wouldn't be much of a loss to Abbie, for those two were as much strangers to her as Sadie.

There were also photographs of Maureen on the walls: backpacking and travelling, on her gap year, a woman so carefree it was like looking at a different person. There were pictures of her parents' wedding dotted around their house too, of smiling guests and a younger Maureen and her father in full morning suit and her grandparents dressed up and beaming but the straight line of where her dad's arm should be was too harsh, cut away and resized.

Her mother had been erased.

The only photos she had seen of her mother were from the internet, reporting about the murder. In those they always printed the most sinister it seemed, the picture taken when her mother was scowling or brows knitted together in a suitable *this woman is a murderer* head shot. Only then did she see the resemblance, only then had she understood why they looked at her the way they did.

Even though silence surrounded her family, little observations would escape Maureen: *your father used to say that*, or, *don't give me that look, it's exactly how your father would act when he was annoyed.* It was usually in her failings when she mentioned him, so her father hung over her like a threat, dangling in judgement and warnings.

At the service, the priest spoke of Abbie's father as if he was a friend and he was, the pictures of the two of them arm in arm on her grandparents' wall proved it. Abbie let his voice take her away.

After, Maureen stood at the church doors, regal and ramrod, clutching her clutch, looking awkward when someone leaned in to console, or show affection, reluctantly shaking hands with a stream of friends and the members of Knockfarraig that loved to remember the worst thing to happen in the town. Her hair was perfect as always, her make up pristine, wearing her best jewellery, with the most expensive twinset she owned, the one with the brooch that clasped at the top, which made Abbie smile remembering Sadie's comments. Abbie picked at her clumped mascara and wished she had remembered to change into her new boots. From the scowls coming her way from Maureen, she wished so too.

Once the crowd dispersed, her grandparents made their excuses to go, saying they couldn't stand any longer. Maureen nodded, 'We'll see you in about an hour.'

Abbie checked her watch. The mass had taken over an hour.

Not to worry there's still plenty of time.

'Where are we going for lunch?'

Maureen fiddled with the sleeve of her twinset, pulling it free from her heavy watch. At first she didn't answer, Abbie knew better than to repeat the question.

'We're going to The Oak Tree.'

'What? In the city?'

Maureen pivoted, still holding her cuff. 'Why, are we keeping you from something more important?'

'No. Just told Shawna I'd study with her later for an exam next week.'

Maureen freed the watch. Then tugged her cardigan over it. 'I'm sure your study won't be ruined by one night off. If we make it back then grand but I'm not rushing away from your father's day all right? It's once a year Abbie, so show him the respect he deserves. Are we clear?'

With a sinking feeling in the pit of her stomach, Abbie nodded in agreement, already knowing she would not get back in time, already knowing Sadie would wait in that hotel for nothing.

And there it was. Abbie couldn't recall another person she hated as much as Sadie, yet she hung off every word the woman said. As much as her presence riled her, Sadie held the key to the answers she sought.

Abbie wouldn't ring the hotel and let Sadie know. Despite the storm, she would wait, just in case by some miracle they finished early, because even if she had to run to Crookstown, even if she only got five minutes with the book, it would be worth it.

Hours later, in the taxi after the tedious meal, after she watched Maureen sipping wine after wine, Abbie braved the question she had wanted to ask all day. 'Maureen, did you know my mother?'

Maureen's back stiffened but her lips had loosened. 'What do you mean? Of course I knew your mother.'

'Before my father, I mean. When you were a kid.'

Maureen swiped at the air, as if swatting a fly.

'No. Why are we talking about that woman?'

'It's her anniversary too.' Abbie said in almost a whisper, yet as soon as the words were out she knew it was still too loud.

A pointed finger stabbed dangerously close to her nose.

'The only reason there is an anniversary at all is because of that woman. She was evil Abbie, evil. Don't you ever forget that.'

Maureen dropped her hand, and all her energy seemed to whoosh out in the gesture.

'Why would you bring her up? On today of all days.'

She wrapped her arms around her thin waist, and her eyes watered.

'Now I have a migraine starting.'

The rest of the journey carried on with only the sound of the radio. The taxi driver didn't try to make small talk, and sensing the atmosphere between the two women, he turned the volume dial up a notch whistling softly in time to the songs.

Looking out the window, Abbie thought about how Maureen always reacted that way whenever she asked questions, valid questions she had a right to ask. As soon as she started a sentence regarding her mother, Maureen would become upset forcing Abbie to retreat, as if she didn't have feelings too, as if her feelings didn't matter. Before meeting Sadie, Abbie believed her aunt was too sensitive, after Sadie, she wondered if it was a form of manipulation. She looked at her watch. Five o clock – still time. The journey would take about forty minutes, an hour at the most and then she would have to get to Crookstown but maybe, if she was lucky she would get thirty minutes. Maybe if she made it, she could persuade Sadie to stay later.

By the time they pulled into Mariner's Park, Maureen was snoring lightly. Abbie took some money from Maureen's clutch and paid the driver and despite his offerings to help, she reassured him she could manage. Maureen stood without resistance but kept her eyes closed, allowing Abbie to lead her to the door.

'Your chair or bed?' Abbie asked.

'Bed,' she muttered. 'I can't cope with this migraine.'

More like the five glasses of wine Abbie thought, but said nothing, concentrating on opening the door then, leading her up the stairs. It was easy to manage Maureen, the woman was as light as a feather. Even if she had stayed asleep, Abbie would have managed to carry her. In all their years together, she had yet to see Maureen eat a full meal; the woman was a nibbler, a picker, never seeming to enjoy anything she ate and only eating for sustenance. At the bedroom door she went to unravel herself when Maureen clung on to her arm.

'Will you stay with me until I fall asleep? I don't want to be alone.'

What could she say? That she had somewhere better to be? That even though Sadie irritated the hell out of her, she already preferred her company? That she wanted to find out the truth about her parents?

She couldn't.

With a heavy heart and a ticking clock, Abbie pulled back Maureen's duvet. She plumped her pillows, smoothed the creases from the sheet, then helped her aunt, her carer, her substitute mother into bed. Once the woman settled, Abbie closed the curtains so the room darkened, then, settled in the chair beside her.

In an unprecedented move, Maureen shifted her hand to the edge of the bed, reaching, searching for her niece's. Abbie placed her own on top, stroking Maureen's skin with her thumb, hoping to soothe, to soften the passage to sleep, even though every part of her wanted to jump up, to run, to check her phone and ring reception and beg Sadie not to leave, she knew if she did, Maureen's eyes would snap open from the intrusion of light or noise and the process would have to start again. Instead, she concentrated on the strokes, making invisible lines on her aunt's skin, wishing with every touch to lull, to remove some of the sadness that blocked and stayed in Maureen's head and heart. Until finally, she heard her breathing change, become lighter, unburdened.

As she slipped out of the room, she was already holding her phone. The display read six fifty. Out the door she did a quick search for the hotel and dialled the number. Her walk became a trot as she rushed for the bus stop.

The phone rang and rang and Abbie was about to hang up when a shaky male voice answered.

'Is she still there?'

He didn't try and pretend not to know and for that Abbie liked Jim even more.

'I'm sorry Abbie, she left. She told me to tell you she'll keep her promise, that she hopes it will be next weekend.'

Turning back around, Abbie wiped at her face and realised it was the first time that day she'd cried. Not for her father, not for her mother, Sadie or Maureen. Her tears were for her, for letting the truth slip through her fingers.

Butterflies

Abbie

In the week that followed, time dragged to almost a stop. Abbie held on to her phone at all times, checking the status of the battery, making sure it wasn't on silent. With no contact from Sadie, no text or call, she clung to what she could remember of the book. Her mother's words drifted through at random times.

Her harshness can have a bite, but kindness will kill it.

We were opposites, but in so many ways, the same.

I've already decided when I die, I'm going to the sea.

As the days wore on, Abbie's desperation increased. Turning those pages, meeting Sadie, awakened a need in her she hadn't known she'd craved. Thoughts that Sadie wouldn't return bombarded her until full-blown jittery panic set in towards the end of the week. What if Sadie died in an accident? The truth would die with her and Abbie would never know the rest of her mother's story. Helpless, she cursed her stupidity for not insisting on taking Sadie's number. She didn't even know what county the woman lived in, or if she lived in another country even. With a location, she could have monitored the local news at least. Until Sadie contacted, all she could do was wait. Sadie had all the power, and the woman liked it that way.

Abbie was under no illusion. The story wouldn't give her the closure she needed, for how could it? Gabrielle couldn't have written the end of her story in that book. It wouldn't have been possible. Anyway, there could be no happy ending in her parents' story. No, what was to come would be painful, of that, she was sure. Necessary, yes; the time away from reading had solidified her need to know. Where she stood now was torturous, left in an ignorant state, aware of some of the story but not all, the book granted a new perspective without knowing yet if the writer was reliable, without access to all the facts, she couldn't be sure.

On the page, Gabrielle seemed rational but there was plenty of ground to cover still, the rest of Abbie's history had yet to be revealed, leaving her hanging, suspending her in the air almost, half way between truth and lies, between belief and outrage. What she had read poked at her.

Even with only half the story, life was different; examining what had come before, what she had taken as fact was now compared to Sadie's or her mother's point of view. Abbie scrutinised the life that surrounded her. Why was she never allowed to ask questions about her mum? What made Maureen and her grandparents cut off half her history like that? Why had Maureen lied about knowing her mother as a child? Or was Sadie lying? What if Sadie was just a crazed fan and had written the book herself? Stranger things had happened. There was so much hidden, with many opportunities to distrust.

Each night she searched the internet, scrolling through incognito pages of images of her mother. It hurt more than she could ever imagine. No longer a stranger, Abbie scrutinised every photograph. Had she been happy in that one? It was only on the second night she realised she was searching for Sadie. In most, if there were other people in the picture, it was usually her father, standing next to Gabrielle, his hand coiled around her waist, or holding her hand, touching her somewhere, always. They made a beautiful couple.

Looking at them now, side by side, she could see her resemblance leaned more to her mother.

On the third night of scrolling, she stopped. In the background of one, holding hands with her mother, was Sadie.

The screen displayed the truth better than any page or mouth could; Sadie had known her mother. After that, Abbie saw Sadie everywhere, hovering in the background, sometimes only a blurred image, sometimes only half a face, or even just a finger on her mother's arm. Still, it was her, recognisable by the same bracelet, or by the same colour top, or by those perfectly shaped fingernails Abbie had already come to know. The pictures with Sadie's face always looked in Gabrielle's direction. Sadie, young and different, her smile broad and white teeth showing. Happy. Beaming.

With every answer, more questions rose to the surface. Abbie wanted to show each picture to Sadie and demand the story behind it.

She took out her journal from her bedside locker, scrolling through the near full book. All the thoughts, all the dreams inside those pages. She stopped on one page.

Why do I feel the need to write?

Am I just like her?

She flipped to the first blank page she could find.

Dear mum, she wrote before snapping the book closed. There was nothing to say.

Avoiding home as much as she could, she trailed the beach each evening to hang with the others on the pier wall, even though it was cold down by the water. For months she had fought an attraction to one guy, to Joe. Afraid of Maureen's wrath, she avoided him when he tried to get nearer, even when he had made it obvious he liked her back. Now she wanted a little of her mother's courage. Or Sadie's brazenness. What could she lose? She smiled at him. It sent a little thrill through her when he smiled back. On cue, Joe noticed her shivering and offered her his jacket. She took it, saying 'thanks.' When she threaded her arms through, the shivering continued.

'Here,' he said, wrapping an arm around her and giving her a side hug, Abbie rested her head on his shoulder, hoping he'd see it as a sign of her interest. He smelt of sea salt and soap and sand. With floppy, dark blonde hair that always tousled around his face, it was screaming for a hand to run through it, but she held back. At sixteen, she was still unsure of how to show a guy she liked him, waiting instead for him to make a move. As they sat like that, chatting to everyone else with his arm around her and her head on his shoulder, she tried to recall the last time someone had held her. It had happened, she was sure of it, yet she couldn't bring up any single given time Maureen had embraced her. Her grandparents hadn't, not ever. It must have been her mother, or her father, it must have been, because she could remember the feeling, the smell of skin, the warmth of a hug, the yearning for another.

The weight of Joe's arm comforted Abbie. How long had she longed for any human touch? She wondered if someone wanting to hold her could become her normal. Had it been like that for her parents? When had they met? Her mother, at the point in the story she'd read, was older, going to clubs. Had her mother felt butterflies for her father like she felt for Joe? She wished she could ask. Boys were definitely one of the forbidden subjects on Maureen's list. Along with dead mothers, or murders, or anything before Abbie was six.

Joe whispered, 'want to go for a walk?' She tipped her head in answer. He jumped down from the wall and splayed his hands out to catch her. For a moment, it felt symbolic, like it wasn't just Joe asking, that his open arms represented much more; the chance of love, the chance for answers. There was no other option for Abbie. The life she'd had before him, before Sadie, before the book wasn't one she wanted to stay in, so she slipped her hands into his and jumped. They walked along the pier with hands held. As they rounded the corner at the end, he pulled her behind the wall and kissed her. She closed her eyes and hoped she did it right. Soft, fleshy skin on hers. The taste of orange from his lips. Abbie could get used to kissing Joe. When he kissed her neck she didn't stop him, lost in the sensation of stubble on her, finally discovering what it felt like, the experience of breath in her ear invasive, so intimate it was almost unpleasant, and when his hand cupped her breast, over her coat, she didn't protest, she said nothing because she liked him. It was normal if he wanted more.

Her phone beeped and before checking, she was already preparing to leave because, even though she was kissing a guy she had wanted to kiss for months, there was only one person that text could be from. She broke away to check it, mumbling something about her aunt. Once confirmed, they went back to kissing and as pleasant as it was to feel Joe's touch, his kiss wasn't enough to tether her attention.

Tomorrow, tomorrow, tomorrow.

Sadie was on her way.

Cards

Abbie

She closed the car door with a gentle click, and Sadie tipped her head in greeting. To anyone else there wasn't an obvious softening, and could be interpreted as hostile, but to Abbie it said: *I'm glad you're here*, it said: *I might actually have missed you.*

Sadie drove and Abbie didn't question this time where she was taking her, for they both knew it didn't matter where the surroundings were. Abbie itched to ask for the book but didn't want to sound too eager. Tensions might have softened but not enough to lay all her cards on the table.

Instead, she asked, 'How long are you here for this time?'

Sadie kept her eyes on the road. 'I'm off for two days, so I'll have to head off tomorrow evening.'

Abbie nodded, flicking her eyes to the window. Two days. It was doable. By tomorrow evening, she would close the book. Tomorrow night, she would have answers, know her parents' story. A shiver ran up her. Sadie inclined her head.

'You need me to turn up the heat?'

'No. Someone walked over my grave, is all.'

Sadie snorted. 'More like we're visiting theirs.'

'True.'

Bushes and trees, walls and sides of road whizzed past, two constants stayed in Abbie's eyeline, the sea and the sky and even when a tree or a multi storey house blocked her view, she closed her eyes so the sea was still there. On a normal day, there was comfort in living by the water and seeing that view, but right then, all Abbie wanted was to sit in a room inhaling a vague smell of mothballs and mould with a book on her lap.

It didn't take long.

Second Sight

Gabrielle

For Maureen's eighteenth birthday, the entire class were invited to her party. Held at her house, it was the first time Maureen asked Sadie and I over. Open-mouthed, we entered the grandest house we'd ever seen with high ceilings that reached for the sky, with chandeliers and pianos and dining rooms that actually housed a proper dining table.

It was a glorious day, and I used the excuse of sunshine to wear my new white dress. There were people everywhere, all milling and moving, drinks splashing and clinking, loud music thumping in the background. The first sight that made me gasp was the view of the sea, which looked like the garden dropped straight in, sloping from green to blue.

Surrounded by people, Sadie pulled at my arm and with reluctance, I turned from the view. The crowded space parted and a man on the other side of the room stood straight in my line of vision. He didn't break his stare when I caught him, didn't look away. The second sight that made me gasp was your father.

First came recognition, for I had seen him months earlier on the street and wondered for weeks who he was.

His concentration made me more aware of my body than ever before; I brushed away my hair from my face, my cheeks betrayed me by flushing, *not cool.* It was as if the whole room watched me, even though the only eyes I noticed were his. Sadie's words faded away, even though I was aware she was still talking, I relegated her words to unnecessary. My only focus was on him.

Throughout my life, I have replayed that moment. What made it different from any other exchange? What was it about the sight of him that cut through every other being in that room rendering them insignificant?

At first, his stare was serious, penetrating even, yet innately I understood it as nonthreatening. I didn't want him to look away. Then his features softened into a smile that said so much, that spoke words I instantly understood. Words like: *come here*, like: *what's your name?*

A violent pull tugged at me, as if invisible bungee cords attached between us, my body wanted to move, wanted to get nearer. Before that day I never believed in instant love and it wasn't Abbie, it wasn't. What I saw in him was someone with kind eyes and shy mannerisms. What I felt was a compelling interest, and a definite attraction. Love needs to be developed, it needs depth to become true but Abbie, there was something, bigger than I'd felt before. A drawing close. More than that, even.

In later years, I often wondered if it was the white dress that attracted your father, or rather the innocence it represented. Even then, on that first glance, he knew who I was, what I could be. *I* didn't though. Yet, I saw him too, in the way he stood, rigid, with his neck jutting forward like he claimed every inch of space in order to be nearer, his arms hanging by his sides like he had forgotten what to do with them. Whether from the way he stood, or his body language, or the way his eyes met mine, I could tell he was damaged, hurt in some way, and instead of repulsing me, it made me more interested. My love for the underdog wanted to heal the hurt inside him. All that in a glimpse. For people like Sadie and your father, they need a person to love them no matter what happens. Looking at this beautiful man, I discovered what I needed was for someone to need me.

And then the crowd swarmed and we were hidden from each other and when they shifted back again, he wasn't there, his shape replaced with an empty space. Before we ever uttered one word, I'd lost him. How can you lose something you never had? I did though Abbie, I felt the loss.

Sadie spoke in a constant stream, pointing out the fancy napkins, or shoving food in my direction, forcing me to try this or taste that or pulling me away to avoid someone or towards someone she wanted to see. No matter where I looked, I couldn't find him.

After an hour, Sadie and I sat in the garden, her needing air and me needing a closer look at the view. It was even more stunning from outside.

'Wanna head back in?'

I shook my head. 'I'm happy out here but you go.'

'I'll just get us some drinks or something. Keep my seat.'

I closed my eyes and tried to imagine what it would be like to hear the sea while sitting there, an impossible feat with the noise from barely adult voices allowed drink for the first time. When I opened them again, my view was your father. I blinked in case it was some type of mirage.

'Falling asleep? Is the party that bad?'

He grinned now, cradling a beer, dulling that unnerving energy.

'Maybe it's the company,' I said.

'Maybe I can do something about that,' he said, pointing at Sadie's empty seat and waiting for my nod before sitting down.

'You a friend of Maureen?'

He scrunched his nose. 'I wouldn't say a friend exactly.'

I reddened, changed the subject. 'Before you came over I was trying to imagine what the sea sounds like from here.'

'Oh, sorry for interrupting.'

Grinning, he went to stand. I touched his hand.

'Don't go.'

He sat back in the seat, surveyed the view.

'You won't get to hear the sea today. Can't say I've listened myself lately.'

I didn't ask how he would listen, didn't want to know how he knew Maureen, not yet wanting my hopes dashed. Up close, he had stubble on his chin; the hairs poking through his skin almost blonde from the sun. He took a swig of his beer and I waited for him to look at me again. Only then did he seem to notice my empty hands.

'You dry? Do you want me to get you a drink?'

'No, you're fine. My friend went to get me one, but I'm not drinking, not alcohol anyway.'

He wiggled his bottle. 'You against it?'

I shook my head. 'Just wanted my head clear.'

He turned to me then, gave me the full extent of those green eyes. There were flecks of brown there, too. Colours I hadn't seen before, hadn't noticed on anyone, ever.

'Clear for me?'

Afraid to give myself away, I shrugged. Sadie appeared with two drinks but after getting a get lost look from me, swivelled in the other direction.

He turned sideways on the chair and I mimicked his movements, so our knees were only inches away. We leaned closer, our hands on our laps, pushing into the space between us, until we were almost touching.

'See, that's where we differ. I took one look at you and knew I couldn't approach you until I had a few.'

'Why?'

'I don't know yet.'

139

'I feel it too,' I said and to this day it is still the bravest sentence I have ever spoken. I followed it with the second bravest. 'I thought I'd lost you.'

He shook his head. 'Only because I wanted you to.' He swayed his bottle of beer. 'For someone like you I needed some help.'

'Someone like me?'

He tipped his head and laughed. 'If ever there was a hint at wanting a compliment.'

'You seem like you know how this works.'

He turned serious. 'Do I?'

'Don't you?'

He drained his beer, his mood darkened. 'I know nothing.'

'I doubt that.'

He smiled.

'Well, for one I don't know your name.'

'Gabrielle. See? Now you know something.'

'That I do.' He sat back in his chair, closed his eyes and mouthed, 'Gabrielle.'

'What?'

'Just imagining what it would be like to say that without anyone else here. We can all dream.'

'My dreams get me in trouble.'

He opened his eyes, shielding them from the sun with his hand, tilted his face towards mine.

'How's that?'

'I dream too much.'

'"A dreamer is one who can only find his way by moonlight, and his punishment is that he sees the dawn before the rest of the world."'

'Who said that?'

'Oscar Wilde.'

'You're a reader?'

'Not so much now since I moved but when I lived in Knockfarraig I read plenty.'

'Reading keeps me sane. Whose your favourite author?'

He laughed. 'That's a deep question and an impossible answer. It's like asking a parent who their favourite child is.'

'No, it's not.'

'It is, and the truth is, nobody gives the truth. They give the answer they think will impress. They size up the person asking and go with that. Like, if I was trying to impress you I'd quote Oscar Wilde when really I read it on a fridge sticker and my favourite author is Stephen King.'

'Nothing wrong with Stephen King. He's an absolute genius.'

His eyes lit at that, but then he pursed his lips.

'Let me guess, you watched *The Shawshank Redemption* twenty times and think you know all of his work.'

'Now whose judging me?'

'All right.' He put his hand to his chin, in an exaggerated thinking pose. 'Bet you your favourite is *Different Seasons.*'

'Cos of *Shawshank*? Or *The Body*? Not at all.'

He eyed me, held out a finger as if thinking.

'I know. It's *The Green Mile.*'

'You got me.'

He clicked his fingers.

'Hold on now though, in case you think you have me summed up. My second favourite is *The Dead Zone.*'

'Impressive.'

'I've a particular fondness for *Gerald's Game* too.'

'That's the one where the wife is tied up? And the husband dies on her at the start?'

'That's the one.'

He grinned. 'Well, you're a dark horse. Mine's *It.* Have you read that one?'

'Skipped that one. Clowns creep me out.'

'It's so much more than about clowns, though. The combination of friendship, grief, standing up to evil, facing your fears, that book has everything.'

'Fine. You've sold me.'

'Really?'

'How could I not read it now?'

He grinned and my stomach flipped.

'I know your favourite book yet I still don't know your name.'

'Liam,' he said.

I closed my eyes and mouthed, 'Liam.'

And when I opened them, his face was closer, hovering an inch from mine, nearly touching, waiting as if asking permission. In answer, I edged closer and with that move, his lips were on my lips, soft, trying it out, lingering on my bottom lip, pushing mine apart. I poured myself into him, lips and tongue meshing, my arms draped around his neck, his fingers clenching my face.

'Liam!'

We broke apart at the screech. Maureen stood in front of us and with a sinking in my stomach I waited for her to announce he was her boyfriend.

'What are you doing with my friend?'

'Getting to know her,' he answered in a voice that implied he was talking to a child. 'It is a party, Maureen. Isn't that the reason other people are invited? To talk, to get to know new people?'

'To talk, not to shove their tongue down my friend's throat. You do know she's in my school? You do know how young she is?'

My cheeks burned with shame. He flicked his eyes at me but then recovered.

'There's a big difference between how some people act. Take you

142

and her.' Liam pointed between us. 'It's night and day Maureen. You are a child, this here is a woman.'

He took my hand and kissed it.

'I'm warning you Liam, leave my friends alone.'

His smile dropped but he kept my hand suspended. 'Why?'

'Because... because...'

I waited, hanging on her next word.

'...you'll hurt her.'

'You really believe that?'

Maureen straightened, but her face didn't look that convinced.

'You'd really say that about your own brother?'

Only then did the penny drop. Before that night, I'd heard Maureen mention Liam's name in passing countless times but because of the distance between our houses, I'd never seen them together. He hadn't enrolled in Knockfarraig secondary, but attended a school in the city instead. From her, I'd formed an image of a guy with porn magazines under his bed, a jerk who refused to get off the phone when he knew she was waiting on a call from a date, so, when I conjured up a picture of her brother an image of a nerdy, annoying posh boy with jam jar glasses, who masturbated in his room all day came to mind. The Liam I heard about teased her all the time and sounded mean. The Liam in front of me looked like he would never do such a thing.

'Are you OK with this?' Maureen asked me and when I mouthed yes, she turned on her heels.

We talked until the night became morning. Older by four years, he acted way more mature than any of the guys in my school and the fact he worked in the city, only coming home some weekends, made him sound even more sophisticated.

As the last shufflers left, we exchanged hesitant goodbyes, promising to meet up the following Saturday. Liam didn't ask me to stay over, and I liked him more for that, for showing respect, for not trying it on, for wanting more from me than just a one night occurrence. Yet it was impossible to unravel ourselves from each other, only doing so when the cab driver, sick of waiting, beeped his horn. With reluctance, I slipped into the car. Liam leaned in.

'Keep her safe for me,' he instructed Sadie, closing the door.

She didn't answer, just scowled. For once I didn't care about her opinion.

'Watch him Gabs he bites,' she said as we drove off.

'Why? cos of what Maureen said? You know the wrong side of Maureen better than anyone Sade. Bet you though if we asked her she'd put a good enough spin on your arguments that would convince even you she was in the right. We both know Maureen isn't a very nice person.'

'Yeah, and the way you're acting, you're looking at making her your sister in law.'

'Look at this face.' I pointed at my smile which was so broad I had an ache in my cheeks. 'When was the last time you saw me like this? Can't you be happy for me?'

Sadie slumped. 'I'm just saying. Maureen has a mean streak, maybe it runs in the family.'

'You of all people shouldn't be comparing family members. How's your family lately?'

She nudged me. 'Shut up Gobby.'

But she placed her head on my shoulder and we continued the rest of the drive home in silence.

A day later, a signed copy of *It* was posted through my letterbox. There was no stamp, just a brown envelope with my name on. Inside was a handwritten note.

I hope you love the book as much as I do.
Looking forward to comparing thoughts.
Can't wait for Saturday.

Love Liam.

Our first date was in a bookstore and I knew right then I could love him. We walked in separate directions, him to the horror section, me to the contemporary. Every few seconds I looked in his direction and found he glanced my way each time. As he lost himself in a blurb of a book, I thought, *I could look at that side profile beside me forever.* And what a profile Abbie. Your father had this way of delaying looking back, so by the time he did I was desperate, I needed his eye contact, needed his validation. It was as if he timed it so he was the perfect combination of not too eager but not too cocky either.

I had spent the week reading *It*, staying up late the night before so I finished.

'You were right,' I said behind him, in almost a whisper.

'About?' he asked, leaning his head back to my ear, so my mouth touched his skin. My lips tingled with the contact.

'The book. I loved *It*.'

He turned and wrapped his arms around my waist. In front of the whole store he didn't hesitate, didn't seem one bit self conscious, and I loved that, that he wasn't ashamed to be with me in front of anyone, that he was proud to be seen with me.

'See? I knew I was right about you.'

'In what way?'

'That you would be my kind of girl.'

'What kind is that?' I laughed.

'Cool,' he said and kissed me.

In that store full of books, love blossomed.

Before he ever tried to touch me intimately, Liam wooed my mind. He took me on dates to the theatre, to museums, or the library where we would set the task of picking a book for the other. Each time I would marvel at his choice, wondering how a man I barely knew could see into my head like that. It was a revelation to speak to someone about books. The only thing Sadie enjoyed to read was the back of a crisp packet.

With Liam, there were no signs of cold feet, no looking for an excuse not to meet or ignoring his calls. There was a rightness to the relationship, a natural progression, a feeling of belonging with him. A lack of pushing away from what I had previously with anyone else. Anywhere we went, I felt his eyes on me and my eyes were drawn to him too. I searched for him in every crowd. Used to false proclamations of affection from men, with Liam I found sincerity.

We moved quickly. In a short space of time, I fell completely. Cutting off the bungee cord on my feelings, I found when he wasn't with me, I got jumpy, craving to hear his voice, smell him, see him, to feel his skin on my skin. We got physical early; there was no need to wait, or no catholic guilt as far as I was concerned. How could love be sinful? How could something that felt so good be wrong?

Our lives have more than one beginning. For me, there was my actual birth, moving to Ireland was the beginning of a new life, Sadie was new friendship and then meeting Liam was the beginning of romantic, sexual, all consuming love.

It changed everything. I won't go into sex, I'm sure that would be surplus information for a daughter to read about. All I'll say is when he touched me, it was as if he was checking I was real. Content to just stroke me, he would run his fingers through my hair, trailing a line from my temple down along my jaw then starting again from my forehead down. Awakening nerves that had no reason to exist before. It wasn't normal surely for a man to want to do that. It felt powerful, to be seen as precious, to have someone worship my body that way. He touched me as if I was fragile, as if too much pressure might shatter me and I liked that he regarded me as this delicate beauty. In his touch, I understood my role – I needed to be precious, needed to be delicate.

I was attracted to your father through a love of stories. The interest deepened with the books we discussed. But, it was only when he confided in me with his own story, when he trusted me enough to tell it, that I fell in love.

We were sitting reading, our backs to each other, when he spoke. 'I like that I can be silent with you and not need to fill the space.'

I put down the book. 'I like it too.'

'Before meeting you, I couldn't stay in a quiet room. I'd have to turn some background noise on or something. Now hearing you breathing or the page turn, seeing you there is enough.'

'Are you saying I breath too loud?'

'I'm saying the sound of your breathing is perfect,' he said, kissing my nose.

'Silence never bothered me. It's when the ideas come. When I get to make up stuff, invent stories.'

'There was a time I clawed anything I could to avoid it.'

'Why?'

'It was a punishment. Silence was used against me.'

He stood. 'Let's get out of here.'

I touched his arm. 'Let's stay.'

Liam looked at me, pained and questioning. He sat.

'My father would use silence against me. He would make Maureen and my mother ignore me too. Weeks could go by without them saying a word. I would talk but they would act like I wasn't there, like they couldn't even hear me. If I waved my hands in front of them they would side step past me.'

'Liam, that sounds awful.'

'The hardest part was it made me doubt myself. When no one acts like they can see you how do you know you are there? It wasn't so bad at school times cos then there were other people but in the summer, up in that big house where no one visited, I often thought I'd either gone crazy or died and was some ghost or something.'

'That's evil.'

Liam looked at me with eyelids half closed as if afraid to look at me fully. There was such vulnerability there, all the hurt evident in a stare. Right then, I knew I would never want to hurt him and wanted to wipe away the damage they had inflicted.

'When it was time to go to secondary school, they didn't even tell me they enrolled me into St Augustine's in town. It was a boarding school you know?'

I shook my head. I hadn't known.

'More confirmation they didn't want me. If you asked them it wasn't the case, swore blind it was only because it was the best school around but why did Maureen go to Knockfarraig when it was her turn then? The sad thing is, I still don't know why they were like that with me. Or why they hated me so much.'

He flinched when I placed my hand on his but he didn't pull away. We both stared at my hand, then he trailed his thumb up my knuckle, tracing the line of each finger.

'You were only a child, it wasn't your fault. There wasn't anything you could do.'

He kissed me then and I knew I would never want another man to kiss my lips again.

Falling in love changes how you see the world. People say love is blind, what I found was it illuminated every flaw of my other relationships. When you get used to love being the priority, any lack of love is highlighted. I became selfish with my time, wanting to spend it all with him, whenever he was free and Sadie called over, she was like gristle, getting into the cracks of my teeth. After Liam, I looked at Sadie with narrowed eyes, she was too negative, too intrusive, too hostile. It was the same with my family. I saw what Liam saw when he called over: the messiness, the scuffs on the wall from my brothers' skirmishes, the marker stains and fingerprints and discarded dolls from Lily. The

148

unrestrained conversations that didn't have any borders in our house compared to the politeness and order in his own. How much did I love your father? I wanted every second of every day to be filled with his image. I wanted him closer, even when he was inside me. At all times I was desperate to know what he was thinking, wishing to burrow into his brain and find the reason why he wanted me. One look from him was enough to make me ready.

As an eleven year old, I believed once Sadie removed herself from her family, the pain would stop. I also believed love would fix everything. Pain doesn't just end like that Abbie. It follows. Other relationships become reflections of her pain. Fragments of the same hurt entered her life from different components because it filtered from the one source, from the one common denominator: Sadie. It all came from her belief that there was something wrong with her. In most interactions she was reminded of it – in the way strangers bristled when she spoke, in the rolling of the eyes when she made a point. In the sighs when she walked into the room. Being ignored or blanked or talked over. In the folding of arms or the looking away. In smirking or coughing or the rubbing of temples. For someone else those signs would go unnoticed. Not Sadie. Each reaction was logged and added to the 'everyone hates me' pile. It was merited, in fairness. But then she played on it too. Expanded it. Made sure that if those sighs or eye rolls were just a coincidence, by the time one of them would leave, it would be warranted. Purposely difficult, she would complain or moan or turn loud in a quiet place or become quiet in a loud one. Sadie wanted to irritate, giving them what they wanted, or what she believed they wanted. I understood it was a shoot first before being shot scenario so I would stay quiet and try and reason with her after.

Sadie was not afraid of criticism. We would decipher where she went wrong and talk about ways to do it that would make life easier but then the next time would be exactly the same, as if I never spoke to her and talking afterwards would be like I was explaining it again for the first time.

The year of our Leaving Cert, Sadie ramped up her search for a man. Desperate to leave her house, she jumped into relationships quickly. You can imagine the type of boyfriends she had. If there were twenty identical men stood in front of Sadie, with every one of them gazing up at her with doleful eyes except one who looked everywhere else but at her you can guess which one she'd go for.

One guy brought another girl into their bed while Sadie was sleeping. One guy left her on the side of the road a mile from home in the middle of a storm. One guy kicked her out on Christmas Day. The thing was, Sadie would tell you herself, she didn't know how *not* to fight. Another opposite of me.

On reflection, moaning stopped Sadie from going insane. Telling anyone who would listen, her latest drama, over and over until she grew tired of talking about it. Once voiced, she'd let it out, passed it over, passed it on to someone else, diluting it. Whereas I internalised mine. I couldn't speak ever about my pain, but all pain has to come out eventually. She would tell me the horrible things the latest guy done, and I would be horrified, thinking it was the worst thing ever, not realising it was nothing compared to what would happen to me.

Christmas Day

Abbie

'Did a guy actually kick you out on Christmas Day?' Abbie asked, placing the book on the bed as carefully as if it was a sleeping baby.

Sadie jerked as if she just woke up. 'That would be a gentleman called Warren.' She sucked in a breath. 'He was not a keeper.'

'What did you do?'

Sadie shrugged. 'Called your mum, of course. It wasn't snowing or anything, but it was freezing cold and the dickhead actually kicked me out wearing just a t-shirt and my knickers. I'd only picked up the phone to throw it at him. Didn't even have shoes on. How embarrassing is that?' She shook her head. 'Which meant there was no way I was ringing a taxi. I kept talking through the letterbox, trying to reason with him, asking for at least my clothes. When that failed, I lost it. By the time your parents pulled up, I was bleeding and sporting a broken toe from trying to kick the door in.'

Abbie's eyes widened, and when Sadie met hers, they smiled.

'I wouldn't mind, but I only moved in on Christmas Eve. Your parents had only just lugged all my stuff there. Less than twenty-four hours later we were over, with the turkey I bought still cooking in his oven. I'd only asked him if he was going to help me with the veg when all hell broke loose. Happy fucking Christmas.'

Abbie couldn't help it. The image of Sadie in her knickers kicking at a door was too much.

She let out a giggle. 'You must have freaked out.'

'Freaked out? I was livid. Honestly, I didn't even feel pain in the toe until later.'

At that, Abbie burst out laughing. When Sadie started, there was no stopping them.

'It's still wonky now,' she said through gasps.

'What is?' Abbie managed.

'My toe, you eejit, stick with the story.'

Abbie held her side. 'I thought you meant the door.'

Sadie wiped away a tear. 'He wasn't even the worse of them. Your mother wasn't joking about my dating history, I met some stinkers. One guy wanted me to dress up in a dashiki and head wrap and kept calling me his African queen. Three drinks in to our date and my Cork accent's getting louder and more pronounced and he still doesn't get the hint, so I lost it and ended up shouting, "I've never even been on a plane, you dumbass, don't you know all our pussies look the same?" That got me kicked out quick enough.'

Abbie's jaw ached from laughing.

'He was worse than the guy who kicked you out in the storm?'

Sadie waved her hand. 'No, he was an utter shit. Gabrielle just didn't mention the other one, so I gave you another.'

Hearing her mother's name was like a stab to the heart, stopping Abbie mid chuckle.

'I wish I could do that, drop her name casually.'

Sadie cleared her throat, as if to demand order from her body. 'You can talk about her with me.'

'But that's just it. I have no stories to tell, none of my own, none just mine. The only thing I have is what that book or you tell me.'

'The memories might come back. Reading might trigger something.'

'You think?'

Sadie shrugged. 'I hope.'

'Yeah, I hope so too. There may already have been something. It was just a hug, but I think I remember it being her.'

Sadie propped the pillows so she could sit straighter. 'That would be your mum, all right. Never met such a hugger.'

'Really?'

'God yeah, any opportunity and the woman would hug you. I hated it, well I used to say I hated it, but I loved it really. Your mother would just know when I needed one, or when anyone needed it.'

'Maureen isn't a hugger.'

Sadie made a face. 'No, she never was.'

Abbie ran her finger along the spine of the book, trying to picture her mother as a moving real image rather than one of the generic ones taken from online, but there was nothing.

'So, you think if I read on, I might remember more?'

'It can only help. You haven't got to the part about you yet. Reading about myself brought so much back to me, things I hadn't even noticed back then. It might do the same for you.'

Abbie thought about the things she had already learnt. The Ellis's had mistreated her father. Growing up, she believed it was just her they had a problem with, but the son they now celebrated each year, who they idolised on the walls of their home, they had once ignored; they had once sent away. Abbie knew it was true, because they had ostracised her, too. What else was there to learn?

Opened Doors

Gabrielle

'Sadie's coming over,' I said, one evening, reading her text. We had finally finished our exams; I'd threw down the pen three days before while Sadie's last ended that day and we had promised to celebrate with a slice of cake at mine.

'Right so,' Liam said, slapping his legs and jumping from the seat. My parents were gone out, celebrating a football win. My brothers were asleep or pretending to be in their rooms.

'You don't have to go.'

'Sorry Gabs, but I haven't the energy for her tonight.'

'What do you mean?'

'Sadie takes over everything. The conversation, the couch, the mood. Listening to her go on about some problem or other now is more than I could take.'

He stroked my face. 'There's no problem. The lads have been on about catching up for ages. A night down the pub would suit everyone. Let you have your girl chat, sure I'll see you tomorrow.'

Even though I knew Liam going to the pub shouldn't bother me, the thought of even a night away from him made little sparks of panic jitter in my body. If he was going to the pub, I wanted to go. It never bothered Liam if I couldn't meet up or if he needed to do something, not like me, anyway. Every time he left the room felt like a loss, when I couldn't see or touch him, I felt like I'd forgotten something, an important part of myself, constantly missing. I resented anything that took him away from me and this time it was Sadie.

He flew out the door smelling of cologne and I paced, waiting for my friend, trying to work out why I felt the way I did, why it was such a big deal, when time apart was good for the relationship, and maintaining my own friendships was healthy and the right thing to do. I told myself all of that Abbie, but I was riled, I was shaky and vulnerable and woozy from how much I loved him and scared that he didn't love me at the same level. By the time Sadie opened the unlocked door and walked in without knocking, I was in a contrary mood. Any other time if she had rang the doorbell I would have told her off for not just walking in but this time her familiarity grated. As usual, she came in talking so fast I couldn't understand. It wasn't Sadie's fault that Liam left, what upset me was between the two of us, yet her excitement only added to my annoyance. Going straight to the fridge she took out the cheesecake I'd made to celebrate and without asking stuck her finger in to taste.

'Do you mind?'

Sadie scooped up a handful of the cheesecake before I could stop her, shoving it into her mouth and spitting biscuit crumbs everywhere. 'Mind what?'

I pulled out the drawer with more venom than I intended and handed her a spoon. 'You didn't wait to eat it together.'

Sadie dived in with the spoon taking a massive chunk. It wasn't a scoop but more like a shovel. I blew out a long breath. *It's Liam your angry with, not Sadie.*

But was it though? Wasn't it selfish to take something from someone's fridge and not ask before diving in? Wasn't it because of her annoying habits that people didn't want to be around her? Wasn't it because she was argumentative and in Liam's face that he would want to run?

'Where's Liam?' She said pointing upstairs and winking.

'Pub,' I said. With the form I was in I was tempted to add, to avoid you, but didn't.

'Drinking on a school night. Pity, I wouldn't have minded winding him up about the win.'

'Why would you do that?'

'Do what?' she said stuffing more cake into her mouth.

'Wind him up.'

'For the laugh.' Bits of cheesecake fell into the cake tin as she spoke.

'Christ, you could at least cut a slice and eat from a plate.'

I opened the cupboard again.

'No need, I'm done.' She threw the remnants of the cheesecake into the fridge.

'You may as well have finished it, the state you've left it in no one else will want it.'

'Too full now, I'll take it home with me.' She grinned, then seeing I was serious, grimaced. 'What's eating you anyway?'

That was enough for me to blow.

'You. The way you act. Coming in here not even asking. Not even knocking. Taking what isn't yours. Why is it you love to rub people up the wrong way? You know if you said something to Liam about the match it would make him feel bad for being out injured. Yet you would still say it. Why Sadie? You're so blind you don't even see the impact of what you say. You wouldn't see how it affects him after, how it would cut Liam deep.'

I didn't add that he would sulk for about three days.

'Well, if he can't take a joke that's on him. Not my fault if he's a bore. And when did you become so serious all of a sudden? His old man stuffiness is rubbing off and it doesn't suit you, that's all I'll say. Coffee?' she asked. Picking up the jar.

The heat rose in my chest, moving all the way to my face. My outburst hadn't even fazed her. There were many times Sadie had pushed my buttons but never this much.

'The only reason it doesn't suit you is because I normally put up and shut up with you. Like, look at you, asking me if I want coffee in my own house! You have no boundaries at all and then you wonder why people get annoyed. Why do you have to be so difficult all the time Sadie? Why can't you just be quiet and conform, for once in your bloody life!'

Sadie slammed down the kettle.

'Make your own coffee so, I was only trying to be nice. I can't believe you're starting on me today of all days. Anyone else I get but you… you're were meant to be different to other people.'

She poked me in the chest. 'Being with him has made you the same. Liam and his snotty family, hanging around with him and Maureen, they've changed you, and you've let them so Liam will love you, so you fit in. You're boring now you know that?'

I poked her back. 'I'm the boring one? Says the one who does nothing but hang around making me feel guilty for wanting a life with other people.'

Sadie seethed, searching for the ultimate put down.

'You're just another stupid girl who has to have a guy on her arm to feel good.'

The thing with close friendships is that they see into the heart of you. A best friend discovers what makes you tick, what you love, what you dislike, sometimes better than you can understand about yourself, tidbits of truth that no one else can see. When you confide in your best friend it helps you bond and sound out the problem but if you ever fall out, they can use the truth against you. Because of this, her words stung, the truth felt as stunning as a slap.

'You're jealous,' I said.

Sadie crossed her arms and smirked to rile me. For once, being on the receiving end of her tactics, it worked. 'Of ye? No thanks I'd rather stay single.'

'What's wrong with him?'

'Nothing.' Sadie shrugged. 'It's how you've changed that bothers me. You jump. You grovel. You're like a whole other person. The Gabs I love was cool.'

'Maybe the only reason I was cool was because I never challenged you. No wonder I run to Liam. At least he doesn't talk about himself constantly. Or complain. All the time I've known you it's been you complaining or moping, or getting into trouble, with me having to mop up your problems.'

Sadie clamped her fingers open and shut. Open, shut, open, shut. I could feel the heat burning in my cheeks, and I knew if I looked in the mirror the skin would be purple.

'Sorry, am I waffling?'

She puckered her lips and smirked, in a classic Sadie move.

'You want to know the truth Sadie?'

Her hand stopped moving, interested in my lowered tone.

'It's exhausting being your friend. You're like a leech, sucking the energy out of me. A parasite is what you are, feeding off my life, taking all my nutrients, my goodness. Anytime I suggest we do something you say no. Any fun, it's a straight up no. I want to be around fun people and Sadie, you-just-aren't.'

It hit a nerve. Sadie arms fell loose. We stared at each other for the longest time. Then, Sadie clenched her fists.

'Sorry about that. Sorry if I'm not the loudest at the party but we both knew there was only one allowed that position. You'd take over everything, insist I do this or go there even if I didn't want to.'

'Like where?'

'Like druggy nightclubs full of scum bags.'

'Hold on.'

Sadie put up her hand to stop me. She hadn't finished. 'Sorry, that you got everything you could ever want when I got nothing. Parents who love each other, who love you, brothers and sisters who care you're alive, a house you can relax in, and now you hit the jackpot with a boyfriend to screw you as well.'

'You are jealous.'

Sadie pointed a finger in warning to stop talking.

'Even when you mess it all up, even when you stayed out all night they fell over you. The golden child. The butter wouldn't melt girl who somehow still turned it all around, who still landed on her feet. I mean, even when you came home fucked off your face they forgave you and dangled a trip away if you just behaved, when I couldn't even go out past ten.'

'Is that what this is about? We asked your mum if you could go. We wanted you to come with us.'

'You're not listening. It's not about the trip. You didn't care how much you hurt them, didn't give two shits about the hassle you put them through as long as Gabrielle O'Neill was having a good time. That club was boring. Those so called friends wouldn't know how to have a conversation if you wrote it out for them, I mean, Royce can't even string a sentence together.'

'You're not exactly known for your stimulating conversations with people either.'

Sadie's nostrils flared. 'I don't bother with people who don't get me.'

'Well maybe I'm one of those people now.'

We stared at each other again. In all my life, I have never been so mad as I was in that moment. When Sadie spoke next her voice was devoid of anger.

'Admit it, you've loved it really, having a miserable friend to lord it over 'cause no matter how bad your life seemed all you had to do was look at me and know you were still better than someone.'

I gasped at the truth in her statement, at how true she believed it was. Sadie's nostrils flared wider, her sign that she was in it now, the temper completely unleashed. 'And now you're in a relationship you think that's another thing that you're doing better than me but sorry to tell you, darling, your boyfriend doesn't give a shit about you. I've said nothing, keep it zipped watching you fall all over the boy, pandering, running around in circles after him. It actually makes me sick, there's been times I've actually upchucked in my mouth. You were meant to be cool Gabs, you were cool, the coolest girl I ever met and now, you just aren't.'

'Get out,' I said.

'Get out? With pleasure and don't think I will be back either. I'm done with this town. Done with everyone in it.'

She stormed to the door.

'Go on yeah, run away then. The problem is Sadie, you can't ever run away from the person you really need to. You can't lose yourself,' I roared.

Swinging the door open, Sadie stepped out and just as she was going to slam it, she stepped back in. Instead of being angry though, her cheeks were soaked. 'You weren't meant to be like them. I could handle everyone else thinking it or saying it because I always knew you didn't.'

In an instant my anger left.

'Sadie, I'm sorry.'

All the heat in my body cooled at the way Sadie looked at me.

'You're not. You meant every word. From now on I'll get out of your way, I'll let you have fun.'

Sadie closed the door without another word. Even though I knew I should, I didn't call out to her to stay, I didn't run out after her and ask her to come back in. The sad truth is I wanted her gone, quickly I got ready, putting on some makeup and made my way to the pub, even though I was meant to be babysitting. Only when I saw Liam smile did my nerves settle. Liam put an arm around me and listened as I told him I never wanted to talk to her again, relishing his attentiveness as I spoke. Back then, I thought I was just unleashing, speaking of my grievances so they wouldn't stay inside, and once out they would lessen and dissolve and one of us, probably me, would contact the other and we would sort it and go back to the way we always were.

If I knew what she had called over to tell me, I would have listened. I would have sat down with my friend and said nothing about what annoyed me, but I never gave Sadie the chance. She never got to tell me her news, never got my advice on the decision she was trying to make. Our argument made the decision for her. That was the last time I saw Sadie for five years.

Drag

Abbie

She peeked over the pages of the book. Sadie was scrolling through her phone.

'You didn't speak to my mum for five years?'

Sadie stopped scrolling. 'Yip. Five long years.'

'How could you walk away like that? After my mother showed you such love?'

'It was because of that I had to walk away, Abbie.'

Abbie shook her head, not understanding, needing more.

Sadie tsked, picked up the phone, then dropped it again. 'She'd had enough. For a long time I could tell, even before your father came along. I dragged her down. Now, I can see what she said that night was true. I was a misery to be around. For a long time, I expected other people, mainly your mother, to make me happy and, well, it wasn't happening. All I did was rely on her and that drained us both, I think. Your mother couldn't help me and I hated that, hated her for that.'

'You *were* jealous.'

'Course I was jealous. Even before she started writing, your mother had everything I wanted and no matter how much I tried, even when I acted upbeat like her, it just fell flat. It was false cos I didn't know who I wanted to be. Leaving meant I would have to find a way to, just like, deal with myself. Leaving meant I couldn't expect her to sort my problems out anymore.'

'Did it help?'

Sadie sat on the bed, looked straight at Abbie. 'It did.'

'Did you miss my mum?'

'Losing her felt like someone had drilled a hole in me and left it wide open.'

'Where did you go?'

'Ah, let's not get too ahead of ourselves here. I don't want to ruin the story.'

'Don't think you need to worry about the spoilers here Sadie, I know how this book ends.'

Sadie picked up a nail file, bowing her head to her nail, but flicked her eyes up.

'The ending doesn't make the story. It's all the little bits that come before that make sense of the ending. They are the bits you need, they are the bits that will help you.'

'You think I need help?'

'Oh, I know you do.'

'You're infuriating, do you know that?'

Sadie ran the file straight across her nail. 'Yip. Been told that all my life. It's kind of my party piece at this stage.'

'Will I regret it?'

Sadie tilted her head. 'What?'

Abbie spoke low, afraid to say it too loud. 'Reading the rest.'

Sadie held the file in front of her, thinking, then went back to her nail. 'Truth? I don't know Abbie. Like you said, there is only one outcome.' She pointed at the book. 'Let's not pretend, yeah? We both know you *have* to finish it. Anyway, you've come too far now not to know the truth.'

Date night

Gabrielle

Were you ever told how your father saved my life?

Twice.

Remember the story about my mother sitting on the step and promising if I didn't touch drugs anymore they would book the whole family a trip around Europe? They kept to their word and every week I stayed at home and studied, they threw at least a fifty note into a jar. We planned the trip of dreams. Starting in France, we would spend a week in Paris, moving on to Amsterdam for a week, then inter-railing to Italy, stopping in various places along the way. Venice, Florence, Tuscany, Pisa and Rome.

Then I met your father and every hour away from him even in Knockfarraig was too much. The thought of leaving for over a month made the bright brilliance of the trip fade to a dull light. As the days leading up to the trip neared, Liam became quieter and distanced, making excuses not to see me, changing plans at the last minute, avoiding my calls. Convinced he was breaking up with me, I kept asking him what was wrong, and he would flare up, telling me there was nothing, that I was creating an issue when there wasn't one. For me, there was no other explanation. The night before I was due to leave, we went on a date and, just as I suspected, Liam was quiet. He yawned ten times in five minutes. He kept looking at his watch, or the menu, or anything but me, and a dull ache churned in my stomach. Who was this person? The Liam I loved would have held back tears and grabbed my hand, declaring confessions of love, begging me to stay. The Liam that night acted as if he was over us already. There was a coldness, in the way he spoke with stunted tones and one syllable answers, with no emotion in the way he regarded me, as disinterested as someone looking at a painting he'd grown used to and tired of, where the colours grated, turned garish and regarded as an eyesore. He acted like he was going through the motions, bored with our interactions. Bile lodged in my throat. Could he be sick of me? Food wouldn't pass, so I just moved it around my plate.

He spoke about work, about an important project he needed to finish, and how his boss was being a stickler for details. I spoke about my brothers getting caught trying to jump from the top of the roof for a dare. Neither of us mentioned the trip. It was as if a line had crossed between us; I couldn't mention it in fear that he was going to use it as an excuse to break up, but why couldn't *he* mention it? He didn't ask why I wasn't eating, but when the waiter took our plates away and asked if we wanted to see the dessert menu, he shook his head and asked for the bill instead.

Our date was over.

Outside my house, in his car, he leaned over and kissed my cheek.

'Have a good time.'

I couldn't say nothing. I had to confront him.

'Is that all?'

Liam looked down at his hands. 'I don't know what else you want me to say.'

'How about that you are going to miss me?'

He jerked his head. 'Well, I would have thought that was a given.'

'Nothing is a given. Why are you acting like this?'

'Like what?' He rubbed his stubble. 'I'm just tired.'

'Come on, Liam, you won't see me for over a month. Instead of making the most of the time we had, you've avoided me. You won't miss me at all.'

'That's not fair. What do you want from me? I have to protect my feelings, Gabs. You'll go over and meet a guy and I'll be the dope sat around waiting for you.'

'No, I won't. You know me better than anyone. You know I won't look at anyone else.'

He shifted in his seat, smiled at me as if he was talking to a young child. *Silly Gabrielle.*

'You say that now. And I know you have every intention of keeping it that way, but I understand Gabs. I get it. Two weeks in, you'll be out there in some restaurant and some guy will show interest and that will be it, open sesame.' He put his two palms together and opened them to get his point across. I cringed at the visual.

'No, they won't. Stop.'

He tapped on the steering wheel.

'Look, I've been thinking about this a lot and what's best for you is if we broke up. That way you can be free to meet other people and I won't drive myself demented in the meantime wondering if you've hooked up with someone.'

'You can trust me.'

He stopped tapping, looked at me. 'I know I can, Gabs. It's the other people I don't trust. A few drinks, a bit of sweet talk. Christ, look at you, any guy would be stupid not to try it on and I won't be there, and it will drive me crazy. If we're meant to be together, we will when you get back.'

He ran his finger slowly along the steering wheel. 'If I'm still here.'

'Still here? Where are you thinking of going?'

'Work is talking about moving me to Dublin. It's a promotion, more

166

opportunity, more money. They hinted at it before, but I wouldn't even consider leaving you. If we aren't together though...'

'If we aren't together, what?'

'You're the only thing keeping me here, so if I don't have you, why not go?'

'Dublin? Why am I only hearing about this the night before I go away?'

He rubbed at his face. 'I wasn't planning on saying anything tonight. It's been weighing on me, Gabs. I didn't want to trouble you with my own problems or take away from your excitement. You should be excited for going away, it's a once in a lifetime trip. It's why I've avoided you, cos I knew you'd prise it out of me and I didn't want you to carry the burden. Now that you pushed, it's come out and I see we can't go back. My parents are going through a tough time, my dad... it's come out the house is in trouble, so I might not even have a place to live anymore. The move to Dublin would sort that. The extra money will help. You know what?'

'What?'

Now that I've said it, now the words are out, it's clear we have to do this. Gabrielle, we have to break up.'

'Liam, no.'

He wiped at his cheeks as if trying to remove the strain from his face.

'I've made my decision. We both need time to think, to plan our life. Go enjoy yours and don't hold back. Have fun. Enjoy your trip fully, live in the moment and I'll do the same. I'll suss out Dublin. Get a taste for living up there and afterwards, well, we can see. Four weeks is a long time. Hopefully, we won't have moved on.'

'I can't believe you're doing this. Are you trying to make me stay?'

'No Gabs.' His eyes were sincere when he spoke. 'Like I said already, it's a trip of a lifetime. I could never stop you. I'll miss you and from a purely selfish point of view, I wish you weren't going, but I can't stop you or sit around and wait. It'll hurt too much.'

'Liam. What if I asked my parents if could you join us?'

He shook his head. 'It's too late for anything like that. Maybe if you had suggested it a few weeks ago but work wouldn't give me the time off or I wouldn't have enough money to pay my way.'

'I could ask my parents for a loan or...'

'Stop.' His order made me jump. I'd never heard him raise his voice before. 'I've made my decision. Please don't make it worse. I think you should get out of the car.'

'No, I...'

Liam opened his door and strode around to mine and swung it wide. With a clenched jaw and an expression like steel, he looked at the sky, waiting. Confusion made my body as fixed in place as concrete and my fingers clung to the underside of the seat. My brain reeled, trying to process. It all felt like it was happening in slow motion, that it was unreal, that I was in a bad dream, that he was going to turn around and say he was joking. He blew out a breath, angry now. 'Don't make me drag you out. You have to go. Don't make the last time we see each other turn horrible.'

I looked up at him, but he wouldn't meet my eyes, still staring at the sky. My brain whirled, trying to find the right words to make it all better.

'Go,' he shouted.

This startled me into motion.

With limbs full of lead, I stepped out of the car. Liam didn't even look at me as I did. He slammed the door and strode back to his side of the car before I could touch him or say another word. Once in, he drove off without even looking at me, without looking back.

Trip

Gabrielle

That night I climbed in to bed in shock. My worst fears had come true and Liam had ended it. How could he have been like that? How had a trip of a lifetime turned into something awful? After that, I raked through the memories of our relationship. Everything had been perfect between us before I mentioned the trip. How had it turned? How could he just close the door of the car?

Sleep wouldn't come. My brain raced as I sat up and cried and tried to find a way to resolve it. Due to an early morning flight, my mother knocked on my door while it was still dark, stepping into my room, she reeled at the mess of a girl she found.

'What's wrong, love?' she said, rushing to me.

'I don't want to go.'

'What do you mean? You've wanted this all your life.'

'I can't leave him. I know we'll never get back together.'

My mother's eyes flickered. 'Did ye have a fight?'

I nodded, cried in her arms. 'Gabrielle, if you're meant to be, he'll be there when you get back.'

What I couldn't tell her was that was what worried me.

'I love him,' was all I said. Leaving out about Dublin or how he said four weeks was a long time, I only mentioned my feelings, my decision.

'I don't want to go anymore.'

'Gabrielle, you can't give up a trip of a lifetime for a guy you've been with for a few months.'

'Why not?'

She tilted her head. 'Would he give it up for you?'

'Yes,' I said, my answer sounding more convinced than I believed.

'We spent a year planning this. You can't throw a decision like this at us the morning we leave.'

'Why not? You got what you wanted. We did this for me to knuckle down and study and stop partying, and I did. The trip was the bonus. You can still go anyway, you won't lose out.'

'Course I'll lose out if you're not there.' Her eyes bulged with frustration. 'Gabs, I can't believe you would throw away a holiday like this for some guy.'

'Like you wouldn't have done the same for dad.'

She sighed.

'Dad would never have let me stay.'

'Nor will Liam. He told me to go. He wants me to, but we left it really badly, he wants me to be free, to just have fun and not worry about him but he won't be there and I'll be miserable and all I'll do is drag your fun down.'

'So what? You'll stay in the house here on your own?'

I shrugged.

'No way is that happening. You're going.'

'I'm an adult, you can't force me.'

Her shoulders slumped and all the fight went out of her. 'Oh, honey, I know you love him and I like Liam, I do. If you stay though you'll make the biggest mistake of your life. You'll forever regret not going.'

'What if I go and forever regret not staying? What if I come back and he's taken the promotion, and I lose my greatest love and twenty years from now, I still haven't met anyone?'

'Christ, Gabrielle, talk about being dramatic.'

'This is how I'll be for the complete trip if I go. I can't help it. I love him.'

Mum stared at me. Noise erupted from the landing. The boys were up and, from the sound of it, were fighting.

'What if I delayed your flight? Got you on a different one tomorrow or in a couple of days?'

'How would that help?'

'It would give you time to sort it with Liam, to make up and say a proper goodbye.'

I shook my head. 'It won't change anything.'

'Well then, how about we book him a flight to come for some of it? For Italy maybe?'

'You'd do that?'

She grabbed my arms and rested her nose on mine. 'I'd do anything for you.'

My mother smelt of coffee when I hugged her. When we broke away, I ignored how hurt she looked, telling myself it was the best solution for everyone.

The boys only shrugged when told, not bothered if it didn't affect them, like sixteen and fourteen-year-olds do, but, alone in the hall, Sam punched my arm playfully and Darren hugged me and whispered, 'free gaff you lucky thing.' Lily cried on hearing but distracted with a present of my new nail varnishes I bought for the trip, she soon forgave me. Dad took longer, his hurt resistant to any distractions.

'Why can't you just ring him to tell him and he can follow us over?'

I shook my head. 'You don't understand how we left it. I have to see him.'

Writing this is hard to admit, but after that, I was dying for them to leave. Once decided I would stay, I just wanted to run to Liam, to show I chose him. At the door, I stood and waved them off, wanting to speed up time, wanting the door to close faster. As the car pulled away, it halted, and for a second I thought my father was going to get out and drag me into the car. It was my mother who got out , who ran and didn't stop until I was in her arms and she was again stroking my hair.

'Talk to him and sort it out. Tell him he can go for the whole trip if that makes you happy. I don't care. I'll find a way to pay for it all, just as long as you come.'

'Are you sure?'

'It's the things you don't do that you regret, Gabrielle.'

As we hugged, I breathed her in and said goodbye. With one last squeeze, she let me go. Even though I knew I broke her heart by choosing Liam, my mother still loved me. Even then, she didn't judge. Only a mother loves with no conditions.

I waved at my family. With a mix of disappointment and impatience, my father waved once, then looked away. Darren's red beanie hat almost covered his eyes, he laid his hand flat against the window and smiled as they drove away. Sam blew on the glass and Lily drew a heart through the condensation with her finger.

As I waved my family off, I thought of your father. Without a backward glance, I let them go. We all knew it; when given a choice between them, I chose Liam. Over the family who would do anything I needed, who would book a holiday to save my life, who loved me no matter what I did, who loved me enough to let me go.

As soon as they were at the bottom of my drive, I rang Liam.

'I stayed,' was all I said.

At my door within ten minutes, his chest heaved as if he ran all the way. His hair stuck up in places and his eyes were as red as mine. He kissed me hard on the lips and scooped me into his arms and I dropped everything: my phone, my bag, my shoes on the floor, not caring about anything but him and when he carried me up the stairs, there was nothing I wanted more.

Losing someone, or feeling the loss of someone for even a second, is enough to hold them tighter when found again. We found each other that morning; we searched each other. He kissed every part of me, kept saying 'I can't believe you stayed' and, 'I thought I'd lost you' and 'I can't believe you chose me.'

We talked about the trip and how he would convince work to give him time off, how he would turn down the promotion, how we would make it up to my parents. He told me the extent of his father's gambling battles, how the banks were foreclosing on the house. Liam told me he had saved some money and would take my family out for a meal and promise to pay them back and then, after all the day's drama, and tired from staying up all night, we fell into a deep sleep.

I picture their journey now. An early flight meant they drove on pitch dark roads with a notoriously steep hill to the airport. My father, upset with my refusal, must have been distracted and flustered. My refusal to get ready made them late. The delay must have caused a need to speed, making him drive faster than usual to catch the flight. His disbelief, his hurt, had to cloud his judgement. They say he may have looked at something in the back, or in the ditch nearest the passenger side. Whatever it was, the car drifted onto the other side of the road, right into the path of a juggernaut.

They say that something in the car distracted him, but I know better. It was me, Abbie; I was the distraction. I killed my family.

To say they had quick deaths would sound easier, sliding over the horrific details, but I promised you I wouldn't lie. The autopsy ruled four of my family: my father, the first man to love me, the first man I loved, that strong man who made me laugh, who carried me on his shoulders as a child; Sam, whose playful punch in the hall left a bruise for weeks after I picked out his coffin; Darren, the highest tree climber, with his red beanie hat and a full life still left to live; Lily, with her finger on the glass still trying to show me love despite my abandonment, all died from thermal injuries, showing signs of smoke inhalation. They would have died in minutes, but how long is a minute when you are burning to death? What are seconds when your skin blisters and charrs until you are only bone? Does the smell of your singed flesh invade your nostrils before your body gives up, before it gives you the mercy of dying? There is no doubt they suffered, that they died in horrendous pain.

They found my mother half in and half outside the car with a phone in her hand. With third-degree burns, she climbed out of the car and collapsed on the road. Phone records show she tried to ring me, but it rang on the floor of the hall. Even in her dying seconds, my mother thought of me.

It keeps me up at night thinking how they must have screamed and clawed at the car as their bodies burned. I have nightmares about my mother dying in the middle of a road, with strangers around her, trying to get near a burning car. I picture their last breaths and how, as they were taking them, as the air from their lungs filled with smoke and left their bodies for the last time, as they screamed in agony, I was gasping in pleasure.

Breathe

Abbie

Her breath wouldn't settle. Here it was: this was the reason she had no family. The O'Neills, all her mother's family were dead.

Oh, mum. You lost them all.

She wanted to cry. In a few lines, over a few inches of paper, she had lost five relatives. Not just five, for she had lost the hope of meeting the descendents of those five relatives too.

How could Gabrielle live through that guilt? Abbie couldn't imagine. Not after refusing to go, not after the decision Gabrielle made for love. What must it have felt like to carry that guilt for the rest of her life? How had it affected her parents' relationship?

Hole

Gabrielle

What happened straight after is a blur. There is a vague recollection of a Garda uniform, of wondering why there was a Garda even at the door. Brief snapshots of time have stayed, of watching as the man's lips made movement but his voice didn't compute, of Liam catching me, of being brought to bed, of being given something to sleep.

After that I went into shutdown. Because no matter what anyone said, no matter what they tried to placate me with, I caused their deaths. My family embarked on that trip for me. Because of me. And I didn't go when I should have died beside them.

Sometimes I wonder if I would have been better off, but then I think of you and I smell your hair as you hug me, and I know I could never wish that. I would take every bit of that pain for you, Abbie.

One thing I know for sure, if Liam wasn't with me I would have joined them. First, your father saved me from the car crash and then he saved me from the depression that tried to kill me as well. He organised everything: the insurance, the red tape phone calls, holding my hand as I picked out the coffins, guiding me towards the cremation when they said they couldn't bury five bodies in the one grave at the same time.

They wouldn't allow me to confirm their bodies, insisting their dental records were enough. They spared me, I know. Yet, there is a reason for being able to confirm, for disclosure, to say goodbye. One minute they were there and the next I was told they were dead. A writer's imagination goes deeper than most, which is good for a story, but not good for over imagining the worst-case scenarios of life. Every time I closed my eyes, I pictured them lying motionless in the morgue, their mangled, charred corpses side by side.

I must have broken their hearts. Sometimes, even years later, when I'm lying in the dark, they demand answers for letting them down. As I've already mentioned, the night always scared me, but after that, the turning of the day brought an indescribable horror. It terrified me to be alone. I stopped sleeping and became catatonic. Liam stayed to help me. There was a hole left from where my family's love had been.

Liam made me get up, made me accountable for the day, found reasons to force me out of bed. The way he picked me up, dragged me into still living, sat and held me as I cried. Without him, I don't know if I would be around to write this.

There would never be another day that I would see my mother's smile again. Or hear my father's laugh. No more times to tease my brothers or assure Lily that everything would be all right. Nothing would ever be all right again. My family's absence would mark and taint every occasion. For months after, I lay on their bedspreads and didn't move for hours, inhaling my mother's perfume, my father's smell of wood, the smell of football boots and a faint whiff of hash from my brothers. I would have given anything to have them back. I would have sold my soul for an hour.

From then on, I saw Liam differently too, for as much as I was grateful to him for doing the things he done, I hated that because of him, because of the decision I made, my parents died.

There was no way to redeem myself. No way to make it up. When I woke up screaming, the only way to counteract the nightmares was to ignore the truth and instead slip into unreality. By imagining false scenes, I could survive. The only relief came from carrying on their journey, conjuring up images of us all huddled together for a picture in front of the Eiffel Tower, or shouting at each other to keep up as we rode bicycles over the bridges in Amsterdam, sweaty and bored on the trains throughout Europe where we fought and bickered and laid our heads on each other's shoulders. The pleasure I took from picturing how we would have eaten tagliatelle over candlelight in Rome, or nearly capsizing the gondolas in Venice. Or how the churches in Florence would have echoed with their laughter, knowing I would have tried to ignore the dirty looks of the serious spectators come to have a look at the frescoes. Even though it was a form of insanity, this fracture of reality carried me through my days. Without realising, it opened the door to my writing too, because playing with imagination allowed stories to slip through later.

For a brief time, people are in your life and the next they are gone from existence. They have a word for losing both parents, but none for losing a sibling. From that day on I lived with the label of orphan but I was also Lily, Sam and Darren less and the only person left was Liam. Sadie didn't contact. As much as I'd hurt her, as close as we had always been, I couldn't believe she wouldn't come to the funeral. Each time the door swung open in the church, I turned around, expecting it to be her.

A month after the funeral, with swollen eyes and unbrushed hair, I called to her mother's door.

Mrs Jennings looked surprised to see me, and her appearance was a surprise for me also, for her blonde hair was now replaced with mostly grey and all resemblance to the once glamorous woman was gone. Even though she was surprised, she held the door open wide to enter. For the first time, she offered me a seat, on the coveted couch, now minus Sadie's brothers, who had moved on and out.

'What can I do for you, Gabrielle?'

'I was just wondering if you have any way to contact Sadie?'

'I would have thought you would have more chance of knowing that than me?'

I shook my head, my emotions so fragile and near the surface, they threatened to unleash.

Mrs Jennings sat opposite me. There was no offer of refreshments. With no one else to witness, the use for pleasantries was gone.

'Is everything all right Gabrielle?'

I shook my head again. 'My whole family is gone.'

For a moment I thought she hadn't heard me, but then the woman nodded. 'How?'

'A car crash. By the airport.'

And then Mrs Jennings did the complete opposite of what I thought she would ever do. She softened.

'That must be a terrible blow.'

I bowed my head, afraid if I opened my mouth I would lose my composure completely.

'I know how close you were to your family. It was enviable, really it was. I wished I had such a bond with my children but...' she looked out the window. '... it wasn't to be.'

Just after the funeral, I wasn't in the right frame of mind to answer or pick up on what the woman had said. Now I wonder, could I have said more, could I have challenged her, or supported her, but then all I could do was drip tears into the tissue I was holding.

'Do you know where Sadie is?'

Mrs Jennings continued to stare out the window.

'Mrs Jennings?'

The woman startled. 'Yes?'

'I asked, do you know where Sadie is?'

Teeth touched her bottom lip, moving from one side to the other.

'She's never been back. Never said a word that she was leaving, or even left a note, just took all her clothes and disappeared.' Mrs Jennings straightened. 'I know what your family thought of me, that I was a terrible mother, but you've no idea what type of a child she was. Sadie was hard work from the day she was born.'

Being raw and broken left me without restriction. There was nothing to hold back anymore. Abbie, I'm proud of what I said next.

'Anything that's worth having is hard to get. Sadie was always worth more than you gave her.'

'Excuse me?'

'It's because of you she left. She couldn't wait to get out of this house and now I have no friend and I miss her so much and I should have said something long ago to fix it. I should have stood up to you. Back then I should have rung child services.'

'Ha, that's a hoot. What for, providing a roof? For being well fed?'

I wiped at my nose.

'Just because she didn't like the food. She might have made out she was starving, but the girl never stopped eating! We provided her with clothes, washed by me. There was never any neglect.'

'There was never any love, Mrs Jennings!' I shouted.

'Get out,' she said, standing. 'You might be grieving but that doesn't mean you get to insult me in my own house.'

She followed me as I rushed to the door. Even then I knew the rage in me was really for my family, but rage was better in the moment than grief.

'Your house. That's how you always made Sadie feel, like it was never hers. You say there was no neglect, but you hurt her. You hurt her every single day.'

'Out now.'

She pushed me out the door with such force I nearly fell backwards. As she went to slam it. I caught it with my hand.

'Look, I'm sorry. I just want to see my friend,' my voice cracked. 'To tell her what happened. You know how much she loved my family.'

Mrs Jennings' hands on the door went limp.

'She loved them, yes. More than she ever did me.'

'Will you tell her? If she rings or contacts you, will you let her know I called?'

Mrs Jennings nodded, then closed the door.

Texts

Abbie

'Maureen never told me about the crash. This is the first time I heard my mother lost her family.'

Sadie's face was a question: *why would you think any differently?*

'All these years, I wondered why my mother's family weren't in the picture. I can't believe I didn't know. How come I didn't read about it online?'

Sadie bit the inside of her lip. 'Don't know. It was there. The headlines covered it for days after your mum died, making out like it was a family curse or something. Maybe we don't see what we aren't looking for?'

'Someone should have told me. Someone should have let me know what happened to them. They were my grandparents, my uncles, my aunt, and I didn't even know their names. Up until last week I didn't even know they existed. And now I find out I lost them too. When I read about Darren and Lily and Sam, I kept thinking, kept hoping there might be this whole other family out there that you were going to hook me up with, that they might have had kids and I'd discover long-lost cousins hidden somewhere and just like that, they're gone too.'

'It sucks,' Sadie said, looking out the window.

'How can you be sad about people you never met?'

Sadie didn't turn around. 'It's still a loss. Still your loss. You thought you were gaining a family and now you've learnt it isn't to be. No shame in feeling that.'

Abbie wiped away a tear before Sadie turned.

'She lost everyone, like me. My mother lost her father and mother too. How could she hurt my dad knowing what that loss felt like? She knew how lonely that would make me.'

There was a pause before Sadie spoke, as if she was thinking of what to say.

'She did lose everyone. Your mother often spoke about the other side of pain, about how loss can make you appreciate what you have. She swore the pain made her a better writer. Losing everyone meant she wasn't afraid to speak out or hurt anyone's feelings. The pain helped her go deep into her thoughts, made her question the big questions, made her take chances, made her want to record the moments. Have you read any of her books?'

Abbie shook her head. 'Even seeing the covers make me angry. And anyway, where would I read them? They're banned in Maureen's house and she'd cut my hands off if she saw me holding one outside. In the library or a bookshop, it's too public. Everyone knows who I am, so it's like I can feel them holding their breath waiting to see if I'll pick them up. If I order it online, Maureen will see the package.'

'You've thought about it then.'

'One time I even took the bus to town and went to a bookshop but even seeing them on the shelf made me break out in a sweat, like I was going to get caught, full sure someone from Knockfarraig would see me, as if I was stealing or something. It felt like a betrayal to Maureen and my father. Still, I flipped to the back of one and read the description, but that just made me angry. How hypocritical that she could talk about the power of love and then kill my father. That pissed me off.'

'This time read them. After you're done with this one I mean, when you've finished, read them. You'll understand way more.'

'Have you?'

'Every single one. And I'm not a reader, never have been, but I've read them all. Reading her books returns her to me. They aren't her life, they are different stories, but her voice is there. If you wanted, I could get you some, so you don't have to worry about anyone seeing you buying them in the shop?'

'You'd do that?'

Sadie shrugged. 'See it as making up for all the godchild presents I didn't send.' She looked at her watch. 'Tell you what, I'll leave you read for a bit and I'll go into town and get them. Give you some space. I'll bring back some lunch.'

'Cool.'

Sadie gathered her keys and wallet and left without another word. Abbie immediately took out her phone and checked her messages. One was from Joe.

See you later?

Any time she thought of Joe, she smiled. The night before, she'd told him she had to meet a family friend so couldn't hang out that day but might be around that night, not wanting to presume if Sadie had plans. Or if the reading was intense, they would need a break from each other.

Hope so, but not sure. Might have to entertain later, but will try to sneak out. Will let you know?

Abbie bit down hard on her lip as she hit send. Was the question mark too needy? Her stomach flipped when a text beeped almost instantly.

Hope it goes my way. Want to see you.

Abbie held the phone to her chest. She wanted to see him, too. Conflicting thoughts ran through her: excitement, anticipation for what would come next with him, competing with her need to stay, to find out more, to pick at Sadie further for stories.

The more she was finding out, the more she felt she was still only skimming on the surface. Sadie always gave her the impression she was leaving out the juicy parts, skipping the bigger, deeper details. Hadn't Gabrielle written about how Sadie deflected from the truth? From the little Abbie knew about Sadie, she was sure of only one thing: Sadie was used to keeping secrets. All Abbie had to do was figure out what would make her talk.

Cling

Gabrielle

After the funerals I stopped answering calls from friends and neighbours, sick of hearing the sympathetic tones which sounded insincere and nosy. Everyone just wanted to see the orphan, touch the drama of it, catch a piece of the tragedy so they could relay the gossip. For some time, I hated people, hated everyone because they lived and my family died. Friends who called to the door meant well, but I felt like punching them when they spoke about their love lives or where they were going out on the weekend. After a few minutes, I would clam up and show them the door. A lot of doors were closed on relationships then. The one person I didn't push away was Liam. Instead, I clung. If I woke up, I followed him around the house, needing him next to me, to remind me what to do. Incapable of any clear thought or direction, I needed him to navigate my day as much as oxygen.

My Leaving results arrived and stayed unopen, same with the college applications. Liam worked out that my parents' insurance would cover the mortgage and even though it would take time, his job could supplement me. You don't know how much that meant. Far distanced aunts and uncles, relatives that I had known my whole life, said all the right things at the funeral, but then they were gone, and their offers of help disappeared.

It's important you know your father cared. That he honestly saved me.

On the days he worked, time would pass in blank spaces, and I wouldn't be able to explain what I had done with the hours. For a while, he was my only contact with the living world and his face the only feature I could handle seeing. Once he walked in, I ran to him, relieved that he was finally back. It was my favourite place, tucking in to his open arms. There, I would lay and shut out as much as I could. There, I concentrated on his touch, on his lips, reducing the world to his skin, his breath, our wants. In those hours, all I needed was him.

When I wasn't in his arms, Liam gave me the space to allow my sorrow to pass until it was manageable. He would sneak to the kitchen as I closed my eyes and after a while, I would smell wafts of garlic or meat. When he called me, he would lead me from the bed to the table where he would place a plate in front, handing me a glass of wine and I would cry with gratefulness. Snatches of happiness came, so fleeting and brief, all down to Liam. Instead of tears of wretchedness that consumed me during the hours without his presence, around him the tears I cried were of possibility, because if I could smile, surely happiness could be available in the future.

It wasn't easy. The burden of my grief, the sudden change in the relationship dynamic, hung over us. I wasn't exactly a catch. Overnight he had become my carer, my cook, as well as my lover. Enormous pressure for a man in his early twenties. With no buffers anymore, no people on my side to sound out the relationship, or talk my troubles over, no fresh updates about the antics of my family to laugh over my conversation dried. When all your days are the same, you have nothing new to say. When grief overtakes you and threatens to pull you under, there is no point making any effort.

As weeks turned into months, Liam's enthusiasm waned and who could blame him? His visits became less frequent. The times his eyes flicked to the door increased, as if wondering when he could leave. There was always something else he had to do: help his mother with her charity work, help his father with the court paperwork, help Maureen move her stuff, play sport, meet the lads, anything, everything he could use he did, and the gap broadened between us.

'You want to break up with me, don't you?' I asked one day.

He took a deep breath, then dragged the curtains apart. 'You need to get over this, Gabrielle.'

'How?' I croaked, wiping the raw skin under my eyes. 'How would you get over it?'

He considered my question. By his expression there was no need to answer, because we both knew he would, he would carry on, maybe not as normal, but there would be no staying in bed, no closing of the curtains for Liam.

He sat down opposite me with a sigh, raking his fingers through his hair.

'I can't keep on seeing you like this. It's not working anymore. At first I understood you needed time, but now I don't know how to help and I don't recognise who you are.'

'Your whole family dying will do that, Liam.'

'Don't you think I know that? That's why I'm here. The guilt, it's awful. I know it must be killing you.'

'You stayed with me because you were guilty?'

'No. But I owed them to at least try.' He clicked his tongue. 'Don't you think it played on my mind that I might have caused their accident? That our fight might have upset them, distracted them?'

'I thought that was just me.'

'Not at all.' He looked at the ceiling. ' Look, call me heartless, make me the villain, but this isn't living and I can't watch you die anymore. I won't.'

He shifted on the bed. 'I love you Gabs, but I won't watch you give up. I didn't sign...'

'Sign up for this. Is that what you were going to say?'

He sighed. 'Well... yeah. It all got so serious and, look, I know that isn't your fault, and you never wished for any of that, and if you could have your family back in a heartbeat, you would. Trust me Gabs if I could get them back I would. It's just... I can't go on like this, if I have to open those curtains once more I think I'll crack. It's getting to the stage where I can't bear to walk in the door anymore. You don't wash or eat unless I force you... I just don't know what to do.'

'I know I need to change, but I can't, Liam. It's too hard to move. Don't you think I see that I'm losing you? All you do is avoid me.'

'Would you blame me?'

'No,' I said, my voice a croak.

He stood up. 'Look, I'll give you some time.'

'All I have is time. Please, Liam, don't leave me as well.'

He opened his arms, at a loss. 'I don't want to.'

He was prepared to go, to walk away from me forever. My whole body shook. Before my family died, we might have drifted apart naturally. We might have taken the trip around Europe and discovered we weren't compatible. After their deaths, there was no going back. With no family or Sadie, Liam was all I had left. It sealed our fate. For I would not lose him too even if it meant doing everything in my power to make him stay.

'I'll start getting up, getting out.'

'I don't want to force you if you're not ready.'

'I'm ready. I can be ready. Just don't go now. Please.'

He stuffed his hands in his pockets.

I smoothed my hair back, wiped away my tears. 'If you want, I'll have a shower right now. I'll get ready. We can go for a walk or hang out, whatever you want. Let me show you I can be Gabrielle again. I can be the person I was.'

'The person I love?'

'You still love me?'

He sat back on the bed, leaned in, kissed me. 'I wouldn't have stayed unless I loved you.'

Little by little, I ventured outside again. First, I braved walks on the beach at quiet times or in the evening we would sit in the garden counting stars. Liam led me for picnics outside, eventual meals in restaurants, winter visits to remote pubs sitting beside log fires and ordering stew and hot toddies. He brought me back to living Abbie, another silent way he saved me. Until one day I woke and there was a familiar stirring, a bubble of excitement, a hunger. That day I planned an elaborate meal, a retro prawn cocktail, sea bass with mushrooms, fudge cake for after. It took me all day to prepare, and as I finished the final touches of the starter, I looked at them with pride. For the first time in months, I had accomplished something. After that, I got dressed and took time with my makeup. In the forefront of my mind was Liam and how I wanted to pay him back for all he had done, to show him how he helped. I waited for him, with growing anticipation, when I heard the key in the door, I stood for his appraisal. The look he gave me wasn't what I had hoped for. Instead, he rocked on his heels, as if given a blow. His unexpected reaction threw me. I stood self-conscious and unsure.

'I made you dinner as a thank you for everything.'

He sat down at the table and scratched his chin. 'You should've told me. I'm after eating a late lunch.'

'Oh. I'm sorry. The prawns and cake will keep. I should have rung, it was just for the first time I felt able to do something and I wanted to thank you, to surprise you. It wasn't about the food.'

He flicked his eyes over me, over my heels, my bare legs, the short dress.

I wanted to wipe off my makeup, rip out my earrings, curl up on the sofa.

'You look lovely. There was no need to go to the trouble.'

'I like to, though. I'll do anything to make you happy with me again.'

Liam studied his hands. 'Sorry Gabs, I just had a hard day. I've always been funny with surprises. That must have taken some effort. Tell you what, if the prawns will keep, how about I find room for the main?'

I beamed at him, Abbie; I beamed at him with gratitude.

Orphan Abbie

Abbie

It was hard to compute that her mother became an orphan, just like her. *Everyone just wanted to see the orphan, touch the drama of it, catch a piece of the tragedy so they could relay the gossip. I hated people, hated everyone because they lived and my family didn't.*

That was exactly how Abbie felt.

If anyone had known what it would feel like to live on after your family died, it was Gabrielle. Then why did she make Abbie do the same?

Sadie entered the room, swinging a bag of books.

'Is my mum telling the truth here?'

Sadie cocked her head. 'Her truth, yes.'

'What does that mean?'

'There are things I told your mother that she never put in the book.'

Abbie shook her head as if to ask her to elaborate.

'When I read it, I asked her why.'

'You could do that?'

Sadie looked confused.

'Are you saying you got to read this book before she died?'

'Course. We had to get it bound. Your mother was a perfectionist about her books. There would have been no way she would have trusted me with that task, as much as she loved me.'

If Abbie wasn't sitting down, she would have needed to.

'That answers that, so.'

'Stop speaking in riddles. What are you going on about?'

'If she finished the book before she died, then it's not possible to find out about that day. Their last day.'

Sadie hardened, her eyes focused. 'Don't worry, she lets you know.'

'Really?'

Sadie nodded.

So I will find out the truth.

'Why did she leave things out about you?'

'It was in case I needed to apply for custody. In case the authorities needed to read it. As proof.'

'Proof of what?'

Sadie shook her head as if saying, *you know I won't say yet.*

'Can you at least tell me what she left out?'

'A few years in to moving to Galway, I had a breakdown... a bad, bad breakdown.'

'How bad are we talking about?'

'As bad as it gets, really. Bad enough that I tried to stab one of the not so good guys. As if that wasn't enough, I panicked and drove into a wall. Ended up in hospital, then court. Not my finest hour. But in the end it saved me, because it forced me to get help. Proper help. If Gabrielle had been around, I would have just leaned on her, got her to bail me out. All alone, I couldn't do that. The judge saw right through me, ordered me to go to anger management. With a stranger, a counsellor, it was easier to make sense of everything. It wasn't like I couldn't talk to Gabs, it was just, I'd never been ready to. Gabs took me out of reality. In childhood, to survive, I needed that from her. If I told her all the things that were done to me, it would mean it was real. Hilary, my counsellor, taught me that the world wouldn't explode

THE SISTERS YOU CHOOSE

if I admitted what happened. Anyway, that was in the end how your mother discovered me. In the book she made out it was just on instinct, but the truth was she found me from the court records.'

'You tried to stab someone?'

'Don't freak out. It was only a butter knife. My nails would have been sharper. He also had just punched me, so he was lucky it wasn't a steak knife I grabbed. The guy didn't press charges or anything. When the guards saw my bust up face, they wanted me to go after him. It was the dangerous driving I got in trouble for.'

'So it was Galway you ran to?'

'Dammit, I keep giving away the story before it happens.'

'Like I care about you ruining the surprise. What bothers me more is how she swore she would tell me the complete truth.'

Sadie rolled her eyes.

'Her truth. Your mother knew you'd bring that up, so I promised her I'd explain. She felt strongly that I should be the one to explain my details myself.'

'An omission is still a lie.'

'Believe what you want. Your mother was thinking of me, but she was also thinking of you.'

'Of me? How?'

'Because she wanted to make sure if it came to it, if I needed to fight for custody, then that was possible.'

'Why would you need to fight for custody?'

Sadie let the silence answer.

Traits

Gabrielle

First things first, here are some of the many traits I love about your father: I love the way he says my name like it is the sweetest word he has ever spoken, how it spills from his tongue like he coated it in syrup. How he kept me alive after my family died, by insisting I get up, giving me tasks, giving me reasons to live. I love him most for giving me you.

There are many ways he shows his love, in simple things like knowing when I say I might choose the salad what I'm really looking at on the menu is the dessert, so he tells the waiter we're skipping the mains or when he comes home with extra pens because he knows I probably lost mine again and I can't go an hour without one. I love the way he looks at me when something happens, a hidden exchange, a covert language where we don't need words to say anything, we just know. I love how we can sit in silence with each other and not feel uncomfortable. I love how he supported me when I started to write, how he encouraged it even or how he can't walk past a bookstore without bringing home a book for me he thinks I'll love and always nails it. Most of all Abbie, I love the way he loves you. How his eyes brighten and expand when you walk into the room, when he holds his arms out wide as if he wants to make the space inside himself bigger, opening up to make room, to allow you into a place no one else gets to visit. I love him more for loving you.

They are only a fraction of the parts of him I love. I tell you them now because very soon I will get to the parts I hate and I need you to see, in advance, that your father isn't just his faults. Those few sentences above are why I stay. Those sentences mean everything.

From early on, even before my family died, I made Liam aware marriage was important. We talked about it many times – about the possibilities, about the reasons it meant something, for the opportunities it would open up in regard to having a family.

He proposed with a wedding dress. One day I walked into the bedroom and hanging outside my wardrobe was a white gown, with beading embroidered into fine lace on the scalloped neckline, the skirt flowing out, covered in tiny beads. I had to sit on the bed when I saw it for it was the most beautiful dress I had ever seen. There was a note pinned to the hanger, saying 'would you wear this?'

On the bed was a jewellery box, inside sat my mother's engagement ring. Both fit me perfectly. When I opened the door, Liam stood on the stairs with a bunch of flowers and a bottle of champagne. He looked straight at my finger and when he saw the added jewellery, he grinned.

'I didn't know if you would want to wear your mother's ring. If it's too painful, we can go out and pick another one.'

I shook my head. 'It's perfect. Exactly what I wanted.'

He lifted me into his arms and carried me to the bed and we didn't leave for the whole day.

If I had my way, I would have married the next day in the registry office in Cork City. In a plain square room with carpet on the floors, magnolia paint on the walls, a mahogany desk in the middle and cheap plastic chairs lined up in rows with the officiant stood looking at her watch in a plain black suit. I would have loved that room and all it represented. Marriage to me, meant Sunday mornings with family wrapped around, someone to cuddle when the fear gripped me in the dark, a person to share life's troubles with, a hand on the small of my back when I was stressed. There was no one else I wanted children with.

Instead, Liam's parents insisted we make it a big celebration. By choosing my dress, Liam spared me the hurt of shopping for one without my mother. Despite my soon to be mother in law and Maureen's complaints that it was bad luck for the groom to see the dress beforehand, I saw it as another sign of his love.

For my sake, Liam insisted on only immediate family at the ceremony. There was no way I could have held it together seeing the seats full on Liam's side compared to the empty spaces on the church pews where my mother would have sat dressed up in her finest or where my brothers would have stood on Liam's side. Where Lily would have trailed flowers before me guiding me to soon to be husband, the same aisle my father would have walked me down. Instead, we broke tradition. Liam waited outside the church for me and we walked in together holding hands. There was no doubt on my behalf, not one bit of hesitation.

The wedding breakfast was held in a five-star hotel overlooking the water where we ate a seven-course meal until we thought our bellies would burst with three hundred guests in attendance. Tradition was broken left and centre - the speeches were scrapped as I couldn't have kept it together knowing I would never hear the one I needed most. My father's voice had long gone from my memory, no matter how hard I tried, I couldn't recall it. His face I could picture, the words he would say I could imagine but I couldn't replicate the sound of his voice, or the tone.

No longer a daughter, or a sister, all I could dream of was being a wife. When I strode up that aisle it was for one purpose. What I wanted more than anything was to be a mother. What I needed in my life was you, Abbie.

We went home to my family home, our family home now. We had chosen a new bed to put our own touch on the house and it was here we went straight to. Contraception was thrown in the bin and we stayed there for four days. Sorry Abbie, it's probably too much information but it's important too, for it shows you how much we loved each other. You'll need that.

The week after we boarded a plane for Malta. The honeymoon should have been idyllic. Good food, late nights and late mornings. There was no place we had to go, no more wedding lists, no more requirements, which at the time had been stressful but had served me well, kept my thoughts busy, distracting me from memories that only highlighted the loss of my family. At the wedding the absence of them could not be ignored and on holiday it was all I could think about. For the sake of Liam, I tried to keep it together, but every detail reminded me. Boarding the plane I remembered the time Lily screamed out in the aisle that she'd dropped her doll, when the hostesses saw her bottom lip quivering, they delayed the flight until security found it. Or as we walked out of the airport my first sight of palm trees jolted me back to a trip the family made to Lanzarote two years before they died, when we were gathering up the luggage, we couldn't find Sam, and then Lily pointed to the sky and there he was, scaling one of them, waving at us from his perch. The loss of them was everywhere, there was a heaviness in my chest, carried on my shoulders, darkening my days. Liam tried his best to distract me, and he succeeded some of the time. Your father was the best distraction.

Two days in, on a boat trip to Gozo, we stopped at the blue lagoon in Comino, with its turquoise clear water. Laying out two towels, I let the suns rays hit me and dug my feet into the blonde, fine sand. A woman in the water stood in my line of vision, she held her hand out towards a child, stopping the little boy from going further. In the clear water you could see her full profile, her legs opaque and ghostlike. The way she stood, the way she stopped the boy, reminded me of something I couldn't place. Taking the boy's yellow bucket, she skimmed the water in front. The boy stepped back further, afraid. The woman waded further out alone, taking slow, careful steps, until she had gone at least ten feet. Only then did she empty the contents back to its home. From the tentative movement of the other people in the water and the fact not one of them was swimming, I stood and saw the surface was full of floating jellyfish.

All the best moments have the possibility to sting.

When the woman turned back to the boy, it was in the way she leant to him, took his hand again, her mouth close to his ear saying words I knew reassured, calmed, placated that was so familiar. It was as if my mother was there again. Liam kissed me lightly on the shoulder, then handed me an ice cream.

'What happened?' he whispered.

'Nothing,' I said, forcing a smile.

'Then why are you crying?'

I hadn't even realised I was. As I wiped away my tears, I watched as that woman gave up trying to clear the copious jellyfish floating nearer and led the boy out of the water. She was low, talking in his ear, trying to appease but the boy's disappointment was too much, his face was contorted with tears. I stood and walked towards them, meeting them at the waters edge.

'Would you like an ice cream?' I asked the boy.

He stopped crying, shocked at the offering. He looked to the woman.

'I saw you in the water. You were very brave to keep trying. My husband bought me an ice cream but I'm not hungry and I thought you might like it.'

His eyes widened at the woman, in a question. She smiled in agreement. The tears left the two of us. The boy took the ice cream and licked the melted areas that had nearly reached the cone. He ran to his towel, up the beach a little. The woman didn't move. Close up she was nothing like my mother, the age, the hair colour, the eyes were all off, yet it still felt like I was looking at her, like this woman understood somehow. She regarded me, then touched my arm.

'Thank you. Have a good holiday.'

It was all she said. Those words unlocked a part that had twisted shut. My parents would not have wanted me miserable; all my mother ever wanted for her children was their happiness. Remembering that, was enough to help me live. One day, if I was lucky, I would have my own child and would pass on the love she showed me. Her legacy would be love. My life hadn't ended. There I was, in a beautiful place, with a man to call my husband, a man that I loved and a whole life ahead.

We settled into our version of marriage and we formed our own pattern. Due to my family's life insurance, I never had to work. Money wasn't an issue so it left no roadblocks for children. I thought I would get pregnant straight away. For so long before we were married I was terrified that 'that' one time would get us caught so when we began trying I was convinced it would be instant. It wasn't. Hindsight is something isn't it? I see now I was desperate to emulate my own upbringing. Having a baby would, in a way, bring my family back. It's a good thing I didn't. It wouldn't have been fair on a child. To expect another to take away my pain. The truth was I needed to grieve for my family. I needed to get over what was to come first.

Early Sparks

Gabrielle

Happiness grew. Domestic life gave me a focus. Cleaning, cooking, making improvements to the house all kept me busy. Busy was good, as it meant not over thinking. After my chores I would walk the beach and sit on the wall and speak silently to my family. I would ask them to forgive me making quiet pleas to help me create my own family.

As the days turned into months, each one laced with the pain of discovering another bleed, I became consumed with getting pregnant. When the months turned into seasons our sex life turned into home-work, and if truth be told, hanging around the house left me bored.

Maureen called a lot those days, and on her own, with my full attention, she was different from school. Packing for her trip around the world, which made me bite the inside of my lip every time she mentioned it, distracted me from my families trip that never was, I handed over some of the holiday outfits I bought for the honeymoon.

'Do you want some books?'

Maureen raised an eyebrow. 'I don't plan on doing much reading.'

'When I go on holiday all I want to do is sit and read.'

'What a waste. Anyway, it's not a holiday, it's an adventure. Why don't you do that now?'

'What go on an adventure?'

Maureen laughed as if the idea was ridiculous. 'No, read.'

'Read? In fairness I spend most of my day doing that.'

'No, I mean, get a qualification. At least you'd have something to show for it.'

'I don't think you can get a qualification for just reading.'

'You're always scribbling in some journal. Why don't you do some creative writing course? If it was me I'd crack up in the house all day.'

The idea of doing a course sprouted wings, fluttering at my brain until I could see no reason not to. Excited I couldn't wait to tell your father, bringing the conversation up over a coffee.

'So, me and Maureen were talking today and she suggested doing a creative writing course.'

He didn't look up, kept scrolling through his phone. Straightaway I felt the energy shift, grow more hostile.

'Right.'

'What do you think?'

'I think if you're planning on taking a creative writing course you'd want to watch your grammar. Me and Maureen, come on Gabrielle, that's basic.'

'Sorry I didn't know I had the grammar police on me. Anyway speech is different, there's no rules there.'

'What, you're an expert now that you've read a few books?'

'I think it helps.'

He laughed. 'Do you think you're gonna be the next King? Or have you moved on to better writers?'

I looked at him as if seeing him for the first time.

'I don't know this Liam. Who are you? The Liam I know would want me to try and live again, to get out of the house, to do anything but wallow. It's like you want me to stay and mourn. It can't suit you to have me just sit and rot here?'

He put down his phone. 'No. That's not what I want. What I want is for you to be happy. I thought you were, here with me, I didn't know it wasn't enough.'

'You're enough for me, it's me that isn't enough. What's inside me isn't whole, I'm not content with who I am. Look, I don't even know if I'm going to like it but out of everything it's the only subject that interests me.'

'Why didn't you tell me you were feeling this way?'

'I'm sorry, I kind of thought it was obvious.'

'So I'm a fool now? You lost your whole family, I thought you were grieving.'

'I am grieving, I just don't think sitting around the house they lived in is helping me heal.'

'So how will this work then?'

'There's an MA course in UCC. It's only one year, and I figured I could drive up with you each morning.'

'I'm working from home more now.'

'On those days I could bus it or I'll learn to drive. I haven't figured out the times yet but I'm sure I could still get home in time to make dinner.'

'What about our plans?'

'What plans?'

'Come on.'

I rubbed at my arm. Words on paper are so much easier to write than vocalised.

'Well, I know we've been trying but I thought maybe it was, it's been, too much pressure. Maybe if I enroll in something like this I wouldn't be so obsessed with getting pregnant, and it might happen naturally, like a watched kettle and all that.'

'You haven't changed your mind?'

'God, no. I want a baby more than anything.

Liam closed his eyes in relief. Then he held my hand.

'What if you get pregnant?'

'It's only a year, so there's time to work around it. It's only a year Liam, maybe we could delay trying for a few month?.

He dropped my hand, shoved his seat back, then stood. 'There you go, you haven't even started the course and already you're changing the rules.'

'We're married, I didn't think that meant we needed to be chained together.'

Before I knew it he caught my top and wrenched me closer to him, so when he spoke his lips almost touched my face. 'Leave then, if that's what you want. Give up on our dreams of a child without even consulting me.'

'Liam, let go,' I said slowly, enunciating the words.

He released his grip, but held his gaze. 'I don't want to be around you.'

He stormed out of the room, and then I heard the door slam.

My head reeled with confusion. I thought he would be happy for me, for finding something to do with my days. How did happy news turn into that? My chest heaved with hurt, and shock. It was like being with a stranger. What had just happened?

For hours I sat at the table trying to figure it out, trying to work out how I felt about it but the truth was I was stunned. Full sure he would come back and apologise I waited but as the hours turned from day to night, my resolve faltered. By the time night fell, I started to worry. Was I wrong? We had spoken many times of wanting children and we had tried but why couldn't I have it all? Why couldn't I study and try for a baby? The only thing I could see I did wrong was not speak to him before Maureen but it was only because of that conversation that the idea materialised. The rivalry between them may have hurt, that she had known first. But was he blind? Liam saw me writing in journals, scribbling my thoughts and observations down any chance I got. He saw the books on every available surface, the need in me to dive into stories, surely he could see I wanted to be a writer? Surely it was his job as my husband to push me to the best for myself. As partners weren't we meant to lift each other up rather than hold the other under the water? I oscillated between feelings of utter loss to smugness. As the days went on with no word from Liam, all anger subsided and genuine worry took over. He had left his phone on the table and ringing around, no one had heard from him. By the third day I was in full blown panic. He walked in as I rang the guards.

I hung up and ran to him and he caught me as I did.

'It's not about the course. You are a writer, I know that, you should be a writer. It's just that I don't want to lose you.'

'You can't lose me.'

'Promise?'

'I swear.'

'On who?'

'On all that's come before me and every person after.'

I ran my fingers through his hair and kissed his almost full beard and he carried me into the bedroom and we made up the only way we knew how.

I didn't ask where he had been, I didn't ask why he left me. There were no apologies then or ever. That day in bed he was different. Just as gentle, your father never treated me badly there, but this time he was firm, straight to it, on a mission and when he came inside me, I understood, he needed me to keep my side of the bargain and he was going to do everything he could to make sure I was pregnant before the year was out.

There was a sadness in that I couldn't explain because I had wanted a baby more than anything, yet something in it hurt.

The course was a breath of fresh air. During the day, my classes made me fall in love deeper with words, with composition, with creating characters, with the form, with prose.

During the night the arguments got worse. No matter how much I placated, I couldn't get it across to Liam that it wasn't a choice between him or the course, I wanted both.

'You're taking something aren't you? Are you hiding the pill on me?'

'Course not. The doctor said not to even worry if it takes longer than a year. With everything that happened to my family, the grief probably had an effect. He said it will happen naturally. If you want, there's sticks you can get, to check my ovulation, maybe we're trying at the wrong time?'

He arched an eyebrow. 'We're trying every night.'

'Yeah but maybe that's where we're going wrong, maybe we need to build up the anticipation.'

'You think I'm shooting blanks.'

There he was, reverted to a little boy, blaming himself.

'Not at all. There's nothing wrong. Let me get the sticks and we can see.'

There was no need for the sticks. The next month my period didn't come.

Abbie did the math on her finger and a sinking feeling swam around her stomach.

At first, there was no problem being pregnant on the course. Watching my period like a hawk, the doctor only reckoned I was five weeks when I found out so there was plenty of time ahead. I've never seen your father so happy. Men can be very strange creatures but this I understood, he was virile and wanted everyone to know it. Parading me to his parents we told them the happy news and honestly I felt like I was on top of the world. Until the sixth week when I was struck with non-stop morning sickness. Barely able to hold my head up, sitting in a bus for an hour was not possible. Days were missed. On the days I did manage to attend, all I had to do was catch a whiff of someone's tuna or cigarette smoke and I would have to jump up and spend the next hour in the bathroom. Once I started it wouldn't stop and I would have to ring Liam to collect me and in the car, I would look at him and wonder how he could be so ecstatic when I was so miserable and then I would place a hand on my stomach and think of the little bean growing inside me, the little gift of magic.

When the bleeding started, at first they reassured us it was just spotting, that most women don't even notice. Liam lay with his head on the bed, talking to my flat stomach. My heart tugged at his words, with his pleas, with his promises that we would be good parents.

It wasn't enough.

The cramps came and the bleeding increased and hours later our magic bean expelled from me. I examined every bit of blood, trying to find our baby, but each clot looked like just a clot, when it was so much more. Life and dreams and a future and now that it was gone we fell apart.

By that stage I had missed so many classes I didn't think I'd catch up. The thought of carrying on, acting normal was just too much. Liam didn't push me, didn't try to persuade me to go. If I was of sane mind it might have annoyed me, but he could barely cope himself. Distraught, he booked holidays from work and for two weeks we stayed in the bed, next to each other, two lost bodies lying motionless. At first our backs were against each other, separate in our grief and then, as the days elapsed, with each cup of tea made, or takeaway ordered, slowly we turned to face each other, until there was a day we could look each other in the eye, wipe away our tears and make love again.

The Woods

Abbie

'I can't see straight. My eyes aren't used to reading this much.'

Sadie noted where the open pages stopped. 'Information overload?'

'You could say that.'

'How about a drive? You could close your eyes on the way to give them a rest.'

'A drive sounds good.'

Sadie parked overlooking a wall of trees. She stayed still, even after if became awkward.

'Will we get out?'

'That's the plan,' Sadie said, unlocking her seat belt.

She walked ahead, on a mission, past the other cars, the picnic area, the lake, only stopping at a bench.

'Is this the woods Gabrielle wrote about?'

Sadie sat, inclined her head.

'On the days mam allowed me I'd come with the O'Neills. I never hiked with your granddad or your mam, there was always this feeling of it being sacred between them. If I'd asked they would have let me, your family never stopped me doing anything. No.' She tapped the seat. 'This was the spot I wanted, beside your grandmother. Now that you've read what you have, now that you know what happened to them,

I wanted to come here, to talk, because this story is as much about honouring them as it is about your parents.'

'What were they like?'

'Your grandmother was kind. She was one of those rare people that seemed to live for making others happy. If everyone was smiling around her, she was satisfied. Growing up in my house... it wasn't what I was used to. Your mother wrote about me loving her family, sometimes worrying if it was them I wanted not her, and I did Abbie, I would have given anything for your grandmother to have been my mother but never to replace Gabrielle. What I wished for was to be adopted by them. To be loved. Over time, I learnt I didn't have to live with them for them to love me. They proved over and over they did.' She inhaled loudly, the air dispelling out of her in a whoosh. 'Love is a strange possession when you're not used to it. It's not like it's an object you can pick up. You can't hold it in your hands yet you feel it. I felt it from them all the time. We would sit on this bench and talk and she would gently tease out all my niggles. She never made me feel like she was doing me a favour. Your grandmother acted like she enjoyed my company, like she valued my opinion. To have someone, an adult, show they cared was... strange.'

'What was my grandfather like?'

'Strong. Never backed down from an argument, although with him disagreements were rare. He could hold his own in conversation. Most of all, I loved the easy way he made me laugh, made me see the lighter side. I could storm into his house, my mood as dark as I'd ever experienced and somehow he'd turn me, make me smile. Until I had to leave again at least. Sam, Darren and Lily, I often wondered if I would have been as accepting of a stranger as they were with me. They never complained, never gave out about me. They gave out *to* me plenty, but that was inclusion, you know? That meant they were arguing *with* me. As far as I know they never didn't want me. That was huge to a kid who felt unwanted. They would poke and laugh and rip into me and I loved it because my own brothers acted like I was a ghost, they just didn't care at all.'

'Details please. Give me something about each of them.'

Sadie looked to the sky. 'It was a long time ago.'

'Anything. Give me anything.'

'You interrupted me. What I was going to say was even though it was a long time ago, their details stay. They are still vivid in my memory. Imagine, I can remember the softness of Lily's hair even now?'

Abbie gulped at the thought. Sadie smiled at a memory.

'She had these bright pink sandals with a rainbow flower attached to the middle. Adored is too small a word. As soon as she got them she refused to take them off. Instead of fighting with her, instead of insisting, your grandmother agreed, so Lily wore them in bed, on the beach, even splashing them in the water. Everywhere. They only lasted about a week until the strap broke. As Lily bawled her eyes out, do you know what your grandmother done? She got up from her seat and pulled out a brand new pair from the cupboard. When she handed them to Lily, she bent down to her level and said, "These were the only pair left in the shop. If you want these to last we have to take better care of them, yeah?" Well, Lily wiped at her eyes and pure determined like, said, "I'll look after them." After that Lily only wore them on special occasions, that pair lasted her until she grew out of them and even after that she kept them where she could see them, playing with them often. Her magic shoes she called them. That's the kind of woman your grandmother was. In my house, I would have spent the week grounded and barefoot. Your grandmother saw what the lesson was before it happened and let it play out.'

Abbie bit down on her lip. She wouldn't speak for words might distract Sadie from continuing.

'Sam had a serious addiction to sweets. You know like, sherbet lemons, cola bottles, strawberry laces. If the guy lived, I would have bet a tenner on him developing type two diabetes by the time he was twenty. Once, I caught Darren mocking Sam, saying he had a crush on me. Poor Sam, he must have only been about twelve, turned puce. So, I gave him a kiss on his red cheeks and said, "Here's your first kiss." He flapped me away but after, every so often his hand would touch his skin as if remembering. Darren, he was a cheeky one. A pure rogue. He was getting to the age where he was experimenting, I often caught him toking a joint hanging out his window. Full of nature though, kind like his whole family. Whatever any of them got they would half with me without a second thought. That red beanie hat your mother mentioned?'

Abbie nodded to show she understood.

Sadie chuckled, away in thought. 'I bought him that. For Christmas. I meant it as a joke, festive like. Saved up my money and bought all the family gifts and they knew it was a big deal for me to do that, so I thought at first he was just humouring me, but when it became almost part of him, when he'd never take it off, I can't tell you how much I loved that.' She suppressed a shudder. 'In the end though, you could see the grime around the rim. He didn't care, no way would he take it off. Every time I saw him with it on, I felt proud almost, like I'd got one thing right.'

She pointed at the wild flowers beside them. 'Your grandmother loved these. Lily used to spend ages picking them, holding them up to her like they were a trophy. Rose, your grandmother, took them from her as if they were a prize. I said to her one day when Lily was out of earshot. "They're only weeds." Not my finest moment, must have been one of my grumpier days. Rose held the flowers out in front of us and said, "You may see weeds Sadie but what I see is a gift from a little girl who has no money in her pocket, whose only possession is time and energy, who saw a thing of beauty and offered it to me. You see weeds. I see love." *That* was your grandmother.'

'You must have missed them when you left Knockfarraig?'

'The loss was like a death. I thought being away from them had an expiration date though, that all I was losing was time. The plan was to return a better person, to come back as someone they would be proud of. Finding out they were gone forever, I could never get over that. They were my family.'

She stood as if about to walk away.

'Is that why you brought me here?' Abbie said, hoping to keep her talking.

It worked. Sadie's hands went to her hips and her shoulders raised as if taking some deep breaths. Once composed, she sat on the bench again.

'Reading the book forced me to have a conversation with Gabrielle. There was much we didn't say when we were younger. My fault. Gabrielle tried many times but I couldn't, I wouldn't let her. After reading the passage about what Gabrielle witnessed in these woods, with my mother, we had a heated conversation. Imagine, if I'd been able to confront my mother? To have the proof would have been something.'

'What would you have done?'

Sadie pursed her lips. Shook her head. 'That's the thing. I don't know if I would have said anything. Whether it would have made a difference. Didn't I know on some level my whole life? Back then I couldn't talk. By the time I read the book, the opportunity was gone. We did some digging after we spoke, your mam and me, asked around but if my mam was anything, it was discreet. No one heard of him, no one willing to talk about it, anyway.'

'That must have been upsetting.'

Sadie picked a wildflower and examined the purple petal. 'How can you miss a person you never knew?'

'I do,' Abbie said. 'I miss two strangers.'

Sadie handed her the flower.

Snapshots

Gabrielle

Brace yourself. I'm allowing one chapter to speak of this and then I will avoid any mention for the rest of what I write. One chapter will cover years. Are you ready? I'm sorry Abbie, for you will never be ready.

I can't remember the first time Liam hurt me. It must have been an arm pull or a shove or a threatening voice. No matter how hard I try to bring the memory to the surface, it won't come and I don't know why I can't remember something so significant as the moment that crossed between an equal, loving relationship to what we became.

I'm known for having a good memory.

Under the guise of my research, I have investigated memory loss and think there is some form of PTSD going on. Dissociative amnesia to be more precise. Our bodies find it hard to deal with trauma, but when that trauma is repetitive, when your fight or flight response is activated all the time then the body can go off kilter. Maybe I've blocked it, maybe I needed to block it. Not all memories have disappeared though and I will give you some snapshots here. What I do know is that I made a choice on one of those early days to stay with him no matter what he did. Because I see now, with that first time, I let him know that my love could be pushed, that I would take whatever he dished out.

If my parents had lived would have I taken it? If Sadie had stayed would I have been stronger? Or did Liam see my loyalty that first day, wearing that white dress? Did he see a capability in me to take anything he doled out?

Abbie, here's a lesson for you. The first time a partner hurts you, know it is a test. It won't seem like one at first. What it will feel is shocking and wrong and as if a line has been crossed. It is in those few moments that you know the truth. The voice inside will whisper *that isn't love*, and your logic will tell you that it will only get worse, that you have to leave because every second you stay makes it harder to go. If you hesitate, you will be reminded of the good inside him or her, you will remember all the times love flowed between you, you will recall how unlovable you are. Ignore the excuses they give you, for they themselves don't know yet what they are capable of. It is in the allowance, in your allowance, that they will discover how much they can hurt.

Don't think that means I just gave in. In the early days, I fought back, I shoved after he shoved. I met snarl with snarl until it sunk in that the only person still sore the next day was me. Endless drunken arguments led to shameful Sunday mornings with sore limbs and memories and the feeling in the pit of my stomach that life should not be like that. Love shouldn't hurt.

Also, it was clear to me that the arguments were only hiding the real reason he was angry. Still traumatised over the miscarriage, over the absence of children, over his own childhood, he found other ways to release the hurt. How could we bring a child into the world once violence hung over us?

Each argument would end with a warning from me; I wouldn't take it anymore. Yet when we went to bed to make up, I couldn't help thinking I'd whored and cheapened my body in the name of love. Outwardly, my stance and the words I used were strong but my actions spoke differently. Without saying the words, without confronting the real reasons, I began refusing nights out. Liam still went. When the door closed, I couldn't help thinking he was on the other side of it delighted. Alone, I cried on those nights, listening to the creaks of the house, with the dark descending because no matter how I tried to reason or decipher his actions, I couldn't understand this type of love, couldn't accept it. Love to me was letting the other thrive, supporting them and being there on the low days. I didn't understand his need to rip into my personality, or his anger, or the hatred when he spoke to me at those times. I learnt those two emotions – love and hate, were not all that different. Instead of being opposites, they ran on the same scale and could slide into each other. You might wonder why I didn't instantly turn off him. Each incident was clocked and put away, yet that little fight for the underdog wouldn't leave me, it never has.

I would help him. Even if it killed me.

It was easier to hide than you'd think. Silence worked. When you're known for your honesty it is easy to lie. Because you've built up an idea of who you are, labelled in a box. People forget you can change.

This is one of the reasons why I picked up a pen for the first time and started the novel. In case my life was cut short, in case it ended one day without warning, I didn't want to die having not accomplished anything. When your father hurt me, I wrote to escape.

Here's some snapshots of our life:

2004

Walking home from the pub.

After a night of laughter, I linked Liam's arm. We waved off John, his soccer buddy and his wife as they passed in a taxi and I leaned into him, prepared for the short walk home.

'That was fun,' I said, snuggling my face into his shoulder while walking at the same time.

'You looked like you were having fun all right.'

There was slight sarcasm to the way he said it, making me look at him. He was smiling though, so I carried on.

'There was a time I thought I wouldn't ever enjoy a night out again.'

'Don't get maudlin now.'

There was that tone again. Not sarcasm, more contempt.

'I won't, I didn't mean it like as if I was going to say anything sad. If anything I meant it as a compliment. It's down to you that I'm happy.'

'Seems to me plenty makes you happy.'

I stopped walking. 'What's wrong? What did I do?'

'You tell me if you think you did anything?'

'What, tonight?'

He stuffed his hands in his pockets, shrugged. 'Dunno. You tell me.'

'Liam, what are you on about. You were laughing two minutes ago. We had a good night, I...'

'You had a good night. Who said I did?'

'I say. I just saw you having a laugh with John and Matt in the corner. Ye couldn't stop skitting.'

'Did you ever think I could be putting a brave face on things?'

'For what?'

'If you can't tell then we have bigger problems than you think.'

He picked up the pace, faster than I could keep up in heels. As fast as I could I tried, but the gap grew larger until I gave up and walked and thought.

I ran through the events of the night. Everyone had been in good form, there had been no awkward conversations, no put downs, no nasty comments, no inappropriate behaviour. I flicked through my memories, running chronologically through the order of the night. There had been one thing, one look from Liam, one pucker of the lips, one indent at the bridge of the nose when his eyebrows furrowed as I passed for the bathroom. That was it, all I could think of.

As the shape of him got smaller and more distant, I dreaded his reaction when I walked in the door. Would he go to bed, or would he sit up, waiting to have it out? The sense of foreboding weighted my walk, dragging my heels. The lights in the house were off but the door was unlocked when I pushed against it. Taking off my heels from my sore feet by the stairs, I startled when he moved on the couch.

'Why get so close to Matt?'

'I didn't.'

'First lie. You telling me you weren't talking to him for ages up close chatting? You know he fancies you.'

'He does not! Liam he's one of your oldest friends and he's getting married next month. We were talking about bridesmaid dresses for goodness sake.'

'What, I'm dumb then?'

'No, I'm just saying you have nothing to worry about.'

'Who said I'm worried? I trust you. Still though, you're giving off the wrong impression. You didn't see Nikki, she was livid behind your back.'

This got to me, I'd hate to upset her.

'She has no reason to worry, I wouldn't cross any line.'

'Don't tell me, tell her.'

After that I started to be more wary about what I said and did. As I write this I sound text book, but that's not the way it seemed at the time. They were all my own choices. He planted a seed and I sowed them for sure. If I thought a conversation could be construed as flirty, I stopped mid sentence, leading to awkward pauses. Every action was monitored. Was I leaning in too much or spending too long talking to someone or was I talking into someone's ear when the music was too loud and could that be seen as conspiring? It was me who cut friendships short for the people he didn't seem to like. Hadn't I done the same with Sadie even though I loved her as a sister?

I stayed because I loved him, but there was also a shame in that love, because whatever he had done to me, I played a part in that decision.

I chose the monster I lived with. Understand, I'm not implying he brainwashed me. He didn't. He couldn't. I wasn't a woman who began to believe what her abuser repeats. No, I saw clearly that what he was doing was wrong but I loved your father in spite of those things. Because I was always trying to replicate what I saw in him that first day. Kindness, love. Not love at first sight but the possibility of love. The availability of it. That look he gave me was the truth of him. Truly him. I honestly believed I could draw it out again.

At some stage of your life, people, not necessarily partners, will tell you, in order for them to be happy you will have to do something for them. They will need you to alter, to adapt, to fit into the mould of what *they* need you to be. And even though you know intrinsically there is something wrong with that belief, you do it anyway. Every time you do, you chip away the truth of who you are, until you are left with their perfect replica of who they wanted. After all that, you will discover they are still unhappy and worse, you don't remember how to be the person you once were.

2005

'Why do that to me Gabrielle? Why disgrace me like that?'

I felt the lash to my head too late to react. I slammed against the wall. The shock of it hit me more than the blow. The reeling in my ears as my whole world hollowed out.

2006

The put downs weren't obvious. They were jokey, a grab of an ass with a comment, 'that's more than a handful' or looking up my body and lingering on my stomach or my arms.

'Do you think I don't notice all your hints? How much weight do you want me to lose? A stone? Two? Three? Or will you not be happy until I waste away?' I stood puffing over him, my chest heaving with passion and indignant rage.

He sat back, with shock on his face as if I had just over reacted. But I meant everything I said.

'I don't think you're fat Gabby, not at all, you're beautiful.' He pulled me onto his lap and cuddled me. 'You're just naturally curvy. All woman. It's not your fault.'

'I eat salads while you tuck into chips. I walk instead of driving, I swim everyday.'

'Shh,' he hugged me tighter. 'I know, I know, you just have a low metabolism. You should try exercise that burns it off. Come to the gym with me.'

'No thanks,' I said, getting up from him and moving to another seat.

'Don't be like that, I love you no matter what size you are. I just want you to look your best, so you're happy with yourself.'

'I love you Liam, but I'll be damned if any man tells me what weight I should be.'

I stormed out of the room saying under my breath, 'what I do I'll do for me and only me.'

That was such a lie. Fired up, I played into his comments not realising that was the desired effect. It still planted a seed. I got the hint that I wasn't good enough, the thing I secretly worried about my whole life. Coupled with my need to people please, I tried to be better, while concurrently hating him for not loving me just as I was. Every bite of something deemed bad was eaten with guilt, every time I looked in the mirror I scrutinised my muffin top or the hint of cellulite in a certain light. My insecurities amassed.

The up and down-ness of the relationship derailed me. I couldn't understand how one moment I could be so in love, he be so in love and the next he would look at me with such hate. It was confusing. It was the dropped comments that gained momentum, it chipped away at me. The grinding down of a personality. Of self-worth. That happened so slowly I didn't notice, or rather the gradual decline was so consistent it became a new normal, it became part of my day. Until all that I worked on for confidence was worn away.

2006

We were late. The car drove fast with Liam behind the wheel. I sat next to him worrying about everything from our lateness to how fast he was driving. When the list of worry was over I took a breath. I could tell by the way Liam's eyes kept flicking to the front mirror he was gauging me. I took a breath and tried to distract myself with positive thoughts: the fertility visit would go on regardless, whether we were late or not. But still. It was annoying how I got up early and had everything ready, yet we were still in this situation. Liam still left it to the last minute to leave, humming while shaving, even though he knew we should have left ten minutes earlier. Did he do it on purpose? Surely he couldn't want to argue about this? It felt like he did, so I didn't speak. I would not allow it to seep in, I would be the epitome of sweetness and light. He swerved into the spot and we both rushed in. The rooms were closed, I heard babble coming from the room, people were in there. In the waiting room, Liam sat and folded his arms. We waited. Twenty minutes later we still waited.

'Did you not confirm the appointment time?' he said.

'I did. When we weren't here they must of went in with someone else.'

'They can't do that.'

'Course they can. I know people who purposely come super early so they can slot in if someone's running late.'

'Like who?'

'Alma, next door, she...'

'Oh, fuck off.'

'What? She does, she arrives early so she...'

He stood. Looked around in case anyone was about to appear. When he spoke it was hushed. 'You know what Gabs, I'm sick of your attitude.'

'What attitude?'

'This butter wouldn't melt pretense thing you've got going on. Like you're better than me or something, this kind of smug righteousness.'

'What? All I wanted was for us to get here.'

'Denial as always. That's all I get from you. Well I'm not doing it, I'm not taking it.'

'Liam, you're scared about the appointment.'

He pointed a finger at me. 'Fuck you. That's not what's going on at all. At this moment I don't even want this appointment, all I want is to be away from you. In fact, I'll wait in the car.'

'Liam, don't.'

He slammed the door on his way out.

The thing that prickled at my skin was knowing as bad as the drive had been, the return would be even worse.

If I complained, if I showed disapproval, if I said anything deemed as negative, hell rained down on me and I was attacked verbally or violently. Always harshly. He would never falter in his right to feel the way he did. Or how wrong I was to have changed his good mood. It always threw me. His potential to twist was always erratic. The times I expected him to blow he would be unusually calm. The times I was confident in how much we were connected with each other he blew. It left me wary most of the time.

As I sat and waited, as I apologised on my own for our lateness, for keeping them waiting, as I made excuses for his absence, I plastered on a smile and carried on, despite the fear that lay in the bottom of my belly, settling as a quiet rumble.

Fertility check over, I slid into the car, determined to stay silent. I didn't get the chance, he asked me a question before he'd pulled away.

'Are you going to apologise?' he asked. Said in a way I knew required an answer.

I took a breath, knowing I would have to face this. I braced myself for the onslaught. I would be the voice of reason. 'Liam, you are the one who stormed out.'

'Typical you. You act like a cunt and try to pin it on me.'

I've always hated that word. Hated the way a man can take a word labelled as a part of a woman's anatomy meant for pleasure, meant for birthing babies, a place representing the center of life, of miracles and they twist it into a put down.

'A cunt? Wow Liam.'

'You are a cunt.' He hissed. 'Putting me down. Here I am bringing you to your appointment and you're sat in the car sucking lemons. Fuck that. Fuck you. You *are* a cunt.'

There were no tears, at that stage I was used to it. Not that word, that word always stunned me, even though he had used it before. But by then, I was accustomed to his unpredictability and at that stage, had started to see it for what it was. His guilt at being late put him on the defensive. His fear of infertility made him run from the appointment. His anger at still having no children meant the second I said anything negative he would jump down my throat. Inevitable. The only thing I could do was ride the storm until his anger abated and hope not to put myself in the crossfire. I was guilty too, because I should have known to shut up, known the way he would react to the appointment. When cornered, your father would always react like a rat – he'd go for your neck.

His anger didn't abate when we got home.

After, there were no apologies, no flowers. A day later, he seethed still. I could feel the prickles of resentment coming off him, the embers of anger still ignited and ready to flare. It would be so easy to stand over him with my bruises and list all the reasons he was wrong but they never sunk in, never got me anywhere but exhausted.

'Have you left yet?' He didn't look up from his phone.

Even after what he did I didn't want to leave. Being alone was worse. I didn't want to meet Nuala on the street and tell her that I was divorcing. To admit to anyone that my whole life, the relationship I had poured everything into was a failure. What I wanted was the best version of your father, the man I fell in love with to come back. He was in there, I was sure of it and I did everything to prise it out.

Sitting on his lap, I asked him to look at me. At first, he resisted. *It shouldn't be you begging Gabrielle.*

I did anyway.

Cupping his jaw with my fingers I tilted his face to look at me and when he did, his eyes were childlike and lost. I cried then, for how much he must have been hurt in his past, how his family had hurt him enough to hurt the woman he loved. With that thought, I kissed him, carefully, mindful of my swollen lip and when he didn't reciprocate, I moved my head back.

'I love you Liam. We can get through this.'

What always threw me was how unapologetic your father was. All the movies with abused wives show the man begging them to stay. That wasn't the case with us. He would be adamant he was right to do the things he did. Instead, he would ignore me and act like it was my fault. All I ever wanted was his love yet I could never get it fully. He would blank me, ignore me, walk out with indignation when I would hobble in. Or slam doors, leave, drive away. It worked. It confused me enough to wonder had I been wrong. Was it all my fault?

He never really fooled me, Abbie. In spite of all his insults, I always refused to believe the hurtful claims he made. A strength hid inside me, and I would remember who I was and that I didn't have to take it. On many occasion, I asked him to leave. Days later, when I started to miss the good times, I would get a knock at the door or a text begging me to give him one more chance. I always did. I always left him back in.

It's always hard in a movie to watch a person fall for an abuser, it doesn't seem realistic because how can you portray how it happens in an hour and a half? It is subtle, slow, bit by bit. No woman falls for a guy who treats her badly. No woman sets out to love a monster. They are kind at the start. They treat you better than anyone ever has. They see you, see all your faults yet they still want to stay. It isn't like the abuse starts early on because that would be simple to walk away from. It starts when you are invested, it begins when you have already dug yourself into such a hole you wouldn't know how to claw yourself out even if you wanted to. And you don't want to Abbie, because at that stage you are completely and utterly in love; your life has wound around theirs, connected and grown roots, tangled and twisted together.

Let's be clear, there was a part of me to blame. On occasion I gave back, when we would fight and bite, lick and claw and spit and afterwards I would decide there was something wrong with me, because before he even touched me, right in the second he was just about to, I would get a buzz, just before he hurt me, a thrill ran through. Not because I was a sadist or invited pain but because I was right to doubt him all along.

There was no pattern or sense to the turning of mood. Its random, illogical appearance would always throw me off kilter. It would become him against me in seconds. A good relationship shouldn't carry that much negativity. Many times, I wished for someone who could advise me, but the only person I had was Liam. My family and Sadie were gone. Even Maureen by that stage was on her travels.

As I've said before, I've always been scared of the dark. Then, when the darkness gripped me I would lie awake with the fear clagging in my throat, afraid to breathe too loudly as he walked up the stairs and would question if that night would be *the* night, of reaching the tip of no return. In the dark there was a motion to the fear, a conclusion already decided and mapped out. It felt as if I was being dragged towards it, with my nails helplessly scraping along the floor.

He never beat me. I wasn't a victim, you understand? Even though I should probably list the parts of my body that weren't hurt instead of what did. There were no blows.

Only pokes. Twists. Tugs. Digging fingers. Pulled sleeves. Scrunched up faces.

Still. Years later the threat lingered. Of what he could be capable of. Of what was possible. Never beatings but arguments. Arguments we were both involved in. For the majority of the fight we would be equals but then the scale would tip in my favour with the writer's strength of my words, when my point would be made so eloquently I should have won.

Abbie, I never won.

Left with the only option about how he could be the winner, he'd finish the argument the only way he could, in the only way he could be sure to win.

I always thought if someone loves you yet hurts you, they say sorry, but he never did, he always acted like it was my fault, that I made him. That he wasn't like this with anyone else. Like he was disgusted with me for provoking him.

Looking back on my life, I understand why I stayed. Falling in love for the first time at eighteen, then I became a woman full of self-loathing after my families death. Dealing with the guilt for how I treated them before, for the continuous mistakes I made. Then I was a wife who couldn't fulfill the only dream we both desperately wanted for children. Of course a woman like that would tolerate his anger, reason the violence. It wasn't just reasoning, I accepted it.

Even though I drew a line each time: each mark, each bruise, each scrape and friction burn reminded me of my ignorance, of my naivety that love would win. Instead of running, I hardened, and my skin thickened enough to become shell and the shell hardened enough to become wall.

Until I stopped. I couldn't live a life with walls but I couldn't leave him either. So, I learned to tolerate and turn over. To let the anger of how unfair he was to fizzle out. Anger never stays. It always dissolves and if you let it get you, if you react, even if you had reason, even if you are in the right, all you're left with is regret and injury.

Remember when I told you to pay attention to the story in the bathroom Abbie? Well, here you go. Years later I was in a different bathroom with a different man but nothing else was the same because the man who was attacking me was my husband. I couldn't kick him in the balls and run away. If I did kick him and run, where would I go? What would it do to get him that angry for by then I was in no doubt he was capable of killing me. It was there, in his eyes, every time he attacked. Even as a writer, I find it hard to explain how you can love someone you are afraid of. But I did. I saw the damage, the hurt and the wounds and at the start, I believed love would fix him. Abbie, I was wrong, you cannot fix anyone else, only they can. Later, I stopped trying, because the person who was getting hurt was me.

What I've learnt about your dad is never to challenge him. If you say nothing life will keep going, if you ignore the voice inside you that wonders why it has to be the way it is. If I settle for the scraps he gives me, life will keep plodding along but if I say a word, the only person that will be blamed is me. Knowing this I found a way to navigate through peace. Were there times I hated who I'd become? Yes, is the short answer.

The coldness that overcame Liam, switching me to his ultimate enemy, I never understood the hows. How could he hate the person he meant to love? How was he capable of wanting to scare me with the threat of violence? How he could carry out his threat.

After he was violent, after he calmed down, he changed back to caring Liam. Once the man with bulging eyes retreated, without a sorry, seeing him want to brush over the incident, I would allow my own anger to flush. Safe then to vent, I would show him the bruises, silently screaming, *see what you did to me?*

And he would take my skin as if I'd offered it up instead of the rebuke it was intended and he would kiss the spot, stroke or soothe and I would weep with the gentleness of the act while he drew circles with his finger on my skin, slowly moving the circle up or down depending on where he hurt me, each time ending in the same place, where he would slip that same finger inside. This was when I would hate myself most. For being weak. For compromising my beliefs, my standards, for allowing a man to manipulate me. For whoring my body in exchange for his control. When I should have shoved his hand away, walked out, shouted at him or roared, when he reached my underwear, even though I would turn my face away, not wanting to see him, too hurt still, I allowed his fingers, let him touch me, wanted him to touch me. Those same fingers that once choked, gave me pleasure, knowing the exact rhythm, the exact pressure, the very spot until I was almost begging him to enter. After, he would fall asleep in an instant while I would stare at the ceiling, trying to make sense of it all, thinking there must be something wrong with me.

2006

After another night of Liam's accusations about not wanting a child, I lay in the dark pleading for sleep for if I was unconscious, Liam might leave me alone. What rest I got was fitful and hours later, when I heard his footsteps on the stairs, I was alert once more. By the sound I could always judge what way he'd act. Tonight, the speed of his feet on the wood, the clip as he lifted every step told me he wasn't done. Liam was looking for more. Sure enough, when he entered the room he didn't stop at his side of the bed but walked around to mine, where he stood over me. I kept still, my eyes stayed closed but I could feel his presence as if the space between us condensed. It is an impossible task to stay still when your body is screaming at you to run. Terror clawed at my cells. I lay as still as a dead woman, praying that my eyes wouldn't flicker and give me away, trying to make my breath thick and some bit ragged to imitate what sleep would do, all the time prepared for a shove or even a smack. It's the most vulnerable you can be, to lie with your eyes closed, as a person whose hurt you before stares at you. I willed him away, sending him silent messages to, *just go to bed, just leave me alone.* All the while I breathed through the panic, even though my heart was racing. The worst thing I could do was to make him aware that I was awake. My side of the bed groaned with the weight of him and heat flushed over my face and chest while simultaneously I suppressed a shiver. Was it possible to die from fear? *Please just go to sleep.* A finger jutted my upper arm.

'Wake up.'

My bones withered from my muscles. *Retreat Gabrielle, anyway you can.* Stubble scratched at my ear. He kept his voice low enough not to wake any neighbours but loud enough to hurt my eardrum.

'Liar.'

I didn't move.

'Get up.'

Stay small, play dead.

'Get-up-now.'

Pretend you're somewhere else.

'Gabrielle... I'm warning you. Get up.'

How do I fix this?

'You arrogant bitch.'

He's going to get louder. You're going to make him angrier if you don't say something.

He leant closer into my ear, his nose grinding into my temple. He spoke louder. 'I'm warning you. Get up. Now.'

'Get out of the room Liam.'

Before I could filter it, the words rose up in me involuntary. There was no satisfaction from standing up to him, only fear, pure muscle numbing fear. All that time my eyes stayed closed.

Oh, you done it now girl.

Silence thickened the air in the room, hanging between us. Liam leaned over again, close enough the alcohol on his breath made my nostrils burn and I had to fight the urge to turn away. A hand pressed over my mouth and nose, blocking my airways. There was no way to breathe. Only then did I open my eyes and his were furious and gleeful because here was his payoff, for he had found a way to win, to intimidate. There it was, the reason I kept my eyes closed because what I saw in them scared me most of all. The man looking back would be happy for me to die. The Liam who caressed me, who whispered in my ear, the man who brought me to orgasm, who kissed every section of skin was gone, exchanged for a monster I didn't know or want, who delighted in my pain and distress.

'Don't ever tell me to leave my bed again,' he said, his teeth glowing in the dark. He kept his hand over my mouth, in control. Then, I struggled under him, fighting, because this time he would kill me. With one hand he caught hold of my wrist, twisted it, shoved it down, pushing hard on both my hand and my mouth. In seconds, I felt my body lifting, losing consciousness, and I could see my body below and I knew with certainty, I was about to die.

The grip released and I sucked in a delicious breath. The mattress bounced back as he left the bed, then room. Without his presence I shook all over. My lungs, aware of what they nearly lost, now fought for deep intakes. Within a minute he was back.

Foolish girl, you knew it wouldn't be that easy.

The crescendo, the climax was coming. Liam stood over me again. Can you imagine what it's like to lie down in the dark with someone physically stronger, angry and ready to hurt? In that position you are disadvantaged, more so than if you're standing facing each other. I would never win against Liam in a fight anyway, but lying down would be impossible. He leant right over me until his nose touched mine and I squeezed my eyes shut.

'You're nothing but a scumbag.'

Then spreading his fingers wide, he pushed my face into the pillow. I kept my eyes shut, afraid, so terribly, terribly afraid thinking, *please god, don't let him kill me* and I held my breath, waiting, just waiting for the next hit but apart from the burning skin from where his fingers dug in, there was nothing. I listened and when I heard no sound I still didn't open my eyes. Done before, he had fooled me by staying silent until I reacted, only to lay into me again. Only after the spare bedroom door slammed did I open my eyes.

I stayed still until the dawn. My wrist ached from where he twisted it. My face burned from where his hand pushed down, from the amount of tears that had slid across them since. His words stabbed at me. *Liar. Arrogant bitch.* Anyone that says words can't hurt are lying Abbie. It seeps and burrows, it stays and sticks, forming a thick layer in your gut until you carry it around.

That morning I just wanted to end the pain. As Liam snored in the next room I imagined getting dressed and opening the back door as quietly as possible, at the the beach I would wade into the water, and curse my bodies reflexes for fighting against the cold, where I would push past the cold splinters of pain and let the water take me. I'd walk deep enough to drop, then breathe my final breath and slip under. It must be beautiful to let go of that last exhale, I thought, to know in a few minutes all the pain would be over. I got dressed and stopped at the doorway of the guest bedroom. Liam slept soundly, his mouth slightly open, his closed lids moving, in the middle of some dream. He could sleep while I imagined taking my own life. It hit me then, that I was the only one suffering. It hit me that I didn't want to die.

If I stayed, we would eventually make up, even if I held off for weeks, something would make me soften because I was hopeless with him, even though he could hurt me enough that I would want to kill myself, I still loved him. While he slept I packed, and this time I walked out of that house and boarded a bus to Galway.

Keys

Abbie

The page wasn't visible through her tears. Sadie was on her in a second, wrapping her close. 'It's all right.'

'He could have killed her,' Abbie said, her face resting on Sadie's chest. 'How could he be like that? How could she accept it?'

'It happens gradually. It's never overnight.'

'The guy in Galway?'

Sadie chewed on her lip. 'Among others. When you don't like yourself, you kind of attract it.'

'Was that what happened? Was it my fault? Did my mother kill him because of me?'

Sadie wiped her tears. 'Nothing was ever your fault. You brought the light to her days Abbie, you made everything bearable.'

'But did she do it because of me? Did he hurt me?'

Sadie straightened up. 'You need to hear what happened from your mother's mouth. I promised her that. What I will do though, is tell you some things she didn't think to include, that she left out.'

'Like?'

'Like, your mother was always too hard on herself. Do you remember the key her parents gave her after my mother made us stay out in the rain? Well, she didn't mention she never kept it, not even for one day.

233

She gave it to me so I would never have to stay outside again, to let myself in no matter what the time. When school was too much, I let myself in during the day when they were all gone out. I wouldn't walk around the house or anything, just stay in her room and draw or read. I never told your mum, but of course she missed nothing. She began leaving me notes on the bed.'

'Like what?'

'Like, there's a chocolate bar and a can in the second drawer or Mum is home at twelve today. Also, she could keep secrets. I didn't understand how much until I read the book. Another fact, when she got sick, she never complained. When it got bad, she'd close her eyes and take a breath and then look at me and say, "tell me something good, Sade."'

'She got sick?'

Sadie baulked. 'Christ, there I go again. I knew I'd say too much somewhere. No more talking. Read on.'

She gets sick, Abbie thought.

Search

Gabrielle

Sadie wouldn't live far from the water, it was the only thing I was sure of, which was why I ended up in Salthill. Along the road by the beach, I trailed slowly remembering the last time we had come here, in our teens, when her mother surprised us by letting her go away for a weekend together, chaperoned by my parents. Thinking it had more to do with plans she had that weekend rather than giving Sadie any leeway, we still took it with glee. Instead of it being the best time, Sadie spent it pensive and moody, and for most of it kept her distance. It didn't matter what we did or how much we tried to coax her – on the beach, while we swam she dug holes in the sand as if she was trying to find the other side, at the fun fair, even on the rollercoaster, her lips stayed like thin slits, at the many restaurants we dined at, she only picked at her food. The more we laughed, the more she retreated and by the last evening all I wanted to do was shake her. Sitting beside her on the rocks of Salthill, as we watched the day leave, I said.

'I don't get you, how long have you waited for one weekend away? When you get it you act like you want to go home.'

She just looked at me, her eyes bright and her hair dancing in the breeze and said, 'Do you think I could stay?'

I picked up a stone and fired it in the water. 'I know it's hard but you're nearly there. Go properly. Go with a job and money behind you Sade. You stay here and what do you have? Galway's so far from Cork.'

'Not far enough.'

'There I was thinking you hated the trip. I thought you were quiet because you were bored.'

Sadie shook her head, picked up her own stone and fired it in the water, 'It hurts to see the way your family is. My normal isn't your normal. My normal isn't anyone else's normal. What if I don't go back?'

'She'd probably come straight up to Salthill and drag you to Cork.'

'Why though? It's not like they love me, it's not like they care. My dad couldn't stand me enough to even live with me anymore. She hates me but she won't let me leave either.'

I bit down on my lip hard. Maybe I should have argued that they did love her but I couldn't, there wasn't one instance I could use as evidence of their love. For me, their relationship was about control but seeing Sadie's pained expression, I couldn't hurt her anymore. The confirmation wouldn't help, it wouldn't change anything, it would only make her feel more helpless.

'You are nearly there. Only a year to go and you can run wherever you want. Study, get a scholarship, then move out. Move the right way.'

There had been no scholarship, and she didn't wait to move the right way. That weekend, the way Sadie acted while there, was the first lead I had and I went with my gut feeling.

It was different to what I remembered; the promenade was more modern and it looked smaller. First, I walked around aimlessly, my mind fragmented and I knew I wasn't thinking clearly. Exhausted from the night before, I sat on the same rocks from years earlier and tried to think like Sadie back then, about where if I was her, would I go. How could you find someone who didn't want to be found? Getting on the bus, I hadn't thought of a backup. Without Sadie, I didn't know if I could go through with my plan, I didn't believe I was strong enough to contemplate a life without Liam. Having the hindsight to take some money out of the ATM before I left Cork so there would be no trail, I had come too far to panic. With or without Sadie I would figure out what to do next – starting by booking in to a hotel and getting myself something to eat. With the promise that if, by the end of the week I couldn't see any hope I would finish what I started in the water of Salthill.

It wasn't as hard as I expected. Even though Ireland had come a long way since I moved there twelve years before, Sadie still stood out as the minority. It only took showing her photo in one shop to get pointed in the general vicinity of where Sadie worked. The shop girl wasn't positive of the exact restaurant, only that she definitely worked in one.

On the strand, I moved from window to window, scanning each menu to see if anything stood out. When I saw a listing for cinnamon pie in one place, I went straight in.

They sat me at the window; it was that awkward time for eating, too early for dinner but too late for lunch so it meant the restaurant was empty. There was no need to pick up the menu, my choice was already made. The cinnamon pie. It was Sadie's go to recipe, if she wanted to show thanks for anything, that was how. Passed down from generations, Sadie knew how to bake that cake since she was a little girl. I had never heard of anyone else making it before or since. To see if it was hers, I needed a taste.

'Hi ya,' the girl asked that approached my table. 'Do you know what you want?'

'The cinnamon pie please,'

'Good choice. You're in luck, there's some left, usually the lunch crowd devour it but the chef made extra for the rush.'

'The chef? She wouldn't happen to be called Sadie Jennings by any chance?'

The girl looked confused. 'Sorry.'

'I am too. I was so sure.' The tears spilled out before I could stop them. A tear for each failure: my relationship, my losing and failing to find Sadie.

The young waitress hovered, uncomfortable. I picked up a napkin and dabbed my eyes.

'Sorry. My dog just died.'

'You poor thing. Are you OK?'

'I will be. Sorry.'

'No worries,' she said leaning in. 'It's grand and quiet at this time so you take all the time you need. Sometimes a good cry is needed.'

'Thanks. Can I ask is there a hotel…'

I trailed off for I had just saw a ghost. Sadie's ghost. Walking from the kitchen a woman with her hood covering her face had passed quick as a flash out the door. In a wide road with a million people I would still know that walk anywhere.

'Actually sorry, cancel that order.' Grabbing my coat and bag, I ran from the restaurant.

And just like that, there she was. Galway produced her, and it wasn't even a real surprise; with Sadie there was always this weird serendipity; this draw to each other, this inner silent navigation centre that guided us to the other. Her back was to me as I opened the door. When I called her name she stopped as if electrocuted. She turned and I got to see her for the first time in years. If she was shocked, she hid it well. Sadie looked at me as if she always expected me to turn up one day. There were no hugs exchanged, no exclamations of happiness. She just stated my name, in the breathless way of a lover, as if she had longed for me for the longest time.

'Gabrielle.'

In the years I hadn't seen her, Sadie had grown – upwards and outwards. Her hair was long, longer than I'd ever known it, reaching halfway down her back and the black curls branched out at the shoulders, framing her face. She was taller, nearly reaching my height and although she was still thin, she had curves. Like a flower's petals unfurling, away from the poison of her house, Sadie had blossomed.

The way she folded her arms told me I wasn't off the hook. It also told me she didn't have a clue about my parents.

'The girl said you didn't work there. She didn't know your name.'

Sadie didn't move. Didn't react.

'I'm so sorry Sadie. I've missed you so...' I burst out crying. Not little sobs but loud uncontrollable, unrelenting ones. She frogmarched me to a bench.

'Gabs, not here.'

'Sadie, it's been hard without you.'

She flagged down a taxi and sat in the front, giving the driver instructions for what I assumed was her apartment. She didn't try to talk, and I knew better than attempt to so I settled in the seat and watched the sea stay but the road turn more rural.

Her apartment was small, but full of art, her art. Abstract pieces that reminded me of the painting that lay beside mine all those years before in Miss Simpson's classroom.

'These ones have colour I see,' I said pointing to the largest in the hall.

Sadie threw her keys into a embossed gold plate, on a stylish grey console table, then continued until she reached a comfy looking grey sofa, where she sat with force, puffing out the cushions on either side with her impact.

'Why have you come?'

Still in the hall I hovered, unsure to sit without invitation or to tell her my story from where I stood. In the end I did neither, walking to the window I looked at the view. Over the other rooftops was that familiar line.

'I knew it,' I said, smiling. 'If there was one thing I was sure of it was that you would find a way to see water.'

Sadie's smile wasn't a nice one. 'You always thought you knew me so well.'

'You don't think I did?'

'I think you thought you did.'

'Where did I go wrong?'

It was my turn to fold my arms. This time I didn't fight the anger that rose.

'The last time we spoke ended badly but I hoped you would be at least happy to see me.'

'Ended badly? That's an understatement,' she scoffed.

'What I don't understand is, why *you* are acting hard done by.'

Sadie stared. Sadie seethed.

'OK then,' I said. 'You're right. I did think I knew you so well but I was wrong. Because the Sadie I thought I knew would have moved heaven and earth to see me again, would have forgiven everything that went between us, would have given me a hell of a better welcome than you have. I guess that girl stayed in Cork or like you said, I never knew her at all.'

Sadie wouldn't look in my direction. Fired up, I strode across the room and opening the door wide, slammed it behind me. My breathing was ragged and as I ran down the stairs, I fought back tears. I walked blindly, in a rush, not caring which way I went or where I ended up for there was no where for me to go anymore and I didn't care, for I was done with taking everyone's anger, of being the punching bag, of taking what life threw.

'Wait.'

Sadie was bent over, pressing her hands on her thighs, catching her breath. 'Christ, you're fast.'

I waited, still too angry to speak.

She straightened and held her hands out wide. 'I'm sorry, OK? You threw me, just turning up like that and after the way it ended between us… I went on the attack before you could.'

There. There was the Sadie I remembered. Some people's fire sparks early and fizzles out. That was me, there was no fire left inside, no fight or want to fight. Sadie took time to smoulder but when it did catch alight she burned brighter than anyone.

Back in her apartment, we sat facing each other, each one skirting around what to say. There was no offer of coffee, no softening the edges of the conversation we needed to have, Sadie always wanted to get right to the point.

'Did you come here straightaway after you left Cork?'

Sadie nodded, looked out the window.

'After our fight there was nothing else keeping me there. There was no point waiting for the Leaving results, I was never gonna have enough points for anything. All year, before the exams, I kept an eye on the job classifieds, away from Cork. One in Galway City advertised for a kitchen apprentice and they were willing to take a chance on a girl with no credentials. That night I'd wanted your advice on whether to stay or take it. Our fight was the flip of the coin I needed. When I went home that night, I packed a bag and hopped on a bus the next morning. The money was shit but it was a start.'

She picked at her nails.

'It was tough. The job didn't pay enough to get anywhere to rent so I had some fairly sketchy nights hiding in the shadows.'

'Oh Sade,' I groaned. The image of Sadie walking around Galway City on her own in the middle of the night was too much. 'I shouldn't have let you leave.'

She cocked her chin. 'If I remember it right, you weren't the one that forced the situation. No need for pity. It got easier. The owner copped on what I was doing when he caught me robbing some food and instead of kicking me out he found me a hostel, and in exchange for paying for my digs, I came in earlier and cleaned the place. I worked my way up and when he told me he was opening a place in Salthill, I begged him to let me work there. Now, I'm head chef.'

She jutted her chin, proud.

'I always knew you'd make it.'

Her chin lowered, studying me. 'You're different. Quieter.'

'It's been a rough few years.'

'You still with Liam?'

I nodded, then shook my head. 'I've left him.'

'Is that a ring?'

I twisted the bands. 'We married two years ago.'

'Big do I suppose? With everyone from Knockfarraig but me.' Her mouth twisted as she finished her sentence, upset.

I couldn't do it, I couldn't break her heart yet.

'You don't think I wanted you there? You're a hard girl to find. Do you know how heartbreaking it was to look around the aisle and not see your face? How could you do it Sade? All these years with no contact. Every time post arrived, my heart did a little flip because the letter might be from you. Every time. Do you know how many nights I thought about you, about where you might be, about the last time we saw each other, about how much you must hate me? I called up to your mother's but she said she didn't know where you were, that you didn't contact her either. Was that the truth?'

She nodded, then sparked up a cigarette. 'You knew when I turned eighteen I was out of Knockfarraig. I only hung on to finish the exams.'

'Yeah, but we were meant to go together.'

She blew out a long line of smoke like a sigh. 'Please. Let's not pretend. There was no way you were going anywhere. You were different the moment you met him. Liam changed you. There was no way you'd leave him, days into the relationship, I could never compete. You would always choose him over me.'

Wasn't that exactly what I did with my parents? Every suppressed thought hit me, as I remembered memories I tried to block. Of husbands who hurt, of dead parents and siblings long gone, of a baby that didn't want to stay with me either, of the journey to look for Sadie, the searching, the finding. It all became too much.

'You all right?'

'I'm just... I'm so tired.'

'You look it.'

'Thanks.' My eyes welled.

'Come on, I know what you need.'

She took my hand and led me into her double bed and tucked me in as if I was a little girl. Abbie, I didn't even look around. The tiredness covered me like a shroud. Knowing I found her, knowing Sadie was near calmed my frayed nerves. Even if she didn't want to sort it out, or we never fixed the friendship or she kicked me out later that day, for that moment, it felt like I had family around again.

With that comfort, I slept soundly for hours and despite the impending dark, I slept, even when Sadie came in during the night and lay down beside me, when her arms wrapped around my body, I snoozed with streaming tears because I had missed that feeling, of being home, because Sadie was home to me, and I had missed her.

To wake next to Sadie made me smile. In the early hours, I watched her shallow breathing. Lying in bed, her hair hidden under a silk hair wrap, a much more expensive version than the one I'd presented her with all those years ago. I stroked the material, not wishing to wake her, but needing to prove she was real. My lightest touch was enough for her to stir. She opened her eyes and gave me the full rays of a Sadie smile. Taking my hand in hers, she brought it to her face to kiss it but stopped when she saw the bruising on my wrist. I flinched, not noticing it before and tried to cover the bruises with my other hand, then when that didn't work, slipped them both under the duvet. Instead of asking, instead of demanding, Sadie understood I wasn't ready yet to talk. In her gift of silence, I finally understood the need for Sadie's quiet all those years before. Back then, the silence wasn't from her shame that they hurt her; the shame came from allowing it to happen at all.

Sadie let me have that. She allowed me the silence and I needed it, desperately, because my head was so jumbled, filled with a million thoughts, with a million paths to take and each option was massive. Too big to comprehend, too overwhelming to say out loud.

When you give yourself space, it helps you see clearly. I began to. Being out of the claustrophobic hold we'd titled as love liberated my opinions, my wants, my soul. The next day it was as if we had spent no time away from each other, as we sipped our coffee and ate our toast. Sadie and I walked the beach and talked about anything except the reason I might have turned up. In the evening we drank wine and cooked meals. When she worked, I read books I'd bought from a store in town. Thankful I left my phone in Knockfarraig, there were times when I was alone in Sadie's apartment that my resolve waned. In weaker moments, an image of Liam at his most loving would flitter into my consciousness, bringing my decision into question. No matter how many years have passed Abbie, no matter how much I have tried to reason or make sense of it, I've never understood how quickly he flipped from love to hate because even during his worst actions, I loved him.

One night, while eating a takeaway from the restaurant, Sadie chewed, then coughed.

'So... I'm seeing someone.'

'Oh yeah?' I watched her squirm. 'Is it serious?'

'Two years, so I'd guess so.'

'I would say that's pretty serious.'

'You know me Gabs. There are times I wonder if I'll ever be capable of love.'

'You're capable. You've always shown me love.'

'You know, I really believed when I left Knockfarraig it would feel like a weight lifted and I would feel free, but I didn't. I felt lost.'

'Course you felt lost. You were so used to being told what to do. Rules were the bricks of your foundation. When you took them away, you must have felt open and vulnerable. When you were never allowed to learn to be independent, the world must have become very scary all of a sudden.'

Sadie nodded, taking a bite of curry.

'At the train station I couldn't even make a decision about where to sit. You're right, I didn't know how to be an adult. I've learnt though. Although, in fairness, it still takes me forever to make a decision on anything. But then, when I do, I'm proud.'

'I'm proud of you too.' I nudged her shoulder. She pointed her fork in my direction.

'You've changed. You're quieter. Sadder.'

'A lot has happened. And I had no one to talk to.'

'You had more than me. At least you had your family.' Sadie stabbed at the food, piling up her fork.

It was time. I had to tell her. I tried to think of the least dramatic, the least shocking way to say it but there was none, all ways were going to break her heart.

'Sadie I'm so sorry, but I didn't. I don't. Not anymore.'

'What's not anymore?'

'All my family are gone.'

'Where?'

My fortune has been made from conjuring words. Hours have been spent thinking of the structure of a sentence. Words consume my life.

I have written sad sentences, ones intended to uplift, ones meant to have the reader shed a tear but let me just say, the hardest sentence I ever composed was telling Sadie what happened to my family.

'Sadie,' I gulped. 'They died. They died in a car accident.'

Sadie stood, rigid, her fists turned to balls. 'You're lying.'

'I wish I was.'

Sadie's legs went but I caught her. 'No, no, no, no.'

Each no felt like a punch in the stomach. I sat her down.

'Tell me your joking.'

'I would never joke about that.'

'Your parents?' she said.

I nodded.

'Sam? Darren? Lily? All of them gone?'

One nod dispelled three lives.

Sadie rocked, hugging her body. 'How? When?'

'About a month after you left.'

'All this time you were on your own? Why didn't you find me?'

'I tried Sade. After the funeral I called to your mother, but she said you didn't contact her.'

Sadie wiped her tears and flopped her hands to her side. She let out a yelp.

'What?'

'I rang her every Christmas. The first person I asked about was you. About your family. She told me the last she'd heard you'd moved away.'

'Your mother promised me if you ever contacted, she would tell you.'

Sadie covered her face. 'Even miles away, the woman had to win.' She grabbed me and when she spoke again, her words came out ragged and trembling. 'I'm sorry, I thought I was doing what was best for you. You know I would have never stayed away if I heard that happened. You know how much I loved them.'

We held each other, and both sobbed.

'It must have been so hard,' Sadie said. 'To have that kind of love and lose it.'

I nodded into her hair, I couldn't even speak.

'And then my mother, full of hate, gets to live. Gets to spread her nastiness. Even when they died, she made it about her.' She pulled away, wiped at her eyes. 'I hate her Gabs. Do you see why I had to get away? She's a disease. She eats away at you like cancer.'

I wiped the tears from her until my hands were wet. 'Only if you let her. Hate uses energy and your mother doesn't deserve ours.'

'I'll drink to that,' Sadie said walking to her kitchen, opening a bottle of wine. After she filled two glasses, she drained one, then handed me the other. 'How did you cope?'

'I didn't, I fell apart. Nothing made sense. Nothing mattered. The hardest part of missing them is not seeing them, not getting to pick up the phone and hear their voice or their noises. The house was way too quiet after, full of silence and you weren't there either and I missed you too, I grieved for you too.'

Sadie threw her hands up in the air, openly weeping. 'See, even trying to do the right thing I fuck up.'

'It wasn't your fault.'

'It wasn't yours either.'

'That's where you're wrong.'

I picked up the bottle and poured myself and her another glass, draining mine.

'Dad was upset with me. He wasn't driving in his right mind, wasn't alert. Again, I let them down. I'll never forget their faces, their disappointment.'

'They could never have been disappointed in you.'

I shook my head. 'Like you said before, I didn't care about the hassle I put them through as long as I got what I wanted. I broke their hearts

247

that day. We were meant to go together, you know on the Europe trip?'

Sadie's hands covered her mouth.

'At the last minute I refused. Because of... I didn't go because of Liam. You were right the other day when you said I picked him because when it came down to the choice I even chose him over my family.' The rest of the words came out in a stream. 'When they needed me I wasn't there for them, I wasn't, I wasn't, I wasn't.'

Sadie wrapped around me, shushing and soothing, listening to me cry, and splutter and empty. When the cries softened, she spoke.

'No family loved better than yours. It hurt to see it when I first met ye and I probably should have resented you all because I never felt that loved by anyone. But I couldn't. Your family taught me love wasn't restrictive. Ye showed me there was enough love for me too.'

She tilted my face to look at her. 'They knew you loved them Gabs. Yeah, they may have been sad that you weren't coming with them, and they probably *were* disappointed but they loved you enough to give you space, knowing you would have made it up. You would have sorted it out.'

I took a gulp of air. 'Yes, we would.'

And I believed her Abbie.

She shoved her half full plate away.

'Since we're talking, are you ready to tell me what happened with Liam?'

'It's complicated. I needed some time away to think things over. The love, my love is still there. Would I have stayed if my family were around? He was a rock after they died, I wouldn't have made it without him, but he changed.'

'In what way?'

Here was the moment. To finally admit to someone what was happening. Even after all we'd said, even after how liberating, how healing it was to say the truth about what happened to my family, to say out loud what Liam had done was different. I couldn't. If I vocalised it, that would make it real. Forced to answer something, I went with the half-truth.

'Sometimes when he gets angry, he crosses a line. Verbally.' I blurted out. 'So I stay away until he learns a lesson. Or until I guess I decide I've had enough.'

The expression I had wanted to avoid was there. The judgement. The pity. I hated it.

'You can imagine after what happened I wasn't the easiest to live with. Sadie, I wouldn't even wash. Then we tried and tried to get pregnant and...' I trailed off, lost in grief as if it had just happened all over again.

'You know you can stay for however long you like. Permanent even. It's been good having you here.'

'I don't think Kieran would be too happy for me to keep sharing your double bed.'

'D'mind Kieran. Seriously Gabs, if you'd like to stay we could get a bigger place. I know of work in the kitchen if you need money? I never said it to your family and now it's too late. They saved me. You and your family saved me no exaggeration. If it hadn't been for ye I don't know what I would have done. All those years, ye gave me an outlet, a bit of fun when everything else was just... shit. When I met you, I hated every minute I was alive. It was normal to be told I was worthless. Everyone couldn't stand me and then, all of a sudden, I would come down to your house and I was important. When you looked at me, I was someone. Do you know what that feels like when you've spent your whole life being ignored? Being told you're annoying?'

I didn't answer.

'You were there for me. When *you* needed me, I wasn't. Never again. If you ever need anything I will do it. No matter what. Gabrielle, I will follow you anywhere or I will do anything you ask. Even tell you the truth when you don't want to see it. I'll lay it out even if you don't want me to because we are adults now, and there is no one who can stop us from speaking our truth. When you say Liam gets angry, I know that it's more than verbal; I saw your wrist the other morning. I understand your family's death would have an affect on you, but you are a whole new person. You seem fucking scared and that Gabrielle is a stranger to me.'

'Did you ever think I may have hid my fears from you? That one of us had to be strong because I knew you needed me to be. Did you ever think that it could be the other way around? That this is the real me and I hid who I really was from everyone. Because no one likes the truth, Sadie. Somebody needed to be the strong one.'

'Bullshit and you know it. You always wore the truth on your face. You could never hide it. If you were sad your features changed. You had a million different facial gestures and I learned every one of them. Don't even pretend it's any different. Don't lie to yourself. Or what, you're going to go back to him to play happy families?'

I hesitated before I spoke again. 'That's the thing about someone that's been labelled honest. It's so easy to get away with lying. I need a walk.'

Sadie stood up. 'I'll get my jacket.'

'No Sade, I want to be on my own.'

There was a reason for my walk. On the way back I picked out a bottle of wine. Taking my time, I traipsed around Salthill, delaying going to the apartment. When I let myself in, Sadie was gone to bed already. Leaving the bottle of wine on the table, I went to the bathroom, then climbed into the bed. Sadie stirred into me and we lay holding each other. When I said I forgave Sadie everything, know this Abbie: Sadie always forgave me too.

In the early hours, I gathered the little items I'd brought. When I was ready to leave, I left a note beside a pregnancy test on her bedside locker.

I'm sorry for taking the cowards way. If I told you in person, you'd talk me out of it. I have to go back. Liam needs the chance to be the good father I know he can become. Being here with you, it's reiterated my belief that if love is shown to a person, they too will love. You've done so well. You've thrived. If you can thrive with the little bit of love we showed you, so can he. Love fixes everything.

Please forgive me. Please don't stop talking to me again.

Gabs.

Going back home, I was sure Sadie would never talk to me again. How wrong I was. With the decision I made to go back to Knockfarraig, with the news of the positive pregnancy test, by turning up on her doorstep and spilling my problems, then leaving, I made the decision for Sadie too. Two weeks later, she followed me home, came back to Knockfarraig, to the place she despised. Maybe it was because she wanted to keep an eye on Liam. Or help with the pregnancy. Or maybe it was more selfish than that. All I can say was how happy it made me, because I think we both only realised after spending time together again that home was each other. Sadie gave up her home in Galway, her job and Kieran so she could be nearer to me. A selfless act, but one that would have consequences for all of us.

Unbuttoning

Abbie

The rumble from her stomach startled her, and was noisy enough for Sadie to notice.

'Time for some grub?'

'Could do with some, yeah.'

'Do you want to go out?'

Abbie shook her head. 'I want to read on. Toasties would do me just fine.'

'Here, or will we walk down?'

'Getting out of the room might help reawaken my bum.'

Sadie stretched. 'Same here.'

As they walked side by side in the corridor, Abbie stopped. 'I didn't know her at all, did I?'

Sadie shifted her feet. 'You knew her, Abbie.' She took Abbie's hand on the girl's chest. 'It's still there inside you.'

'She mentioned some type of amnesia, with trauma and stuff. Do you think I might have that?'

Sadie shrugged. 'Don't know, maybe.'

'Why can't I remember her? Was I there, when it happened?'

'No.' Sadie looked solemn. 'You were at school.'

'I keep trying to conjure her up, but there's nothing.'

They walked on. 'Maybe that's the problem. Maybe you're trying too hard.'

At reception, Sadie gestured to the chairs after seeing a group of women entering the doors. 'You grab them and I'll do the ordering.'

Abbie didn't need to be told twice. Draping her jumper over one chair, she sat in the other, and without checking on Sadie, she opened the book.

Gabrielle

Back in Knockfarraig, the house was as if a rubbish bomb exploded inside, with takeaway cartons on every counter. Empty cans fired all over the floor. All the blinds were closed. The rooms smelt of stale smoke. Liam sat slumped, surrounded by his mess, his hair unbrushed, the silent television flicking images in front of him. It put me on edge, made me alert, walking into such a dishevelled room, seeing such a mess of a man. On the bus journey when I imagined the scenario, I expected a different welcome, of standoffishness, of pleads from me to soften his anger, of having to break down the walls. As horrible as it is to admit, seeing his disarray, brought a sliver of enjoyment, to discover he had struggled without me. In uncharted territory, I was unsure of his reaction, so was relieved at his relief.

He clambered from his seat, stumbling over cans and wrappers. When he reached me, he cupped his hands over my face. A patchwork of red lines occupied the white of his eyes.

'You came back.'

In answer, I closed my eyes. When he kissed my cheek, his lips felt soft against my skin, I couldn't help but let out a groan. Everything was conflicted; I hated and adored him more than anyone ever; I wanted to leave or run and I wanted to stay forever; I wanted to shove him and hit out and refuse him, yet, still; I wanted him to take me in his arms and hold me and lay me down on the bed. Most of all, I loved him, and for that, I hated myself.

'You came back,' he repeated. 'I wasn't sure you would or if I should stay here anymore. I was afraid if I left the house that would be it, we'd be over. Staying... if you came back, I could try to talk to you.'

'Things need to change Liam.'

'They do, you're right. I hate us fighting.'

The 'us fighting' grated.

'There was no us in what happened. I can't go on with this. Your anger terrifies me. When you get that angry, I think there will be a time when you go too far. You hear of men killing their wives, Liam.'

'Stop. I would never do that.'

'How do you know?'

He closed his eyes and sucked in his lips, as if he was trying to keep his cool.

'See? We can't even have this conversation without you losing it.'

When he opened them, his eyes were wet, filmy.

'All I see is black. It's like I step out of myself.'

I shook my head.

'That's not... I'm not trying to excuse it. I know I went too far. Please, Gabs, listen to me, it's not all my fault.'

I folded my arms. 'How's that now?'

'You're the only person who does this to me, who I react that way with. Look at every aspect of my life, I don't fight with anyone else.'

That was true. On every other level, Liam was the perfect worker, the perfect brother, the best friend. With our marriage and money, Liam's work friends told us all the time how lucky we were, usually as I pulled down my sleeve or tried to breathe through the pain.

He held my hand. 'We both need to be better.'

I snapped my hand away. This was the usual way he got round me, to caress in all the right places, knowing I craved the affection, knowing how to make me purr. It helped in the moment. To dilute the pain with pleasure, but I despised myself also, for lying down to it, to him, for accepting what he had done, for responding to his touch, for being this vulnerable, wanting thing, this sexual, needy girl who needed to find pleasure by his hands, who needed him for what I needed. *No more.* If I wanted to change our relationship, a line had to be drawn.

'I'm not taking that, Liam. You act like a bully. How do I need to be better when it's you hurting me?'

'You hurt me too.'

'How?'

'When you say things, they cut into me. They feel like an attack and before I know it, I'm losing it.'

'Don't justify it. No matter what way you spin it or what you say you will never convince me or change my opinion. It is never OK to put your hands on me. Do you get that I wasn't coming back Liam?'

He nodded, his brows burrowed in pain. His bottom lip trembled, trying to keep from crying. My instinct was to go to him, to take away that pain, to soothe and console. Instead, I stood straighter.

'I'll do whatever it takes to keep you.'

'How much are you drinking lately?'

'I drink because of what's happening. Losing you is killing me and I don't know how to fix it, fix us.'

He saw my look. 'Fix me, I meant fix me. I'll lay off the drink.'

'You have to this time.'

'I will.'

'You don't understand...'

'Make me understand,' he said, slipping down the strap to my top, ready to distract me, ready to push my buttons.

'This is serious. I mean it this time, something has to change.'

He nuzzled my neck. 'It will.'

Here's the truth: I smiled then, because I knew what I would say next gave me power. Even if he thought he was winning me over, I was going to floor him with what I had to say.

'I'm pregnant.'

His hands went up to his mouth.

After everything we'd been through, I still loved instigating his smile. Giving him that gift of a baby, that happiness made my heart thump. Although a little voice said: *now he has you.*

He picked me up and swung me around. 'This is exactly what we need. This is the change we're looking for. Sure, that means no more drink, anyway. We'll do everything different from now on. A baby in the house means we have to cop on. Settle down.'

'We have to make sure this doesn't happen again. You get so angry and you take it out on me and...'

His brows furrowed and my stomach lurched with regret for thinking it could be any different. Just as quickly, he smiled and hugged me.

'This is our second chance, Gabs. Everything is gonna be great.'

He dropped to his knees, lifted my top, exposing my stomach. Liam inhaled the skin by my belly button.

'We will do everything to make you happy, I promise. Just stay and I'll prove it.'

I wasn't sure if he was talking to me or the baby. I raked my hands through his hair and smiled.

Like I said, Abbie, I went back to your father to give him a chance but also, I felt you were enough, that you to save us.

And you did.

Glass Walls

Gabrielle

Your father saved my life twice Abbie, but you need to know you saved my life before you were even born because you, my beautiful, gave me something to live for.

The pregnancy was hard. From six weeks along severe morning sickness attacked; I bloated from the moment I conceived. Any smell was enough to make me run to the bathroom. Health wise, I was miserable, but my heart was ecstatic.

Like the other time I suffered, your father rose to help. He rubbed my back and held my hair while I vomited. When I couldn't stomach anything else, he ran out for broth. We became closer than ever. That was all I'd wanted: to be on the same side, to show he loved me. It's the simple things that are life altering and Liam kept to his word, he stopped drinking, joining me in bed for early nights. We lay in the dark, my back to him with his hand resting on my growing bump and spoke about our plans for the baby long into the night, about our deepest wishes.

'This baby is going to get what I didn't.'

He kissed my back, right in the center, between my shoulder blades. 'Love.'

I shifted my body to face him. 'Oh, Liam.'

'Why didn't they love me? Our baby hasn't even arrived and the love I feel for him or her is enough to knock me on my knees. How could they treat a little kid that way?'

I stroked his hair. 'I don't know.'

'Did I ever tell you the story of when I was about eight, when the whole family stopped talking to me?'

I propped up on my elbow. 'No.'

'We were talking about a ship coming into Cobh, one of those huge liners and my father said it was arriving at two. Without thinking I butt in saying, "no, the paper said it's gonna arrive at one." The conversation went from there. With my father things escalated quickly, you could be having a normal chat, then in a flash, he would turn. You were helpless to stop it, even if you saw signs beforehand.'

'Like what was happening to us?'

Liam stiffened in the bed. 'I know I got upset with you but believe me, when he flipped, there was no holding back.' He lay on his back. I let him think.

'What I did to you was never acceptable. Believe me though, I tried to keep it in check.'

I placed my hand on top of his. 'I know.'

'Whatever my father said went in our household. He announced he wouldn't talk to a liar and rest of the family shouldn't either and they did exactly as told. Even Maureen, who was only about four ignored me. After that, if I walked into a room, they all walked out.'

'How long did that go on for?'

'Weeks.'

'Did you ever confront them? Since you became an adult, I mean.'

'Once. He denied everything. Told me I'd want to get psychologically assessed.' His breath hitched. 'There's no point. He twists everything. When I was a kid, he used to lock me in a room, in there I used to dream of the day I was old enough to hurt him back. It was pitch black in there, couldn't even see my fingers. In that dark room, I dreamt of pushing him in and locking the door and leaving him there, but then I got older, and once he didn't have any power over me the dynamic changed. I hate him though, Gabs. I hate him and love him at the same time. Maybe that's where the anger comes from? From little me wondering why in hell he's still in my life, why I didn't stick up for myself. All that anger and instead of taking it out on the people I should have, I took it out on the woman who showed me the most love. I'm sorry.'

I snuggled into him. 'I'm sorry too for what you had to go through.'

'It stops now.'

'I know.'

He turned on his side, lay his face next to mine. 'I mean it, more than I've ever meant anything. They ruined my childhood. I will not ruin my child's life.'

'Good. I'll hold you to that.'

'I'm going to give this baby the best.'

'The baby doesn't need the best, the baby just needs you and me and every bit of love we have.'

He chuckled. 'Fine. I'll give this baby everything I have.'

I loved him more for trying. After what happened to my family, after the miscarriage, I was astonished that I'd been allowed this gift. Life revolved around long walks for fresh air. We thrived in my nauseous misery.

What I've come to believe, is pregnancy is purposely long. For one, it's allows the baby to develop. Two, it also gets the mother ready. Pregnancy gives continual hints that life has more than you to consider. Also, it gives you time to become self-less, at least some of the time. It's a starter for what is coming. The more miserable and harder the pregnancy, the less of a shock it is when the baby is born because you've already sacrificed, you've already learned there will never be just you again. You can walk out or divorce a partner, but your child will always be your child. Your own blood will always run through them. Your cells made their cells and you never forget that.

Still, coming to that conclusion, didn't prepare me for you.

I won't describe the labour - you do not need to know anything except it was the worst day of my life, and then the best. It left me stunned for weeks. Pain often leaves a gift. In that case, I got a bargain.

Even though your father for a time was my greatest source of anguish, he was also my protector and in the hospital he was helpless, for he couldn't ease the pain, couldn't do anything but hold my hand. In my agony, his uncomfortableness was a concern.

When they handed you to him, I thought he would crack open with love, his eyes wide and wet, his mouth blowing out in disbelief. You, baby girl, melted your father's frostiness in a second of meeting. In that bubble of love in that delivery room he was the perfect man.

And then he handed you to me. Finally we arrive at the best part of my story. You.

The one I waited for. The one I spoke to, prayed to, soothed when you kicked. It felt like I had waited for you since I first took a breath, like finally my life, my real life, could begin. It didn't matter what had come before, the pain was left behind. You squirmed and snuffled and I stroked your puffy face with my own puffy fingers.

'We did it,' I said.

You looked right at me Abbie, with wisdom, with recognition and I looked back at you with love.

At visiting time, Sadie was the first through the door, and even though she knew why she was in the room, it was as if the sight of me holding a baby, shocked her into stopping. Her hands went to her mouth, her eyes wide with concern for me but hopeful too, happy too.

'It's OK, come on,' I said.

On tiptoes, she moved slowly, as if afraid to make noise. Sadie didn't make a sound, but the tears streamed down her face and she looked like she was finding it hard to breath. She smiled at Liam, mouthed congratulations, handed him a gift, but then turned her full attention on you Abbie. She was transfixed. Sadie fell in love for the first time. The obsession was mutual. Asleep until then, you opened your eyes and stared back at her. Sadie stroked your skin and when she touched your fingers, you coiled yours around hers.

'How can I feel this much love for a stranger?' Sadie whispered.

'She has that effect all right,' Liam said. Sadie broke her eye contact for the first time to look at Liam.

'She makes me want to be a better person,' he said.

Sadie nodded, Liam nodded, and then she smiled. For the rest of the visit all eyes stayed on you Abbie.

Holding

Abbie

The smell of the toasties wafted over. Jim wobbled the tray and this time it was Abbie that jumped from her seat to help him.

'These look great,' she said.

'Get stuck in so,' Jim said. 'I'll leave you be. I can see ye're busy.'

He pointed at the book. Abbie's heart swelled for the gentle, soft-spoken man, who saw lots but said little.

Sadie poured the tea. Abbie pulled apart the toastie, letting wafts of steam coil beside her fingers.

'The way my mother writes about my birth, you'd swear you loved me or something.'

Sadie kept pouring, but flicked her eyes to Abbie. 'Fishing for compliments again?'

'Funny how I would, when I know I'll get none.'

'I remember what that feels like,' Sadie said, sliding a cup in Abbie's direction.

'Did my dad honestly change?'

'When you came along?'

Abbie nodded.

'We all did, Abbie. From the day you were born, you were a whirlwind upturning all of us.'

Abbie picked at her toastie.

'In the best way, I mean.'

Abbie smiled. 'Mum makes out he changed before that. Once she told him she was pregnant.'

'She wouldn't lie. I didn't see it much.'

Abbie straightened.

'Not like that. It was just things were frosty between me and your father. I was protective and I suppose your dad was guilty maybe, knowing Gabs had confided in me when she ran away. We kept the peace not wanting to stress your mother out but we avoided each other as much as possible. Once you came along, that wasn't the case. Nothing was keeping me away from you, father or no father.'

'Was he that bad?'

Sadie tilted her head, thinking.

'You might not get this, but I understood him. We had more in common than you'd think.'

Abbie screwed her face.

'You don't believe me? For one, we both had parents that totally ruled our life. For another, I never heard of anyone else who used to be locked into a room. I swear our parents must have known each other and passed out notes.'

'So they did lock you in?'

'In that house, I spent more time locked in my room than out of it. Unlike your father, at least I had light, and even though my mother only let me keep the barest of things, I always had my sketchbook and a window. Remember, I was in the Ellis's big house, I saw the room they kept him in. It was tiny. He wouldn't have even been able to lie down. No wonder he attacked when he felt caged in.'

They locked my father in a room.

'In the house they live in now?'

'No. They didn't become homeless, but they lost the big house. Your father tried his best. In the end, they made a deal to sell it, pay off what was outstanding and buy a smaller place.'

'My parents were happy with me?'

Sadie blew on her tea, then took a sip. 'Honestly? Happier than any other couple I know.'

She laughed. 'Before you get up on your high horse, my word, could you scream. It was enough to curdle milk. There were times I had to leave the house and go for a walk just to give my eardrums a break. Liam would join me outside, jumpy, trying to gulp back air. When you got upset, the whole place knew about it. Your face would close in on itself, contort into lines until your eyes were only slits and you would roar until you were purple. It wasn't pretty. If you'd asked me while you were screaming if I loved you, I would have told you I was reexamining my choices. Your mother though, she put us to shame. She would rock you and sing and I'd wonder how she could keep patient. And then you would calm and fall asleep and we would gravitate back to you, the three of us just staring. Then you were beautiful. All again forgiven.'

'Where was Maureen?'

'Still off, who knows where. We didn't miss her.' Sadie blew on her tea again. 'Maureen wasn't known for her maternal side.'

'And my grandparents?'

'They did the obligatory visits. Your father tried to distance you from them. There was too much pain there. Believe it not, we bonded through that. Both of us grew up unhappy, both of us changed by the love from the same woman. Once, when your mother was having a shower or something and it was just the two of us, your father cradled you and said to me, "how could they look at us with anything but love Sade?" and I got him totally, because after you were born I used to wonder the same thing. You were innocent, and it made us see ourselves as innocent, too. Seeing you made us see ourselves.'

264

Scribbles

Gabrielle

After you were born, on the car journey home from the hospital, I fretted. Why were the cars driving like they were racing? Why couldn't they stay in their own lane? Was your neck going to get hurt if we braked too quickly? Every car was a potential accident and you were the most precious cargo. My neck craned so many times to check on you, Liam pulled over.

'Gabs, go in the back.'

'No, I'll be fine.'

'Go on, I want you to, I can't see how she's doing either and it's stressing me out.'

I got out quick, afraid he'd change his mind. You were asleep, so I placed my hand on your chest and kept it there for the journey in case you stopped breathing and I wouldn't know. If I could help it, you would never come to any harm. As time moved on I relaxed for there has to be knocks and falls along the way still I'd like to think I protected you from the worst. That whole journey I watched you, the outside passing by in unnecessary blurred images.

Nobody tells you how erratic raising a child is at the beginning. The highs are unimaginable, but the lows sink you lower than you ever thought possible. They run concurrently and are the rites of passage

265

for motherhood. Life becomes about liquids. You are urinated on, vomited on, leaked on by milky breasts that pour out most of the time. It becomes about cleaning bums and bodies and constant feeding, all done through sleep deprivation coupled with the frustration of how you have to do everything when you can barely keep your eyes open. There is an undercurrent of deliriousness, of hysteria all the time.

Has anyone ever explained the origin of your name? It shouldn't be hard to figure out but you may have wondered. It was the only one your father suggested that I didn't hate. Abbie means my father's joy, and that was exactly what you were. As you know, I was often called Gabs or Gabby. Your father wanted a name that represented us both. Because you were always the best *of* us, and you brought out the best *in* us.

As a toddler you had this thing with my hair. You were obsessed. Other babies have blankets or a favourite teddy but your favourite thing, your comfort blanket, was my hair. Going to sleep you would twirl it in your fingers until it resembled a birds nest of woven interlocking straw that would stick up on its own. Then you would put a strand across your nostrils and sniff. If upset, I could calm you in an instant by placing a strand across your forehead.

Fun fact: you barely crawled. You would prefer to be held in my arms or in the pram ferried around. If you wanted to move you would stand and I would have to hold you by the two arms where you would waddle away until I had to give up from the ache in my back. Instead of crawling you would scoot everywhere on your butt. Don't get me wrong, you could crawl, I had seen you, you just chose not to. The best place in the world according to you was in my arms. The hard ceramic floor downstairs was an obstacle, you eyed it warily from the perch on my hip so we changed it to floorboards instead. The day it was laid you tapped me on the arm to let you down on the floor and standing, you walked the length of the kitchen stopping at the cupboards, where you turned around by yourself and then walked with arms out to me. Not walked, ran. You ran the day you learnt to walk. You ran into my outstretched arms with such glee, skitting at your shocked mummy. Even as a baby you amazed me.

You were a fun baby. Always laughing, always looking for devilment. In a second of quiet I'd jump up because it would mean you were up to something. Sure enough I'd find you, scribbling on a wall or stuffing some object somewhere, or smearing some liquid. Always with a big smile. I would pretend to be horrified and tell you off and you would tilt your face to the side and give me your wider grin and I would just burst because you had my traits. The ability to rebel was born in you just the same.

You are the reason I became a writer, Abbie. When you were born, during the night feeds, when I was forced to stay awake, I found a way to still dream. Since your birth, I was consumed with a need to leave something behind. Your eyes were a mirror. The silent hours of breastfeeding gave me time to reflect. As you suckled, I contemplated my life. I hated that I had lived so many years on the planet and had nothing to mark my time. One day, I swore, you would look back at me with pride. One day you would read my words. Before you, I never braved following through with a story. You made me brave Abbie. You reignited the spark of fire in me.

So much time passes where you have to sit and do nothing with a small baby, when you're breast feeding or rocking them to sleep, or comfort them if they have wind or are unwell. It forces you to stay, to stick, to no longer run away. In this time, I stopped fighting the silence and let my mind wander. Once I did, ideas started to form, small at first. You awoke a want, to prove my life meant something, so I started to run through what I could do with the rest of my life that wouldn't take time away from being with you. From there a story idea bubbled, a character formed. This pushed me on to at least try.

When I began writing, I rediscovered words and their power. Words matter Abbie. Words can be parasitic, they can spread and devour everything in their path. They can multiply and grow roots, turn into weeds, rot your self-worth. Or if the gardener, continually plants words of hope, flowers bud, then blossom your self belief.

Many say in order to write you have to close the door on everything going on around you. I agree. Although, if I waited until I got a chance to close the physical door, I would still be writing my first manuscript. The urge to write became stronger each day. I felt a pull. A need. I started to write when you were only a few months old. This urge to create something tangible, to prove to you I accomplished something with my life pushed me on. When you were toddling I only wrote when you slept, so wrapped up in you I couldn't contemplate writing. At night I would be so tired I could barely do anything except sit in a vegetative state and watch television. Creative juices definitely didn't flow. Then one day I made a decision; I would write every day, no matter what, even if I only managed a line, I would sit down and try. For the most part I kept to my promise. I learned to close the door in my head. I would still be there present and aware if someone, if you, needed me but if you were drawing or playing with your dolls I would go into my characters' world in an instant. There was never any writers block for me. Always ready to write, it was time that stopped me. Until the act of writing became more.

When there were moments in my life I didn't enjoy, I slipped into plots and characters. In a queue, I went there. When I was rubbing your back as you puked, I pictured how my character would react to the same scenario and I would play the game: what if. What if her child was sicker? What if this sickness was permanent? What if the child was diagnosed with something? What if the husband couldn't cope and ran? From those questions my characters were born. Through them I escaped. It saved me at times. It became my sanity and saviour.

Have you read any of my books Abbie? I wonder if you've looked for answers in my words. You won't find them if you do. People believe what you write has to be true, that it comes from part of your life for it to be real on paper, but that's not my experience. There are similarities, there are inspirations, but the details are not mine. Your imagination can take you away. It can take you away from what's happening in your life, it can take you away from the life you don't want to live. On paper, you can experience the life you wish you led, you can play it out safely on the page, with no harm to anyone else, just as if you lived it. In this way, you can live a million alternatives. The brain is easily tricked.

When I was little, I wanted to be an actress. I enjoyed the playing out of someone's life. But I found learning lines didn't come easy, the thought of standing on stage made me queasy for days. As a writer, my characters allowed me to slip into their lives. For them, I could be brave. Through them anything was possible. On the page, I could do things I was too scared of. My characters allowed me to go where I would never. I didn't set out to write any of them. They just appeared like little poofs of imagery and, through allowing them space to appear, they revealed traits and complexities. The story would unveil itself as I scribbled or typed. You asked me once, stared up at me with those big eyes and asked. 'Is magic real?'

And I leant down to you and said. 'Magic is everywhere if you let it in.'

It wasn't a lie. Writing is the closest I've come to seeing magic. When times became hard, I would go someplace else in my head to distract. I fell in love with my characters and willed for a happy ending, in the dark as much as any reader, until the plot revealed itself. Of course, some of the things that happened in my life were inspiration for my stories, I would think about them in that situation and go to my characters. What would Annabelle Reece do? How would Sabine get herself out of this one? What would Darragh say? Some I used in my next book, some I buried down within me. Until now.

Then when the last word was written, and I knew their endings and their outcomes, I went back to the start and made sense of it all, gave them the story they wanted told. By the end I was sorry to say goodbye, but my characters never leave. They are all my children, after all.

When the first book blew up, I wanted to protect you, in interviews they always wanted to know about my personal life and my books, well, they helped a lot of people, but they also attracted a lot of troubled souls too. Giving reporters a different name for you was easy. Lying is always easy Abbie, living with a lie isn't. In this case though, the lie was virtuous and something I was willing to carry.

Sadie loved being around you and as much as she hated Knockfarraig she learned to be around the place. She made her peace with it. Even with her mother. I never understood why she called back up to her. She never spoke of how those meetings went, only that she was pensive and down for days after.

Sadie was great with you, as you gave her an excuse to be silly, for you were the child she never got to be. Times were harmonious then Abbie, your father and Sadie accepted each other. I think they both recognised the hurt the other went through. She became part of our lives, spending Christmas, new year, birthdays together. For a while we were family.

Then Sadie's mother got sick. On one of her visits, she noticed blood on a tissue after Mrs Jennings coughed. It was enough. She sprang into action. In a way, it was the chance Sadie had always waited for. A way to connect with her mother. Calling a family meeting, it was revealed her mother had stage four throat cancer. Sadie was the voice of reason when they all fell apart. When her mother needed round the clock care, her brothers came to her separately, giving their various excuses for why they couldn't help out she took their time on also. At first, she cut her hours as head chef but as her mother's illness progressed and her siblings retreated further, she resigned. As the hours spent with her grew longer, she moved in to be nearer, back to the house she despised enough to run from. After a week of not answering her phone I knocked at the door. Her mother was nearing the end, on seeing the woman, unconscious, on morphine, I softened. She wasn't the Mrs Jennings I knew, who was strong and cruel and beautiful. She was an old woman, in pain and losing against death. Sadie looked exhausted, insisting she take a shower, I sat with the woman.

After some time, Mrs Jennings opened her eyes. On seeing me, closed them again as if annoyed I had turned up. Even dying, the woman hated me.

'I'm glad you got time with Sadie. It must be good for you to have each other again.'

Mrs Jennings moved her mouth but they seemed stuck together. I leant over and placed a tumbler of water, resting it on her bottom lip. She took a sip.

'We manage.'

I wanted to say, you wasted words with that sentence. There were many sentences that could pass between us, many I wanted to say, to hurt that woman for the lifetime of pain she caused her daughter, for the scars that were still evident in adulthood. Instead, I asked a question.

'Why Mrs Jennings?'

The woman didn't move, didn't even flicker, she stayed vacant and impassive. There was no give, no softening, no remorse. It all came to the surface, the time she had wasted, the lessons she never learned.

'You could have loved her. It was all she wanted. But you chose hate every time you dealt with her. She was a child and you treated her like scum. That time I spoke to you, when I said I should have rang child services, you said there hadn't been any neglect, I didn't answer, didn't get a chance to confront you about the bruises. You hurt her, I saw the bruises and I wish I had the courage...'

'Gabs don't.' A wet towelled Sadie stood at the doorway.

'Why not? Someone needs to say it.'

'Out here. Now.'

I followed her out to the hall.

Sadie shook her head. 'Why don't you say all the things you haven't said? Last chance Sade, if you don't say something it will get buried with her and then you'll be stuck with no answers and no reasons, only questions, only continuous questions that will haunt you forever. Ask her. Ask her how could she be so cruel to you, how could she hit you.'

'She never hit me.'

'Yes she did.'

Sadie slowly shook her head. 'No she didn't.'

'Fine maybe she didn't hit you but she hurt you, I don't know how or what with but I saw the bruises.'

Sadie shook her head again.

'I saw them Sadie, don't deny it, don't pretend.'

'She never gave me any bruises Gabs.'

'Well then who did?'

Sadie wouldn't answer.

'So, she didn't hit you. That still don't make the way she was with you any better. Ask her how she could be so unkind. Cos she was Sade, she was fucking unkind.'

'Stop Gabs.' Sadie adjusted her towel. 'There's no point. Don't you see there's no answer that would justify it? There's nothing she can say that will make it right.'

'Then why look after her?'

That Sadie tilt, full of defiance, looked right at me. 'Because she's still my mother.'

I dramatically looked around at empty space. 'Where's her boys?

The one's she treated right because we both know she didn't treat you like a mother should.'

'Maybe I'm doing it as a way to forgive her? Or in the hope that before she dies, she might say she loves me. She can stuff her apology, all I ever wanted, all I needed was her love.'

She flapped at the air, her hand fanning her face as if drying the possibility of tears. Then she grinned.

'Or maybe it's my revenge. It must kill her to have a daughter she hates wiping her arse now.'

We laughed and then we rested our foreheads on each other.

She whispered. 'Gabs, I don't know why I'm doing it, I just know I have to.'

Sadie didn't get the conversation or the apology or the declarations of love she was looking for. There was no hand holding or long lists of regrets. Her mother died with the same disdain she carried all her life for Sadie. Even still, my best friend done the right thing. As the time became final, she made the phone calls then stood to the side as the others descended and took over. No thank you's were mentioned. Even in death, her family treated her like she wasn't a part of them. At the funeral, the brothers hugged each other and cradled their partners.

It was me that marched her up to the top of the church and made her sit alongside them, asking them to budge up when they didn't move. Even though they all sat on the same pew, their body language veered away from Sadie. There was no recognition. They done exactly as she expected them to do, just not what she hoped. It was me who held her hand as she tried not to cry. It was me who squeezed hers as we stood side by side as they lowered her mother in the ground.

'You holding up?' I said as we watched the coffin descend into blackness.

Her eyes were clear of tears. 'She has no hold over me anymore.'

Of course she meant it, but emotions aren't that easy to control.

273

The legacy of hate her mother bore lived on after her death, carried through her siblings. I don't know if it was jealousy or guilt or just learned behaviour that caused them to be that way. I've given up trying to work that family out. This I know, an hour after the funeral ended, the two brothers went back to the house they barely visited as adults and riffled through the musty drawers until they found the will and deeds. Sadie wasn't mentioned in them at all. That day they also rang the locksmiths. After dropping the last guests home from the hotel, Sadie discovered she was homeless. Along with jobless. Even in death her mother found a way to still ostracise her. From then on, Sadie moved in with us.

Flowers

Abbie

'Just gonna pop to the bathroom,' Abbie said, splaying the book on the empty table. She hadn't even noticed when Jim or Sadie cleared it, for she had been so wrapped up in reading.

In the bathroom, she splashed cold water on her face. It was too much. The scribe contradicted everything she grew up believing. All the evidence pointed to the fact they had loved Abbie. The confirmation felt strange. For she had always thought it was just hope niggling deep inside. At her core, the certainty of once being loved strengthened.

She looked in the mirror. The resemblance was enough to use.

'Why did you end it all? Life would have been different with you around.'

There could be no answer here. The only ones available were on paper out on the table and all those words in the book were in the past, Gabrielle's past. The answers for Abbie wouldn't come. She was preparing for that, she needed to prepare for that.

She reached for a petal on a vase of flowers by the hand towels. White lilies. Soft petals. Reminding her of a question she wanted to ask the one person who could give an answer.

When she returned, Sadie was reading the page she left open.

'It's been bugging me about the flowers you left at the grave. Why rainbow?'

Sadie smiled, remembering.

'I asked her once what her favourite flowers were. She pointed to her temple and answered, "the ones in here. It's where the best things are." When I asked what did she mean she said, "the ones I dream about are better than any reality." So I said, "if you could imagine anything into existence, what would they be like?" She closed her eyes and said, "The colours of the rainbow would run through every flower." After she died, I was walking past a florist and there they were, Gabrielle's dream flower. Every time I visit, I bring them.'

'Did she ever get to see them?'

'I don't think so, not with me, anyway. It was years later when I spotted them. The people around must have thought I was a complete nut job because I was jumping and laughing. I even picked up a woman in the middle of the street. It made me feel close to her again, like your mother was showing me a sign or something, letting me know she was still around cos when she used to talk about those flowers, I would say it was impossible and she would wiggle her finger at me and say, "one day they will be real, one day they will be a thing Sadie wait and see." I looked into it, you know? How they make them because I couldn't get my head around how they could invent a flower with so many colours.'

'I wondered the same. Are they coloured? They didn't have that hard feel you'd get if it was sprayed.'

'That's cos they aren't. They're dyed. They take a white rose and make cuts into the stem and then place the flower in a vase of coloured water. As the rose absorbs the water, the petals change.'

'That's cool.'

'Sure is.'

Sadie's smile left.

Abbie pointed to the book.

'Just been reading about your mother dying.'

'I see that,' Sadie said, handing the book over.

'That must have been tough.'

'Funny enough, the dying part was the easiest bit. It was living with her that was harder.'

'How were you able to be there for her? You should have let her die alone.'

Sadie cocked her head. 'You know, every time I talk to you, I hear more of your mother.'

Abbie picked at her sleeve, feeling her cheeks flush. 'Don't say that.'

'It's true. You just read what Gabrielle thought about me helping my mother.'

'Did you ever forgive her?'

Sadie blew out. 'Forgiveness is a big word. Can I accept the things she did to me? Never. When she died, there was no chance left for an apology. It's taken some time to accept that. It's ongoing, actually. But I've come to the realisation that when I get angry at her, the only one who feels it, the only one who suffers because of it, is me.'

'If it wasn't her causing the bruises, who was?'

Sadie shook her head, closing off.

'Your brothers?'

'Not even close. Why rake it up?'

'Because I need to know.'

Sadie shook her head.

'You owe me that.'

'I owe you nothing.' Sadie said.

'You owe me ten years of not knowing. You owe me ten years of hell.'

Sadie bit down hard on her lip.

'Your father then?'

'Nope.'

'Why are you hiding it? Why would you protect the person hurting you?'

'Because they are closer to you than you think.'

'My mother then? Or my father?'

'No, and no.'

'Or what was that girl's name in the woods, Melissa or something?'

'You won't leave this go, will you?'

Abbie shook her head.

'See your mother's stubbornness?' She tilted her head to the ceiling. Thought for a while. 'All right, screw it. I don't know why I am protecting the person. The girl in the woods was called Marissa, but your mother changed who she was. Marissa was Maureen, and she was the one that hurt me for years.'

Blow

Gabrielle

We fell in to a pattern after Sadie moved in. Liam left for work, I wrote while Sadie looked after you. Abrasive and standoffish with strangers, Sadie was a whole other person around you. Giggling, speaking your own secret language, I'd emerge from my little office to find the two of you huddled in a corner, playing dolls, or beauty salon, where Sadie would have a perfectly normal conversation while covered in the amateur garish colours my daughter had bestowed on every available space of skin.

My first story was about an everlasting friendship that could overcome any obstacles. I wrote about the power of love and how it could redeem the harshest acts. Sabine was Sadie and I gave her the ending I wished for her: the conversation she would never have with her mother. In that story my parents didn't die. In that book, I got my wishes too. It wasn't hard to write, I just wrote the book I always wanted to read, yet it wasn't easy either, for I gave everything to that story; every free moment, every mundane task, was swollen with thoughts about Sabine, about what was happening to her, about what was unfolding. At night, I would see her just before I fell asleep, sitting on my bed, as if waiting for me to wake up again to continue.

Back then I didn't know it would resonate with so many or how

279

massive it was going to be. Back then, I simply wrote that book to right the wrongs that were done to my friend in the only way I could. On paper, I achieved what I couldn't in real life; I could change history; I could erase all of the ugliness and rewrite it with a better outcome.

After Sadie moved in, I completed the book in two months. Before, I had grabbed moments of time here and there, little bits whenever I could but after, I could properly close the door. If I was going to do that, if I was going to lose precious time with you it was going to be with something to show for it. When I wrote The End it was coming into summer, so I shelved it for a month for distance and we spent those moments bringing you to the sea. I loved those times, Abbie. Hearing you whoop and cheer as the cold water sprayed you. Seeing your delight in making shapes in the sand as Sadie made elaborate sandcastles. Adding your feet to the line of ours as we wiggled them in the water. We were happy then Abbie, I swear, we were.

After the month was over, I went back to my office and getting up early, made sure I only missed your breakfast. Edits were hard. Passages that at the time had made me proud, I cringed at after, wanting to delete the majority. But then. Then I would find one singular sentence that would take my breath away and it would spur me on, because for one moment of reading, I believed I was a writer.

As you grew older, Sadie looked for work again in the evenings and landed the head chef role at a five star hotel in Cork City. Many prestigious people called her out to the restaurant to compliment her. One such person, a frequent visitor, happened to be an editor for a publishing house. In exchange for a private, six course free taster meal for ten guests of her choosing, Sadie bartered for the woman to take a look at my manuscript, winning the woman over with the first lines of the novel. A five minute conversation changed our lives.

It scares me to think my whole career hung on that one decision, swayed by chance. We make our own luck Abbie, although sometimes

I wonder if the sun chooses to shine on us or hide behind the clouds. Whatever the reason, in one month of her reading it, I had a publishing deal. The world didn't change with the advance, that came after the fourth print, when they offered me an advance for my second book that left me with my mouth gaping for days.

Do you know how long it takes to get a book out in the world Abbie? Years. There is no quick turnaround in traditional publishing. It didn't matter as I already had an idea for another.

The seasons changed but my routine didn't. No matter the weather or the whereabouts I got up before dawn, writing until I heard the patter of feet or laughter coming from the kitchen. My only regret is that I didn't wake up more with you, at the time I saw it as a small price to pay, for the chance to be financially independent, for the opportunity to fulfill the urge to splay out the words, to tell the stories that haunted my days. On the other side of life, I wonder.

Happiness is not a given and as grateful as I was, I worried it would end one day. All things do.

By the time the book released, I had two more written with ideas for another four. This was a blessing, for now I see if I hadn't been so invested into my other characters and stories I would have been so overwhelmed with the scrutiny, I would have given up.

The publishing house built the hype, booking me everywhere for signings. The publicity tour didn't stop there, every day I had to go somewhere, talk to someone, go to interviews, put on my best outfits. By that stage you were in preschool so I had one strict rule – I would travel anywhere that got me home for dinner. By launch day, the preorders were already record breaking. The book blew up, to this day I'm not sure why. There are so many better writers. The readers that wrote to me said it resonated, that the characters stayed with them, that they loved them as people, I would go to sleep that night with their words swirling around.

There were some parts of my new fame we found hard to take. One day your father came home and threw a white set of what looked like drawings down on the table.

'What's this?' I said touching the corner of the top page. They *were* drawings, like architectural sketches.

'It's our new home,' he said, beaming at me.

'Yeah right,' I said laughing.

'Look at it,' he said, turning serious.

I pulled the drawings towards me and took a breath.

'I don't understand.'

'It's for a plot overlooking the water. You've always wanted that haven't you? It was what you loved about my place. Here we could plan the whole thing, have our dream house. What do you think?'

'Leave here?'

His face looked impassive but his knuckles were white as he gripped the chair. He wanted this.

'Why not Gabs? A fresh start. People know this house, there's weirdos calling all the time.'

'Ah, they're sweet.'

'But what if they're not? What if it isn't safe for Abbie anymore? A lot of them are quirky to say the least. Some are unhinged.'

'That's why I didn't give Abbie's real name out.'

'Like that would make a difference Gabs, all they have to do is follow her. Or break in here. At this house we would have gates, security cameras.'

'This was my family home though. I feel them here.'

'We don't have to sell it.'

'Course we would.'

'No, your fancy books make sure we don't. It's more than that though. There's too many ghosts here.'

He saw my look. 'Not your family, I mean my ghosts. Of who I was.

So many rooms remind me of who I nearly turned into.'

There it was. His vulnerability was all I needed. Understanding Liam needed something, a way to claw back some power over what was happening, I took the sketches and pored over them.

'Let's do it,' I said.

Oran was the architect we called in to make plans for the plot of land we wanted to build overlooking the sea. There was only one speculation from me; I wanted it to be wall to wall glass so nothing interfered with my view. Your father wanted walls to keep people from looking in. Oran was our compromise. He worked out a way to have a normal house facing the road with a glass wall overlooking the water as a living room with tinted windows so no one could see in. Each time he called, Oran's visits became longer, his interest spiked whenever Sadie and you walked by. In my ignorance I thought it was that he loved kids. The fact he wore a wedding ring gave me reason for that.

One spring day, I came home early after an interview was rescheduled. My word quota already met meant my imagination was already spent from waking at dawn to write so I decided to use the time to catch up on some cleaning before collecting you. Grabbing clothes from each room for a wash, I opened the bathroom door and there was Sadie, her leg dangling over the side of the bath, with a man between her, lying on her, the water swishing over her breasts, slopping over the side of the bath. Transfixed on Sadie, not on her nakedness or as a voyeur, I stood immobile. With her eyes closed, and her mouth open as she let out a moan, I realised I had never seen her at anywhere near that level of pleasure before. The man was Oran. Shocked, I backed out, banging my elbow on the door. Sadie jolted. Her eyes sprang open. I rushed out of there, nearly falling down the stairs, taking the steps three at a time, my hands shook as I tried to lean on the kitchen counter. Noises followed me, Sadie appeared, covered in a towel.

'Sorry, sorry, sorry.'

'What the hell Sade?'

'I didn't think you'd be here, I'm sorry you saw us.'

'Saw? I don't care about that. He's married,' I hissed.

'Not happily,' she hissed back.

'How do you know? That's what every adulterer in the whole history of being an adulterer has said.'

Sadie laid her hands on my shaking ones.

I groaned. 'Oh Sade. Why? And don't say you love him.'

'I do though.'

'He's not single. Has he told you he loves you?'

She nodded.

'If you really loved each other you could have waited. Why doesn't he leave his wife?'

'I am,' Oran said, dressed now. He ran his hand through his wet hair, slicking it back.

Sadie's face shot up. 'You are?'

He nodded. She ran to him, kissing him with such passion I didn't know where to look. When they turned to me, they faced me as a couple.

'We tried to fight it.'

'We did. I kept out of her way.'

'But we ran into each other one night.'

'Where?'

'At The Millstone.'

'Oh, funny how he accidentally ran into you at your restaurant, Sade.'

'Hands up I didn't know she worked there. It was only when I went outside for a smoke and she was there and I thought, there she is.'

'How beautiful,' I said, shocking myself with the scorn that dripped from me.

The door slammed. We all jumped.

'Gabs, you home? You'll never guess what happened.'

Liam paced into the room, the jubilant expression left him, all thought for whatever good news he wanted to share disappeared. His brows knitted together, the look I tried to avoid at all costs was there. It was me he addressed.

'What's going on?'

I saw how it looked. Sadie was half naked, Oran's hair was wet and I was in the middle of them when I said I would be gone for the day. A sliver of panic sliced at my stomach. It would be easy for Liam to overreact, to blame me. Instead, I threw them under the bus.

'I've just walked in on the lads in our bath.'

Liam turned to Oran. 'I was just talking to your wife this morning.'

'Chill Liam,' Sadie said.

'Chill.' Liam nodded thinking the word over. The way he said it, the way he contemplated it sent shivers along my skin. 'Chill?' he repeated but the sound was totally different. This time his voice was raised, indignant, angry. 'Are you having a laugh?

'I love her,' Oran said, tilting his jaw.

It was the wrong move. The jaw was like a bullseye on a target for Liam. He gave him an uppercut that lifted Oran off the floor and then back down again.

Sadie screamed, she ran to Oran. I froze to the spot.

'What have you done?' Sadie roared. Oran came to, holding his jaw.

'What have *I* done?' Liam shouted, moving quickly until he was hovering over the two of them. 'You screw him in my house and you're asking me what I have done?'

'It's meant to be my house too.' She screamed standing up to him, facing him off. 'The only reason I'm here is to make sure you don't touch her.'

Liam rocked up to her, got right in her face. 'What do you mean touch her?'

Sadie didn't flinch, didn't lower her voice. 'You think I didn't know the things you did to her? That I didn't see the bruises? I know exactly what kind of man you are Liam. When things don't go your way you'll blame someone else. And now here you are judging Oran? The only reason I've stayed is because it put you on your best behaviour. Don't you think I could have moved out long ago? I stayed for Gabrielle, and Abbie, not you. If I had my way she would have left you a long time ago.'

'Get out of my house,' he said.

'Liam,' I said.

He pointed a finger at me, and for a moment I thought he would hit me in front of them. 'Stay out of it.'

He turned back to Sadie.

Torn, I hesitated. If I let Sadie go I knew Liam would never let me see or talk to her again yet if I stood up for her, he would bring his wrath on me.

'Liam, they said they are in love. Oran is going to tell his wife.' I placed a hand on his shoulder. He was on me within seconds, pinning me to the wall, banging my head. His spittle landed on my face. 'You think that's the right way for a husband to act? You think marriage should be treated that way? He said vows Gabrielle, he swore he would love that woman till death and what does he do? Shack up with the chef. Would you like to have an affair? Is that what this is about?'

'Liam,' I said in the most unemotional, docile voice I could find. *Show no fear. Act calm. Be the voice of reason.* 'This isn't about you or me, this is their choice and they are saying they are in love.'

Sadie pulled Oran up to standing. 'Liam, I'll get my gear, just let her go.'

'You won't,' he said, swivelling around. 'You'll go right now. I'll gather up your shit and throw it out on the porch and you can get it after.'

He charged at them. 'Go on, get out.'

Sadie stood her ground and I thought, *that is what being unafraid looks like.* Our eyes met and she must have seen the terror in mine because she nodded once and I knew she made the decision to concede, for me.

'Come with us Gabs?'

Liam laughed, then flipped altogether. 'Get out,' he roared and shoved Sadie. Oran went to hit him but Liam ducked his punch, then shoved him, sending him off balance for the second time.

'You're the big man hitting someone when they aren't expecting it. You'll get your comeuppance Liam, just you wait. I'll find you down a dark alley one day.'

Liam's fists clenched. 'Looking forward to it. I'll still have you then.'

Sadie and Oran retreated, not taking their eyes off Liam.

'I'll look forward to reporting you to the trade association too for sleeping around on the job while I was paying you.'

'Do that Liam. Whatever gets you going,' Oran said.

'Gabs?' Sadie asked again.

No words passed my lips. My tongue was dry and immovable. My legs were cemented to the ground. The only part of me that wasn't paralysed was my head. I shook it, slowly. *Please don't ask me to leave him.*

A sob escaped Sadie, and I fought back my own tears because we both knew Liam would insist on the friendship being over. I knew this Abbie, I knew this from the bones of me yet I still didn't go.

Gates

Abbie

'Did my dad really kick you out?'

'Ah, you're there.'

'Did it happen like mum wrote?'

'Pretty much. Although your mother was quite forgiving in the way she described how he pinned her to the wall. He didn't just pin her, he vaulted her. Your dad was a fit man, strong out. If he wanted to, he could have killed her easily.'

'You said that was why you had stayed in the house. What did you hear?'

'As far as I'm aware, there were no physical altercations after you were born. Still though, sometimes I would hear him through the walls and the hairs would rise on the back of my neck. When he used to get heated, I'd get scared that would be the time he'd flip so I would go outside their door to make noise. It usually worked. At the time I thought that. These days though I reckon he just didn't care. In his house it was his rules.'

'He sounds like a monster.'

'Hmmm.' Sadie picked at her nail. 'Your mother handled him well. Only when I put my ear to the wall would I hear her voice, always soft, murmuring. Most times I wouldn't even have to make noise, she could soothe the agitation right out of him. When I asked her the next day what had riled him there wouldn't be one bit of worry on her face, she would shrug and say, Liam blows up but deflates just as quick. Her lack of worry stopped mine. This will sound weird coming from what you just read, but in spite of what your father was capable of, he lived his life with morality.'

'Sounds like you're defending him.'

'Just saying how it was. He was very good with you and you only had eyes for him.'

'Did Maureen see some of this?'

Sadie snorted. 'Maureen knew what her brother could be like, believe me. She won't tell you that though. When they immortalised Liam they wiped away all his faults. He was a good father though, I'll give him that.'

'What happened to your father?'

'Which one?'

Abbie widened her eyes, Sadie rolled hers.

'Yes, Abbie, I knew. Not at first. I mean, early on I could tell I wasn't the same, my skin being a different shade to my whole family made sure of that. But my mam always made out I was just this freak of nature, like they didn't know where the difference came from. If anyone questioned my skin colour, mam spouted off about the Black Irish, about the survivors of the shipwrecks from the Spanish Armada who married locals, about a genetic kink that had showed up on me decades later and I accepted that. When Gabs gave me the present of the hair scarf, my doubts fell away. Before that, I knew I was different, course I did, I wasn't stupid, I wondered if I was adopted but apart from my skin colour I looked like my mam. But the way she treated me, the way all the family did, made me wonder if there was something else. Back then I thought it was just that she hadn't wanted another baby, but the penny dropped when Gabs acknowledged my race.'

'Was that a good or bad thing?'

'Neither. Remember, finding that out meant I lost my father and gained a stranger, a man that was never in my life. Anyway,' she clapped her hands together. 'You asked what happened to them. My father, Mr Jennings, left one day for work and never came back and to be honest, it wasn't such a loss. With him, it was like I was invisible, for entire conversations he would pretend not to hear my part, like I wasn't there. When that happens more than once, with enough people, well, you start to wonder if you really exist. Or you invent a way for people to acknowledge you, which is what I did.'

'Sounds like what happened with my father.'

Sadie looked confused.

'The way he was ignored by his family?'

'Yeah. Our upbringing was scarily similar. You'd think we'd bond more over that but I think we were too similar. The traits we didn't like in the other were traits we had too. I met him once.'

'Who?'

'My real father. No one told me it was him or anything. It was before Gabrielle moved to Ireland. Outside the school gates, one day, there was a man standing there. I'd never seen a man with such dark skin, much darker than mine even but skin more the colour of mine than anyone else. On my own, I looked around to see if he was waiting for someone but the man smiled on seeing me, as if he knew who I was. It put me on edge from the start. In his hands were a pair of roller skates, something I had been begging my parents for years to get me. He came towards me, held out the skates. Abbie, I didn't care who he was, mistaken identity or not, I was taking them. He stroked my hair when I leant in. When I looked up to say thanks, he was crying. That totally freaked me out. All I thought about was stranger danger and what my mother would do if she caught me talking to one, so I ran. Before we spoke a word, before I gave him a chance to talk. I think about that day a lot, about what I should have said, about what I should have asked. If your mother was there she would have, my word when she started asking questions!' She tsked. 'Didn't even get a full day with those skates. Until my other father, Mr Jennings, spotted them. When I told him the story, he got so mad he threw them in the fire. The place stank of rubber for weeks, mam had to fish the metal out. At the time I thought he was angry with me for taking them from a stranger, but after your mother pointed out I had a black person's hair, it all made sense. I'd always known really, but I would have fought anyone else to the death denying it before she handed over the scarf. Gabrielle wouldn't hurt me. After that, I remembered that man. For the first time I accepted he was my father. My hair had been just like his hair.'

'Did your mother say anything?'

'Once, around that time, I came straight out and asked if my father was black. She slapped me across the face and screamed at me to never ask her that again. It was the only time she hit me.'

'Didn't any of the school kids say anything? In my school, they didn't stop reminding me what my mother did.'

'Oh, they let me know every day I was different. Growing up, there were these chocolate bars made in Cork called macaroons which had little white flecks of coconut inside. That's what everyone called me. The rumours always floated around, but I didn't listen. When I was smaller, I didn't fight. After the girls attacked me, I learnt I had to. It never mattered if they won, which they always did, cos I was usually the smallest. What mattered is they wouldn't say it again to me, not to my face anyway.'

'I know we're not the same, like what you dealt with, the racism isn't the same and I can't imagine how much it must have sucked. It's just, in Knockfarraig, everyone knows who I am. If I go anywhere, all heads turn. Your skin singled you out and what my mother did singled me. All my life people have watched me to see how I react to anything, as if I'm about to do something crazy and it's shaped me because I do the opposite of what they want, of what they expect and don't react. Like I'd rather die than start a fight.'

'Maybe you need to start, then.'

'What, like you?'

Sadie raised her shoulders. 'It helped me.'

'I'm not you. Like, I look at Maureen now with all this new information and it's changed how I see her. It's like I've been living with a stranger all these years. Why has she lied? Why has she only told one side of the story?'

Sadie shrugged again. 'I guess only Maureen can answer that.'

'There's so many questions I'd love to throw her way, I want to get to the end though before I confront her.'

Sadie shifted, looking uncomfortable. 'That's wise. Until you read everything, I wouldn't go there yet.'

'Did you do jigsaws with me?'

Sadie folded her arms, smiled at the memory. 'Only every damn day.'

'Did one have something like fish scales or something on it?'

'Mermaids. You were obsessed.'

Abbie picked at the edge of the book. 'I see it.'

'Some things are coming back?'

'I think so. Did you used to have a green ring, on your middle finger?'

Sadie gulped. 'Yes.'

'I remember that ring.'

'Your mother died with that ring on.'

Clap

Gabrielle

After Sadie left, it's important you know that I didn't just stay. It's vital you understand I didn't just accept the way your father was. You probably have many questions, wondering why I didn't leave him. Earlier I wrote I would only keep one chapter about your father's anger, but yesterday as I wrote what happened with Sadie and Oran, after I wrote about your father pinning me to the wall, I thought long into the night about who I was protecting by restricting what I wrote. It wasn't to hide or condone or brush over his actions. The reason I kept it to one chapter was down to how much it hurt to write. If it hurt a wife to write it, those words would hurt a daughter more to read. There are a few things I want to make clear though.

It is an enigma to outsiders when someone stays with a partner that hurts them. They can never understand. Before I fell in love with Liam, I was one of them. The outsider might never admit it, but they search for the excuse, thinking some of the blame has to lie with the abused person, even if it is just for staying. It's human nature to rationalise why someone can hurt another. There must be some fault, some flaw in the victim that made them stay, whether it's stupidity, or an addiction to drama, or just lack of self-esteem. Abbie, I knew my worth and I knew I deserved better. Here's what I know:

You stay for the good in the person, the good you see inside them, wishing to make it the permanent trait. You fall for the potential, you strive for it, for the glimmer you experience on the best days. If you only try harder, if you are kinder, if you don't fight back you can help bring that side out. Maybe, you think, if you only show love, it will cure them. For love is the answer to every problem.

The question should never be why does the woman stay, but why does the man act like that?

Women are nurturers. It is in our nature to love. That is why we stay. We stay because we don't want to give up on the person we love. We stay because we see they are so much better than their actions. We stay because we are invested, because we are loyal and once we love someone we will never leave them. We stay because we promised we would, because a vow means something, means everything. We stay because we are ashamed to admit to anyone that we failed. We stay in the hope it will change. Until it changes us. We can avoid the onset of anger if we make ourselves smaller. If we quieten and take every bit of pain, every put down, every accusation thrown and don't retaliate.

You may not believe me, but doing that made me stronger. Quietening made me go inside, quietening made me impenetrable. It distanced me until I saw him as a scared, lost man. Deep down, I was stronger than him.

As careful as I was, I never got it right. On any issue that arose, Liam would stay ambivalent when I approached the concern, he would change the subject, deflecting the answer. When I was forced into making an on the spot choice when the concern became a reality, it would always be the wrong decision. Over time, it became such an regular occasion I saw it for what it was, an excuse to rage instead of a reason. There was a strength in that, in knowing that no matter what I did, it would be wrong.

When I read years later about disassociation, the concept hit home.

Every point described the memory loss. My subconscious had learnt to lift my thoughts out of the situation, to go somewhere else in my brain, so much so, that after a confrontation with him, I wouldn't be able to recall a single word spoken, from him or me. Sometimes even while he was still talking. If he'd asked me to repeat the sentence back, I wouldn't be able. It wasn't not listening, it was different from that, it was as if my mind shut off communication. It reached the brain, because I knew I understood it as it went in, but it was as if the sorting office decided to dump it the instant it entered. It wasn't allowed to stay. In the worst of times, that was my only way to survive, to stay living in the house, because if I remembered, if I stacked them all up in my memory, I would have left that very day.

All the times I fought back in the early days, I only matched his anger. Anger never resolves the situation. It only fuels more anger.

Knowing this, learning this, I stopped. He didn't. Then, I tried something new: when he got angry, I chose to show him love. When that didn't work I removed myself from the situation until he calmed down. Unbelievable as it sounds, I found a way to get through. After you were born, apart from the time he discovered Sadie and Oran, your father never touched me.

It won't help to go into more details of what happened, to chronicle how many bruises I received in our relationship, to list the exact injuries or give more examples of what was done. It won't help you or me and I don't want to leave you with a one sided view of who I was. Yes, your father hurt me on many occasion, yes I stayed when I shouldn't have, but I don't want you to close this book thinking of me as a victim. If I do my job here right, you will at least see how your father was not a monster. He was capable of terrible, wrong acts and carried them out but he was also the kindest person I ever met. It doesn't make sense, I know, but I promised you my truth and this is it: I chose to stay. I chose for you to be around your father because the joy from the two of you was worth it. I stayed because when it was good it belittled the pain. I stayed because I loved your father more than I feared him.

For a long time, years, his violence has been dormant. After I didn't leave him, even though Sadie and Oran witnessed what he was capable of, it dispelled the secret, was no longer a hidden fact. It is only inside a lie that the truth has no power. The day I stayed, I choose love, and it worked, Abbie. His anger subsided. Under no illusions, I treat it like a volcano, to this day I watch it warily. There is never a time I completely forget his eruptions. Even dormant, his potential runs alongside my subconscious, tainting any action, any decision I make. Every word and gesture is carefully chosen not to offend. For I know it was me who changed to keep order; it was me that bent and moulded to fit his needs. Liam didn't change; I just gave no reason or excuse for him to react.

After the altercation which caused Sadie to leave, I decided Liam had to prove his change was permanent. Determined to fix us, I set boundaries. The threat of losing Sadie again was enough to say enough. In order for me to stay after he pushed me against the wall, I insisted he undertake counselling, focusing on anger management. For the first time he agreed.

Monsters are born from sad stories. Every evil act, every despicable person is manufactured from a previous action. Layers of hurt, of abuse, of neglect and pain build up, altering a good person. And if that child never learns how to process that pain and turn it into love, then they mimic how to transfer it, on to a partner or another generation.

After his second session with the counsellor, Liam sat down and started talking. Under his eyes were almost black from lack of sleep.

'I would never have got with you if I'd known I could hurt you. You are the best thing that has ever happened to me.'

'I believe you Liam.'

He examined his hands. '*I* believed I was rotten.'

'You weren't.'

'Please Gabs, let me speak.'

I motioned zipping my mouth.

'In counselling she keeps getting me to talk about my childhood. What's your first painful memory? When were you scared? Were you ever exposed to violence? There's so much I stuffed down Gabs. I told you before about how they ignored me, how the whole house used to pretend I wasn't there but that wasn't the worst of it. It wasn't like he ever laid a hand on me so why complain? If I spoke out of turn, if I slighted him in any way, he banished me. They banished me. Silence was his weapon. Solitude was my punishment. There was a room in our house, when you would have saw it, it was a tiny toilet.'

'By the cupboard?'

He nodded. 'Before it was a toilet, we stacked junk in there. Hating anything to exist without purpose, my father designated it as the bad room. Anything that warranted punishment meant a trip in there. It didn't even have a working light bulb. If he deemed it bad enough, I could be in there hours. Fighting it didn't work. He would call out from the other side that the more I fought, the longer I would stay in. Course, I still did. I banged with my feet, tore at the wood until my fingers bled, until one time the inside of the door wore through and I managed to kick a hole in it with my foot. It didn't matter, he just replaced it with a metal door for the next time.'

He sucked in a long breath, shuddered.

'It was a tiny space. After a few seconds, the air seemed to leave, my chest would press in on itself and no matter what I did, no matter how much I begged, no matter how good I tried to be, I always ended up in there.' Liam's voice cracked. 'I've never seen darkness like it, where no light got through at all. Each time I swore I would do anything not to go in there again. I tried to be like him. To act strong, to be what he wanted, but it was never good enough. My mother would just look on, would back him to the hilt, her only concession was shoving some snacks in there when he wasn't around in case I was in there too long without food or water. The worst was when I heard them getting ready to go out, when I would hear them laughing as they put on Maureen's coat as if they didn't have another child locked in a room. The panic would rise because how long were they going for? Or what if something happened, and they never came back?'

'Oh, Liam, I'm so sorry. Did your mum or Maureen do anything?'

'Mum never challenged him at all. If he said the sky was green she'd agree and what could Maureen do? She was years younger. At first, she used to stay on the other side of the door, trying to calm me down but after dad threatened her, saying if he caught her there she'd go in there on her own, she didn't try again. Then she hardened. I'd see her acting smug, smirking even. It made me hate her but I guess dad wanted that, loved it.'

He flicked me a look. 'Laurie thinks it's why I couldn't handle being challenged. If I felt cornered she said it took me right back to being locked in that room again. Before getting hurt, I lashed out. Not that it excuses it.'

He stopped talking, cupped his hands over his face. 'Nothing can ever excuse what I did. Gabs, I wouldn't blame you for walking away, I'm damaged and I've hurt you.'

I prised his hands away from his face. He looked at me, waiting.

'I'm not going anywhere. I see the work you're putting in, it's not easy talking about pain but you're sticking with it. I've always seen the good in you, now it's your turn to see it.'

He gave a lopsided smile. 'I'll try.'

I sat back. Took a breath.

'One thing though. The deal is I won't give up on you but I won't give up on Sadie either. You can avoid her, stay a million miles away if you want, but don't make me choose. Sadie has her faults but so do you. I won't give up on either of you.'

He pursed his lips, nodded. 'OK.'

That was all that was needed to reinstate Sadie into my life.

By not giving up on your father, for the first time in his existence, he felt unconditional love. That was my gift to him.

And by doing that, he could be the person life always meant him to be, the person who wouldn't hurt another, because there was no need to anymore. That was his gift to me.

When the second book released and the world seemed to know my name, life was good. I had set out to do something and achieved it. I had kept going and was now reaping the rewards. We were a couple in love, with a beautiful daughter, who had faced our demons and still stood together. The world was at our feet. At the National Book awards, when I won book of the year, there was no one as proud as your father clapping for me in the crowd. And Sadie stood right beside him.

Diving

Abbie

Only noticing how dark it was outside, she checked her watch. It was just after eight.

'You wanna go home?' Sadie asked, noticing.

Abbie shook her head. 'Were they good together?'

'Your parents? They made it work. In my eyes Gabrielle was too good for Liam, but I would have thought that about any guy, I think.'

'Were they happy?'

Sadie nodded. 'Yeah, they were. The happy you can't fake too. When I stayed with them, the times I heard them argue were rare. I'd go to bed early sometimes, to give them some space, I'd listen to the sound of their laughter and I would wish for that, to have a man I felt comfortable enough to be myself with. Laughter wasn't one of my requirements for a relationship before that.'

'What was?'

'Don't ask. You wanna read on?'

Abbie checked her phone. There was a text from Joe.

Got the house to myself if you're free.

'Could you maybe drop me to a friend? Some laughter would be good.'

'You saying I'm not funny?' Sadie leaned away from her with a smirk.

'Hmm, funny isn't a word I'd use for you. Sorry.'

'You're lucky I'm not easily offended. Come on then, get up. We'll get back to it tomorrow.'

'Will you be all right?'

'What on my own?'

Abbie nodded.

Sadie grinned. 'Don't worry about me Abbie, I can entertain myself.'

'I'm not worried.'

'Good. Wouldn't want you to catch feelings for me now,' Sadie said, chuckling as they reached the door, holding it open for Abbie to pass through.

'No fear of that,' Abbie said.

When they pulled up at Joe's, Sadie nodded at the house. 'Guy or girl?'

'Guy,' Abbie said.

'One nighter or more?'

'More, I think.'

'Does he make you laugh?' Sadie raised a brow.

'He was a friend first.'

'That doesn't answer my question. A friend can change when they become more.'

'Only one way to find out,' Abbie said, opening the car door. 'Sadie?'

'Yeah?'

'Is it going to be awful?'

She didn't have to explain what she meant. They both knew she was delaying the end of the book.

'I'd say brace yourself. Whatever you think might be to come, whatever you know, it's still going to shock.'

An hour with Joe was enough. Distraction was the aim, and with Joe, it was easy to achieve. All she had to do was give every bit of herself, and once she did, as she stripped off, as she let Joe see all of her, after he kissed every inch and dived into her for the first time, her mother, father and Sadie disappeared and Abbie enjoyed the brief few minutes of silence it released.

Ditch

Gabrielle

It started with spasms in my hand. At first, I put it down to writing, blaming it on overuse. When the foot cramps began and then the thigh twitches, I dismissed it as my body asking for more exercise after sitting in a chair most mornings. Then, on waking I couldn't shake the tiredness. After an hour's writing I needed to lie down. Some days it was a struggle to speak, my mouth moving slow and uncoordinated as if I'd drank alcohol, as if my tongue muscle was too relaxed to work properly. When my balance failed a number of times causing me to stumble, I gave in and visited the doctor, thus setting in motion a flurry of tests, MRI'S, CT scans, then finally, an EMG which involved plunging a needle into my muscle at various points, then sending an electrical current through to gauge the response. Basically, electrocution. Then, one day the dreaded phone call to come back into the surgery.

Abbie, I already knew.

The exact diagnosis was a mystery but I knew my symptoms enough to make sure you were in school when I went for the results. It was Sadie I asked to accompany me, who held my hand as the doctor gave me the results. It was Sadie I wanted beside me, for what was going to be said would devastate Liam and I needed time to deal with it.

303

Always aware of the power of words, this time I was on the side of them I didn't want. Each word spoken by the doctor was unwanted, hurtful, terrifying. Here are some of them:

ALS

No cure.

Life expectancy of two to five years.

Never seen it in someone so young.

When he listed the symptoms of the four stages, I let out a moan. My grip, my voice could, no would, be affected. As a writer can you imagine? The thought of living with all those stories inside me, with no way of getting it out. It was the very worse affliction I could contemplate.

As he spoke, Sadie straightened until she stretched enough I thought she might snap. Her hand stayed on my hand but I could see she wanted to pick a fight.

I stood, said 'thank you Doctor.'

'Wait, there is medication I can recommend.'

'Will it cure me?'

'Well no, but there's one to help with the slur, or the balance, or one they are developing may prolong your life for three to six months.'

'What's the side effects?'

'Well there's the chance of dizziness... '

'Huh.' I strode to the door.

'Wait we haven't talked about physical therapy or other options.'

I waved my hand at Sadie.

'Not now doctor, she needs time to process this. We'll ring you tomorrow and schedule another appointment.'

I didn't hear anymore. I moved as quick as I could to the car. Gasping for breath, I looked around for something to punch. When I stopped, Sadie wrapped her arms around me from behind. My legs buckled. She caught me.

'My grip Sadie, my voice. It's the worst thing that could happen. My stories.'

'That's the worst thing? Not getting out your stories?' She opened the car door, gestured for me to get in, then offered an arm to lever down. 'Don't worry about that, we'll hire someone to transcribe if your hands go.'

'What if it's my voice?'

'Then you use your hands.'

'What if it's both?'

She looked at me. 'Gabs, we'll find a way.'

'It's not about the stories,' I said.

'I know.'

It took her forever to move to the other side of the car, as if all the strength had left her movements, as if it took everything till then and now all her energy had seeped out.

All I could think about was you Abbie, about what my sickness would mean; how it would impact your life. What I couldn't contemplate was leaving you. In that car, in the time it took Sadie to walk from my side to her side, I vowed to defy the doctor's words, to make my own miracle. Although Sadie's eyes were brimming, she smiled on sitting. My Sadie, still trying to be strong. All I felt was numb. She drove.

'I don't care what that doctor says I'm not dying from this. I'm going to get better.'

Sadie kept her eyes on the road, but broke into a grin. 'Then it doesn't have a chance. Once you make up your mind it's screwed,' she squeezed my hand. 'That's my girl.'

Despite my words of determination, the tears came and I allowed them because that was the start, to heal I needed to remove the clogged emotions from my body. I would be kind tomorrow, I would nurture and heal and find ways to laugh and talk and release, but for that moment, I would allow myself the right to feel sorry about the diagnosis. Before you saw me Abbie, I would cry and let go.

Sadie pulled into a ditch and we leaned into each other and cried. She let me roar and wail. She matched me tear for tear. We stayed that way until it felt better to stop. Exhausted, we went home, where Sadie tucked me into bed and waited for you and Liam to return.

When I woke from a beautiful sleep, for a moment all was fine with the world. Then a heaviness formed in my stomach as I remembered. *I'm dying of a terminal disease.*

In the living room, the sounds of you playing meshed with Liam and Sadie's hushed voices. The urge to go join you was strong. Instead, I turned on my phone. Most of the information was horrific. Articles spoke of joints becoming rigid, of saliva drying up making the act of eating impossible, of disturbed emotions, like uncontrollable laughter or crying for no reason. Later stages read like a horror story: stage four listed possible causes of death from swelling in the lung muscles causing no way of air to get through. Ninety per cent of patients at that stage were paralyzed, most with speech gone too. So no movement, no way of speaking and possible suffocation.

The tears wouldn't stop. Yet, there was no way I was leaving that room without a plan. My family would look to me for the answers like they always did, and I would find them. Not for them, for me. It was time to do the things I needed to get better. I kept searching until I found something plausible.

They stood when they saw me. Suspecting something was going on, you ran into my arms, the smell from your hair strengthened my resolve.

'You know?' I asked Liam.

'I just said you went to the doctors, I didn't go into details,' Sadie said.

'Why didn't you ask me?' Liam asked, stroking the stubble on his chin.

There was no right answer. Instead, Liam chose another question.

'How bad are we talking here?'

'I'm not going to even acknowledge any negative. Anyway, it'll only start me off again. Why don't you explain Sade, while I make a coffee. Abbie, let's get you something yummy from the kitchen and turn on a movie. Then, us three are going to talk.'

Liam's eyes were red veined, the skin underneath looked thinner, inflamed even when I appeared again from the kitchen. Abbie, you didn't have a clue, licking your ice cream while watching your favourite show on the big screen. Liam put the coffee down as soon as I handed it to him, took me into his arms and sobbed into my neck. Sadie grasped her coffee from my outstretched arms. Then, I hugged my husband back.

'Sit,' I said as soft as I could. They both did.

'Forty eight people. That's the number of people recorded as reversing ALS. I know what I have to do, where I've been going wrong. I want you to listen to me and then you can speak.'

They stayed silent.

'For so long I kept everything bottled up. Liam, there is so much buried inside I can't even go there. The facts state that it's neurodegenerative and that they don't know how it's caused but I think I know how I got it. Ex-military are more likely to be diagnosed. Why do you think that is? What have people in the military got in common?'

Sadie and Liam looked at the other, confused.

'Trauma, that's what.'

Liam's head jerked up and the fear in his face was clear.

'There's so much I haven't dealt with. Starting with how my family died. Leaving England, losing contact with you Sadie for years, how we were, Liam.' I tapped my temple. 'Writing helped me escape but it's all still buried inside here. First step is to talk to someone about it, so I'm going to start counselling too. Then I'm going to book some holidays.

Life has been serious for too long. I want fun. I want laughter and it starts with the two of you burying the hatchet, for real, this time.'

'Gabs,' Liam said, with urgency.

I held my hand up. 'You are only tolerating each other for my sake but I need her Liam, and if you try and force me the other way I'll walk. That goes for you too Sade, you need to be friends with each other. You have to find a way to make it work. Because I'm sick of the stress. I'm sick of having to be between the two of you. I love you both and I'm tired of being forced to take sides or feel pressure to choose. Because the truth is, now, from this moment on, I choose me.' I pointed to the other side of the room. 'I choose me and Abbie.'

Sadie nodded. 'Whatever you want.'

Liam followed suit. 'Whatever it takes to get you better.'

I became a woman on a mission: taking theracurmin as most who reversed had, lifting weights to strengthen my muscles, replacing sugar with fruits and vegetables, eradicating alcohol from my life, taking long walks on the beach and swimming on the nice days. Endless comedies were watched as I no longer wanted any seriousness in my life. We went on day trips, saw beautiful sights, made many memories. When tired, I slept.

Stripped back to basics, the preciousness of life becomes more apparent. I spent hours watching as you played with your toys, or coloured, or while you slept, sending silent thanks to whoever was responsible for allowing me to witness such a sight. Each another day, was a blessing. Life simplified. My sole purpose was to remove any rot that festered inside, through meditation, breathing exercises, counselling. Long lists were wrote: of mistakes I made, of wrongs done to me, of forgiveness, of wishes, of dreams. I read copious self-help books. The counselling helped. For in the talking it through, I didn't just talk about forgiveness but actually forgave. Knowing the gift of my hands might disappear, I used them as much as possible, rooting out my brushes again to paint, something I swore I didn't have the time, or energy, after you were born. Most of the paintings were of you, my darling.

What this illness has taught me is there is always time for the things you love; time is never the real issue, allowing what you love to be your priority is.

On down days, when my muscles tightened or seized, I scooted down the steps from our house to the beach on my bum, my bad leg, the left, leaving long lines in the sand as I dragged it behind. If the beach was deserted, I screamed at the waves and kicked at the water, at the sand. I screamed for the wrongs done to me. I screamed for the wrongs I did. I screamed for the unfairness of developing a disease that was wreaking havoc on my body, burrowing into my nervous system. I wanted it gone.

At my three month check up, the doctor was shocked to find it hadn't advanced, the theracumin or the self help work or the muscle therapy had stalled the spasms and when I walked out of that surgery I would have put money on that I had the disease licked.

I finished writing the next book in a month. You were in school until one thirty by then, so I had plenty time to write. I couldn't stop the words on the page, they poured out as if they were always inside, just biding their time until I was ready. Instead of shelving the novel for a few months to create distance like I did with the others, I began editing straight away. From the first line I knew the book was different. It was a love story for my fans, giving them what I knew they would want, saying all I wanted them to know. It was heart and soul and blood and guts; it was everything inside me; it was all my knowledge; all the lessons I'd learned; all the words I wish I'd heard; all the love I wish I'd received. As I read it back, I knew I had produced something special. If I came across a particularly poignant line, shivers would run up and down my arms and I knew I had captured something in that sentence.

The publishers didn't want to wait the usual amount of time to process the novel, claiming the book was so cleanly written there wasn't a need for in depth editing like previous works. Secretly, I wondered if it was more to do with marketing a book by a tragic, dying woman the press could still interview, rather than a dead one who couldn't be pictured holding the book. Whatever their agenda, I was proud of what I wrote, proud I managed to finish.

Even though it was my fastest work by far, since its release, it has already become my biggest bestseller. Advance critics have classed it as my masterpiece.

Before any confirmation, I felt the turn, the deterioration. When I would pick up weights and couldn't manage as many lifts as the day before, or when you spilt your crayons on the floor and I couldn't make my fingers pinch to pick them up. By the time my speech slurred, I had already accepted there wouldn't be a cure. Acceptance was the hardest of all. I couldn't speak of it, until it became impossible to ignore the possibility of dying.

In secret, once I finished the novel, I worked on a second project: your book, this book. Reasoning, if I had my life documented while I still could, if I worsened and lost the use of my arms or voice, or if I died, there would be something in my own words for you to read, or, if I got better you would never have to see it because I could tell you the stories in person. God, Abbie as I write this, I hope you never see this book. The hardest part of accepting I might die is understanding that means leaving you. All I can think about is how I've failed. For the only job I had to do was stay alive.

Here's a snapshot of my present day. After I write in the mornings, when you run in the door, I close the computer and enjoy our time. We spend our afternoons in café's or on the beach or going for drives or play dates. I sit back and observe and even though sometimes I use a wheelchair now if I get too tired when we are out, I'm thankful. Every single moment is in focus. For the first time in my life, I am completely present. Liam is back to being the man I fell in love with. I wake up to cooked breakfasts or if the spasms have kept me awake, he leaves me in bed and takes you to school. It helps. Sadie comes everyday. Maureen even helps.

When I felt the tremors increasing, I relaxed my diet and allowed for an occasional glass of wine on our balcony overlooking the view. For the day will come when I will not be able to even hold the glass. One day I will not be able to swallow. Life is more beautiful when death hangs over you Abbie, not less. I only wish I knew that before.

Today they confirmed it was progressing at lightning speed. I sat alone. No one held my hand because if they had, afterwards they would have sent me to bed, they would have watched me like a hawk and then I wouldn't have been able to carry out my plan.

And here it is, for I'm sure now you will read this:

As I write, there is a time bomb on my words. Soon I will no longer be able to pick up a pen or tap at a keyboard. As it is, it is taking much longer to write. Even when that does happen, I will still get to see you every day, will still get to stay with you. At what cost though? Will you only remember me as the silent, immobile body that stares from the bed? The woman who freaks you out? No. A better person would. From the start I told you I would only write the truth.

What is the value of time if you cannot spend it the way you want to live? What is time if you are consumed with pain?

The doctor explained when it was the end it would happen quickly. Some organ would expand or stop. Hearts would attack, airways would swell and suffocate, throats would block. Death would only take minutes but the life before it would take longer to deteriorate. That is the bit I cannot bear.

Those extra months in between have been the best of my life. Your father will find it hard, he has moments where he is snappy but I know it is because he can't fathom life without me. My days of trying to fix it, fix him are over. I've relaxed my diet, drink if I feel like it, eat what I want. On borrowed time there's no point trying to be healthy. Isn't it ironic that for the first time since being a teenager I'm enjoying my food, I'm limited to what I can swallow? That's just how it goes.

As much as I can, I laugh. This time not to heal or for any agenda but just simply because I want to. The undercurrent through it all is knowing I will have to leave you. The thought of not being there for your big occasions floor me. It's why I wrote this.

Every book I've wrote has been to make you proud of me. Out of all of them, the one in your hands now is the one I want you to read most. Here, I'll admit it: I won't get to see you grow up; I won't get to be there on your wedding day or watch your own child, my grandchild, grow. Coming to terms with it is ongoing. This has helped, writing it down. It has helped me see where I went wrong. Abbie, I kept everything inside, I thought if I ignored the pain, it would disappear and that would be it but it festered and grew. All the pain I tried to bury. Yet, I also know I couldn't do it any other way. To do it differently, I would have needed to turn into another person.

This book is meant as a record. It wasn't written as a way for me to leave your father or even to turn you against him. After I'm gone, you can make your own opinion of who I was, of my mistakes and faults but also as a sign of my love, as a way to stay with you. Words are the only way I know how to achieve it. Doing so has been cathartic, a way of forgiving myself for the stupid turns, for the wrong decisions. Also, as a way to relive the happiness. Complete confession, the truth will help Sadie to get joint custody after if needed. I don't want Sadie to take you away but I want that safety net Abbie, because I worry about the outcome of when you get to the age of answering back, when you won't be the sweet girl he expects, when I can't be the buffer who softens out his reactions and his anger.

Also, I wrote this book for Sadie, as written proof of how much I loved her. I wrote this for me too, for Gabrielle, who needed to believe love could fix everything.

Remember when I spoke of the water calling? Please understand my last actions. Before it gets too bad I will go. Please know I wouldn't leave you until then. Every day I have with you now is a bonus. A death sentence hangs over me but at least I've had time to prepare. It's strange to think I will be in past tense when you read this. It does scares me. Your father's reaction after worries me; I don't blame him Abbie, please don't either. He always did what he believed was right, even when he was completely wrong.

For a long time I focused on being a victim. A lost soul on drugs, an orphan, an abused wife. Learn from my mistakes Abbie, because I forgot there was a choice. That I didn't have to accept it. I told myself my love was stronger than the hurt and even now, I believe it was. To this day, I love your father. Love diffused our arguments. When I found a way to get a handle on it, we both thrived. In order to get a handle on it though, it meant submission. It meant showing him love when I might not want to.

In a way, I was right. Love can change people. It did soften your father, it took the fight from him. What I didn't factor was while he softened, I hardened. While his walls crumbled, I picked up those bricks and built my own around me. This I believe, caused my illness.

The past can destroy us or it can be our greatest lesson. For a very long time the past hung around all three of us, tightening its coil, rotating around our lives, influencing our decisions, leading us into situations.

I want you to know nothing mattered more to me than you. I would have ripped up every manuscript I wrote if it bought me another year. I would have taken a million more bruises, a billion more put downs. I would have taken that disease over and over if it meant I would save you from the pain of seeing me die. If it meant walking away from both Liam and Sadie, I wouldn't have even looked back.

A shift has begun in your father. The closeness that came with the diagnosis is waning. Instead, a separation is beginning, splitting the bond. A distance is growing between the gap of us. I know why. For I'm doing the one thing he most feared, the thing I always promised I wouldn't, I'm leaving him. There is no comeback from this one. Neither of us can fix it. So, instead of declarations of love, like you see in the movies, there's a pulling away; of conversation, of affection, of emotion. Avoidance has taken over. He doesn't want to be in the same room as me anymore. If I'd hoped for announcements or confessions or shared emotions, I'll have to take that into the ground. It doesn't matter. I've resigned myself to it now. Liam is dealing with it the only way he knows. It's the only protection he can give himself from the onslaught of hurt he will feel after.

Every day, while you're at school, I make my way to the water. Some days I have to lean on Sadie, others I manage on my own. The doctors have advised me to stay in bed, to reserve my energy but until my dying day Abbie, I will find a way to rebel. We sit on the beach by the water's edge where the tide and sand meet, we wiggle our feet at the brim like we did when we were kids. Nothing has really changed since then. We knew everything that was important. I look at that water and I have forgiven myself all my wrongs. It takes up too much energy to hold on to now.

The water calls out to me day and night. Soon I will go. In taking my own life, I hope there has been no shame for you. I hope the reasons have at least been explained about why I left the way I did. My time is soon, I can feel it in my breath as it struggles to catch in my chest, I feel it in my muscles when I attempt to lift my arm to stroke your hair. My bones are weary. You wince when I ask you to cuddle, because you see I'm breaking down. That, I cannot accept.

Writing my life down on paper has been cathartic. There was so much shame in what I let your father do - for what I allowed him to be. Now I see I set a basis for how I should be treated because of how I viewed myself. I still don't understand why I disliked myself so much. Writing has helped me forgive your father's mistakes. It has helped me come to terms with my own.

The time is upon me to act. If I leave it much longer I won't be able to do it. My speech is slow. It takes forever to say what I need now if I don't use an app or the computer. To write, I have word prediction so I don't have to type as much. Also, I have a laserwriter now, a device that hooks to glasses or a hat where I point a laser at a board and it turns to speech. At night, I need oxygen, for I struggle to keep a steady breath. With difficulty swallowing, crunchy foods are impossible, my food is starting to resemble baby purees. They have scheduled a tracheotomy which I have no intention of carrying out. It has given me an end date.

Don't feel sad. It will be quick. These days I like to focus on only the good, on the sound of laughter, on the sight of the sunset, on the memories that make me smile, on the beauty of you. Wrapped in a blanket, I sit on the balcony, sip tea, watch the ocean. Or on the beach I watch as you dance and cartwheel on the sand and am grateful. I truly lived. I experimented. Danced until the sun rose. Consumed every drink that exists. Experienced a living being growing inside me. Gave birth and survived. Spent time with the most beautiful child this world could produce. I was born into a family who adored me, who were mine for a while and then weren't. My dream to write became real. More money than I could spend came my way. I tried to look fear in the eye. I loved freely. Too much, maybe. It could be argued that sometimes I loved to my detriment, but it doesn't matter, for I will leave this earth never regretting how much I loved you. Or how much I told you I loved you. Or how much I hugged and kissed you.

That's what matters Abbie.

My hope is that you remember how much I loved you. For my love to ingrain enough while I was alive to carry it with you after my death. I hope you feel it now.

After I'm gone, read my books. Earlier, I wrote that you won't find me there but you will if you search, because how could I not be? My life is in the little details: when Sebastian takes a trip to France and stands under the Eiffel Tower, I fulfilled my families last journey; when Nathan wears a red helmet during his fight against his enemy it was a nod to Darren who was fascinated with gladiators and adored his red beanie; when Sabine, the girl who never gave up turned into a beautiful woman, into a beautiful mother, it was my ode to Lily, the only way to complete her life. Or when the Peterson's took a train through Italy, or the Martell's honeymoon in Amsterdam. It was my way of making up to my family, of giving them an outlet to achieve their dreams. A way to apologise too.

Behind the words, behind the happy endings, behind the characters' pain, I'm there. Hiding, reliving, remaking, redoing. I'm there dreaming, surviving, enduring. On reflection, it's a place I'll still exist. With each book I left a piece, a grain of identity, entwined in each sentence. And a part of you Abbie, because you are evident there too. You are the children who my characters love, you are the reward at the end of the story, you are the prize, the happiness they all strive for. You are the joy, the love, the life force. You are the reason for every word.

At the right time I will go. My family wait for me, I feel that now, I hear them calling and if I can, I will wait for you too. Don't come too soon.

Goodbye my sweet, beautiful girl. I love you. Mum xxx

Abbie

Blank space filled the rest of the page. Abbie flipped. Page after page of white until she reached the hardcover. All that was left was empty. Then she roared.

She thought she would choke on her tears.

'It can't be it. That can't be the end. Sadie... please.'

Sadie's arms wrapped around Abbie's and she held her until her tears stopped. As they rocked, Abbie continued to sob.

'Do something. Make it stop, make it better, please. I've lost her. I've lost her all over again.'

When they broke apart, for the first time since Abbie met her, Sadie seemed afraid.

'There's more.'

More

Abbie

Sadie reached into the inside of her jacket, she hesitated, then handed Abbie a sealed white envelope, browned a little at the edges.

'This is the last of it. I don't know what is inside. At the same time, I know exactly what it will say.'

The handwriting on the front of the letter was identical to the inscription at the front of the book. On closer inspection, the brown on the edges wasn't from age but blood.

For Abbie.

'I'm going for a walk. I'll leave you be. When I come back, if I can, I'll answer whatever questions you have,' Sadie said.

She wrung her hands once and picked up her jacket. 'Or if you don't want me, I'll be on the strand.'

Sadie closed the hotel door with a soft click.

Before she ripped it open, Abbie hesitated, noticing the ominous feeling that had come over her. Here was the truth about what happened between her father and her mother. Did she really want to know?

With shaking hands, Abbie opened the letter. It was typed.

Abbie took a deep breath and read the first line.

Split Second

Gabrielle

It happened fast. Sadie helped me climb the steps from the beach. On seeing your father through the glass, she waved goodbye as she was rushing to work.

Your book lay open on his lap. The picture on the wall was gone, the safe behind it prised open by a knife abandoned on the floor. The deeds to a house in Galway lay next to it. Before I closed the door, he ran at me, caught me by the throat.

He looked so hurt, like I'd betrayed him. Maybe if I'd said something, anything, I could have calmed him down, but I was in shock. I couldn't breathe.

He tightened his grip. I tried to step away. When I couldn't, I slapped at his hands, trying to free his from my throat. There was a struggle, we fell to the floor with him on top. I placed my hands on his hands.

'Me, speak,' I managed.

He softened his grip but stayed sitting on top of me

'You're leaving me,' Liam said, his voice catching.

It took forever to get the words out.

'Sadie's... house. Abbie's... after. I... *am*... leaving... ' His eyes widened. '...to... die.'

Madness flashed in his eyes.

'You promised you'd never leave. You're a liar. That house is for you, to run away with Abbie. I'll lose her too.'

'No,' I said.

'Why would Sadie need custody then? I read what you said about me in your book. She's going to take her off me. You want to break us up, you're afraid I could hurt her. How could you think I would hurt my daughter? Isn't it enough I'm going to lose you without taking her as well?'

He tightened his grip until black dots appeared. I hit at his hands, tried to unclasp them, but he only squeezed tighter.

'How could you write down what I did? Abbie will think I'm a monster. It's not how it happened. You exaggerated, you... '

I heard a noise, a wet noise, a squelch, and then your father groaned. He let go and I could breathe again. But then I couldn't, because all his weight fell on me. A multitude of expressions ran over him: fear, regret, love. There was a knife sticking out of his neck. Liam pulled at it, I called out to stop but by the time the words came it was too late, for the second he pulled it out, blood spurted everywhere. My hand couldn't stop the blood, no matter how much pressure or how much I tried to cover the wound, it leaked through my fingers. Liam gargled. His eyes went glassy. Sadie stood behind us in shock.

'Get... towel.' I shouted.

Sadie ran to the kitchen, coming back with a dishcloth. I took it, placed it over his neck, but by then the gargling had stopped. The blood Abbie, the blood. Ten seconds was all it took. Ten seconds for the one I loved, the man I trusted, my lover, my friend, to die.

'I'll ring an ambulance,' Sadie said, running for a phone.

The breath was leaving me from his weight. 'Help.' I managed.

Sadie squatted down but hesitated to touch him. His body lay on me, heavier now.

'Lift,' I said between wheezes.

She shook her head, the horror of what she had done sinking in.

'I... can't... breathe.'

Sadie pushed his shoulder away, turning Liam's face to her. It was too much for her to see, she dropped his shoulder, Liam's jaw crashed down on my nose.

Sadie helped me push him and then I was free. My Liam, your daddy, my beautiful husband, lay lifeless on the floor. I checked for a pulse. None. I checked for breath. None. I knew it was pointless, but I did anyway. He was gone Abbie, and my insides tore.

Sadie was crying, saying sorry over and over. I made sure not to touch her.

'I... always... said... I'd... go... into... the... water. It's... time.'

Sadie looked at me.

'Let... me... take... the... blame.'

'No way. He would have killed you. It was self defense.'

'You... already... have... a... suspended... sentence... for... a... knife. You'll... never... get... custody. No... hospital... bed. No... op. My... way.'

Sadie rubbed the tears away and bucked up her composure. Her voice was steady when she spoke again. 'If that's what you want, then I go into the water with you.'

I knew she meant it. I knew how stubborn she was. 'OK,' I said.

Liam's blood covered us. 'People... will... see... blood... and... stop... us. I'll... shower...then... you. I'll... text... Maureen... to... pick... up... Abbie.'

Sadie nodded. I went to the bathroom and turned on the shower, but didn't go in. My bathroom has a second door to our bedroom, so I slipped in there and used the time to write this note.

This is what I am about to do. As Sadie showers, I will wipe the knife clean and then cover the handle with my fingerprints. I will lay it next to your father at the angle it would have fallen. Then I will kiss him on his cheek and tell him for the last time I love him. I will dress in mine and Sadie's bloody clothes, then I will take the book and put this note inside. On top of the clean clothes I've left, I will leave a note for Sadie.

Please understand she killed your father out of love. Out of love for me. She did it to save me, Abbie. There was no hate involved in killing your father. She did it to end his hate. End his anger. It was my fault. If I had told him the truth about the house, he wouldn't have thought I was leaving. The omission ended your father's story. Ended my story.

Whatever is in the afterlife, I'm not sure. All I know is it's time to go. Your father shouldn't face what's on the other side alone. I don't expect you to understand the choices I made. With Liam, I always saw past the bad times, the man I saw craved love. He was the real Liam.

One decision can change your life. If Miss Simpson directed me to a different seat or if I said nothing when Maureen hissed at Sadie that first day. It changed the course of our lives. It set out a path for what was to become. Or if I hadn't gone to Maureen's house that day and met your father. If I had sat in the car with my parents. Or what if they lived? What if Sadie hadn't picked up the knife?

I couldn't help Sadie back when we were kids Abbie, I couldn't take away her pain. Here I can. This is the way to right the wrongs that were done to her. This is the way to right mine and your father's wrongs.

No matter what, I have to leave you, there is no say in that anymore. In Liam's death, I had no choice either. Sadie's only choice was between Liam dying or both me and her, because if she had tried to pull him off, he would have killed us, I am sure. The last bit of sanity I used to reason with him had gone. The only choice she had was who would die and if it came down to me or Liam, she would always choose me.

The only thing I can choose is the aftermath.

Why let Sadie suffer? Why punish her when all she got so far was shit? That was why I bought the house, I wanted to give her a place no one could take away, a house she couldn't be locked out from, or locked in. A house that was hers no matter what. The mistake I made was hiding it from your father. Look at what it caused.

I hope you can forgive me. I hope you can forgive your father, too. He *was* a good man; he was just flawed like us all.

More than anything, I hope that you forgive Sadie. If you're reading this, then she already knows the ramifications of this letter. You could tell someone, and they would still prosecute her. If you're reading this, it means she took the chance anyway. However old you are now, in her note, I asked her to give it to you when you're old enough to understand. I bought her some time to live, Abbie. Gave her a chance to love. She always deserved that.

Sadie's shower will finish any minute, so I have to go. When I put this pen down, I will go to the sliding door with the sea view. I will walk down those side steps, touch sand, go finally to the water. I like to think I won't hesitate, but I know if I do, it will only be because of you. A second more on the same earth as you is everything. I love you, Abbie. I'm so sorry.

Open

Abbie

Was it possible for a heart to crack? All those years of blame and her mother hadn't killed her father and after everything she had been told or read about and thought of as fact, she hadn't known her mother at all. Even at the very end, facing death, despite everything he did, her mother had still loved Liam.

All the hatred from Maureen, from her grandparents, from neighbours and strangers and the news was undeserved. They were all wrong. And then there was her father, a very different person from the saint Maureen would have her believe. A man who was deeply flawed, deeply troubled but who had loved her mother, had loved his daughter, and had died believing his wife betrayed him.

What broke her was picturing the lonely walk her blood-soaked mother made into that cold water.

What hurt most of all, was that it was over; there was no more to read; a blank page represented what she would get from her mother from now on. Nothing. No more words.

Abbie sobbed until her throat hurt, her voice went hoarse, and it pained her to swallow, reminding her even more what it must have been like to be her mother with ALS. The energy drained out with her tears. After a while, she sat, sated, and rested her head on the headboard.

After what seemed like hours, the door opened. Sadie stepped in, closing the door behind her, she stood against it.

'If you don't want me here, I'll go. Or if you want me to make a statement or...'

'Why did you go into the house?' Abbie's voice came out scratchy.

'I heard her scream. I was...'

'I don't want to hear how you killed my father. Tell me what happened after.'

Sadie nodded, knowing now for sure Gabrielle had revealed all.

'We were meant to go into the water together.' Sadie said, sitting opposite Abbie. 'Your mother insisted we have a shower because she said we would get noticed if someone saw us covered in blood. As I waited for your mother, I sat next to your father in a daze. One minute he was there and then he wasn't and it was all my doing. It was shock, I think, cos if I was thinking clearly I would have offered to help your mother in the shower. When she shouted to go in, I followed her instructions on autopilot, not wondering why I couldn't see her or why she left the water running for me or how she kept it so clean. Under that hot water, I washed off your father's blood and tried to understand how I could have killed a man. How I could be so evil that I didn't even regret it. In the shower, I saw sense. We couldn't go into the water. The more I thought about it, the clearer it got. There was only one thing to do and that was to hold my hands up and admit what I did. Your mother could testify that he was going to kill her. In the shower I realised I didn't want to die, but I didn't want to live in guilt either, so I would do the time and once served, I would get on with my life. The hot water was magnetic, its force kept me to the spot, knowing what was to come, how I would have to convince your mother, how I was going to have to face your father's body again, I prolonged leaving, letting the jets hit me with its heat. As I stepped out of the shower,

Abbie, I swear, I thought about you, on your own, with only Maureen and those horrible grandparents. It wouldn't take much to convince your mother that at least I could fight for custody when they released me. Gabrielle always chose the right thing to do.'

Sadie wiped at her nose.

'There was a note on some clothes on the bed and I knew from the bloody fingerprints it was from your mother.'

Sadie let out a single sob, catching her breath.

'Keep going,' Abbie urged.

Sadie nodded, taking deep breaths until she was steady.

'She asked me to collect you from school. She had texted and answered from my phone so the records would show a conversation. Stacked underneath was the book and envelope for you and the deeds to the house in Galway. She had already given me the keys. She had even laid out a clean change of clothes for me. I changed and as I heard sirens, I looked out at the beach. A crowd had formed by the water's edge, and I knew Gabrielle had done it, she'd walked in. I was too late. My clothes were gone. I couldn't stay in that house with your father lying dead so I sneaked out the front, and I walked up the road, to my shame Abbie.' Her voice caught. 'Even in death, your mother had the last say between us.' She shook her head, as if trying to gather the strength to speak.

'On autopilot, I did as your mother instructed. I picked you up, then I went to Maureen. She pulled you inside, said to me, "that bitch killed my brother." I offered to mind you while she went to the Garda station, but she tried to shun me from the door. I told her Gabrielle would want me to have joint custody. That was my mistake. She said, "who told you Gabrielle is dead?" I stuttered that I didn't know, that if Gabs did it she would go to jail but Maureen could always see through me. She took one look at me standing at that door and smelt my guilt. She said. "You did something didn't you? Trouble follows you wherever you go.

You dirty everything, you taint the world with your ugliness. Did you do something to my brother?" I shook my head. I backed away. "If you did I'll make sure you never see Abbie again." Maureen always knew how to intimidate me. I told her I'd heard it on the radio that people said a woman went into the water, and only brought you to Maureen's in case something was going on in Scart's End. As soon as I got away from that door, I panicked, and ran straight to Galway. What I should have done was stay and fight. The right thing to do would have been to tell the truth but I didn't. Instead I freaked out and let your mother take the blame. I left you. Back then I was a coward, but I'm here to make amends. Whatever you want to do now, I will respect. You deserved to hear your mother's side. I'm sorry.'

There were many things that ran through Abbie's mind to say. To go for the jugular like Sadie went for her father's. To attack the source of all her pain.

'If you're looking for my forgiveness, you won't get it.'

'I'm not.'

'You will always be the person who took my father and mother from me.' Abbie squeezed the bridge of her nose, trying to halt a headache. 'Just because she would have died anyway doesn't make it right. The world thinks she's guilty of something she didn't do. Because of you, I wasn't there when she died. I should have been sitting in a hospital and holding my mother's hand. You robbed me of our last goodbye. You ruined my good memories of her and you took away both my parents.'

An opaque tear ran down Sadie's cheek, staining the skin dark brown.

'But you took away your friend too, and you wouldn't have done it unless you had no choice.' Abbie let out a shaky breath. 'I want one thing. Leave me the book, let me keep her voice. If you give me that, I won't let anyone see and I'll keep your secret, Sadie, but I won't forgive you.'

'Abbie, if you want to go to the guards, I'll go. You can show them the book. I can't live with the guilt anymore.'

When Abbie looked close enough, she could see the little girl with the matted hair waiting for Gabrielle.

'My mother was right. They punished you enough.'

Once the truth was out, there was nothing more to say as far as Abbie was concerned. Her mother was gone, and she wanted Sadie gone too. Too stunned to speak, and drained from what she read, they kept silent in the car, and when she arrived near her house, she closed the door of the car without a goodbye.

Sadie left that night.

Before, After And When

Abbie

It seemed to Abbie that her life could be divided into three different sections: before her parents' death, after, and when she learned the truth. Since, every single person, relationship, and place had altered. Maureen could never be viewed in the same light. Nothing was the same, nothing could ever be the same.

It was hard to drag her body from the bed most days. How could she feel fresh loss for a woman that was gone from her life for ten years? She did though, it was as if her parents' death had created a split inside her heart and only when the book had filled the space, had she noticed it was missing. The words had satiated her but now they were gone.

Her mother walking in to the sea haunted her. Her father's eyes as the knife plunged in, thinking Gabrielle had betrayed him replayed in her nightmares. And then there was Sadie, holding the knife, the one who changed her parents' story, who changed Abbie's life forever. She felt the loss of Sadie too, because with her visits there had been an underlying hope of finally getting the answers she was afraid to ask. Now there were no more questions, there were no more answers.

One warmer than usual morning, she cycled to the furthest point of Knockfarraig, where she locked her bike on a pole and walked along the beach. Ignoring the stares of locals, who no doubt knew why she was there, which was the exact reason she had long avoided the stretch. Now though, she didn't care, she trudged the sand and thought, *let them gossip all they want, I know the truth.*

Eyeing the houses at the top of Scart's End, she spotted the house which once upon a time had been hers, with its black glass peeking out above the cliff edge. She traced the line from the gate of the steps to the sea and sat in the sand halfway between. This was the trail, the line her mother walked. Was the sea calm that day or were the waves violent? She closed her eyes and her nostrils filled with the smell of seaweed.

'You can go up the steps if you want,' a voice said.

A man in his late fifties stood looking down at her. She shielded her eyes from the sun but saw it was Simon O' Doherty, a fisherman known in the town. A pleasant fella usually, she was surprised him of all people would say something.

'I'm grand where I am thanks.'

He didn't leave. Instead he pointed at the sand, to the spot beside her. She sighed, nodded her approval. From his bag he took out a folding stool and sat. He stared out at the sea. 'I was there that day.'

This got her attention.

'I always wondered when you would look for answers. Been waiting for ya, didn't think it was my business to approach ya like, sure I didn't want to cause any trouble and I know how Maureen is.'

'Hmm,' Abbie said not committing.

'For twenty years I've fished here. The salmon love it. If it's a good catch I sell to the hotels in town. Keeps me afloat. Your mother knew me all her life, course I knew Liam too, for my sins.'

'For your sins?'

Simon took off his cap, revealing a circle of bare skin in the middle ringed with floppy hair. He scratched the top of his smooth head. 'Ah, we had a few run ins over the years. He didn't like me fishing around here, said I was a peeping Tom but I swear, I never, I wasn't the sort like.'

Abbie nodded, to show she understood.

'Your mother wasn't like that. She used to bring me tea when it was cold or an iced drink on the hot and always with a scone or some treat.'

Abbie hugged her knees with this information, it was unbelievable how happy it made her.

'Some days she looked very sad like, as if the world was on her shoulders and I kept my distance cos I could tell she wanted some alone time. And then one time her leg was acting all gammy and another time her hands shook terrible as she tried to carry the tray for me, and I said to her, "don't be bringing me any treats anymore", and she said, "I'll tell you what, come up for it instead", and I said to her, "sure how can I there's a lock on the gate up to your house?", and she said, "not to worry I'll give you a key" and she did. And at four on the dot every day I done just that. It got me down when she was getting worse, when she started wearing that thing to help with her speech or when I saw them passing with her in the wheelchair but the days you were with her on the beach were my favourite cos she would be back to herself, clapping and making noise.'

'You said you saw her that day?'

Simon held the cap out in front of him. 'That I did. I was over on the cliff by the new houses with my binoculars, cos I was having a slow day and I was scanning the water for signs of dark movement or bubbles, when I heard the gate go. I looked down hoping to get a wave from her but she didn't look up. She wasn't walking very fast, her leg was dragging and the other one wasn't much better, I thought I'll shout down to her when she sits on the sand. But she kept going which I thought was odd cos she wasn't in her swim gear. By the time I realised she was gonna go in, it was too late. I shouted down to the people on the beach but the wind was strong that day and none of them heard me.

A load of them came out in droves after, talking to the papers about her being covered in blood but none of them tried to stop her, I'll tell you that for something. Mind if I smoke?'

'You're grand. What did she seem like to you? On the day I mean?'

Simon lit his cigarette and took a deep inhale, then spoke on the exhale, the smoke dispelling with every word.

'Determined is what I'd say, I thought to myself, that girl has somewhere she wants to go. Not once did she stop or look around, just walked in a straight line till she disappeared under. And I don't mean like diving or anything, she walked out and kept walking and hopping kinda, bobbing like, as if she was in the deep end of a pool but wanting to go further and when she was well out, only a dot, she just went under.'

Abbie blinked quickly to stop the welling tears from spilling. She could picture the scene, she could see the way her mother did it.

'You said I could go up the steps. How?'

Simon inhaled. With his other hand, he stuck a thumb backwards, so she looked behind.

'Sure, the new owners are scanty bastards. Never changed the gate or the lock. Most of the time they ain't even here, it's their summer home excuse you me, only coming down on the weekend if we see them at all any other season. No one's there now. I always thought to myself, some day Gabby's young one will come looking, so I kept it on me, just in case like.'

He took a deep pull on the cigarette and then standing took out his wallet. 'You wanna go?'

Abbie looked at the sea. 'I'm not sure.'

'Come on, you can see the back of your house,' he said.

As she climbed the steep steps, she imagined her mother having to go down on her bum to reach the beach. She laid her hand flat on the one above. This step had felt her mother's skin, it had known her footprint, her gait, bore her weight, absorbed the dripping sea salt water from her skin as she padded home.

At the top she marvelled at the bird's eye view that had once been her back garden. The view pricked open a memory. She remembered that view. She remembered running down those steps. She remembered the smell of the sea standing right where she was now. Simon pointed into the far distance to the left, at least five houses down.

'I was well over there when I saw her go in, so it took me some time to run down and then the clever girl had locked the gate so I had to struggle to take the key out. By then she had disappeared under the water but I went and I ran, shedding my shoes and my word, the water was cold that day but I kept going, kept diving under and all I could see was the sand and seaweed and the waves were fairly vicious and at one stage I nearly went under myself and then someone shouted that they could see something and I turned around and there was plenty of a crowd after forming and I followed his pointed finger and sure enough there was something kind of floating, and the thought crossed me that at least twenty minutes must've gone by since her head went under but I kept going and went in that direction and it was her hair that was floating, everything else was still underneath and I tried to lift her to the surface but no matter how I tried she kept going back down and she was a ton weight, so I turned her on her back and she was a funny colour and I thought, my word that woman is dead.'

It only takes two minutes to lose consciousness after inhaling water.

Simon stopped to check Abbie's reaction. When she didn't start to cry, he carried on with his story.

'So I tried to swim with her like that but I kept on sinking down and I couldn't put my finger on it but then I thought, sure she has something in her pockets and sure enough, I pulled out these large stone balls that I'd seen in her garden and I tell you, I never told a single soul about that until today. Because you're the only one that should know and do you know what my first thought was?'

'What?'

'That he finally drove her to it. Course, I didn't know your father was up there all murdered like but I'll tell you now, whatever happened up there happened in defence. Your mother was a lady. And a saint. And no matter how anyone else tries to spin it, Knockfarraig was worse off without her.'

'Thank you Simon,' she said.

He wrung his cap then. 'I'm sorry I didn't save her. If only I'd moved when I saw her walking. I knew something was up.'

Abbie placed a hand on his arm.

'Drowning saved her from a much more painful death. You did what she would have wanted most Simon, you found her body. Because of that I can visit her grave. Do you know what?'

'What?' His face was full of hope.

'I think she knew you would. I think she felt you watching her and that gives me great comfort that she wasn't all alone going into that water.'

'You reckon?'

She answered with the truth. 'I really do.'

When he offered to sneak her over the wall to see the outside of the house, she refused. There was no need.

After that, she sought out the places her mother had mentioned in the book, hovering around the old house her mother grew up, every pavement slab was examined, every wall was scrutinised for clues. Going into town, she stood outside the bar Gabrielle wrote about, going anywhere at all that might make her feel closer. Sometimes she wished she asked Sadie for her number, because despite how she felt about her, she would have liked to text to ask her random questions, like what was her mother's favourite flavour ice cream or colour.

One day, when she was walking with the lads in the park, one of them pointed higher at one of the barks in the tree at an etching and Abbie squealed on reading:

Gabs + Sade 4ever

At the beach, she sat on the sand and took off her shoes. She wiggled her feet where the water met beach like she pictured two girls her age doing too. One dark, one pale. Two sisters.

Abbie read the book again from start to finish, taking in more than the first time when questions needed to be answered. The second time the details meant more. With no need to rush, the pieces already knotted together, she found she could picture them as real characters. Once she didn't have to pull apart the meaning of each chapter, she could just enjoy her mother's way with words.

At night she poured over the pages of her mother's novels, as if looking for hidden messages under the typed ink. With the door locked, she read and delighted when she came across a sentence that was as if wrote solely for her.

Every time Gloria watched her daughter Aisling sleep she cried. How many hours had she marvelled at the child? How many times had she lay down beside her and watched her chest rise and fall? How many times had she placed her hand on that chest and waited for the bump of the beat.

Not enough times. A thousand years would never be enough.

Had she ever been that peaceful? Was this what her own mother thought as she slept as a child? Often, she wondered how she managed to birth such a beauty, such an object of perfection, such an exquisite human. Aisling was every good part of her stacked up and multiplied and she would do everything in her power to make sure she believed it.

Her mother had been right. Abbie found her in many lines like this:

The first thing you need to know is love saves us all. Even in death. Even if the cause of death is love. Or in the dying, love can heal the pain. Love can release us.

Another night she read:

Her family let her down over and over but Sabine knew her friend never would. Ursula was more a sister to her than her own. Some sisters are destined never to be friends, forced to exist alongside the other through birth. Then there are others that appear in your life when you need them most. Who stay with you in your darkest days, who stand beside you when you are at your worst. Who still love you when you despise who you are. Who see you when you are blind. They are the ones whose bond can never break. They are the sisters you choose.

In the quest for more, each time Maureen left the house, Abbie went searching. For what she didn't know, proof of the life before maybe? Could it be possible that Maureen destroyed every item from the previous house? The woman was vindictive enough. Still, Abbie held onto some hope, tackling one room at a time, drawer after drawer. Time consuming, Abbie had to be careful to put everything back the exact way in case Maureen suspected anything. There weren't many places to rummage.

Abbie tried to think like her aunt, to picture where she would consider a safe hiding place. After hours in her bedroom rifling through each sock and piece of underwear, she came across one piece of interest in a jewellery box. A small key. Maureen didn't hold onto anything that didn't serve a purpose; whatever the key opened was significant. All she had to do was find it. After searching every nook, and section of the house all she'd found was more frustration. Maureen wouldn't hide anything outside; too conscious of what others thought, anything to do with her mother wouldn't stay anywhere a stranger could discover it. Whatever that box held, wherever it was, Maureen would keep it near.

After two weeks of searching, the only place left to check was the attic. Abbie delayed it for a reason. With no ladder, there didn't seem to be a way to open the attic door. Even ten feet away Abbie could see the key she had was too small. One day when Joe was over, she pointed to it.

'Would you know how to open that?'

Joe shrugged like it was a dumb question. 'With an allen key.'

'Do you have one?'

'My dad has. Why?'

As much as she'd fallen for Joe, she was wary. He had never mentioned her past but that in itself was strange, usually her parents' death was the first subject someone brought up in conversation. The fact that Joe didn't, made her wonder if he genuinely wasn't interested or if he was just biding his time waiting for her to bring it up. In the past there were friends, who months down the line began prodding, taking an interest in her bedroom, the fascination with her stuff, looking for something, anything, that could be used to share. Those friendships didn't last long after that.

Abbie wanted to trust him. She also needed someone's help and if it was going to be anyone, why not him?

'Do you think you could get me a ladder and an allen key?'

'Why don't you ask Maureen?'

Abbie shrugged, trying to seem casual. 'There's some old art stuff up there. She'd probably say it will spread dust or something. You know what she's like.'

'Sure,' he said and Abbie loved him more for not pushing. 'You want me to bring it round tomorrow?'

'Nah. How's Saturday? Maureen's got book club at one so we could do it then?'

Up there, she wasn't disappointed. Canvases were stacked in one corner, most of the paintings were of a child, of Abbie. Hidden under blankets, box after box were labelled Scart's End. Joe pulled open one.

'Woah,' he said, pulling out what looked like a copy book. He flicked through it. 'These are your mother's notes, for her books I'd say. You'd make a wad selling them.'

And there it was. She pushed down the fact that Joe was interested in her mother's death.

'Joe, don't. They're private.'

He threw it back in the box. 'Sorry for looking. What did you want then?'

'Pictures maybe?'

'K,' he said, scowling.

In one, she found a small tin box and inserted the key. It turned.

'What's that?' Joe asked.

His eagerness grated. Asking him had been a mistake.

'Not sure yet.'

She opened it only slightly ajar, blocking his view.

'It's like that, is it? You know what, Abbie, I'll leave you look alone.'

'Joe don't take it bad, it's just... complicated, OK?'

He swung his legs over the hole in the floor. 'Whatever.' He dropped down out of sight.

'Joe!'

The right thing to do would be to follow him. Time pressed on. If she followed him, she would waste precious minutes when there was only a short amount of time until Maureen came back. She looked down at what was in her hands. Joe could wait, she wasn't going to waste the opportunity.

Inside the box was pictures, of Abbie and Gabrielle, in various poses. Of Gabrielle covered in pink make up with Abbie behind her pulling at her hair. This made her laugh. Gabrielle mid kiss, her lips touching Abbie's cheek, the image making her own hand touch that spot of skin. Some were taken at the beach. Pictures with Sadie holding Abbie, of tiny white fingers wrapped around a caramel one. Others were with her father. A handsome man grinning at a girl. A girl who laughed back.

For the first time she got to see the O'Neill family. Her grandparents beaming into the camera, their hands on the shoulders of their children. Darren, Sam, Gabrielle and Lily. The tears came for how alike they were. She stroked her grandmother's face.

'Thank you for loving my mother.'

At the very bottom was her mother's rings, the diamond once her grandmother's too, slipped onto Abbie's finger without effort. There was also a memory stick with an inscription that read: *If ever I should die.*

Abbie clasped it tight. The box was enough for the moment. This was what she had been looking for. When she edged to the hole her feet dangled into air. The ladder was gone.

Rungs

Abbie

Joe didn't come when she called him. Even after the fifth time, there was no sign of him or the ladder. Maureen would be back any minute. Abbie contemplated jumping. The staircase was dangerously close; if she fell she would definitely break a leg, or worse.

She tried her mother's way.

'Please Joe. I'm sorry. All you wanted to do was help, and I acted like a total bitch.'

Within seconds, Joe appeared from her bedroom, leaning on the doorway. He folded his arms and she could see he would make her grovel. *This is what it felt like to be my mother.*

'I'm sorry,' she repeated. 'After going to the trouble of getting the ladder and the allen key, I treated you like that. It's just when I saw those things up there it brought up these weird feelings. It was wrong of me to take it out on you.'

Joe vanished from the doorway. A moment later, the ladder reappeared. Getting down as soon as she could, she sighed in relief once her feet felt ground. Joe sidestepped her, moving up the rungs of the ladder, he shut the attic door. Back down, she hugged him. 'Forgive me?' she said.

He kissed her on the nose. 'Sure. You find anything of interest?'

'Not really. Just a bunch of old junk. Those copy pads are the only things that look like they might be worth anything.'

As they kissed and his arms wrapped around her waist, the memory stick dug into the pocket of her jeans.

One day in May, a letter arrived.

Dear Abbie,

There are things I never got to say that I should have. You needed space. It wasn't right to push more then but I hope enough time has passed for you to have found solace in your mother's words, and will now listen to mine.

It's asking too much to expect you to forgive me, and I want you to know I wouldn't if I were you, but I also want you to know I'll never forgive myself for how your father died. Or, because of her love for me, how your mother dealt with it.

What I'm really writing for isn't forgiveness. It's just that I never got the chance to explain how your mother saved me. We both know how she saved me from going in with her, but I never told you all the other ways. In the book, Gabrielle only mentioned how I helped her.

When I was a child, your mother brightened the darkness around me, turning it to light. Her family home was a safe place, and I wanted to spend every moment with them. As she said that time we fought, I wanted her family, but she was wrong about why, for the main reason was because she was at its centre. What I wanted was to be part of her family. There was something special about your mother. Her family knew it. Liam knew it and I think you know it too now.

When she focused her attention on me that first day, I thought it was a joke because everyone else shot me down. She showed me kindness when all that surrounded me was mean.

She introduced the notion way back then that I was a good person, and I shouldn't listen to anyone who told me otherwise. Your mother pried open a crack so doubt could wriggle in, that what everyone told me growing up was just their opinion and it didn't have to be taken as fact. She started me on the long road of finding how to believe in myself.

In order for me to survive, I was born with resilience, but she strengthened it when it waned. She backed me up when I started to collapse, Abbie.

After I read her book, I looked at the relationships I formed in my past differently. Gabrielle was right about how abuse follows. Every partner treated me like there was something wrong with me. They all used magnifiers on my flaws. My gratitude for whatever affection they gave was cringe worthy. Afterwards, I saw my relationship with Oran as the train wreck it was. But also, I finally understood why I would seek that type of love too. It made me think of the relationship I had with Kieran, who I pushed and pushed and eventually ran away from. In your mother's book she wrote I came back to Knockfarraig for her, and I did, but it had been convenient too. Keiran's love felt wrong because it didn't fit in with what I believed I deserved. He didn't act like the others, which terrified me.

Except for your mother and her family, growing up I didn't know what love looked like. My family were emotionally unavailable. It's taken my whole life to accept they hated me. That I didn't warrant their anger. I was the shit on the shoe, the stain on the dress, the yappy dog in the corner being shouted at to shut up or the big fucking elephant in the room demanding their attention. They never cared for or needed my opinion. They all just wanted me to go away. When I did, when I left for Galway, they didn't miss me. They were glad I was gone and that hurt. Even now it hurts. When I came back, it annoyed them. Your mother saw through them. She'd say, 'They're all delighted you're back because now they have someone to blame for their own shitty lives.'

No matter how many times she repeated it to me back then, it wouldn't go in. I always needed their approval.

After your mother died and Maureen wouldn't let me see you, I fell into a dark depression. The light went out Abbie. The reason for living became pointless. All the fight left me. The one person I could fight back against, my mother, was gone too.

Abbie, your mother saved me many times over by giving me another chance. She told me in that last note I deserved to be happy, that it was her dying wish for me to go out and seek it. Because of your mother, I went to counselling again, because I could hear her voice in my brain clearly after, chanting in my ears until I relented. This time I opened up completely. Before, I was afraid if I told the counsellor the complete truth she would just confirm what the others had known all along: that there was something wrong with me. It was me that was wrong. What they did in my childhood had nothing to do with me. After that, I began to carve out a life. A happy life. I moved into the house in Galway, took a job as a head chef in a hotel in Salthill. After working on myself, when I was ready, I sought Kieran.

He is a good man Abbie. For the first time, I believed I deserved someone like that. Everything got better except the memory of leaving you. You haunted me, Abbie. I don't know if I blocked having children for years, through fear I'd turn out like my parents or that the baby would be as repulsed by me as my family but then I'd think of you, and how much you used to love me, and I'd yearn for that but I'd already abandoned one child, so how could I be a good mother?

And then I met you again, and that first night I could barely speak because it was like seeing your mother when I first met her. Same mannerisms, same eyes. Even though I knew our time was limited, when you would come to the end of the story, would no longer want to be around me, I kept a little hope that one day you might understand. As you read your mother's note I walked to the chemist and the following morning discovered I was pregnant. After years and years of trying, I think it was your mother's gift for facing my fears and finding you.

I know you may never want to see me again and it might disgust you for even asking, but we've decided we want to marry before the baby is born. The wedding is on June the thirteenth, your mother's birthday. I'd love for you to be my maid of honour, or, as a guest would be wonderful even – sorry, I've always had a tendency to push.

Even writing this letter might be a step too far. If it is I apologise. If you can see a way to make it, I would love for you to be there, even if only to see your house.

If you don't want to come, I get it, and I won't contact you again. In case I never see you, I have included a bank card and the pin number to a savings account that is yours that I've kept since you were born.

Even if you don't want to come, you may still have questions. I've tried to think of what they might be and I hope this letter answers some. From your perspective, you might have wondered why I didn't do more, after I knew the truth about your father. I asked her once, after reading the book, your book, after she confirmed some of Liam's ways. The book led us to one long conversation about everything we were at one time afraid to say. We left nothing out. About my mother and both my fathers. About Liam. About the dreams we never dared mention out loud. I asked her to leave him, to come with me to Galway. Your mother just smiled and said, 'Galway is your story, not mine. Mine ends here, with Liam and Abbie.' She grabbed my hand then. 'And, I hope with you.'

I squeezed, trying to ignore the tremor in her hand. 'Always,' I said. 'Or until you're sick of me.'

'Always then,' she said.

Abbie, there are two things I want you to know.

Number one: when you were a child, I lived for your smile.

Number two: your mother was the first person I loved who loved me back, but you were the last.

Sadie.

Trails

Abbie

The sun was only beginning to rise as she followed the path to her mother's grave. It looked different in the daytime, with its green grass cut even and the graves colourful with flowers and pictures. She stopped at one, a child's, with toys dotted around the edge of the stone. Death doesn't end anything. The child was still loved, she thought.

This time, she held a bunch of flowers and didn't falter in her direction. This time, she could find the exact spot with her eyes closed. This would be the last visit she would have to look at that ugly, grey, graffitied tombstone. With the money in her bank account from Sadie, she had ordered her mother a new one.

The night before, when Joe wrapped his arms around her stomach, when he pinched some skin and whispered she had been eating a lot lately, it was the end. Sure, he could argue it was a joke, that she needed to lighten up, but it was the last warning sign. Her father had done the same to her mother.

Abbie had ignored the ladder incident or the time he had called her scabby in front of the lads, or when he had stood her up twice and she'd found him in the park drinking with the others. Even the time when he hadn't wanted to use a condom, making a big deal of putting one on when she insisted, then afterwards, she found it unused in the sheets.

He laughed it off, asking what was the problem when he'd thought he had, that it wasn't his fault if it fell off. He'd been so attentive afterwards, going with her to the chemist to get the morning-after pill. It had been easier to say nothing and go along with it.

With just a pinch of skin, the sharp gesture knocked her out of denial. Her dad had been attentive at first, too. Hadn't her father showed her mother he cared all the time? With all his faults, he had loved Abbie. Abuse wasn't black or white. But nor was love. Did she want the man who loved her to think that way? Was it ever acceptable to put someone down?

Abbie finished with him. As much as she loved Joe, as much as it hurt, as lonely as she would be again, she wouldn't turn into her mother, or let Joe turn into her father. *Love saves us all.* For the rest of her life, Abbie would do everything in her power to avoid that type of relationship.

'Happy birthday,' she said as she set down the rainbow coloured roses. She sat on the grass and laid her hand on the soil where her mother laid underneath.

'Thank you for the book you wrote. And for all your other stories. Thank you for having me. For loving me.'

She pulled out a weed poking through.

'Thank you for the memory stick because now everyone knows the truth. Although, I think you'd be happy I kept Sadie a secret.'

The memory stick contained multiple photographs depicting Gabrielle's injuries taken with a camera with the date displayed in the right-hand corner. Grainy and dated videos displayed the truth. The first time she heard her father's voice shouting, saying the most disgusting things, Abbie curled into a ball and had to stop herself from sucking her thumb.

She leaned in closer, as if it would make a difference to her mother hearing.

'I remember you now.'

She trailed her finger along one of the petals of the flower.

'For a long time, I blanked it, like disassociation. When I heard his voice, it triggered some of it to come back. Hearing you on the tapes brought you back, too. The softness of your hair, its smell, your hugs and how you used to sing to me to get me to sleep. Your whispers in my ear when I was sick saying: *you are strong, you'll get through this, everything passes baby girl.* While I was reading your book, I remembered the fear, your fear more like, how you used to try to hide it from me, but I knew, I *knew* you feared him. Everyone always said how strange it was that I had no memories and reading what you said I get now that I erased them, because the past was too hurtful. To remember your love when there was none from Maureen was harmful. It only reminded me of what I lost.'

She laughed.

'Maureen was livid when I sent the video to the papers. It created quite the storm, especially when I went public with the autopsy report that pointed out your broken nose and bruising on the neck were done before you went in the water. I wish you could see the stir you've made. Online groups have signed petitions demanding justice for women. They are calling on the government to renounce the murder verdict to self-defence. I finally confronted Maureen. Said all the things I should have said years ago and would you believe she just... crumbled. Admitted she had been friends with you, that she knew my father wasn't a saint, that she had been scared of him herself. She argued what good would it have done to have me believe my father was a monster. She flinched when I went close to her, bracing for me to hit her and I could have, it would have been easy to slap her. It would have felt good. But, you'll be proud, I choose to be my mother's daughter, not my father's. You taught me we get to choose who our family is. Like you choosing Sadie to be your sister.'

She smiled, remembering the look on Maureen's face.

'It is kind of funny. I said to her. "All the hurt. All the anger. It was inside you, too. It would be easy to hit you to lash out but then I would be the same as him and I'm not. I would be the same as you with Sadie." She fell back as if I did hit her. Then I did the opposite of what she was expecting, I wrapped my arms around her and whispered, "thank you. I know it hasn't been easy. You're released now, you don't have to look after me anymore."'

Abbie looked at the small suitcase by her feet, with her bag on top and thought, *how can everything I love fit in there?*

'What I want you to know is even when I thought you were a murderer, I never hated you, not really. What I hated was that you left me, that you could leave me. I should have known you wouldn't have done it through choice. I should have remembered your love. Mum, I promise I'll never forget again.'

Abbie thought about the new headstone, an expensive black marble with a picture of her mother laughing on the front. She had kept the inscription short.

Writer. Wife. Mother. Sister. Friend.

Underneath was her quote: *Love saves us all.*

Abbie lay in the grass beside her mother until the sun broke through the sky and the church bell chimed eight. Stiffly, she rose and, dragging the suitcase, with her bag draped over her shoulder, left the graveyard.

On the bus, she pictured her mother years before making the same journey, oblivious to the fact she was carrying a child. Carrying her. This time Abbie felt it the other way round; for now she carried her mother everywhere she went.

In her bag, she rummaged for what felt the hundredth time. When she located the wrapping of the wedding present she closed the bag again, smiling at the thought of handing over the picture frame of two young girls with arms wrapped around each other. If Sadie was going to walk up the aisle on Gabrielle's birthday, surely she would love a memory of her best friend on her day?

It was just an excuse. Turning up would be Abbie's real present, knowing for Sadie, it would represent forgiveness. For Abbie, it would mean gaining a godmother. Whichever way you looked at it, both of them would win.

As she stood on Sadie's doorstep, the giddiness threatened to take over. Sadie didn't disappoint. As she opened the door she reeled backwards, her eyes and mouth wide in surprise.

'Hey,' she said, stepping aside to come in.

Sadie looked different. Her cheeks had filled out and there was a bump where her narrow stomach had been, but she gathered her composure quick enough.

'We hoped you would come. Welcome Abbie, to your home.'

It was hard to hug with a baby between them, but they managed. On the wall opposite the door, were two framed paintings, impossible not to notice. The left one was a pink weeping willow, with a red sunset casting light, creating a sea that rippled with currents of pink and reds. Beside it, in its rightful place, was another painting: a mound of black and blue swirls over the white page. If you looked closely, you could make out a tear.

Together, just as they should be.

Side by side, Sadie and Abbie studied the pictures for a long time, their heads moving closer until they rested on the other. Abbie placed a hand on Sadie's bump and Sadie placed a hand on Abbie's shoulder.

'Let's celebrate,' she whispered.

'Let's,' Abbie said and followed her into the kitchen.

Author's note

I shelved this novel for many years as I did not want to glorify domestic violence even a fraction. Truth told, it was a frightening subject, and I was afraid of the backlash. In the time I put it aside, more young women in Ireland have died from the hands of a man. It wasn't my intention to justify abuse - it is never acceptable to hurt another living being. What made me push on was the thought that I could give the women who have died a voice. As a writer, I'm well aware I won't change the world, but maybe if I can give a gentle nudge, maybe this book can help someone going through something similar.

On April 6, 2020 United Nations Secretary General Antonio Guterres called for measures to address a "horrifying global surge in domestic violence" linked to lockdowns imposed by governments responding to the COVID-19 pandemic1

In Ireland, leading organisations working on domestic violence such as Women's Aid reported an increase in the number of calls to their helplines and the Gardaí reported a 25% increase in domestic violence calls in April/May 2020 compared to April/May 2019.

In the United Kingdom: Domestic violence murders doubled in March/April 2020 compared to March/April 2019.

According to Women's Aid:

One in four women in Ireland who have been in a relationship have been abused by a current or former partner.

In 2021 there were:

28,096 disclosures against women

5,735 disclosures against children

26,906 contacts with Women's Aid

213,206 visits to womensaid.ie

33,831 disclosures of abuse

A 2014 EU-wide study by the European Union Fundamental Rights Agency (FRA) reported that

in 50% of the cases the stalker was a partner (current or former)

14% of women in Ireland have experienced physical violence by a partner (current or former) since age 15

Six percent of Irish women have experienced sexual violence and 31% of women have experienced psychological violence by a current or former partner since age 15

12% of Irish respondents in the study had experienced stalking (including cyber-stalking)

41% of Irish women know someone in their circle of family or friends who have experienced intimate partner violence

The 2020 Femicide Factsheet from Women's Aid shows that:

43 women aged between 18 and 25 years old have been murdered in the Republic of Ireland since 1996

of the resolved cases, 52% of women were murdered by a boyfriend or former partner

Since 1996, 249 women have died violently in the Republic of Ireland. Of the women that were killed:

63% were killed in their own homes.

55% were killed by a partner or ex (of the resolved cases)

almost nine in ten women knew their killer.

There is a misconception that a man who abuses a woman is an obvious monster. That you can tell a violent person from what they look like. There is an undercurrent of blame when a woman is murdered, with people nodding their heads when they say, definitely the partner did it. Like somehow that makes it understandable, like in some way it divides the blame.

I hope my point has not been lost about Gabrielle's story. I wanted to show that it isn't obvious how a man will treat a woman, that it can change years after even.

Speaking to many women of domestic abuse, the undercurrent they all had in common when asked why they didn't leave was the feeling of shame. To admit they fell in love with someone capable of hurting them is terrifying. As a society, we have to change that and this comes from support and understanding.

No one ever has the right to lay their hands on another person. Isn't it about time that when a woman says she has been attacked, or raped, automatically the law should do everything to help her?

Until we change how some men see women, we will continue to see women die.

If you have experienced domestic violence or would like to talk to anyone about emotional abuse, please don't hesitate to contact Woman's Aid.

References

References

2020-06-09_l-rs-note-domestic-violence-and-covid-19-in-ireland_en.pdf (oireachtas.ie)

1 UN News, UN chief calls for domestic violence 'ceasefire' amid 'horrifying global surge', April 6, 2020, https://news.un.org/en/story/2020/04/1061052 (Accessed April 6, 2020).

2 Reported in The Times, Coronavirus: domestic abuse reports rise after people are forced to stay home, March 20, 2020, https://www.thetimes.co.uk/article/coronavirus-domestic-abuse-reports-rise-after-peopleare-forced-to-stay-home-lgz95d9k3 (Accessed April 3, 2020).

3 Reported in The Irish Examiner, Increase in domestic abuse incidents linked to Covid-19 lockdown, June 1, 2020, https://www.irishexaminer.com/breakingnews/ireland/increase-in-domestic-abuse-incidents-linked-tocovid-19-lockdown-1002718.html (Accessed June 1, 2020).

4 UN Women, COVID-19 and ending violence against women and girls. (2020).

Helping You Understand ALS | The ALS Association www.als.org

Enjoy this book? You can make a difference

Honest reviews of my books help bring them to the attention of other readers. If you enjoyed *The Sisters You Choose*, I would appreciate if you could spend a few minutes leaving your feedback. Reviews help the buyer understand the 'feel' of the book so your review could be the difference in whether someone picks it up. It doesn't have to be long – even one sentence helps.

My deepest thanks,
   Natasha Karis.

An Exclusive Gift For You

Want another story?

As a thank you for taking the time to read this book, I want to give you a gift. If you subscribe to the Natasha Karis newsletter, you will get:

The Initiates – A suicide note. Five lost students. One teacher who will stop at nothing to help them.

In the scenic seaside town of Knockfarraig in Cork, five final year students gather in a dingy classroom for a detention. Ignoring the hostility, teacher Alayne Adams has her own problems to deal with and sees the time as a chance to reflect on what to do with her tumultuous home life.

But after discovering a note, Alayne is left with a dilemma. The note states the writer intends to end their life. Looking around, they all seem to have issues.

Ash, a new student at Knockfarraig, was expelled from his last school for a violent act.

Samira tries but fails to hide behind her hair.

Calista, with black circles under her eyes, looks exhausted.

Rian's caustic words goad, but she tugs at her clothes constantly.

Calum jumps every time someone speaks and looks like he'll either burst into tears or run for the door.

The writer could be any of them.

An emotional, heartfelt novel about the power of kindness and never giving up.

Here is some reviews:

'Karis's prose is striking, layered, and poetic.' *-The BookLife Prize* 'A character led story with a strong, emotional message.' *-The Wishing Shelf Book Awards* 'A wonderful, uplifting tale.' *–Amazon reviewer.* 'Absolutely magical, captivating book - it made me laugh, it made me cry & it made me think. I couldn't put it down.' *–Goodreads reviewer.* 'A story that teaches life is so much more than we dream of if we let go of wrong concepts.' *–Goodreads reviewer.*

The Initiation of Alayne Adams - an uplifting novella.

Torn between partying with her friends and doing the right thing, Alayne's life lacks any direction. Until an altercation leaves her spiralling.

Left with nowhere to turn, Alayne tries to find her way. But an encounter in a library opens up new possibilities and a chance to learn. Can Alayne change or will old habits prove too strong?

The Summer Before - an exclusive novella that cannot be bought anywhere else, giving the story that led Calista to the detention room.

You will also be the first to receive exclusive cover reveals, behind the scenes details and giveaways.

Get it today at: https://www.subscribepage.com/initiation

About the Author

Natasha Karis lives in Cork, Ireland, and spends her days navigating between writing and raising her three children. She has been known to write with a child on her knee. She writes contemporary, emotional, uplifting stories. Natasha carries a book with her everywhere she goes, so the invention of eBooks have made her bag lighter at least. Even though she has always been a voracious reader, she wasn't always a writer and has worked as a chiropractic clinic manager, a shoe store manager, and a Dunnes Stores girl.

She is the author of Send Me Home For Christmas, The Breaking of Dawn, The Truth Between Us, The Initiates, The Initiation of Alayne Adams and The Happiness Initiative.

Also by Natasha Karis

Send Me Home For Christmas
An emotional, heartfelt novella about finding your way home.

Four strangers stuck in an airport at Christmas. One snowstorm. Only two tickets home.

Peggy believes in good deeds. In the past, whenever she's felt low, helping people has always turned her good fortune. Lately though, no matter how kind she is to others, she still has no luck.

Desperate to get home to her daughter for Christmas, a huge snowstorm threatens to keep them apart. In the airport, her path crosses with three other strangers who are just as eager to get home. Going nowhere and all longing to get on the last flight, they all stake their claim for one of only two tickets left to Cork.

Each will tell their story.

Each one wishing for a Christmas miracle and hoping that maybe, this Christmas, they may get one.

If you like uplifting women's fiction, this heartwarming short read will leave you inspired.

The Breaking Of Dawn

An emotional novel about finding your voice.

Taken for granted by her boss and friends, Dawn Moloney can never find the right way to stand up to them.

Forced to move back to her childhood home after an attack leaves her bruised and broken, Dawn struggles to adjust.

When her mother suggests she try classes at a local centre for the unemployed, she reluctantly agrees. There, she meets Alayne Adams, who prefers to focus more on Dawn rather than what classes she is taking. Talking about herself is Dawn's worst nightmare, but if she wants to get better, she will have to learn.

Can Dawn finally find the right words?

For readers who love Catherine Ryan Hyde, Kristin Hannah or Mitch Albom.

The Truth Between Us

A make or break holiday. A love that should last a lifetime. A truth that threatens to rip them apart.

When Adaline decides to book a trip away to contemplate her failing marriage, her husband Andrew suggests he join her. As they embark on a last chance holiday to Cyprus, Adaline looks back over her life in the hope to fix what went wrong. But the past contains much pain, and a secret threatens to ruin everything.

Can they confront the truth and still salvage the relationship?

The Truth Between Us is an emotional and uplifting tale about love, loss and hope.

The Initiates

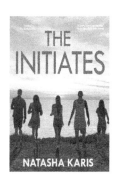

A suicide note. Five lost students. One teacher who will stop at nothing to help them.

When the Principal of Knockfarraig school suggests a series of detentions for some wayward sixth year students, teacher Alayne Adams volunteers. But the discovery of a note reveals one student intends to end their life.

Taking inspiration from a book based on ancient teachings, Alayne embarks on a series of life lessons that encourages each of them to discover ways to heal their pain.

Can she steer them onto a path that will change all their lives?

With characters that will have you rooting and crying for them, this contemporary, emotional novel set in Ireland, will leave you inspired.

The Initiation Of Alayne Adams

What breaks you, can also make you.

Torn between partying with her friends and doing the right thing, Alayne's life lacks any direction. Until an incident leaves her spiralling. Left with nowhere to turn, Alayne struggles to find her way. But an encounter in a library opens up new possibilities and a chance to learn.

Can Alayne change or will old habits prove too hard to resist?

Printed in Great Britain
by Amazon